Paul Doherty was born in Middlesbrough in 1946. He was admitted to Liverpool University where he gained a First Class Honours Degree in History and won a state scholarship to Exeter College, Oxford. While there he met his wife, Carla.

Paul worked in Ascot, Newark and Crawley, before being appointed as Headmaster to Trinity Catholic High School, Essex, in 1981. The school has been described as one of the leading comprehensives in the U.K. and has been awarded 'Outstanding' in four consecutive OFSTED inspections. All seven of Paul and Carla's children have been educated at Trinity.

Paul has written over 100 books and has published a series of outstanding historical mysteries set in the Middle Ages, Classical Greece, Ancient Egypt and elsewhere. His books have been translated into more than twenty languages.

Also by Paul Doherty

The Brother Athelstan Mysteries

The Nightingale Gallery

&

The House of the Red Slayer

PAUL DOHERTY

San Diego, California

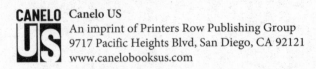

Canelo US
An imprint of Printers Row Publishing Group
9717 Pacific Heights Blvd, San Diego, CA 92121
www.canelobooksus.com

Printers Row Publishing Group is a division of Readerlink Distribution Services, LLC. Canelo US is a registered trademark of Readerlink Distribution Services, LLC.

This edition of THE NIGHTINGALE GALLERY originally published in the United Kingdom in 2021 by Canelo. This edition of THE HOUSE OF THE RED SLAYER originally published in the United Kingdom in 2021 by Canelo.

Published in partnership with Canelo.

Correspondence regarding the content of this book should be sent to Canelo US, Editorial Department, at the above address. Author inquiries should be sent to Canelo, Unit 9, 5th Floor, Cargo Works, 1–2 Hatfields, London SE1 9PG, United Kingdom, www.canelo.co.

Publisher: Peter Norton • Associate Publisher: Ana Parker
Art Director: Charles McStravick
Senior Developmental Editor: April Graham
Production Team: Beno Chan, Julie Greene, Rusty von Dyl

Library of Congress Control Number: 2022934991

ISBN: 978-1-6672-0259-4

Printed in the United States of America

26 25 24 23 22   1 2 3 4 5

The Nightingale Gallery

In memory of Eric

Introduction

The old king was dying. The wind snatched up the rumour and carried it along the Thames. Boatmen whispered about it and the fat-bellied sea-going barges took the rumour further along the coast. Edward was failing; the great, blond-haired conqueror of France, the new Alexander in the West, was dying. Too late for those who had incurred his displeasure, their straggle-haired, blood-caked heads spiked over the gateway of London Bridge, marble white cheeks turning black as the ravens dug for juicier morsels.

The great king, or great bastard depending on your perspective, was reluctantly allowing the spirit to seep from his ageing, smelly body. The court had moved to Richmond in the early summer of 1377 as the winds swung south-west, blowing hard and hot from the dry deserts around the Middle Sea. The plague had appeared in London, with men and women dropping as the buboes swelled in their armpits and, bellies distended, they spat out their life's blood. The king was frightened as Death, assassin-like, crept into his court.

I

Edward braved it well. He tried to paint his sallow face and kept his mouth closed to hide his crumbling, blackened teeth. He dressed in silver and white taffeta trimmed with gold and primped his once golden hair, even though it hung in straggly, sweaty wisps to his bony shoulders. But Death was not appeased. The heat and evil humours from the river wrapped their cloying fingers around his decaying body, and still the king refused to give in. Had he not smashed the armies of France at Crécy and Poitiers? And taken their king captive to ride behind him as he, like a new Caesar, returned to London to glory in his prowess?

Edward sat on cushions in one of his great with-drawing chambers, refusing food and physic. A priest came scuttling round the walls like a small, black spider, a Job's comforter if there ever was one.

'Your Grace,' he insisted, 'you must go to bed.'

Edward turned like an old fox, his lips, twisted by a stroke, curled in displeasure.

'Go away, little man,' he hissed. 'Death will never take me!'

He stayed where he was, staring at his finger where the coronation ring, once so deeply embedded in his flesh, had recently been sawn off. His marriage to the kingdom was dead. He had held the sceptre for fifty years and now must hand it over to another.

He shook his head and glanced at his fingers. Rings of fire seemed to circle them. Death was coming, soft-shoed, shuffling along the corridors.

Edward's great heart lurched and fought back. He stood bravely as he had at Crécy thirty years before. He smiled to remember the way the wind had kissed his face as his captains had shouted 'Loose!' and the archers had sent their black clouds of living death into the advancing hordes of French. He would stand like he had then. Death would not take him if he stood. He did so for fifteen hours before sinking to the cushioned floor, his fingers clenched to his mouth. The priests carried him to his bed.

Hysteria gripped the court and the air was thick with gloom and terror. The gilded courtiers whispered about signs and portents; the River Thames, its waters swollen, broke its banks at Greenwich and flooded the palace. A huge, grey fish, the size of a Leviathan, was beached on the northern shores. The sky turned red at noonday and strange creatures were seen in the dark woods to the north. Voices were heard calling in the shadowy streets and ghostly trumpets brayed from the battlements of the Tower of London and Windsor Castle. One of the ladies-in-waiting saw a tarot card bearing the black figure of Death nailed to a royal chair. Another glimpsed the ghost of the dying king's power in the form of a mystic knight, marching along the moonlit gallery, down the stairs to the great palace doorway.

Edward III, the Lion of England, was dying. Old men recalled their grandparents telling them how the Lion, when young, had seized the throne from his mother Isabella and her lover, Mortimer. Now the Lion's day was done.

The king stirred himself. He asked for music, and a young girl in a tawny dress and lace-edged veil played the viol. The king went back in time as the ghosts gathered around his bed. His father, Edward II, done to death in Berkeley. His mother Isabella, beautiful and passionate. Philippa his wife with her dark skin and tender, doe-like eyes, dead these eight years. And one other ghost: his most precious son, Edward the Black Prince, leader of armies, a Pompey to his Caesar. The general who had taken the banners of England across the Pyrenees into Navarre but came back with nothing except a disease which rotted his body away. All gone! His son was gone.

They brought back the proclamations about the succession and the king knew he was dying. Seals were attached. He was leaving. His retainers melted away. 'Is there no faith left in Israel?' Edward whispered. The palace at Sheen became a mausoleum. The king was left to lie in his own sweat and dirt, alone except for Alice Perrers, his mistress. She swept into the death chamber, her fingers fretted with gold wire, her rich red dress engraved with precious stones. She, with her blandishing tongue and beautiful face, who cared for no one because no one cared for her, sat beside her dying lord and lover, hungrily watching him. The king woke from a dream and saw her hard black eyes and voluptuous lips.

4

'My Lady Sun,' he whispered.

Perrers smiled, her white teeth gleaming as she remembered how she had ridden in cloth of gold up Cheapside, her head held high, her ears closed to the shouts of "Whore!", "Bawd!" and "Harlot!" Now she sat near the king, like a lioness watching her prey. An old Franciscan priest, John Hoccleve, came in but Perrers hissed and drove him out. The king closed his eyes. His breathing was shallow; a dreadful rattle had begun in his throat. Perrers waited no longer but stripped him of whatever finery he had left and fled.

The old Franciscan came back, grasping the king's hand, holding a crucifix up before the fading eyes. He intoned the *Dies Irae* and when he reached the verse 'And what shall I, frail man, be pleading; When the just are mercy needing?' the king opened his eyes.

'Do you wish absolution?' Hoccleve whispered.

'Ah, Jesu!' the king muttered back, and weakly pressed the Franciscan's hand.

'I therefore absolve you…' the priest said, '…from your sins in the name of…' he continued, his voice growing louder as the death rattle sounded in the king's throat like the beat of a tambour. The king turned, his eyes open. One last gasp and his soul went out into the darkness. Hoccleve finished his prayer and looked down at the grey, emaciated face, remembering the golden days when the king had walked in all his glory. He bowed his head, pressing his brow into the dead king's hand, and wept for the sheer waste of it all.

A few hours later in Westminster Palace, John of Gaunt, Duke of Lancaster and eldest living son of the dead king, sat alone before a great, hooded fireplace. He squatted, jerkin open, legs apart, letting the flames of the heated logs warm the chill in his thighs and crotch. The duke had heard the news as he returned from hunting, drenched to the skin after a sudden storm. His father was dead and he was regent but not king. John groaned to himself, clenching a bejewelled fist. He should be king, a man born to the crown with claims to the thrones of Castile, France, Scotland and England. And the only obstacle in his path? A golden-haired ten-year-old boy, his nephew, Richard of Bordeaux, son of Gaunt's elder brother, the feared and fearsome Black Prince.

'A heartbeat away!' Gaunt murmured. Only a short breath between him and the diadem of the Confessor. Gaunt stretched his great frame, his muscled body cracking and straining at the fury within. Regent but not king! Yet the land needed a firm ruler. The French were plundering the southern coats. The Scots were massing on the northern borders. The peasants were surly, demanding an end to incessant taxation. And the Commons, led by their speaker, were abusive and strident when they met in the chapel of St Stephen's at Westminster. Gaunt stroked his neatly barbered moustache and beard. Could he take the step? Would he? He chewed his lip and considered the possibilities. His younger brothers would resist. The great lords of the council, backed by the soft but powerful bishops, would take up arms and call down heaven's anger on him. And Richard – pale-faced, blue-eyed Richard – what would happen to him? Gaunt shivered. He remembered the old prophecy – that when the old cat died, the mice must not rejoice for the new kitten would grow into an even more dreadful monster!

Gaunt, who feared nothing, admitted his silent, grave-faced nephew held special terrors for him, as if the age-old eyes in that ten-year-old face read and understood his most secret thoughts. The Commons, too, would watch him and Gaunt had been careless. He had tried to raise money and the proof was there for the asking. The Sons of Dives had him in their clutches. The secrets they held must never be revealed.

Gaunt shifted in his chair. What was he frightened of? The demons in his own private hell stirred and rose from the black pit of memory. Murder! He stared around. The long chamber was deserted, as only shadows danced silently against the arras-covered walls. Assassin! The accusation seemed to leap from the flames and Gaunt broke into a cold sweat. The demon rose, twisting in his heart, and the duke gulped greedily from his wine cup, hoping its purple juice would drown the demons in its heavy vapour.

Gaunt was right to be wary. After all, Murder was no stranger to London. It stalked the streets, its eyes blind as night as it sought out its hapless victims. Murder tripped along the shit-caked alleys and streets of Southwark, and slid like a cold mist through the half-open doorways of hot, stuffy taverns to squat cold-eyed as men hacked each other to death. Murder lurked in the doorway of the filthy apothecary's house where poisons could be bought: ratsbane, crushed diamonds, belladonna and arsenic. Sometimes Murder would come across the city walls, sneaking along the dark country lanes behind the Tower, but on that night it had chosen a juicier prey and set up camp in Sir Thomas Springall's fine mansion in the Strand: a veritable palace with its tiled roof, black-embossed timbers, gleaming white plaster and freshly painted shield bearing the goldsmith's escutcheon of silver bars, gold trefoils and clasps of gold and silk.

The house itself was silent. In the lofty banqueting hall, the fire had died to popping cinders and smouldering ash. The candles were long snuffed though the air still bore the fragrance of sweet-smelling wax. The tapestries, heavy and gold-encrusted, hung on the walls, shifting slightly in the cold night breeze which pierced the gaps in the mullioned-glass windows. The massive table bore the remains of a banquet and its white lawn cloth, grease marked and purple-stained, still shimmered in the fading light of the fire. The silver dishes had been removed but the platters remained, covered with the remnants of fricassée and jiggets of mutton, as well as the bones of goose, peacock and chicken. Next to these were the deep-bowled cups smattered with the dregs of malmsey, Bordeaux and sack. A stout, long-tailed rat prowled amongst the dishes, its red eyes gleaming, its belly full and heavy, so sluggish it hardly squeaked when the ginger house cat pounced and crunched the swollen body in its jaws. Down the hall a dog heard the sound and stirred, lifting its shaggy, sleep-laden head.

Below stairs the servants slept on, their stomachs gorged, their brains dull with the scraps of food and wine they had gulped. In one chamber lay a maid, the hem of her skirts pushed into her mouth, twisting in mute passion under the hot probing loins of a young groom. She need not have worried about uttering any cries. The wide stairs above were deserted, as was the wood-panelled gallery which swept past the master bedrooms. In one a man and woman lay entwined, their skin gleaming with sweat as they writhed and turned under the blue and scarlet canopy of the four poster bed. A silver candelabra, set on a red- and white-tiled tabletop, gave the room a golden glow which was reflected in the precious silver thread of the wall hangings as well as the costly silk and lace clothes scattered over the floor. Further along the gallery, in the great bedroom of the master of the house, Sir

Thomas Springall, Murder brooded from its ghostly corner. Sir Thomas did not expect it. Oh, no! He ignored the preacher's words: 'In the midst of life we are in death.' Like the rich man in scripture, Springall was planning on destroying his old barns and building new ones, as befitted a merchant who had fingers in every silver pie. Sir Thomas lay between his silken gold-fringed sheets and basked in his wealth. He was pleased the old king was dead. A young boy now wore the crown.

'Woe to the realm where the king is a child!' Sir Thomas whispered, and laughed softly. 'Thank God!' he muttered. The regent needed him and Springall would prosper even more for he knew Gaunt's secrets. Sir Thomas licked his thick red lips. He stared into the darkness, across to the table where the Syrians, his precious chess set, glowed in the moonlight streaming through the casement window. More wealth would come. Springall would have entry to the treasure chambers of the kingdom. And the keys to such riches? The Book of the Apocalypse 6, Verse 8. And the other? Genesis 3, Verse 1. Springall smiled, rolled on one side and stared down at the cleverly carved bed posts. He thought of his wife, she of the chestnut curls, golden skin and eyes blue as a fresh spring sky. But Springall desired other flesh. He gripped the bed clothes and, at that moment, knew something was wrong. He clutched his throat, but too late. Murder was upon him.

Chapter 1

Brother Athelstan sat on a plinth of stone before the rood screen of St Erconwald's church in Southwark. He stared despairingly up at the hole in the red-tiled roof then at the dirty puddle of rainwater which shimmered on the flagstones two yards away from his sandalled feet. He stroked his clean-shaven face and glared down at the small scroll of parchment in his hand.

'You know, Bonaventure,' he murmured, 'and I say this in the spirit of obedience, so don't repeat my words if he ever comes, but Father Prior's remarks about my past cut like barbs.'

He folded the parchment neatly into a perfect square and slipped it into the battered leather wallet on his belt.

'I daily atone for my sins,' he continued. 'I observe most strictly the rule of St Dominic and, as you know, I spend both day and night in the care of souls.'

God knows, Athelstan thought, tapping the flagstones with his feet, the harvest of souls was great; the filthy alleyways, the piss-soaked runnels and poor hovels of his parish sheltered broken people whose minds and souls had been bruised and poisoned by grinding poverty. The great, fat ones of the land did not care a fig but hid behind empty words, false promises and a lack of compassion which even Herod would have blushed at. Athelstan stared around the empty church, noting the dirty walls, peeling pillars, and the fresco of St John the Baptist. Athelstan grinned. He knew the Baptist had been beheaded but not whilst he was preaching! Someone had scrubbed the painting, removing St John's head as well as those of his attentive listeners.

'You have seen my house, Bonaventure? It's no more than a white-washed shed with two rooms, a wooden door and a window which does not fit. My horse, Philomel, may be an aged destrier, but it eats as if there is no tomorrow and can go no faster than a shuffling cat.' He smiled. 'I mean no offence to present company, but he drains my purse. Now, I am not moaning, I am just mentioning these matters to remind ourselves of our present state, so I can advise my prior that his paternal strictures are not necessary.' Athelstan sighed and went over into the small carrel built into the wall near the Lady Chapel where he had been penning his reply to the Father Prior. He picked up his quill, thought for a while and began writing.

As I have said, Reverend Father, my purse is empty, shrivelled up and tight as a usurer's soul. My collection boxes have been stolen and the chancery screen is in disrepair. The altar is marked and stained, and the nave of the church is often covered with huge pools of water, for our roof serves as more of a colander than a covering. God knows I atone for my sins. I seem to be steeped in murder, bloody and awful. It taxes my mind and reminds me of my own great crime. I have served the people here six months now and I have also assumed those duties assigned by you, to be clerk and scrivener to Sir John Cranston, coroner in the city of London.

Time and again he takes me with him to sit over the body of some man, woman or child pitifully slain. 'Is it murder, suicide or an accident?' he asks and so the dreadful stories begin. Often death results from stupidity: a woman forgets how dangerous it is for a child to play out in the cobbled streets, dancing between the hooves of iron-shod horses or the creaking wheels of huge carts as they bring their produce up from the river; still a child is slain, the little body crushed, bruised and marked, while the young soul goes out to meet its Christ. But, Reverend Father, there are more dreadful deaths. Men drunk in taverns, their bellies awash with cheap ale, their souls dead and black as the deepest night as they lurch at each other with sword, dagger or club. I always keep a faithful record.

Yet, every word I hear, every sentence I write, every time I visit the scene of the murder, I go back to that bloody field fighting for Edward the Black Prince. I, a novice monk, who broke his vows to God and took his younger brother off to war. Every night I dream of that battle, the press of steel-clad men, the lowered pikes, the screams and shouts. Each time the nightmare goes like a mist clearing above the river, leaving only me kneeling beside the corpse of my dead brother, screaming into the darkness for his soul to return. I know, Reverend Father, it never will.

Athelstan scrutinised the words he had written, replaced the quill beside his letter and walked back to the chancel screen. He looked across as Bonaventure rose and stretched elegantly.

'I intend no offence, Bonaventure,' he said. 'I mean, Sir John, despite his portly frame, that plum-red face, balding pate and watery eye, is, you will agree, at heart a good man. An honest official, a rare fellow indeed who does not take bribes but searches for the truth, ever patient in declaring the real cause of death. But why must I always be with him?'

Athelstan went back to sit before the rood screen. What use was it to list the terrible murders and scenes of violence he had witnessed? What would Father Prior know of them? Souls sent out into the dark before their time, unprepared and unshriven.

Men with their eyes gouged out, their throats cut, their genitals ripped off. Women crushed beneath scaffolding or horribly murdered in some stinking alleyway. If Christ came to London, Athelstan thought, he would surely cross to Southwark, where poverty and crime sat like two ugly brothers or wandered the streets hand-in-hand spreading their stench. Bonaventure rose and padded gently over to him. Athelstan stared down at the cat.

'Perhaps I should tell Father Prior about you, Bonaventure,' he said, admiring the sleek black body of the alley cat he had adopted, noting the white mask and paws, the tattered ear, the half-closed eye.

'You're a mercenary,' he continued, stroking the cat gently on the top of its head. 'But my most faithful parishioner. For a dish of milk and a few scraps of fish you will sit patiently whilst I talk to you, and be most attentive during Mass.'

Athelstan jumped as he heard a sound behind him. He looked round the chancel screen and realised how dark it was in the church, the only light being that from a taper lit before the statue of the Madonna. He yawned. He had not slept the previous evening. He did not like to close his eyes on dreams where he saw his brother's marble-white and glassy face, the eyes always staring at him. So, instead, he had climbed to the top of the church tower to observe the stars, for the movements of the heavens had fascinated him ever since he had begun studying them in Prior Bacon's observatory on Folly Bridge at Oxford. He had been tired and slightly fearful as well, for Godric, a well-known murderer and assassin, had begged for sanctuary in the church. Since his arrival, Godric had lain curled up like a dog in the corner of the sanctuary, sleeping off his exhaustion. He had eaten Athelstan's supper, pronounced himself well and settled down to a good night's sleep. 'How is it,' Athelstan murmured, 'that such men can sleep so well?' Godric had slain a man, struck him down in the marketplace, taken his purse and fled. He had hoped to escape but had had the misfortune to encounter a group of city officials and their retainers who had raised the 'Hue and Cry' and pursued him to St Erconwald's. Athelstan had been trying to repair the chancel screen and let him in after he hammered on the door. Godric had brushed past him, gasping, waving the dagger still bloody from his crime, and ran up the nave, shouting: 'Sanctuary! Sanctuary!' The pursuing officials had not come into the church, though they expected Athelstan, as clerk to Sir John Cranston, to hand Godric over. Athelstan had refused.

'This is God's house!' he'd shouted. 'Protected by Holy Mother Church and the King's decree!'

So they had left him and Godric alone, although they had placed a guard on the door and swore they would kill the murderer if he attempted to escape. Athelstan peered through the darkness. Godric still lay sleeping.

Athelstan prepared the altar for Mass, laying out the rather tattered missal and two candlesticks so bent they could hardly stand straight. A chipped, silver-gilt chalice, paten and small glass cruets, containing water and wine, were placed on the spotless altar cloth. Athelstan went into the dank sacristy, put on the alb and scarlet cope, crossed himself and went out to begin the magic of the Mass, priest before God, offering Christ to the Father under the appearances of bread and wine. Athelstan blessed himself as he intoned the introductory psalm.

'I will go into the altar of God, unto God who gives joy to my youth.'

Godric snored on, oblivious to the drama being enacted a few yards away. Bonaventure sidled up to the foot of the altar steps. The cat licked its lips, swishing its long tail in anticipation of a deep bowl of creamy milk as his reward for attention and patience. Athelstan, now caught up by the music of the words of the Mass, swept through the readings of the Epistle and the Gospel, reaching the Offertory where he mingled the water and wine. At the far end of the church a door opened and a hooded figure slipped in, moving soundlessly up the darkened nave to kneel beside Bonaventure at the foot of the steps. Athelstan forced himself to keep his eyes down on the white circle of bread over which he had breathed the words of consecration, transforming it into the body of Christ. The consecration over, he intoned the Lord's Prayer: '*Pater Noster, qui es in caelis.*'

17

His voice rang loud and clear through the hollow nave. He paused, as the canon of the Mass dictated, to pray for the dead. He remembered Fulke the warrener, a member of his parish killed in a tavern brawl four nights earlier. Then Athelstan's own parents and his brother Francis… the friar closed his eyes against the hot tears welling there as the faces of his family appeared, clear and distinct in his mind's eye.

'God grant them eternal rest,' he whispered.

He stood swaying against the altar, wondering for the hundredth time why he felt like an assassin. Oh, in France he had killed men whilst fighting for the Black Prince, the old king's eldest son, who wanted to unite the crowns of France and Castile with that of England. Athelstan had shot arrows as good and true as the rest. He remembered the corpse of a young French knight, his cornflower blue eyes gazing sightlessly up at the sky, his blond hair framing his face like a halo, Athelstan's barbed arrow embedded deeply in his throat between helmet and gorget. The friar prayed for this unknown knight, yet he felt no guilt. This was war and the Church taught that war was part of man's sinful condition, the legacy of Adam's revolt.

'Oh, God, am I a murderer?' he whispered to himself.

Athelstan thought once again how, as a novice in Blackfriars, near the western wall of the city, he had broken his vows and fled back to his father's farm in

Sussex. His mind had been filled with dreams of war and he had encouraged his younger brother in similar fantasies. They had joined one of those merry bands of archers who swung along the sunny, dusty lanes of Sussex down to Dover and across a shimmering sea, to reap glory in the green fields of France. His brother had been killed and Athelstan had brought the grim news back to the red-tiled Sussex farm. His parents had died of sheer grief. Athelstan had returned to Blackfriars to lie on the cold flagstone floor of the Chapter House. He had confessed his sin, begged for absolution, and dedicated his life to God as reparation for the grievous sins he had committed.

'A guilt greater than Cain's,' Father Prior had declared to the brothers assembled in the Chapter House. 'Cain killed his brother. Athelstan is responsible for breaking his vows, and, in doing so, bringing about the deaths of his entire family!'

'Father!'

Athelstan opened his eyes quickly. The woman kneeling on the steps was staring up at him, her beautiful face drawn with concern.

'Father, is there anything wrong?'

'No, Benedicta, I am sorry.'

The Mass continued, the *Agnus Dei* followed by Communion. Athelstan took a host down to the waiting woman who tilted back her head, eyes closed, full red lips open and tongue out, waiting for Athelstan to place Christ's body there. For a second he paused, admiring the flawless beauty: the soft golden-hued skin now stretched across the high cheekbones; the long eyelashes like dark butterfly wings, quiveringly closed; the parted lips showing white, perfectly formed teeth.

'Even if you lust in your mind's eye...' Athelstan reminded himself. He placed the host gently in the woman's mouth and returned to the altar. The chalice was drained, the final benediction given and Mass was ended.

Godric, in his little alcove, belched, snorted and stirred in his sleep. Bonaventure stretched, miaowing softly. But the widow Benedicta still knelt, head bowed.

Athelstan cleared the altar. On his return from the sacristy, his heart skipped when he saw Benedicta still kneeling there. The friar went and sat next to her on the altar steps.

'You are well, Benedicta?'

The dark eyes were full of silent mocking laughter.

'I am well, Father.'

She turned, stroking Bonaventure gently on the side of the neck so the cat purred with pleasure. She glanced mischievously at Athelstan.

'A widow and a cat, Father. The parish of St Erconwald will never become rich!' Her face grew solemn. 'In Mass you were distracted. What was wrong?'

Athelstan looked away. 'Nothing,' he muttered. 'I am just tired.'

'Your astrology?' He grinned. They had had this conversation before. He edged closer.

'Astrology, Benedicta,' he began with mock pomposity, 'is the belief that the stars and the planets affect men's moods and actions. The great Aristotle accepted the theory of the ancient Chaldeans that man is a microcosm of all there is in the universe. Accordingly, there is a bond between each of us and the stars above.'

Benedicta's eyes rounded in sham admiration of his scholarship.

'Now astronomy,' Athelstan continued, 'is the study of the planets and stars themselves.' He stretched out his hands. 'There are two schools of thought.' He thrust forward his left hand. 'The Egyptians and some of the Ancients believe the earth is a flat disc with heaven above and hell below.' Athelstan now stretched out his right arm, his hand rigid like a claw. 'However, Ptolemy, Aristotle and the Classics believe the earth is a sphere within a spherical universe. Each star, each planet, is a world in itself.'

Benedicta leaned back on her heels.

'My father,' she answered tartly, 'said the stars were God's lights in the firmament, put there by the angels at the beginning of time.'

Athelstan knew she was teasing him.

'Your father was correct.' He shrugged sheepishly. 'At Exeter Hall in Oxford I studied the greatest minds. In the end their explanations pale beside the creative wonder of God.'

Benedicta nodded, her eyes serious now, her teasing over.

'So why do you spend so many hours there, Father? On top of the church tower at night? We see your lantern.'

Athelstan shook his head.

'I don't know,' he murmured. 'But on a clear summer's night, if you stare at the velvet blackness and watch the movements of the planets, the shimmering light of the evening star, you become lost in their vastness.' He looked sharply at her. 'It's the nearest man comes to eternity without going through the door of death. When I am there, I am no longer Athelstan, priest and friar. I am just a man, stripped free of cares.'

Benedicta stared down, gently touching the crumbling altar step with the tips of her fingers.

'Tonight,' she murmured, 'I will do that, Father. Stare up at the sky, and see what it is like to die without dying.'

She rose quickly, genuflected before the winking sanctuary lamp and walked quietly out of the church.

Athelstan saw the door close behind her and turned to where Bonaventure awaited his reward. The friar went into the sacristy and brought out the expected bowl of milk. He sat and watched the cat greedily lick the lacy white froth with its pink, narrow-edged tongue.

'Do you know, Bonaventure,' he muttered, 'every time she goes, I want to call her back. She comes here to pray for her husband's soul, another casualty of the king's war, but sometimes I deceive myself and believe she comes to talk to me.'

The cat raised its battered head, yawned and went back to the milk.

'The Master was right,' Athelstan continued. The friar suddenly remembered his old novice master, Father Bernard, who had been responsible for Athelstan's spiritual education in the novitiate at Blackfriars.

'A priest's life, Athelstan,' Father Bernard once began, 'has three great terrors. The first are the lusts of the flesh! These will plague your dreams with visions of soft bodies, satin-silk limbs, full sensuous lips and hair which gleams like burnished gold. Yet these will pass. Prayer, fasting and the onset of old age will drive this enemy from the field of battle.' The old novice master had leaned forward and grasped Athelstan by the wrist. 'Then comes the second terror, the sheer soul-destroying loneliness of a priest: no wife, no children, never the clasp of small warm bodies and clinging arms round your neck. But,' Father Bernard muttered, 'that, too, will pass. The third terror is more dreadful.' And Athelstan remembered the old priest's eyes brimming with tears. 'There's a belief,' the novice master whispered, 'that each person is born destined to love another. Now sometimes we priests are lucky – in our early pilgrimage we never meet this person. But, if you do, then you truly will experience the horrors of the dark night of the soul.' The novice master had paused. 'Can you imagine, Athelstan, to meet, to love, but be bound by God's law never to express it? If you do, you break your vows as a priest and are condemned by the Church to be buried in hell. If you remain faithful to your priestly vows, you bury yourself in a hell of your own making for you will never forget her. You search for her face in crowds, you see her eyes in those of every woman you meet. She plagues your dreams. Not a day passes without her appearing in your thoughts.'

Athelstan thought of Benedicta and knew what the novice master had meant.

'Oh, sweet Christ!' he murmured.

He rose and dusted down his robe. Bonaventure, his milk finished, padded across and stared up.

'Catholic or Catolic, Bonaventure?' Athelstan laughed at his feeble jest. 'Is Father Prior playing a joke on me?' he murmured. 'I am past my twenty-eighth summer and I go from pillar to post.' Perhaps his superiors were testing him, sending him from the rigours of the novitiate to the academic glories of Exeter Hall, then pulling him back to menial duties at Blackfriars and finally to work as the Lord Coroner's clerk and parish priest of St Erconwald.

The friar knelt, crossed himself, and began softly to recite a psalm when he heard a disturbance at the back of the church. He rose in alarm, thinking that perhaps the city authorities had sent retainers to take Godric.

Even in the slums of Southwark, Athelstan realised he lived in turbulent times. Edward III was dead; his heir, Richard II, a mere boy. The powerful, noble hawks still had their way in most matters. Athelstan took a taper, lit it from the candle burning before the Madonna and hurried down the church, splashing through the puddles left by the violent rainstorm a few days before. He opened the door, thrust his head out and smiled. The city guards, roused from their sleep, were now locked in fierce argument with Sir John Cranston, who boomed as soon as he saw his clerk: 'For God's sake, Brother, tell these oafs who I am!' Cranston patted the neck of his huge horse and glared around. 'We have work to do, Brother, another death, murder in Cheapside! One of the great ones of the land. Come on, ignore these dolts!'

'They do not know you, Sir John,' Athelstan replied. 'You go round muffled in cloak and hood, worse than any monk.'

The coroner blew his great cheeks out, pulled back his hood and roared at his tormentors, 'I am Sir John Cranston, coroner in the city, and you, sirs, are disturbing the king's peace! Now back off!'

The men retreated like beaten mastiffs, their dark faces glowering with a mixture of anger and fear.

'Come on, Athelstan,' Cranston bellowed. He looked down at the friar's feet. 'And put that bloody cat away! I hate it.'

Bonaventure, however, seemed to regard Cranston as its long-lost friend. The cat skipped friskily down the steps to sit beneath the coroner's horse, staring up at the big man affectionately as if he was the bearer of a pail of thick creamy milk or a platter of the tastiest fish. Cranston just turned his head away and spat.

'Leave Godric be,' Athelstan warned the city guards. 'You are not to enter my church.'

They nodded. Athelstan locked the door and went over to his own house next to the church. He stuffed his battered leather panniers with parchment, quills and ink, saddled Philomel and joined Sir John. The coroner was in good spirits, thoroughly enjoying his altercation with the city guard as he hated officialdom. He damned the city guards loudly, along with goldsmiths, priests and, looking slyly at Athelstan, Dominican monks who studied the stars. Athelstan ignored him, urging Philomel on.

'Come, Sir John. You said we had business.'

But Cranston was thoroughly roused by now. He shouted abuse once more at the guards, kicked his horse forward and drew noisily alongside Athelstan.

'I suppose you had no sleep last night, Brother? What with your damned stars, your bloody cat, your prayers and your Masses!'

'Ever heavenwards,' Athelstan quipped in reply. 'You, too, should look up at the sky and study the stars.'

'Why?' Cranston asked brusquely. 'Surely you do not believe in that nonsense about planets and heavenly bodies governing our lives? Even the church fathers condemn it.'

'In which case,' Athelstan answered, 'they condemn the star of Bethlehem!'

Sir John belched, grabbed the ever-present wineskin slung over his saddle horn, took a deep gulp and, raising one buttock, farted as loudly as he could. Athelstan decided to ignore Sir John's sentiments, verbal or otherwise. He knew the coroner to be at heart kindly and well intentioned.

'What business takes us to Cheapside?' he asked.

'Sir Thomas Springall,' Cranston replied. 'Or rather, the late Sir Thomas Springall, once a powerful merchant and goldsmith. Now he is as dead as that rat over there.' Cranston pointed to a pile of rubbish, a mixture of animal and human excrement, broken pots, and, lying on top, a mangy rat, its white and russet body swollen with corruption.

'So a goldsmith has died?'

'Has been murdered! Apparently, citizen Springall was not beloved of his servant, Edmund Brampton. Last night Brampton left a poisoned cup in his master's chamber. Sir Thomas was found dead and Brampton discovered later hanging from a beam in one of the garrets.'

'So we are to go there now?'

'Not immediately,' Cranston retorted. 'First, Chief Justice Fortescue wishes to see us at his home Alphen House, in Castle Yard off Holborn.'

Athelstan closed his eyes. Chief Justice Fortescue ranked foremost amongst the people he did not want to see. A powerful courtier, a corrupt judge, a man who took bribes and ran errands for those more powerful than he, the Chief Justice's ruthlessness was a byword amongst the petty law breakers of Southwark.

'So,' Cranston interrupted jovially, 'we meet the Chief Justice and then go to examine death in Cheapside. Merchants who are murdered by their servants! Servants who hang themselves! Tut, tut! What is the world coming to?'

'God only knows,' replied Athelstan. 'When coroners drink and fart and make cutting remarks about men who are still men with all their failings, be they priest or merchant.'

Sir John laughed, pushed his horse closer and slapped Athelstan affectionately on the back.

'I like you, Brother,' he bellowed. 'But God knows why your Order sent you to Southwark, and your prior ordered you to be a coroner's clerk!'

Athelstan made no reply. They'd had this conversation before, with Sir John probing whilst he defended. Some day, Athelstan decided, he would tell Sir John the full truth, although he suspected the coroner knew it already.

'Is it reparation?' Cranston queried now.

'Curiosity,' Athelstan replied, 'can be a grave sin, Sir John.'

Again the coroner laughed and deftly turned the conversation to other matters.

They continued along the narrow stinking streets, following the river towards London Bridge, pushing across marketplaces where the houses reared up to block out the rising sun. Near the bridge they met others, great swaggering lords who rode about on their fierce, iron-shod destriers in a blaze of silk and furs, their heads held high – proud, arrogant, and as ruthless as the hawks they carried. Athelstan studied them. Their women were no better, with their plucked eyebrows and white pasty faces, their soft sensuous bodies clothed in lawn and samite, their heads covered with a profusion of lacy veils. He knew that only a coin's throw away a woman, pale and skeletal, sat crooning over her dying baby, begging for a crust to eat. Athelstan felt his own soul dim, darken with depression. God should send fire, he thought, or a leader to raise up the poor. He bit his lip. If he preached what he thought, he would be guilty of sedition and the prior had kept him under a solemn vow to remain silent, to serve but not to complain.

Cranston and Athelstan had to stop and wait a while. The entrance to the bridge was thronged with people preparing to cross to the northern parts of the city to the great marketplace and shops in Cheapside. Athelstan pulled his hood over his head and pinched his nostrils against the odour from an open sewer full of the turds of nearby households, dregs from the dye houses and wash houses, and rotting carrion which had been dumped there. The area was thick with the foul, tarry smell from the tattered cottages where tanners and leather workers plied their trade.

Cranston nudged him and pointed across to where an inquest was being held over a dead pig, and two constables in striped gowns were scurrying about trying to discover whether there were any bawds, strumpets or scalds in the area in order to arrest them.

'Are there hot houses, sweat houses, where any lewd woman resorts?' one of the constables bellowed, his fleshy face red and sweaty.

'Yes,' Athelstan muttered, 'they are all here. Most of them are my parishioners.'

He watched a milk seller, buckets strapped across her shoulders, come up hoping to ply custom, but turned away as Crim, son of Watkin the dung-collector, crept up and without being noticed spat in one of the buckets. The urchin suddenly reminded Athelstan of duties he had overlooked in his haste to join Sir John Cranston.

'Crim!' Athelstan shouted. 'Come over here!'

The boy ran up, his thin, pallid face grimed with dirt. Athelstan felt in his purse and thrust a penny into the boy's outstretched hand.

'Go tell your father, Crim, I am across London Bridge with Sir John Cranston. He is to feed Bonaventure. Ensure the church door remains locked. If Cecily the courtesan sits there, tell her to move on. You have that message?'

Crim nodded and fled, fast as a bolt from a crossbow.

The crowd eased and Cranston kicked his horse forward. Athelstan followed. They went down on to

London Bridge, weaving their way through houses built so close, the road was hardly a cart span across. Athelstan kept his head down. He hated the place. Houses rose on either side, with some of them jutting out eight feet above the river with its turbulent tide-water rushing through the nineteen arches below. Sir John began to tell him about the history of the old church of St Thomas Overy which they had just passed. Athelstan listened with half an ear. He crossed himself as they passed the chapel of St Thomas à Becket, and only looked up when Sir John ordered them to stop so they could stable their horses at the Three Tuns tavern.

'The crowd is too great,' Sir John commented. 'It would be quicker on foot.'

He paid for ostlers to take the horses away and, with Athelstan striding beside him, they made their way up Fish Hill past St Magnus the Martyr church and into Cheapside. The good weather had brought the crowds out. Apprentices and merchants, their stalls now laid ready for trade, scurried backwards with bales of cloth, leather pelts, purses, panniers, and jerkins. They piled their stalls high, eager for day's business. The ground underfoot was a mixture of mud, human dung and animal decay, still damp from the storm. They slipped and slid, each holding on to the other, Cranston mouthing a mixture of curses and warnings, Athelstan wondering whether to protest or smile at Sir John's purple countenance and violent imprecations. The dung carts were out picking up the refuse left the day before. The burly, red-faced carters, swathed in a collection of garish rags, shouted and swore, their oaths hanging heavy in the thick, warm air. As Cranston and Athelstan passed, they heard one of the dung-collectors give a cry for them to stop working as a corpse was rolled out from behind the buttress of an old house. Athelstan stopped. He glimpsed straggly, white hair, a face sunken in death, the skeletal fingers of an elderly lady. Cranston looked at him and shrugged.

'She is dead, Brother,' he said. 'What can we do?'

Athelstan sketched a sign of the cross in the air and said a prayer that Christ, wherever he was, would receive the old woman's soul.

They went down past the Standard and the Conduit gaol with its open bars where courtesans and bawds caught plying their trade at night, stood for a day whilst being pelted with dirt and cursed by any passing citizen. Cranston asked him a question and Athelstan was about to reply when the stench from the poultry stalls suddenly made him gag: that terrible odour of stale flesh, rotting giblets and dried blood. Athelstan let Cranston chatter on as he held his breath, head down as he passed Scalding Alley where the gutted bodies of game birds were being cleaned and washed in great wooden vats of boiling hot water. At the Rose tavern on a corner of an alleyway they stopped to let a ward constable push by, leading a group of night felons, hands tied behind their backs, halters round their necks. These unfortunates were bound for the Poultry Compter, most of them still drunk, half asleep after their late night revels and roistering. The prisoners slipped and shoved each other. One young man was shouting how the constables had taken his boots and his feet were already gashed and scarred. Athelstan pitied them.

'The gaol's so hot,' the friar murmured, 'it will either waken or kill them before Evensong.'

Cranston shrugged and pushed his way through like a great, fat-bellied ship. They walked on past Old Jewry into Mercery where the streets became more thronged. The women there moved gingerly, skirts brushing the mud, their hands on the arms of gallants who walked the streets looking for such custom, in their high hats, taffeta cloaks, coloured hose and dirty-edged lace shirts.

The paths became softer underfoot as the sewer running down the middle had begun to spill over, choked to the top with the refuse dumped there by householders cleaning the night soil from their chambers. The road narrowed as they passed Soper Lane. The heavy, tiered houses closed in. Dogs barked and frenetically chased the cats hunting amongst the piles of refuse heaped outside each doorway. The crowd now thronged into an array of colour; the blues, golds, yellows and scarlets of the rich contrasting sharply with the brown frocks, russet smocks and black, greasy hats of the farmers who made their way from city market to city market, pulling their small carts behind them. The noise grew to a resounding din. Apprentices were busy yelling and screaming as they searched for custom. The taverns and cook shops were open, the smell of dark ale, fresh bread and spiced food enticing the customers inside. Cranston stopped and Athelstan groaned softly.

'Oh, Sir John,' he pleaded, 'surely not refreshments so early in the day? You know what will happen. Once inside, it will take the devil himself to get you out!'

Athelstan sighed with relief as the coroner shook his head regretfully and they moved on. A party of sheriff's men appeared, dressed in their bands of office, carrying long white canes which they used to clear a way through the crowds. They circled a man in a black leather jerkin and hose. His hands were bound, the ends of the cord being tied around the wrists of two of his captors. The prisoner's jerkin was torn aside to reveal a tattered shirt. His unshaven face was a mass of bruises from brow to chin. Someone whispered, 'Warlock! Wizard!' An apprentice picked up handfuls of mud and threw them, only to receive whacks across his shoulders from the white canes.

'Make way! Make way!'

Cranston and Athelstan walked on, past the stocks already full with miscreants: a pedlar; a manser-vant caught in lechery; a foister; and two other pickpockets. At last they turned off the Holborn thoroughfare into Castle Yard. A pleasant place, the houses being fewer, better spaced, each ringed by sweet-smelling rose gardens and tree-filled orchards. Fortescue's house was the grandest, standing in its own grounds, a massive framework of black timber, thick and broad as oaks, gilded and embossed with intricate devices. Between the black beams the white plaster gleamed like pure snow. Each of the four storeys jutted out slightly over the one on which it rested and each had windows of mullioned glass, reinforced with strips of lead. Cranston lifted the great brass knocker shaped in the form of a knight's gauntlet and brought it down hard. A servant answered and, when Cranston boomed out who they were, ushered them through the open door into a dark panelled hall with woollen carpets on the floor and gold-tinged drapes on the wall.

Athelstan noticed how cool the place was as they were led up an oak staircase and into a long gallery, so dark the wax candles in their silver holders had already been lit.

The servant tapped on one of the doors.

'Come in!' The voice was soft and cultured.

The chamber inside was rectangular in shape, walls painted red with silver stars and the polished tile floor covered with rugs; candles also glowed here because the light was poor and the mullioned window high above the desk was small. The candles bathed the area round the great oak desk in a pool of light. Chief Justice Fortescue, enthroned behind it, barely moved as they entered. One beringed hand continued silently to drum the top of the desk while the other shuffled documents about. Like the rest of his kind, Fortescue was a tall, severe man, completely bald, with features as sharp as a knife and eyes as hard as flint. He greeted Sir John Cranston with forced warmth but, when Athelstan introduced himself and described his office, the Chief Justice smiled chillingly, dismissing him with a flicker of his eyes.

'Most uncommon,' he murmured, 'for a friar to be out of his order even, and serving in such a lowly office!'

Cranston snorted rudely and would have intervened if Athelstan had not.

'Chief Justice Fortescue,' he answered, 'my business is my own. You summoned me here. I requested no audience.'

Cranston belched loudly in agreement.

'True! True!' Fortescue murmured. 'But this meeting was arranged by someone more powerful than I.' He smiled mirthlessly and picked up a knife he used for cutting parchment, balancing it delicately between his hands. 'We live in strange times, Brother. The old king is dead and for the first time in fifty years we have a new king, and he is a child. These are dangerous times. Enemies within and enemies without!' He lowered his voice. 'Some people say that a strong man is needed to manage the realm.'

'Like your patron, His Grace John of Gaunt, Duke of Lancaster?' Cranston interrupted.

'Like His Grace the Duke of Lancaster,' Fortescue mimicked in reply. 'He is the regent, proclaimed so by the late king's will.'

'Regent!' Cranston snapped. 'Not king!'

'Some people say he should be.'

'Then some people,' Cranston barked, 'are varlets and traitors!'

Fortescue smiled as if he had tried to go down a path and realised it was blocked.

'Of course, of course, Sir John,' he murmured. 'We know each other well. But Gaunt is regent, he needs friends and allies. Other lords seek his head; the Commons mutter about conspiracies, expenditure, the need to make peace with France and Spain. They object to taxes which are necessary.'

'The Commons may be right,' Cranston tartly replied.

'About others,' Fortescue continued, 'they may be, but the regent is steadfast in his loyalty to the young king and looks for support from his friends and allies. Men like Springall, Sir Thomas Springall, goldsmith, merchant, and alderman of the city.'

'Springall is dead,' Cranston retorted, 'and so the duke has lost a powerful friend.'

'Exactly!'

Athelstan saw the obsidian eyes of the Chief Justice glare at the coroner and intervened before further damage was done. Sir John was a lawyer from the Middle Temple and appointed as coroner by the late king, an appointment confirmed by the Commons and the powerful Guildhall merchants, yet even he could go too far.

'My Lord of Gaunt must grieve for Springall's death?' Athelstan asked.

'He does.'

Fortescue rose and went to a small table in the corner where stood a number of cups. He filled them to the brim and brought them back. Athelstan refused his, as it was too early in the morning for such drink, but Cranston did justice to both of them, draining one goblet then the other down his cavernous throat in a long, gulping sound. After he had finished, Cranston slammed the cups on the table in front of him, folded his great thick arms and looked steadily back at the Chief Justice.

'Sir Thomas Springall,' Fortescue continued, 'was a good friend of the duke's. A close associate. Last night he held a banquet in his house in the Strand. I was there, together with his wife, his brother Sir Richard, and other colleagues. I left after sunset when the bells of St Mary Le Bow were ringing the curfew. A pleasant evening – the conversation, like the food, most appetising and titillating. From what Sir Richard Springall has told me, Sir Thomas retired just before midnight. Although married, he slept in his own bed chamber. He bade his wife, brother and associates good night and went upstairs to his chamber where, as always, he locked and bolted the door. Now Sir Thomas was a fleshly man. Like you, Sir John, he liked a good glass of claret. Every night he ordered his servant, Brampton, to leave one such cup on the table beside his bed. This morning, Springall's chaplain, Father Crispin, went to rouse him and received no answer. Others were called and, to cut a long story short, the door was forced. Sir Thomas Springall was found lying dead in his bed, the cup beside him half empty. The local physician was summoned. He examined the corpse as well as the contents of the wine cup and pronounced Sir Thomas had been poisoned. A search was immediately made.' Fortescue paused and licked his thin lips. 'Brampton's chamber was deserted but, when his chest was rifled, they found phials of poison hidden beneath garments at the bottom. Then an hour ago Brampton was found hanging in a garret of the house.' Fortescue heaved a sigh. 'It would appear that Brampton and Sir Thomas had quarrelled during the day and this reached a climax early in the afternoon. Brampton kept to himself in a sulk. He must have purchased the poison or had it ready, took the cup to his master's room, put the poison in and left. However, like Judas, he suffered remorse. He went up to the garret of the house and, like Judas, hanged himself there.'

'Strange,' Cranston mused, and pursed his lips.

'What is, Sir John?'

'We have a steward who has quarrelled with his master and stormed out. Nevertheless, he remembers his duty and takes up a goblet of wine.'

'If the wine had not been poisoned,' Fortescue replied sharply, 'it would have been a kindness. But, Sir John, a man who offers a poisoned chalice is no friend.'

'So what is the mystery?'

Fortescue smiled thinly.

'Ah, that is for you to discover. My Lord Gaunt thinks there is one. Remember, Springall lent the crown monies. There may be reason to see the merchant's death as a hindrance to the regent.' Fortescue shrugged. 'His Grace has not opened his secret thoughts to me, but he believes there is a threat to his rule here.'

The Chief Justice picked up a scroll tied with scarlet ribbon and handed it over to Cranston. Athelstan glimpsed the purple seals of the regent.

'Your commission,' Fortescue said drily, 'warrants, and permission for you to pursue this matter.'

The Chief Justice rose as a sign that the meeting was over.

'Of course, all expenses are to be handed over to the clerk of the Exchequer.' He rubbed his hands together dryly. 'Though the Barons will question any overindulgence in food or drink.'

Cranston rose.

'My bills will be fair, as they always are, and I will be taking constant refreshment. After all, My Lord, when you listen to some men, their lies stick in your throat and give you a terrible thirst.'

He picked up his cloak; Athelstan, clutching his leather bag of writing materials, followed Cranston's lumbering gait towards the door. The friar did not dare look up and fought to keep his face straight.

'Sir John!'

The coroner stopped.

'The Sons of Dives?' Fortescue asked. 'Do you know of them?'

Cranston shook his head. 'No, why should I?'

'They are a secret group,' Fortescue testily replied. 'Their nature and purpose a mystery. But Sir Thomas's name, so my spies relate, was linked to them. Dives means nothing to you?'

'He was a judge in the gospels, was he not? Rich and corrupt who let the poor starve outside his gates.'

Fortescue smiled and looked at Brother Athelstan.

'Is it true, Friar,' he said abruptly, 'that you atone for your brother's death? Is that why your Order has put you in St Erconwald's church and made you clerk to Sir John Cranston here?' The Chief Justice's grin widened. 'You should sit at his feet, Brother. Sir John will instruct you in the law. He will tell you all he knows. I am sure it will not take long!'

Cranston turned. His steel grey mop of hair seemed to bristle with anger, and his dark eyes held the ghost of malicious mockery as he stroked his beard and moustache.

'I will do that, My Lord,' he said slowly. 'I will instruct Brother Athelstan in what I know about the law and I am sure it will not take long. Then, of course, I will instruct him in what you and I both know, and I am sure it will not take any longer!'

Cranston spun on his heel and, with Athelstan scurrying behind him, choking on his laughter, swept out of Alphen House into Castle Yard and back to Holborn.

'Bastard! Varlet! Lecher! Arse pimple!' Cranston indulged in a succinct summary of what he thought of the Chief Justice. Athelstan just shook his head, caught between admiration of Cranston's honesty and a desire to burst into laughter at the way he'd dealt with the Chief Justice. They paused on the corner of Holborn thoroughfare to let an execution cart rattle by, its iron wheels crashing on the cobbles. Inside a black-masked hangman and a parson, his sallow face covered in sweat, were standing over a pirate caught, so the notice pinned to the cart said, two days ago off the mouth of the Thames. Despite the placard around his neck, the fellow was laughing and joking with the small crowd which followed on either side, chanting a song popular on execution days: 'Put on your smocks on Monday.' The condemned man did not seem to give a fig for his impending death. He was more determined to cut up his scarlet cloak and taffeta jerkin and distribute the pieces amongst the spectators. Every so often he would look up and grin at the executioner.

'You will take no share of my clothes!' he bawled. 'I came naked into the world and I will go out naked. And all the more merrily for knowing you got nothing from me!'

The crowd roared with laughter at this sally and, as the cart trundled up to the great three-branched scaffold at the Elms, broke into fresh chants and songs.

'More like a wedding than an execution!' Cranston muttered. 'The hangman will slip the knot. This fellow will dance for a long time before he dies.'

They crossed the rutted track leading to the shady side of the street for the sun now shone much stronger, beating fiercely down on them. Cranston mopped his sweating face and pushed Athelstan into the welcoming shadows of the Bishop's Pig tavern. The tap room inside was dark and cool with a high, black-timbered ceiling letting the air circulate as it poured through the great open windows at the far end. Cranston and Athelstan sat there, the friar silently wondering to himself about Sir John's constant need for refreshment; the coroner seemed to eat and drink as if there was no tomorrow. As usual Sir John did full justice to himself, ordering two large tankards of frothy dark ale, an eel pie and a dish of vegetables. All disappeared down his yawning throat as the coroner continued to berate Fortescue. At last, the rancour drained from him, Sir John wiped his lips, leaned back against the wall and glanced across at the friar. Athelstan, looking up from his own thoughts about his church, realised Sir John's good humour had returned and now they would concentrate on the matter in hand.

'Was the Chief Justice right?'

'About what?' Athelstan asked.

'About you and your brother?'

Athelstan made a face.

'To a certain extent he spoke the truth, but I do not think the Chief Justice was concerned with that. More with the malicious desire to hurt.'

Cranston nodded and looked away. Now, he did not like priests. He did not like monks. He certainly did not like friars, but Athelstan was different. He looked at the friar's dark face, the black hair cut neatly in a tonsure. More like a soldier, he thought, than a monk. He sighed, wiping the sweat from his throat; every man had his secrets, and Cranston had his own.

'This matter,' he said. 'Springall's death. Do you think there is a mystery?'

Athelstan leaned forward, resting his elbows on his knees.

'There is something strange,' he muttered. 'A merchant is murdered by his servant who then commits suicide. A very neat death, orderly. All the ends tied up like a parcel, a package, a gift for Twelfth Night. Surely two mysteries? The first one is the neatness of the deaths, the second my Lord of Gaunt's interest in them. Yes, Sir John, I think there is a mystery but only the good Lord knows whether we will solve it!'

'There is more, isn't there?' Cranston said, pleased to have confirmation of his own thoughts.

'Oh, yes,' Athelstan replied, sitting up and stretching. 'Gaunt seems frightened that Springall has died, as if the death poses a personal threat. It must be so, otherwise why would he get the Chief Justice of the Courts to interview us? To impress upon us the importance of the task? To test our loyalty and give us a special commission?' He got up. 'If you are refreshed, Sir John, perhaps it is time we found out.'

Cranston rose, picked up his cloak and threw it across his arm. He adjusted his great sword belt round his girth. From it hung a long thin Welsh dagger shoved into a battered leather sheath and the broadest sword Athelstan had ever seen. Once again, he tightened his lips to hide his smile. Cranston waddled through the tavern, shouting goodbye to the landlord and his wife who were busy amongst the barrels at the far end of the room. The coroner's good spirits were restored and Athelstan braced himself for an exciting day.

They walked back up Cheapside. It was now early afternoon and the traders were busy.

'A fine hat for the French block!' one called. 'Pins! Points! Garters! Spanish gloves! Silk ribbons!' shouted another.

'Come,' a woman cackled from a doorway, 'have your ruffs starched, fine cobweb lawn!'

The cries rose like a demonic chorus. Carts rumbled by, now empty after a morning's trade, their owners desirous of getting clear of the city gates before the curfew tolled. A group of aldermen attired in long, richly furred robes were rudely mocked by a troupe of gallants resplendent in gold, satin garments and cheap jewellery, the air thick with their even cheaper perfume. A party of horsemen trotted in from the fields, hawks on their wrists. The fierce birds, their blood hunger satisfied, sat quietly under their hoods. Cranston stopped by a barber's shop, fingering his beard and moustache, but one look at the steaming blood in the bowls beside the chair changed his mind. They continued back up Cheapside.

'You know the house, Sir John?'

Cranston nodded and pointed. 'It is there, the Springall mansion.'

Athelstan paused and took Cranston by the elbow. 'Sir John, wait awhile.' He pulled the bemused coroner into a darkened doorway.

'What is it, Monk?'

'I am a friar, Sir John. Please remember that. A member of the preaching order founded by St Dominic to work amongst the poor and educate the unenlightened.'

Cranston beamed. 'I stand corrected. So what is it, *Friar*?'

'Sir John, the warrants? We should inspect them.'

The coroner made a face, then pulled out the scrolls handed to him by Fortescue. He broke the seals and opened them.

'Nothing much,' he muttered, reading them quickly. 'They give us full authority to investigate matters surrounding the death of Sir Thomas Springall and oblige all loyal subjects, on their loyalty, to answer our questions.' He looked sharply at Athelstan. 'I wonder if that includes the Sons of Dives?'

The friar shrugged.

'You know the city better than I do, Sir John. Every trade has its guild, every coven its patron saint. I suspect the Sons of Dives is a title fabricated to cover the less salubrious dealings of certain of our rich merchants. They do not plot treason but profit.'

Cranston grinned and stepped out of the doorway.

'Then come, trusty Dominican, let us discover more!'

Chapter 2

The house was a fine building, very similar to that of
Lord Fortescue, though today great black banners of
costliest lawn hung from the upstairs windows and
the broad shield of the goldsmith above the main
door was hidden under black damask. An old manservant, dressed like death itself, answered the door; his
face was soaked with tears, his eyes red-rimmed from
crying.

'Sir John Cranston, coroner, and Brother Athelstan,' the friar quietly announced.

The fellow nodded and led them down a dark
passageway into the great banqueting hall, also hung
in black. As they crossed the black and white chessboard floor, Athelstan felt he was entering the valley
of shadows. Black cloths hid the tapestries and paintings on the walls. The air seemed thick and heavy,
not due to the heat and the closeness of the day but
to something else which prickled the hair at the back
of his neck and made him shiver. Cranston, however,
lumbered along, his bleary eyes fixed on a group
sitting round the table on the dais at the end of the
hall. In the centre a great silver salt cellar winked

like a beacon light in the glow of the glittering candles. The small oriel window above the table let in some brightness but Athelstan could not make out the figures clearly. They seemed concealed in the shadows, talking quietly. All conversation ceased as they stared at Cranston's huge form stumbling towards them.

'Can I help you?'

Cranston stopped abruptly, almost colliding with Athelstan as they turned to look at the speaker. A young woman who had been sitting in the window embrasure inside the hall got up and came forward.

'You are?' Athelstan asked.

'Sir Thomas Springall's wife,' the woman replied coolly, stepping into the light.

Sweet God, Athelstan thought, she was beautiful. Her face a vision of loveliness with dark-ringed eyes and the face of an angel like those painted on windows in the abbey church. Her slender body was exquisitely formed, her skin burnished gold. She had dark, blood-red hair and lips as crimson and as lush as a spring rose.

'Sir Thomas's widow?' Cranston asked tactfully.

'Yes.' The voice grew harsh. 'And you, sirs, what are you doing here?'

Cranston glanced up at the group still sitting silently round the table on the dais, and drunkenly doffed his hat.

'Sir John Cranston, king's coroner in the city. And this,' he waved behind him, 'is my faithful Mephistopheles, Brother Athelstan.'

The woman looked puzzled.

'My clerk,' Cranston slurred.

'Madam,' Athelstan interrupted, 'God rest your husband's soul, but he is dead. Sir John and I have orders to examine the body to determine the true cause of death. We are sorry to intrude on your grief.'

The woman stepped closer and Athelstan noticed how pale her face was, her eyes red-rimmed with crying. He noticed that the cuffs on the sleeves of her black lace dress were wet with tears.

The woman waved them up to the dais and the group sitting there rose. They were all dressed in black and seemed to hide behind a broad-chested man, sleek and fat, with a balding head, fleshy nose, and eyes and mouth as hard as a rock.

'Who are you, sirs?' he snapped. 'I am Sir Richard Springall, brother and executor to the late Sir Thomas!'

Cranston and Athelstan introduced themselves.

'And why are you here?'

'At the Chief Justice's request.'

Cranston handed over his commission. Sir Richard undid the red silk cord, unrolled the parchment and gave its contents a cursory glance. He waved expansively to the table.

'You may as well join us. We have business to discuss. Sir Thomas's death is a great blow.'

Athelstan thought Sir Richard looked more the eager merchant than the grieving brother, but they took their seats and Sir Richard introduced his companions. At the far end of the table was Father Crispin, chancery priest and chaplain to the Springall household. He was a young man, gaunt-faced, dark-eyed, clean shaven, his hair not cut in a tonsure but hanging in ringlets down to his shoulders. His dark gown was expensive, tied at the throat with a gold clasp and silver white bows. On the other side sat Edmund Buckingham, clerk to Sir Thomas, about the same age as Father Crispin, but darker, sallow-faced, hard-eyed and thin-lipped. A born clerk or secretarius, a counter of bales and cloths, more suited to tidying accounts and storing parchment away than engaging in idle conversation. He drummed the table loudly with his fingers, showing his annoyance at what he considered an unwarranted intrusion. The two remaining members of the group, Allingham and Vechey, were typical merchants in their dark samite jerkins, gold chains and silver wire rings on fleshy fingers. Stephen Allingham was tall and lanky, with a pockmarked, dour face and greasy red hair. His front teeth stuck out, making him look like a frightened rabbit; his fingers, the nails thick with dirt, kept fluttering to his mouth as if he was trying to remember something. Theobald Vechey was short and fat; his face puffy white like kneaded dough, his eyes small black buttons, his nose slightly crooked and his mouth pursed tight with sourness.

After the introductions, Sir Richard ordered cups of sack.

Oh, God! Athelstan prayed. Not more!

Sir John, already heavy-eyed, beamed expansively. A servant brought a tray of cups. Sir John downed his in one noisy gulp and looked greedily at Athelstan's; the friar sighed and nodded. Sir John grinned and supped that one, impervious to the astonished looks of those around him. Athelstan emptied his leather bag, smoothing the creases out of the parchment and arranging the quills and silver ink horn in his writing tray. Sir John, refreshed, clapped his hands and leaned forward, glancing towards Sir Richard at the head of the table. Cranston's elbow slipped and he lurched dangerously. Athelstan heard the young clerk titter and glimpsed the silent mockery in Lady Isabella's beautiful eyes.

'Yes, quite,' Cranston trumpeted. 'Sir Richard, your account? Your brother has been slain.'

'Last night,' Sir Richard began, 'a banquet was held. All of us were present, together with Sir John Fortescue, the Chief Justice. He left about eleven, before midnight.' Sir Richard licked his lips and Athelstan wondered why the Chief Justice had lied about the hour at which he had left the house.

'My brother,' Sir Richard continued, 'bade us good night here in the hall and went up to his chamber.'

'Lady Isabella,' Cranston interrupted, 'you have your own separate room?'

'Yes.' The lady glared back frostily. 'My husband preferred it that way.'

'Of course.' Cranston beamed. 'Sir Richard?'

'I went to say goodnight to my brother. He was dressed for bed, the drapes pulled back. I saw the wine cup on the table beside his bed. He wished me a fair night's sleep. As I walked away, I heard him lock and bolt the door behind me.'

Athelstan put down his quill. 'Why did he do that?'

Sir Richard shook his head. 'I don't know, he always did. He liked his privacy.'

'Then what?'

'Next morning,' Father Crispin began, leaning forward, 'I went to wake...'

'No!' Lady Isabella interrupted. 'I sent my maid, Alicia. She tapped on my husband's door a few minutes after he had retired and asked if there was anything he wanted.' She smoothed the table in front of her with long, white elegant fingers. 'My husband called out that all was well.'

Athelstan looked sideways at Cranston. The coroner's heavy-lidded eyes were closing. Athelstan kicked him fiercely under the table.

'Ah, yes, of course.' Cranston pulled himself up, burping gently like a child. 'Father Crispin, you were saying?'

'At Prime – yes, about then – the bells of St Mary Le Bow were ringing. It was a fair morning, and Sir Thomas had asked to be roused early. I went up to his chamber and knocked. There was no reply. So I went for Sir Richard. He also tried to waken Sir Thomas.' The young priest's voice trailed off.

'Then what?'

'The door was forced,' Sir Richard replied. 'My brother was sprawled on the bed. We thought at first he had had some seizure and sent for the family physician, Peter de Troyes. He examined my brother and saw his mouth was stained, the lips black. So he sniffed the cup and pronounced it drugged, possibly with a mixture of belladonna and red arsenic. Enough to kill the entire household!'

'Who put the cup there?' Athelstan asked, nudging Cranston awake.

'My husband liked a goblet of the best Bordeaux in his chamber at night before retiring. Brampton always took it up to him.'

'Ah, yes, Brampton brought a cup of claret!' Cranston smacked his lips. 'He must have been a fine servant, a good fellow!'

'Sir John,' Lady Isabella shrieked in fury, 'he poisoned my husband!'

'What makes you say that?'

'He took the cup up.'

'How do you know?'

'He always did!'

'So why did Brampton hang himself?'

'Out of remorse, I suppose. God and his saints,' she cried, 'how do I know?'

'Sir John...' Father Crispin raised his hand in a placatory gesture at Sir Richard's intended outburst in her defence. The merchant looked choleric, so red-faced Athelstan thought he might have a seizure. 'Lady Isabella is distraught,' continued the priest. 'Brampton took the cup up, we are sure of that.'

'Was he present at the banquet last night?' Athelstan asked.

'No.' Sir Richard shook his head. 'He and my brother had a fierce quarrel earlier in the day.'

'About what?'

Sir Richard looked nervously down the table at Vechey and Allingham.

'Sir Thomas was furious: he accused Brampton of searching amongst his documents and memoranda. There are caskets in my brother's room. He found the lid of one forced and, beside it, a silver button from Brampton's jerkin. Brampton, of course, denied the charge and the quarrel continued most of the day.'

'So Brampton sulked in his room, did not attend the banquet and retired for the night – but not before he had taken a goblet of wine along to his master's chamber?'

'So it would seem.'

Cranston had now gently nodded off to sleep, his head tilting sideways, his soft snores indicative of a good day's drinking. Athelstan ignored the company's amused glances, pushed away the writing tray and tried to assert himself. 'I cannot understand this,' he said. 'Brampton argues with Sir Thomas, who has accused him of rifling amongst his private papers?'

'Yes,' Sir Richard nodded, watching him guardedly.

'Brampton storms out but later takes up a cup of wine. A kind gesture?'

'Not if it was poisoned!' Allingham squeaked. 'The cup was poisoned, laced with a deadly potion.' Athelstan felt caught, trapped in a mire. The listeners around the table were gently mocking him, dismissing Cranston as a drunk and himself as an ignorant friar.

'Who was present,' he asked, 'when Sir Thomas's body was found?'

'I was,' Sir Richard replied. 'And course Father Crispin. Master Buckingham also came up.'

'As did I,' Allingham grated.

'Yes, that's correct,' Sir Richard added.

'So you sent for the physician?'

'Yes, as I have said.'

'And then what?'

'I dressed the body,' Father Crispin offered. 'I washed him, did what I could, and gave Sir Thomas the last rites, anointing his hands, face and feet. You may recall, Brother, there are some theologians, Dominicans,' the priest smiled thinly, 'who maintain the soul does not leave the body until hours after death. I prayed God would have mercy on Sir Thomas's soul.'

'Did Sir Thomas need mercy?'

'He was a good man,' Father Crispin replied sharply. 'He founded chantries, gave money to the poor, distributed food, and looked after widows and orphans.'

'I am sure the good Lord will have mercy on him,' Athelstan murmured. 'Now for Brampton. You made a search for him?'

'Yes,' Sir Richard replied briskly. 'We suspected he was involved so we searched his chamber. We found a small stoppered phial in a chest beneath some robes. A servant took it round to Peter de Troyes, who pronounced it held the same mixture found in my brother's wine cup. We then searched for Brampton.'

'I found the corpse,' Vechey interrupted. 'I noticed that the door leading to the garret was half open, so I went up.' He swallowed. 'Brampton was hanging there.' The fellow shivered. 'It was dreadful. The garret was empty and cold. There was a horrible smell. Brampton's body was hanging there like a broken doll, a child's toy, his neck askew, his face blackened, tongue lolling out!'

He gulped at his wine.

'I cut him down and loosened the rope, but he was dead, the corpse clammy and cold.' He looked pleadingly at Sir Richard. 'The body's still there. It must be removed!'

'Tell me,' Athelstan said, 'do you all live here?'

'Yes,' Sir Richard replied. 'Master Allingham is a bachelor. Master Vechey is a widower,' he smiled, 'though still with an eye for the ladies. This mansion is great, four storeys high, built in a square round a courtyard. Sir Thomas saw no reason why his business partners should not share the same house. Tenements, property, their value has increased, and with royal taxes...' His voice trailed off.

Athelstan nodded understandingly, trying to mask his frustration. There was nothing here. Nothing at all. A merchant had been killed, his assassin had hanged himself. At the same time Athelstan detected something. These people were pompous, arrogant, sure of themselves. They walked the streets like cocks, confident of their wealth, their power, and their friends at court or in the Exchequer.

'Sir Thomas treated Brampton well?' Athelstan asked. 'Was he a good lord?'

'A more courteous gentleman you could not hope to meet,' Allingham answered. 'Sir Thomas gave generously in alms to the poor of the parish of St Bartholomew's, to the Guild, and,' he ended contemptuously, 'to friars like you!'

'So why should he quarrel so violently with Brampton? Had he done it before?'

Allingham stopped, wrong-footed.

'No,' he murmured. 'No, he had not. There were just disagreements.'

'Lady Isabella,' Athelstan asked, 'your husband – was he anxious or concerned about anything?'

Sir Richard patted Lady Isabella's wrist as a sign that he would answer for her.

'He was worried about the war, and the increase of piracy in the Narrow Seas. He lost two ships recently to Hanse pirates. He resented the old king's growing demands for loans.'

'And Brampton, was he a good steward?'

'Yes,' Lady Isabella answered quickly, 'he was.'

'What kind of man?'

She made a grimace. 'Quiet, gentle, a loyal servant.' Her eyes softened. 'I saw him just after the quarrel with my husband. I have never seen Brampton in such a state, fretting and anxious, so angry he could hardly sit still.'

'Your husband, did he mention the quarrel?'

'He said he would investigate the matter later. He was surprised more than angry that Brampton could do such a thing. He said it was out of character.' She paused. 'At the banquet my husband broached a cask of his best Bordeaux. I sent up a cup as a peace offering to Brampton.'

'You are sure Sir Thomas thought highly of Brampton?'

'Oh, I am certain.' Lady Isabella shook her head and stared down at the table.

'Shall we move on to other matters? The banquet last night.'

Cranston farted gently. The sound, however, rang through the hall like a loud bell and Lady Isabella looked away in disgust. Sir Richard glared at the coroner whilst Athelstan blushed with embarrassment at the sniggering and laughter from Buckingham.

'Why was the banquet held last night?'

'The young king's coronation,' Sir Richard replied. 'Each guild must prepare its pageant. We were discussing the plans the Guild of Goldsmiths had for their spectacle.'

'So why was Chief Justice Fortescue present?'

'We do not know,' Allingham squeaked. 'Sir Thomas said that the Chief Justice would be coming. He often did business with him.' He smirked. 'Fortescue owed him money, like many judges and lords in the city.'

'Why all these questions?' Sir Richard asked softly. 'Surely the matter is clear. Even a child,' glancing contemptuously at Sir John, 'can see that! My brother was murdered, his assassin was Brampton. Why must we go over these matters, muddying waters, causing pain and grief? We are busy men, Brother Athelstan. Your friend may sleep but we have business to attend to. My brother's corpse lies cold upstairs. There is a funeral to arrange, matters to put straight, business colleagues to contact.'

'Strange!' Cranston stirred and opened his eyes. 'I find it very strange!'

Athelstan looked down the table and grinned to himself. One of the things he could never understand but most enjoyed about Cranston was how the big, fat coroner could doze and yet be aware of conversations going on around him.

'What is strange?' Lady Isabella snapped, her distaste for the coroner now openly apparent.

61

'Well, My Lady,' Cranston licked his lips, 'your husband has a servant, Brampton. Brampton is faithful and obedient, like the good steward in the gospel. Why should he wish to search amongst your husband's papers? What did your husband have to hide?'

Lady Isabella just glared back.

'Let us say he did,' Cranston continued, breathing in heavily. 'Just let us say he did and there was a quarrel – surely no cause for murder or suicide? You have said, Madam, how Brampton was a quiet, placid fellow. Not a man of hot humours or rash disposition who would commit such a dreadful act and then compound it by taking his own life.'

'How else did it happen?' Sir Richard asked stiffly.

'Well,' Cranston said, 'is it possible that Brampton took the wine cup as a peace offering to his master?' He ignored the sneer on Vechey's face. 'Placed it on the table and then left?'

'And?' Lady Isabella asked.

'Someone else went up those stairs during the banquet and put poison into the cup. Or,' Cranston rubbed his fat hands together, now warming to his subject, 'how do we know that Sir Thomas did not have a visitor after he retired? Someone who went up the stairs and along the gallery, slipped into Sir Thomas's room, perhaps engaging him in conversation and, while doing so, secretly poured the poison into the cup.' He held up a hand to still the murmur. 'I am just theorising, as the theologians say, speculating on the nature of things.'

'Then, Sir, you are a fool!'

Cranston, Athelstan and the whole company turned round in astonishment and looked down the hall. In the doorway stood an old lady dressed completely in black like a nun. Her head was covered by a thick, lawn veil arranged in the old-fashioned wimple which framed her sour lemon face in its black lace. She walked forward, her silver-topped stick beating loudly on the hall floor.

'You are a fool!'

Cranston rose. 'Perhaps I am, Madam, but who are you?'

Sir Richard darted forward.

'Lady Ermengilde, may I present Sir John Cranston, coroner of the city.'

The old lady glared at the coroner with eyes like two dark pools.

'I have heard of you, Cranston, your drinking and your lechery! What are you doing in my son's house?'

'Sir John is here at the request of Chief Justice Fortescue.' Sir Richard's voice was soft, almost pleading.

'Another rogue!' the lady snapped.

'I asked, Madam, to whom do I have the pleasure of speaking?' Sir John repeated.

'My name is Lady Ermengilde Springall. I am the mother of Sir Richard,' she stroked Springall's arm. 'My other son now lies dead upstairs and I come down to hear you chatter on about nonsense. Brampton may have been a good steward. He was also a varlet, a commoner! He had ideas above his station. Thomas rebuked him, and like many of his kind, Brampton could not take it. His heart was filled with malice. Satan whispered in his ear, and he carried out his dreadful deed.' The old woman crashed her stick to the floor and held it between her two hands, resting on it. 'At least Brampton did us all the courtesy of hanging himself and so sparing the public expense and the work of the hangman at the Elms!'

Athelstan watched Cranston. The coroner was now in one of his most dangerous moods. He smiled but only round the lips. His eyes were hard and fixed, watching the old lady as a swordsman might an opponent waiting for the next parry.

'Lady Ermengilde, you seem well appraised of what happened. I crave your indulgence. Can you explain more?'

'My chamber is close to that of my son,' she snapped. 'The staircase beyond,' she indicated with a nod of her head, 'leads up to two galleries, one running to the right. At the end was Sir Thomas's chamber and, next to his, mine.'

'Any other?'

Lady Ermengilde's eyes slid towards her daughter-in-law.

'That of the Lady Isabella. There is a gallery to the left, identical to the one I've described except for one thing.' She raised one bony finger. 'My chamber, as well as those of Sir Thomas and Lady Isabella, stands on the Nightingale Gallery.'

'The Nightingale Gallery?' Athelstan asked. 'What is that?'

Dame Ermengilde smiled and walked nearer, her face looking more than ever like a sour apple. Athelstan noticed she was not dressed in black but in the dark brown habit of a nun, though her scorn for the luxuries of this world must have been shallow for the rings on her fingers held jewels the size of birds' eggs. A worldly lady, Athelstan thought, for all her prim face, sour lips and arrogant eyes.

'It's well known,' she continued, her voice tinged with patronising arrogance. 'This house was built on a square, and on the opposite corner of the square are stairs to the second storey.' She waved her hand to the far doorway which stood slightly ajar. Through it, Athelstan could glimpse steep stairs. 'They will take you up to Sir Thomas's chamber,' she added. 'At the top are two corridors. The gallery to the right is the Nightingale Gallery because it "sings" when anyone walks through it.' She must have seen the disbelief in Cranston's bleary eyes. 'This house is very old,' she continued, looking up at the great blackened beams. 'It was built in the reign of King John.' She smirked. 'A time very like our own. A strong ruler was needed. Anyway, one of John's mercenary captains used this house as a base from which to control London. He trusted no one, not even his own men.' Her eyes drifted to Lady Isabella, who was standing behind Athelstan. 'Anyway, he had the floor of that gallery taken up and replaced with special boards of yew. No one can approach any of the three chambers on that gallery without making it creak, or "sing". Hence its name.'

'And the importance of this?' Cranston asked.

'The importance, my dear coroner,' she purred in reply, 'is that I was in my chamber all evening. I am old and banquets bore me. Oh, I heard the talk and the laughter from the hall below. It disturbed my sleep. Fortunately, I need very little.' She glared at Cranston. 'You will find out for yourself, Sir John, age makes you sleep lightly.'

'Just in case Death taps you on the shoulder!' he answered crossly.

'Quite,' she jibed back. 'But Death has a tendency, as you well know, Sir John, to take the heaviest first!'

'My Lady,' Athelstan intervened, 'the events of yesterday... you heard no one go up to Sir Thomas's chamber?'

'Before the banquet people were scurrying back-wards and forwards,' she retorted. 'During the meal I heard the Nightingale sing once. I was surprised. I opened the door and saw Brampton, carrying a wine cup in his hand. I heard him open the door to my son's chamber and then go back downstairs again. I heard no other noise before Sir Thomas's footsteps when he came up to his chamber. Sir Richard followed him and bade him goodnight, then Lady Isabella's maid made her inquiry. After that the house was silent till this morning. Father Crispin came up, I heard him knock on the door, then he went for Sir Richard and brought him back.'

Cranston nodded. 'I thank you, Lady Ermengilde. You have solved one piece of the puzzle. Brampton did take the cup up. Now,' he looked at Sir Richard, 'disturbing and painful though it may be, I must insist that I view the bodies of both men.' He bowed to Lady Isabella. 'Your husband first, My Lady. You have no objection?'

Sir Richard shook his head and led them out across the hall and up the broad sweeping staircase. As Cranston passed Lady Ermengilde, he belched rather noisily.

At the top of the stairs the passageway, or gallery, to the left was unremarkable. The walls were whitewashed and coated with fresh lime, and the woodwork painted black. There were canvas paintings nailed there in between the three chambers, which were now covered in black gauze veils; the doors of each chamber were huge, heavy set, and reinforced with iron strips. The gallery running to their right, however, was different. The doors and walls were similar but the floor was not made of broad planks but thin bands of light-coloured wood. As soon as Sir Richard stepped on them, Athelstan realised the gallery was aptly named. Each footstep, wherever they stood, caused a deep, slightly melodious twang, similar to the noise of a dozen bowstrings being pulled back simultaneously. Immediately to their left was Lady Isabella's room, the central chamber was Lady Ermengilde's, and the last Sir Thomas's, now in utter disarray. The floor outside was gouged. The door, smashed off its leather hinges, stood crookedly against the lintel. Sir Richard dismissed the servant on guard and, with the help of Buckingham, pushed it gently to one side.

Athelstan looked around. The company from the hall had followed them up, making the Nightingale Gallery sing and echo with its strange melody.

'Where is Father Crispin?' he asked. 'Dame Ermengilde?'

'Down in the hall,' Allingham muttered. 'The priest has had a deformed foot since birth. At times he finds the stairs painful. Dame Ermengilde is old. They send their excuses!'

Athelstan nodded and followed Cranston into the death chamber. The room was a perfect square, the ceiling a set design, the black timber beams contrasting sharply with the white plaster. The walls were white-washed, and costly, coloured arras hung from each, depicting a number of themes from the Old and New Testaments. No carpets but the rushes on the floor were clean, dry, and sprinkled with fresh herbs. There was a small cupboard, a huge chest and two small coffers at the base of the great four poster bed. Next to it stood a small table, a wine cup still on it, and over near the window, on a beautiful marble tabletop, was ranged the most exquisite chess set Athelstan had ever seen. Sir Richard caught his glance just as Father Crispin hobbled into the room.

'The Syrians,' Sir Richard explained.

Athelstan, a keen chess player, went over and looked down at them. The Syrians were resplendent in their beauty. Each figure, about nine inches high, was a work of great craftsmanship, fashioned out of gold and filigree silver. Athelstan whistled under his breath, shaking his head in admiration.

'Beautiful!' he muttered. 'The most exquisite pieces I have ever seen!'

Sir Richard, who had followed him over, nodded.

'A hundred years ago, a Springall, one of our ancestors, went on a crusade in the Holy Land with King Edward I. He won a name for himself as a great warrior. In Outremer there was a secret sect of assassins led by a mysterious figure called The Old Man of the Mountains.' He straightened and looked across to where Sir John was now swaying drunkenly in the middle of the room, the rest of the group watching him attentively, only half listening to Sir Richard's account. He smirked. 'Anyway, the members of this sect were fed on hashish and sent out to assassinate anyone their leader marked down for destruction. They had castles and secret places high in the mountains. Our ancestor found one of these, laid siege, captured and destroyed it. He seized a great deal of plunder and, as a reward for his bravery, the English king allowed him to keep this magnificent chess set. My brother,' he added softly, 'was a keen player.'

'He was in the middle of that game last night,' Father Crispin interrupted, coming up behind them. 'Sir Thomas was so angry with Brampton, I persuaded him that a game would soothe his humour.'

Athelstan smiled.

'Did you win, Father Crispin?'

'We never finished the game,' Father Crispin murmured. 'We broke off for the banquet. I was threatening his bishop.' The priest looked up, his eyes smiling. 'So easy to trap a churchman, eh, Brother?'

'Did Sir Thomas think that?'

'No, he was furious,' Lady Isabella interrupted. 'During the banquet he kept plotting how to break out of the impasse.'

Athelstan just nodded and went over to where Cranston was staring at the ruined door.

'Both locked and bolted?' the coroner murmured.

'Yes,' answered Buckingham.

Cranston bent down, crouching to look at it, nodded and rose.

'And the corpse?'

Lady Isabella gulped at his harshness. Sir Richard led them over, pulling back the heavy bed curtains. The huge four poster bed had been stripped as a pallet for Springall's corpse which lay rigid and silent under

70

a leather sheet. Cranston pulled back the cloth. Now Athelstan had seen many a corpse, male and female, with the most horrible injuries, yet he thought there was something nightmarish in seeing a man in his bed, dressed in his nightshirt, eyes half open, mouth gaping like a landed fish. When alive Sir Thomas must have been a fine-looking man with his tawny hair, sharp soldier's face and military appearance. In death he looked grotesque.

Cranston sniffed the man's mouth and gently pushed back the lolling head. Athelstan watched fascinated, noting the slight purplish tinge in the corpse's face and sunken cheeks. Someone had attempted to close the dead merchant's eyes and, unable to, had placed a coin over each of his eyelids. One of these had now slipped off and Sir Thomas glared sightlessly at the ceiling. Cranston turned, waving Athelstan closer to examine the body. He always did this. The friar suspected Cranston took enjoyment in making him pore over each corpse, the more revolting the better. Athelstan pulled back the nightshirt and examined the rest of the body, impervious to the groans and gasps behind him. He looked over his shoulder; Lady Isabella had walked back towards the door, Sir Richard's arm around her waist. Buckingham just stood with eyes half closed. Both merchants looked squeamish, as if they were about to be sick. Outside the Nightingale Gallery sang and Lady Ermengilde, her hands grasping a black stick, her face covered in a fine sheen of sweat, pushed into the room and glared at Cranston.

'Is this necessary?' she asked. 'Is it really necessary?'

'Yes, Madam, it is!' he barked in reply. 'Brother Athelstan, have you finished?'

The friar examined the corpse from neck to crotch. No mark of violence, no cut. Then the hands. They had been washed and scrubbed clean, the nails manicured. The body was now ready for the embalmer's, before being sheeted and coffined and the funeral ceremony carried out.

'Poison,' Athelstan confirmed. 'No mark of any other violence. No sign of an attack.'

Athelstan picked up the cup and sniffed it. The smell was rich, dark, dank and dangerous. It cloyed in his mouth and nostrils. He put it down quickly and bent over the corpse, sniffing at the dead man's mouth from which issued the same acrid, richly corrupting smell.

'Belladonna and arsenic?' Athelstan remarked.

Buckingham nodded.

'A deadly combination,' the friar observed. 'The only consolation is that Sir Thomas must have died within minutes of putting the cup down. Sir John, you have seen enough?'

Cranston nodded, straightened, and went to sit in a chair over near the chess table. Sir Richard came back into the room.

'You have found nothing new, Brother?'

Athelstan shook his head.

'I speak for Sir John. Sir Thomas's body may be released for burial whenever you wish.' He looked round the chamber. 'There are no other entrances here?'

'None whatsoever,' Sir Richard replied. 'Sir Thomas chose this chamber because of its security.' He pointed to the chests. 'They hold gold, indentures and parchments.'

'And have you been through these?'

'Of course.'

'Have you found anything which may explain Brampton's strange conduct in trying to rifle his master's records?'

Sir Richard shook his head.

'Nothing. Some loans to rather powerful nobles and bishops who should have known better, but nothing else.'

Athelstan took one look round the bed chamber, noting the exquisite beauty of the carved four poster bed, with its writhing snakes and other symbols. A luxurious chamber but not opulent. He tapped gently on the floor with his sandalled foot. It sounded thick and heavy. No trap doors.

'Did Sir Thomas have a...'

'A secret place?' Sir Richard completed his sentence. 'I doubt it. Moreover, Master Buckingham and I have been through the accounts. Everything is in order. My brother was a tidy man.'

'Sir Richard, we are finished here. I would like to view Brampton's corpse.'

'Brother Athelstan,' the merchant smirked and nodded towards where Cranston sat, a contented smile on his face, fast asleep. 'Your companion, good Sir John, appears good for nothing! Perhaps tomorrow?'

'Yes, yes,' Athelstan replied. 'But first I must see where Brampton killed himself.'

'I will take care of it, Sir Richard,' Buckingham murmured.

Sir Richard nodded and the clerk left the room, returning within seconds with a candle in its metal hood. He led Athelstan out of the bed chamber, back along the passageway and up to the second floor. Behind them the Nightingale sang as if mocking Athelstan's departure. At the bottom of the second gallery was a narrow, winding, wooden staircase.

'It leads to the garrets,' Buckingham said, sensing the friar's thoughts.

They went up. Buckingham pushed open a rickety wooden door and Athelstan followed him in. The garret was built just under the eaves of the roof. The wooden ceiling sloped high at one end and low at the other. Just inside the door stood an old table, a stool beside it. Buckingham held the candle up and Athelstan studied the stout beam directly above the table. A piece of rope hung from it, scarred and frayed. It swung eerily in the breeze which came through a gap in the roof tiles. On the table beneath, covered by a dirty sheet, lay Brampton's corpse. Athelstan took the candle off Buckingham and looked around. Nothing but rubbish: broken pitchers, shattered glass, a coffer with the lid broken, and a mound of old clothes. The garret smelt dank and dusty and of something else — corruption, decay, the order of rotting death. Athelstan went across to the table and pulled back the filthy sheet. Brampton lay there, a small man dressed in a simple linen shirt, open at the neck, and wearing dark green hose on his scrawny legs. He would have appeared asleep if it had not been for the curious lie of his head. The neck was twisted slightly askew to one side. The heavy-lidded eyes were half open, his lips parted in death, and a dark blue-purplish ring circled the scraggy neck. Athelstan peered closer. There were no signs of violence on the yellow, seamed face. The small goatee beard was still damp with spittle; the gash on the throat quite deep, with a large bruise behind the ear where the noose had been tied. He scrutinized the man's hands, long and thin, manicured like a woman's. Carefully he examined the nails, noticing the strands of rope caught there. Behind him Buckingham muttered darkly, as if resenting his scrutiny. There was a crashing on the stairs and Cranston burst in, the ill effects of the wine readily apparent. He slumped on the stool, mopping his sweaty face with the hem of his cloak.

'Well, Monk!' he called out. 'What have we?'

'Brampton,' Athelstan replied, 'bears all the marks of a hanged man, though some attempts have been made to redress the ill effects of such a death. The mouth is half open, the tongue swollen and bitten, the neck bears the sign of a noose. There is a bruise behind his left ear and Brampton apparently grasped the rope in his death agonies.' He turned to Buckingham. 'So Brampton came up here, intending to hang himself. There is rope kept here?'

Buckingham pointed to the far corner.

'A great deal,' he replied. 'We often use it to tie up bales.'

'I see, I see. Brampton therefore takes this rope, climbs on the table, ties one length round the rafter beam, forms a noose and puts it round his neck, tying the knot securely behind his left ear. He steps quietly off the table and his life flickers out like a candle flame.'

Buckingham narrowed his eyes and shivered.

'Yes,' he muttered. 'It must have been like that.'

'Now,' Athelstan continued conversationally, ignoring Cranston's glares, 'Vechey finds the corpse. He searches for a knife amongst the rubbish,' Athelstan tapped it with the toe of his sandal where it lay on the floor, 'cuts Brampton down, but finds he is dead.'

'Yes,' Buckingham replied, 'something like that. Then he came down and notified us all.'

Athelstan picked the dagger up from the floor. He had glimpsed it when he had first entered the room and could see why it had been discarded. The handle was chipped and broken, and there were dents along one side, but the cutting edge was still very sharp. Athelstan climbed on to the stool, then on to the table. He looked at the hacked edge of the rope. Yes, he thought, Brampton had been tall enough to fix the rope round the beam, put the noose round his neck, and tie it securely with a knot before stepping off the table.

'Master Buckingham,' Athelstan said, getting down, 'we have kept you long enough. I should be most grateful if you would present my compliments to Lady Isabella and Sir Richard and ask them to meet me in the solar below. I would like the physician present. I believe he lives nearby? The servants, too, should be questioned.'

Buckingham nodded, relieved that the close questioning of himself was over, and left Athelstan dragging a dozing Cranston to his feet. The coroner struggled and murmured. Athelstan put one of his arms around Sir John's shoulders and carefully escorted him downstairs. Thankfully, the gallery below was deserted. He rested the coroner against the wall, slapping him gently on the face.

'Sir John! Sir John! Please wake up!'

Cranston's eyes flew open. 'Do not worry, Brother,' he slurred, 'I won't embarrass you.' He stood and shook himself, trying to clear his eyes, jerking his head as if he could dislodge the fumes from his brain.

'Come,' Athelstan said. 'The physician and servants still await us.'

Athelstan was partially correct. The servants were waiting in the small, lime-washed buttery next to the flagstoned kitchen, but the physician had not yet arrived. Buckingham introduced them as Cranston went over to a large butt, ladling out cups of water which he noisily drank, splashing the rest over his rosy-red face. Athelstan patiently questioned the servants, preferring to deal with them as a group so he could watch their faces and detect any sign of connivance or conspiracy. He found it difficult enough with Buckingham lounging beside him as if to ensure nothing untoward was said, whilst Cranston swayed on his feet, burping and belching like a drunken trumpeter. Athelstan discovered nothing new. The banquet had been a convivial affair. Chief Justice Fortescue had left as the meal ended, whilst Sir Thomas had been in good spirits.

'And Brampton?' Athelstan asked.

'He sulked all day,' the young scullery maid squeaked, tightly clutching the arm of a burly groom. 'He kept to his chamber. He...' she stammered. 'I think he was in his cups.'

'Did any of you hear someone moving round the house?' Athelstan queried. 'Late at night, when everyone had retired?'

The maid blushed and looked away.

'No one came through the yard,' the young groom hotly stated. 'If they had, they would have woken the dogs!'

'Brampton – what was he like?' Cranston barked.

The old servant who had answered the door lifted his shoulders despairingly.

'A good man,' he quavered.

'So why should Sir Thomas be angry with him?'

The old man wiped his red-rimmed eyes. 'He was accused of searching amongst the master's papers. A button from his jerkin,' he stammered, 'or so I under-stand, was found near one of the coffers which had been tampered with.'

'What was Brampton looking for?'

A deathly silence greeted his question. The servants shuffled their feet and looked pleadingly at Buckingham.

'Good friar,' the clerk intervened, 'surely you do not expect servants to know their master's business?'

'Brampton apparently tried to!' Cranston snapped, going back to the butt for another cup of water.

'So it would seem,' Buckingham answered sweetly.

Athelstan gazed at the servants. 'These can tell us nothing more, Sir John,' he murmured.

'And neither can I!'

Athelstan spun round. A plump, balding pigeon of a man stood in the doorway. He was dressed in a dark woollen cloak which half concealed a rich taffeta jerkin slashed with crimson velvet. Athelstan glimpsed the green padded hose and the silver buckles on the dainty leather riding boots. The little fellow exuded self-importance. He held his smooth, oil-rubbed face slightly tilted back. A nose sharp as a quill prodded the air like the beak of a bird. In one hand he held a silver-topped walking cane, in the other a pomander full of spiced cloves. Now and again he would hold it to his face.

'You are, Sir?' Athelstan asked.

'Peter de Troyes, physician.'

He looked distastefully at Cranston.

'And you must be Sir John Cranston, coroner of the city? Do you need my help?'

The arrogant physician sat on the corner of the table. Athelstan watched Cranston carefully and held his breath. From experience he knew that Sir John hated physicians and would like to hang the lot as a bunch of charlatans. Cranston smiled sweetly, ordering Buckingham to clear the buttery whilst he lumbered across to stand over the physician.

'Yes, Doctor de Troyes, I am the Coroner. I like claret, a good cup of sack and, if I had my way, I would investigate the practices and potions of the physicians of this city.' His smile faded as de Troyes stuck out his plump little chest. 'Now, Master de Troyes, physician, you inspected Sir Thomas's corpse?'

'I did.'

'And the goblet he drank from?'

'Quite correct, Sir John.'

'And you think it was a mixture of belladonna and arsenic?'

'Yes, yes, I do. The cadaver's skin was slightly blueish, and the mouth smelt rank.' He shrugged. 'Death by poisoning, it was obvious.'

Athelstan walked across to them. The physician didn't even turn to greet him.

'Would death have been quick?' the friar asked.

'Oh, yes, and rather silent. Very much like a seizure, within ten or fifteen minutes of taking the potion.'

'Master physician,' Athelstan continued, 'please do me the courtesy of looking at me when I ask you a question.'

De Troyes turned, his eyes glittering with malice.

'Yes, Friar, what is it?'

'Surely Sir Thomas would have detected the poison in the wine cup? You smelt it. Why didn't he?'

The fellow pursed his lips. 'Simple enough,' he replied pompously. 'First, Sir Thomas had drunk deeply.' He glanced slyly at Cranston. 'Wine is a good mask for poison, and if there is enough in the belly and throat the victim will never suspect. Secondly, the wine cup has stood all night.' He wetted his lips. 'The smell could become more rank.'

'And the phial found in Brampton's coffer was the same potion?'

'Yes. A deadly mixture.'

'Where can it be bought?'

The physician's eyes slid away. 'If you have enough money, Sir John, and know the right person, anything or anyone can be bought in this city.' De Troyes stood up. 'Do you have any more questions?'

Cranston belched, Athelstan shook his head and the physician swept out of the room without a backward glance.

They found Sir Richard's group still waiting in the solar. Athelstan gathered his writing tray, paper and quills, putting them carefully back into the leather bag. He had written very little, but would make a thorough report later. He hurried back to where Sir John, legs apart and swaying slightly, stood leering lecherously at Lady Isabella, who stared back frostily.

'I think,' Sir Richard said quietly, 'that Sir John needs a good night's sleep. Perhaps tomorrow, Brother?'

'Perhaps tomorrow, Sir Richard,' Athelstan echoed, and slipping his arm through Cranston's, turned him gently and walked him out of the hall. Sir John suddenly spun round and looked back at the company, his heavy-lidded eyes half closed. Athelstan followed suit and glimpsed Sir Richard's hand fall away from Lady Isabella's shoulder. Something in the merchant's face made Athelstan wonder if they were more than just close kin. Was there adultery here as well as murder?

'Oh, Sir Richard!' Cranston called.

'Yes, Sir John?'

'The Sons of Dives – who or what are they?'

Athelstan saw the group suddenly tense, their faces drained of that pompous, amused look as if they regarded Cranston as the royal jester rather than the king's coroner.

'I asked a question, Sir Richard,' Cranston slurred. 'The Sons of Dives? Who are they?'

'I don't know what you are talking about, Sir John. The ill effects of the wine?'

'The wine does not affect me as much as you think, Sir Richard,' Cranston snapped back. 'I will ask the question again.' He bowed towards Lady Isabella. 'Good night.'

And, spinning on his heel, Cranston lurched with as much dignity as he could muster through the door, Athelstan following behind.

Once clear of the house, Cranston waddled as sure as a duck to water towards the welcoming, half-open door of an alehouse across Cheapside. Athelstan stopped and looked up at the starlit sky.

'Oh, good God!' he groaned. 'Surely not more refreshment, Sir John?'

Nevertheless, he hurried after; the water had apparently revived the good coroner and Athelstan wanted to clear his own mind and define the problems nagging at him. The alehouse was almost deserted. Sir John seized a table near the wine butts.

'Two cups of sack!' he roared. 'And some—?' He glared at Athelstan.

'Watered wine,' the friar added meekly.

The sack disappeared down Sir John's cavernous throat. More was ordered, and the coroner clapped his podgy hands.

'An excellent evening's work!' he boomed. He nodded in the direction of the Springall mansion. 'A coven of high-stepping hypocrites.' He turned to Athelstan, bleary-eyed. 'What do you think, Monk?'

'Friar!' Athelstan corrected him despairingly.

'Who gives a sod?' Cranston snapped. 'First, I wonder why our good Lord Fortescue was there? I think he left a little later than he claims.' Cranston belched. 'Secondly, Brampton. They say he was rifling through his master's papers, and they have evidence of it, so it is easy to imagine the quarrel between him and Sir Thomas. Springall would feel betrayed, Brampton furious that he had been caught as well as fearful of dismissal.' Cranston drummed his stubby fingers on the wine-stained tabletop. 'But if Brampton was innocent,' he slurred, 'why was he made to appear guilty? There's no answer to that.'

'And if he was guilty,' Athelstan added, 'what was he looking for? What great secret did Sir Thomas Springall possess?'

Athelstan gazed across the tap room, watching two drunken gamblers shove and push each other over a game of dice.

'Even so,' he murmured, 'why should Brampton kill his master and take his own life? Revenge followed by remorse?'

A loud snore greeted his question. Cranston had now fallen back against the wall, his eyes closed, a beatific smile on his fat, good-natured face.

'Was Sir Thomas murdered because of the secret?' Athelstan muttered. 'Or was his wife an adulteress, playing the two-backed beast with her husband's brother?'

Some men kill for gold, he thought, others for lust. And Dame Ermengilde? Did she play a part in this charade, trying to advance the interests of her favourite son, Sir Richard? And the other two, Vechey and Allingham? Strange creatures, battening like fleas on the skill and acumen of Sir Thomas. And, of course, young Buckingham. Athelstan shuddered. He had met men like Buckingham, with their fluttering eyelashes and graceful, dainty gestures; men who preferred to be women but hid their natures under the cloak of darkness lest they be discovered and boiled alive at Smithfield. Finally, the good priest Crispin. Was his leg as malformed as he pretended? When he first met the priest in the solar Athelstan had noticed how ungainly he walked, but when later he had joined them in Springall's chamber, Athelstan had observed how the priest had changed into Spanish riding boots, the heel of one slightly raised to lessen his deformity. In these he moved quietly and quickly.

Sir John suddenly groaned and sat up.

'Oh, God, Athelstan,' he moaned. 'I feel sick!'

The coroner rose and staggered to the door.

Chapter 3

Outside the alehouse Sir John paused to vomit, afterwards loudly protesting he was all right. Athelstan linked his arm through that of the coroner and they carefully made their way down Cheapside. It was raining and had become messy underfoot. They were stopped by the Watch, a collection of arrogant servants and retainers from the households of some of the great aldermen. They would have arrested them both, delighted to pick on a friar. Athelstan, however, informed them his companion was no less a personage than Sir John Cranston, who was now ill, so they stepped aside, doing their best to hide their smirks. As Athelstan turned off Cheapside into Poultry, he could still hear their loud guffaws of laughter.

The coroner's house was a pleasant, two-storeyed affair in an alleyway off the Poultry. Athelstan hammered on the door until Sir John's wife appeared – a small, birdlike woman much younger than Cranston, who greeted her husband as if he was Hector back from the wars.

'The weight of office!' she shrilled. 'It's the weight of office which makes him drink.'

And, grabbing Sir John roughly by the hand, she unceremoniously pushed him upstairs.

Athelstan stood in the hallway looking carefully around, for this was the first time he had been to Cranston's house and met his wife. The room beyond the hall was cosy and comfortable with clean rushes on the floor and a large, high-backed chair before the fire. Athelstan caught a fragrant aroma from the kitchen, the supper Sir John had missed. The friar realised how hungry he was.

Cranston's wife Maude rejoined him, still behaving as if Athelstan had brought her husband home from a heroic field of battle rather than half drunk, his doublet stained with vomit.

'Brother,' she said, taking the friar by the hand, her bright blue eyes full of life, 'this is the first time I have met you. Please, you must stay.'

Athelstan needed no second bidding and sank gratefully into a chair, accepting the meat pastry, mince tart and cup of cold wine that Lady Maude pushed before him. After that, she showed him up into a chamber at the top of the house. Athelstan said his prayers, the *Dies Requiem* for Springall, Brampton, his own brother and others, made the sign of the cross on himself and thanked God for a wholesome day.

He slept like a babe and woke just after dawn. He felt guilty at not returning to his own church but hoped that his few parishioners would understand. Had Simon the tiler fixed the roof? he wondered. Would Bonaventure be fed? And surely Wat the dung-collector would make sure the door was locked and Godric safe? And Benedicta the widow who attended every morning Mass, whose husband had been killed in the king's wars beyond the seas…? Athelstan sat on his bed and crossed himself. Sometimes he would catch Benedicta looking at him, her lovely face pale as ivory, her dark eyes smiling.

'No sin!' Athelstan muttered. 'No sin!' Christ himself had his woman friends. He gazed at the floor. For the first time ever, he realised how he missed the woman when he did not see her. Every morning at Mass he sought her smiling eyes as if she alone understood his loneliness and felt for him. Athelstan shook himself, dressed, and went along to the kitchen to beg from a startled maid a bowl of hot water, a clean napkin and some salt with which to scrub his teeth. After his ablutions, finding the house still quiet, he left and went back down Cheapside to the church of St Mary Le Bow. The bells were clanging in the high tower which soared up to a steel blue sky. Athelstan saw the night watchman douse the light, the beacon which was lit every evening to guide travellers through the streets of London.

Inside, the dawn Mass was just ending, the priest offering Christ to God in the presence of three old women, a beggar and a blind man with his dog.

They all squatted on the paving-stone before the rood screen. Athelstan waited near the baptismal font. When the Mass was finished, he followed the priest into the vestry. Father Matthew was a genial fellow and cheerfully granted Athelstan's request, giving him vestments and vessels so he could celebrate his own Mass in one of the small chantry chapels built off the main aisle.

After Mass and the chanting of the Divine Office, Athelstan thanked the priest but refused his kind offer of a meal and wandered back into Cheapside. The broad thoroughfare was now coming to life. The cookshops were open, the awnings of the stalls pulled down, and already the apprentices were darting in and out, seeking custom for their masters. The friar walked back up to the Poultry and knocked on the coroner's door. Cranston greeted him, standing like vice reformed, sober, dour, and full of his own authority, as if he wished to erase the memory of the night before.

'Come in, Brother!' He looked out of the corner of his eye as he beckoned Athelstan into the parlour. 'I am grateful for what you did last night when I was inconvenienced.'

Athelstan hid his smile as Cranston waved him to a stool, sitting opposite in a great high-backed chair. In the kitchen Maude was singing softly as she baked bread, its sweet, fresh scent filling the house.

Strange, Athelstan thought, that a man like Sir John, steeped in violent bloody death, should live in such homely surroundings.

Cranston stretched and crossed his legs.

'Well, Brother, shall we record a clear case of suicide?'

'I would like to agree with your verdict,' Athelstan replied, 'but something eludes me. Something I cannot place, something small, like looking at a tapestry with a loose thread.'

'God's teeth!' Cranston roared as he rose and went to fetch the boots standing in the corner. He pulled them on and looked sourly across at the friar.

'I know you, Brother, and your nose for mischief. If you feel there is something wrong, there is. Let's be careful, however. Springall belonged to the court faction in the city, and if we put a foot wrong, well...' His voice trailed off.

'What do you mean?' Athelstan asked sharply.

'What I say,' Cranston caustically retorted. 'I stay out of the muddy pools of politics. That gives me the right to insult fools like Fortescue. But if I offend the court, its opponents think I am a friend. If I am partial to them, I am an enemy.' He buttoned up his doublet. 'God knows when order will be restored. The king is young, a mere boy. Gaunt is so ambitious. You know, through his wife he has a claim to the throne of Castile; through his grandmother to the throne of France. And between him and the throne of England

– one small boy!' Cranston closed the parlour door so his wife could not hear. 'There may be violence. For myself I do not care, but I do not want armed retainers terrifying my household by arresting me in the dead of night.' He sighed, and picking up his cloak, swung it about him. 'However, I trust your judgement, Athelstan. Something's wrong, though God knows what!'

Athelstan looked away. He had spoken largely without thinking. He thought back to the visit to the Springall house yesterday. Yes, there was something wrong. Oh, everything was neat and orderly. Springall had been murdered and his murderer had committed suicide, so everything was neat and tidied away. But it was all too clear, too precise, and death wasn't like that. It was violent, cumbersome, messy. It came trailing its blood-spattered tail everywhere.

'You know...' he began.

'What's the matter, Brother?'

'Oh, I'm just thinking about yesterday in the Springall mansion. A strange coven. The deaths were so orderly.' He looked up at Cranston. 'You felt that, Sir John, didn't you? Everything precise, signed, sealed, filed away, as if we were watching a well-arranged masque. What do you say?'

Cranston moved back to his chair and sat down.

'The same,' he replied. 'I know I drank too much, I always do. But I agree, I sensed something in that house: an evil, an aura, a dankness, despite the wealth.

Something which clutched at my soul. Someone is hiding something. Of course,' he smiled, 'you know *they* are the Sons of Dives? They must be. Some sort of coven or a secret society, and I believe they are all party to it. Did you see their faces when I asked the question?' Cranston threw back his great head and bellowed with laughter. 'Oh, yes, and that Dame Ermengilde – I have heard of her. A nasty piece of work, vicious and venomous as a viper! Well,' he smacked his knee, 'we shall see.' He went off into the kitchen. Athelstan heard Lady Maude squeal with pleasure. The coroner came back, grinned at Athelstan, belched loudly, and without further ado they went back into the street.

They were halfway up Cheapside when a small voice called out: 'Sir John! Sir John!'

They stopped. A little boy ran up, face dirty, clothes dishevelled, his breath coming in short gasps so he could hardly speak. Sir John stood back and Athelstan smiled. Cranston always seemed to have a fear of small boys. Perhaps a memory from childhood when a fat Cranston must have been mercilessly teased by others. Athelstan knelt before the child, taking his thin, bony hand.

'What is it, lad?' he asked gently. 'What do you wish?'

'I bring a message from the Sheriff,' the boy gasped. 'Master Vechey...' The child closed his eyes to remember. 'Master Vechey has been found hanged under London Bridge. The Sheriff says it's by his own hand. The body has been cut down and lies in the gatehouse there. The Sheriff sends his com—'

'Compliments,' Athelstan interrupted.

'Yes.' The boy opened his eyes. 'Compliments, and wishes Sir John to go there immediately and examine the corpse.'

Cranston, standing behind Athelstan, whistled softly.

'So, we were right, Brother,' he said, tossing a coin to the boy who scampered away. 'There is evil afoot. One murder can be explained, one suicide can be accounted for, but another suicide?' His fat face beamed. 'Ah, no, Sir Richard may be pompous, Lady Isabella frosty, Dame Ermengilde may strike her cane on the floor in temper, but Vechey's death cannot be dismissed. There is evil here, and you and I, Athelstan, will stay like good dogs following the trail until we sight our quarry. Come! The living may not want to talk to us, but the dead await!'

And, without even a reference to refreshment, Cranston waddled off down Cheapside with Athelstan striding behind him. They pushed their way through the morning crowd: monks, friars, hucksters and pedlars, ignoring the shouts and screams of the city as they turned into Fish Hill Street which led down on to London Bridge. They stopped at the Three Tuns tavern to ensure their horses had been well stabled. Cranston paid the bill. Philomel, happy to see his master again, nuzzled and nudged him. The road down to the bridge was packed so they decided to leave their horses rather than ride.

At the entrance, just near the gatehouse door, Cranston stopped and knocked hard at an iron-studded door. At first there was no reply so, picking up a loose brick, Cranston hammered again. At last the door was opened. A small, hairy-faced little creature appeared glared up at Sir John.

'What do you want?' he roared. 'Bugger off! The gatehouse is closed on the king's orders until the arrival of the coroner.'

'I *am* the coroner!' Cranston bellowed back. 'And who, sir, are you?'

'Robert Burdon,' the dwarf retorted. He rearranged his cloak and stuck his thumb into the broad leather belt at his waist like a wrestler waiting for his opponent to attack. Sir John ignored him and pushed forward into the dank entrance of the chamber.

'We have come to view Master Vechey's body.'

Robert ran in front of Cranston, jumping up and down.

'My name is Robert Burdon!' he shrieked. 'I am constable of this gate tower. I hold my office direct from the king!'

'I don't give a fig,' Cranston replied, 'if you hold it direct from the Holy Father! Where's Vechey's corpse?'

He looked into the small chamber near the stairs where the dwarf probably ate, lived and slept. A small baby crawled out on its hands and knees, its face covered in grime. Robert picked it up, shoved it back in the chamber and slammed the door behind him.

'The corpse is upstairs,' he said pompously. 'What do you expect? I can't keep it down here with my wife and children. The cadaver's ripe.' He indicated with his thumb. 'It's on the roof. Up you come!' And, nimble as a monkey, he bounded up the stairs ahead of Cranston and Athelstan. He pushed open the door at the top and led them out on to the roof, a broad expanse bounded by a high crenellated wall. The wind from the river whipped their faces. Cranston and Athelstan covered their face and nose at the terrible stench which blew across.

'God's teeth!' Cranston cried as he looked around. Vechey's corpse lay in the centre of the tower near a rickety hut, formerly used by guards on sentry duty. The body lay sprawled, its face covered by a dirty rag. Athelstan thought the odour came from that but, looking around, he saw the rotting heads which had been placed on spikes in the gaps of the crenellated wall.

'Traitors' heads!' Cranston muttered. 'Of course, they spike them here!'

Athelstan looked closely, trying not to gag. Like all Londoners, he knew that once the bodies of traitors had been cut and quartered, their heads were sent to adorn London Bridge. He looked closer. Thick, black pools around the spikes showed some of the heads were fresh, though all were rotting, crumbling under the rain and wind which whipped up their oddly silken hair. Large ravens which had been busy, plucking out juicy morsels with their yellow beaks, rose in angry circles above them.

'Their hair,' Athelstan whispered. 'Look, it's combed!'

'I do that!' Robert cried. 'I always look after my heads! Every morning I come up and comb them, keep them soft, pleasant-looking. That is,' he added morosely, 'until the ravens start pecking them, though they usually leave that bit for the last. Oh, yes, I comb their hair and, when I am finished, I sing to them. I bring my viol up. Lullabies are best.' He looked up at Athelstan, his face beaming with pride. 'Never lonely up here,' he said. 'The things these heads must know!'

'God's teeth,' muttered Cranston. 'I need refreshment! But never mind that. This morning I swore a mighty oath not to touch the juice of the grape or the crushed sweetness of the hop. But first let's see Vechey's corpse.'

Robert skipped over to show them the unexpected addition to his ghastly collection. He whipped off the rag which the wind caught and blew against one of the spiked heads.

'You examine it, Brother,' whispered Cranston. 'I feel sick. Last night's wine.'

Athelstan crouched down. Vechey was dressed in the same clothes as yesterday. The soft face was now puffier, its colour a dirty white. His eyes were half open, mouth slack, lips apart, displaying rows of blackened teeth. Vechey seemed to be grinning up at him, taunting him with the mystery of his death. Athelstan turned his head slightly to one side. He caught his knee on his robe and slipped. He felt queasy as his hand touched the cadaver's bloated stomach and noted that the dead man's legs were soaking wet. He inspected the gash round Vechey's neck, which was very similar to that of Brampton; black-red like some ghastly necklace and the dark, swollen bruise behind the left ear. He held his breath and sniffed at the dead man's lips. Nothing but the putrid rottenness of the grave. Then he examined the corpse's hands. No scars, the nails neat and clean, shorter than Brampton's. There was no trace of a strand of rope caught there. Athelstan looked at the dwarf.

'Where's the noose?'

'I tossed it away,' the fellow replied triumphantly. 'I see'd him there, I cuts him down, I loosened the noose and it falls in the water.' His face grew solemn, his eyes anxious. 'Why, shouldn't I have done that?'

'You did well, Robert,' Athelstan replied quietly. 'Very well. You found the body?'

'Well, no, my children did. They were playing where they shouldn't, on the starlings under the bridge. You know the wooden barriers around the arches?' He shook his head. 'So many of them. Nine, I have,' he declared. 'Should be ten but the eldest got drunk and fell in the river!'

Cranston stared in utter disbelief at Robert's potency.

'So you cut him down?' he asked. 'How did you know it was Vechey?'

'I found coins in his pocket and a piece of parchment. It had his name on it. That and someone else's. Thomas...' He closed his eyes.

'Thomas Springall?'

'That's right. Look, I have it here. There's something else written.'

The little guardian of the great gateway dug into his wallet and brought out a greasy scrap of parchment. Two names were written on it: Theobald Vechey and Sir Thomas Springall. Beneath the latter's name, written in the same hand, was Genesis 3, Verse 1 and the Book of the Apocalypse 6, Verse 8.

'Here, Monk,' Cranston muttered. 'You are the preacher, what do you make of it?'

'First, Sir John, as I keep saying, I am a friar, not a monk. And, secondly, though I have studied the Bible, I can't recollect every verse.'

Cranston smirked.

'Was there anything else?'

The little man bobbed up and down.

'Yes, some rings and some coins, but the sheriff's men took them. I sent one of my boys to the Guild-

99

hall, they sent down constables of the ward. That must have been,' he sucked on his finger, 'just after dawn. I heard them say they had sent for you.'

'Well,' Sir John sighed, 'we have a corpse and a scrap of paper, and the sheriff's men have the valuables – and that's the last any one will see of them,' he added bitterly. He looked down. 'The man was just hanging, his hands were free?'

'Oh, yes,' the little fellow replied. 'Just hanging there from one of the beams, swaying as free as a leaf in the wind. Come, I will show you!'

He led Cranston and Athelstan downstairs past the closed chamber where the noise of his large brood sounded like the howling of demons in hell. They went back through the gatehouse, following the line of the riverbank down some rough-hewn stairs cut into the rock and beneath the bridge.

'Be careful!' the dwarf shouted.

Cranston and Athelstan needed no such warning. The Thames was flowing full and furious, the water greedily lapping their feet as if it would like to catch them and drag them under its swollen black surface. The bridge was built on nineteen great arches. Vechey had decided to hang himself on the last. He'd climbed on to one of the great beams which supported the arch, tied a length of rope round it and, fastening the noose around his neck, simply stepped off the great stone plinth. Part of the rope still swung there, hanging down directly over the water.

'Why should a man hang himself here?' Cranston asked.

'It's been done before,' the gateman replied. 'Hangings, drownings, they always choose the bridge. It seems to attract them!'

'Perhaps it's the span which represents the gap between life and death?' Athelstan remarked.

He looked at Cranston. 'Bartholomew the Englishman wrote a famous treatise in which he remarked how strange it was that people chose bridges as their place to die.'

'Give my thanks to Bartholomew the Englishman,' Cranston replied drily, 'but it doesn't explain why a London merchant came down here in the dark, fastened a rope round a beam and hanged himself.'

'Bangtails come here,' Robert piped up. 'Bawds! Whores!' he explained. 'They often bring their customers down here.'

'What does Bartholomew the Englishman say about that, Friar?'

'I don't know but, when I do, you will be the first to know!'

They examined the rope again and, satisfied that they had seen everything, climbed the stone steps back on to the track high on the riverbank. Cranston thanked the gatekeeper for his pains, quietly slipping some coins into his hands.

'For the children,' he murmured. 'Some pastries, some doucettes.'

'And the corpse?'

Cranston shrugged. 'Send a message to Sir Richard Springall. He has a mansion in Cheapside. Tell him you have Vechey's body. If he does not collect it, the sheriff's men who pocketed poor Vechey's valuables will find him a pauper's grave!'

'At the crossroads,' the fellow said, eyes rounded. 'What do you mean?'

'He means, Sir John,' Athelstan interrupted, 'that Vechey was a suicide. Like Brampton, a stake should be driven through his heart and the cadaver buried at the crossroads. They still do that in country parts. They claim it prevents the dead man's troubled soul from walking abroad. But what does it matter? It's only the husk. I will remember poor Vechey at Mass.'

They bade farewell to the gateman, collected their horses from the urchin and, seeing the busy crowds ahead of them, decided to walk up to Cheapside. The throng was thick, massing like a swarm of bees, the noise and clamour so intense they were unable to hear one another speak. In Cheapside, where the thoroughfare was broader and the houses did not press so close, they relaxed. Athelstan, patting Philomel's nose, stared across at a now perspiring Cranston.

'Why should Vechey kill himself?' he asked.

'Don't bloody ask me!' Cranston retorted crossly, wiping the sweat from his face. 'If it wasn't for that poor bugger, I would be getting as pissed as a bishop's fart in the Crossed Keys and you would be back in your decrepit church feeding that bloody cat or watching your bloody stars! Or trying to save the soul of some evil little sod who would slit your throat as quickly as look at you!'

Athelstan grinned.

'You need refreshment, Sir John. You have had a hard morning. The rigours of office, the exacting duties of coroner – they would break many a lesser man.'

Cranston looked evilly at the friar.

'Thank you, Brother,' he said. 'Your words of comfort soothe my heart.'

'Be at peace, my son,' Athelstan said mockingly and pointed. 'Over there is the Springall mansion. And here,' he turned and gestured to the great garish sign, 'is the tavern of the Holy Lamb of God. The body needs refreshment.' He grinned. 'And your body, great as it is, more than any other!'

Cranston solemnly tapped his bell-like stomach. 'You are correct, Brother.' He sighed. 'The spirit is willing, but the flesh is very, very weak.'

And there's a lot of weakness there, thought Athelstan.

'But not now,' he added hastily, catching the gleam in Cranston's eyes. 'Sir Richard Springall awaits us. We must see him.'

Cranston's mouth set in a stubborn line.

'Sir John, we must do it now!' Athelstan insisted.

Cranston nodded, his eyes petulant like those of a child being refused a sweet. They stabled their horses at the Holy Lamb of God and threaded their way across the noisy marketplace. A figure garbed in black, a white devil's mask on its face, was jumping amongst the stalls, shouting imprecations at the rich and the avaricious. A beadle in his striped gown tried to arrest him but the 'devil' scampered off to the cheers of the crowd. Cranston and Athelstan watched the drama play itself out; the beadle chasing, the 'devil' dodging. The small, fat official was soon lathered in sweat. Another 'devil' appeared, dressed identically to the first, and the crowd burst into roars of laughter. The beadle had been tricked, fooled by two mummers and their game of illusion.

'Like life, is it not, Sir John?' Athelstan queried. 'Nothing, as Heraclitus says, is what it appears to be. Or, as Plato writes, we live in a world of dreams. The realities are beyond us.'

Cranston gave one last pitying glance at the beadle.

'Bugger philosophy!' he said. 'I have seen more truths at the bottom of a wine cup, and learnt more after a good tankard of sack, than any dry-skinned philosopher could teach in some dusty hall!'

'Sir John, your grasp of philosophy never ceases to amaze me.'

'Well, I am now going to amaze Sir Richard Springall,' Cranston grated. 'I haven't forgotten yesterday.'

The same old manservant ushered them into the hall. A few minutes later Sir Richard came down, closely followed by Lady Isabella and Buckingham.

The latter informed them that Father Crispin and Allingham were working elsewhere.

'Sir John, you feel better?' Springall asked.

'Sir, I was not ill. Indeed, I felt better yesterday than I do now.'

Sir Richard just glared, refusing to be drawn into Cranston's riddle.

'You have heard of Vechey's death?'

Sir Richard nodded. 'Yes,' he said softly. 'We did. But come, let us not discuss these matters here.'

He led them into a small, more comfortable room behind the great hall where a fire burnt in the canopied hearth; it was cosier and not so forbidding, with its wood-panelled walls and high-backed chairs arranged in a semicircle around the hearth.

'Even in the height of summer,' Sir Richard observed, 'it's cool in here.'

Athelstan smelt the fragrance of the pine logs burning in the hearth, mixing with sandalwood, resin, and something more fragrant – the heavy perfume of Lady Isabella. He looked sharply at her. She had now donned full mourning weeds. A black lacy wimple framed her beautiful white face while her splendid body was clothed from neck to toe in a pure black silk gown, the only concession to any alleviating colour being the white lace cuffs and collar and the small jewelled cross which swung from a gold chain round her neck. Buckingham was paler, quieter. Athelstan noticed how daintily he moved. There was a knock at the door.

'Come in!' Sir Richard called.

Father Crispin entered, his thin face creased with pain at his ungainly hobbling. He caught Athelstan's glance and smiled bravely.

'Don't worry, Brother. I have had a clubbed foot since birth. You may have noticed a riding boot greatly eases my infirmity. Sometimes I forget my lameness, but it's always there. Like some malicious enemy ready to hurt me,' he added bitterly.

Lady Isabella went forward and grasped the young priest's hand. 'Father, I am sorry,' she whispered. 'Come, join us.'

They sat down. A servant brought a tray of wine cups filled to the brim with white Rhenish wine, as well as a platter of sweet pastries. Cranston lost his sour look and satisfied himself by glancing sardonically at Athelstan as he sipped daintily from the wine cup.

'So,' said Sir John, smacking his lips, 'a third death, Master Vechey's suicide.' He held three fingers up. 'One murder and two suicides in the same household.' He stared around. 'You do not grieve?'

Sir Richard put down his wine cup on the small table beside him.

'Sir John, you mock us. We grieve for my brother. His funeral is being held tomorrow. We grieve for Brampton, whose body has been sheeted and taken to St Mary Le Bow. Our grief is not a bottomless pit and Master Vechey was a colleague but no friend.'

'A dour man,' Buckingham observed, 'with bounding ambition but not the talent to match.' He smiled thinly. 'At least not in the lists of love.'

'What do you mean?' Cranston asked.

'Vechey was a widower. His wife died years ago. He saw himself as a ladies' man, when in his cups, a troubadour from Provence.' Buckingham grimaced. 'You met him yourself. He was small, fat and ugly. The ladies mocked him, laughing at him behind their hands.'

'What the clerk is saying,' Sir Richard interrupted, 'is that Master Vechey was immersed in the pleasures of the flesh. He had few friends. Only my brother really listened to him. It could well be that Sir Thomas's death turned Vechey's mind on to the path of self-destruction.' He spread his hands. 'I do not claim to be my brother's keeper, so how can I claim to be Vechey's? We are sorry for his death but how are we responsible?'

'Master Vechey left the house when?'

'About an hour after you.'

'Did he say where he was going?'

'No. He never did.'

Cranston eased himself in his chair, head back, rolling the white Rhenish wine round his tongue.

'Let me change the question. Where were you all last night?'

Sir Richard shrugged and looked around. 'We went our different ways.'

'Father Crispin?'

The priest coughed, shifting his leg to favour it.

'I went to the vicar of St Mary Le Bow to arrange Sir Thomas's funeral.'

'Sir Richard? Lady Isabella?'

'We stayed here!' the woman retorted. 'A grieving widow does not walk the streets.'

'Master Buckingham?'

'I went to the Guildhall, taking messages from Sir Richard about the pageant we are planning.'

'My brother would have liked that,' Sir Richard intervened. 'He would see no reason why we should not make our contribution to the royal coronation.' His voice rose. 'Why, what is this? Do you hold us responsible for Vechey's death? Are you saying that we bundled him down to the waterside and had him hanged? For what reason?'

'The coroner is not alleging anything,' Athelstan remarked smoothly. 'But, Sir Richard, you must agree it is odd, so many deaths in one household?'

'Does this mean anything to you?' Cranston took the greasy piece of parchment out of his wallet and handed it over. Sir Richard studied it.

'Vechey's name, my brother's, and two verses from the Bible. Ah!' Sir Richard looked up and smiled. 'Two verses my brother always quoted: Apocalypse 6, Verse 8 and Genesis 3, Verse 1.'

'You know the verses, Sir Richard?'

'Yes.' The merchant closed his eyes. 'The second one refers to the serpent entering Eden.'

'And the first?'

'To Death riding a pale horse.'

'Why did your brother always quote these?' Cranston asked.

'I don't know. He had a sense of humour.'

'About the Bible?'

'No, no, about these two verses. He claimed they were his key to fame and fortune. Sometimes, when deep in his cups, he would quote them.'

'Do you know what he meant?' Athelstan asked.

'No, my brother loved riddles from boyhood. He just quoted the verses, smiled, and said they would bring him great success. I don't know what he meant.'

'What other riddles did your brother pose?' Cranston asked.

'None.'

'Yes, he did,' Lady Isabella spoke up, pushing back the black veil from her face. 'You remember, the shoemaker?'

'Ah, yes,' Sir Richard smiled. 'The shoemaker.'

'Lady Isabella,' Cranston queried, 'what about the shoemaker?'

She played with the sparkling ring on her finger. 'Well, over the last few months, my husband used to make reference to a shoemaker. He claimed the shoemaker knew the truth, and the shoemaker was guilty.' She shook her head. 'I don't know what he meant. Sometimes, at table,' she smiled falsely, 'my husband was like you, Sir John. He loved a deep-bowled cup of claret. Then he used to chant: "The shoemaker knows the truth, the shoemaker knows the truth".'

Cranston watched her closely.

'These riddles your husband used, when did they begin?'

'The quotations from the Bible? About – oh, fourteen or fifteen months ago.'

'And the shoemaker riddle?'

Cranston noticed that Lady Isabella had become tense and anxious.

'Shortly after Christmas? That's right. He first made the riddle up during one of our mummer's games at Twelfth Night.'

Somehow Athelstan knew these riddles were important. The room had fallen deathly silent except for Cranston's abrupt questions, the equally abrupt answers and the snapping and crackling of the logs in the fire. What did this group fear? he wondered. What was the meaning of the riddles?

'Tell me,' Athelstan spoke up, 'did anything happen in the household to account for these riddles? Anything in Sir Thomas's life? Sir Richard, Lady Isabella… you were the closest to Sir Thomas.'

'I don't know,' Sir Richard muttered. 'My brother liked to speak in riddles, refer to shadowy things, lectures and parables. He was a man who loved secrecy for secrecy's sake and hugged such secrets to his chest like other men do gold, silver or precious stones. No, nothing special happened here.'

'Are you sure?' Cranston turned and looked at him, resting his cup on one large, plump thigh. 'Are you sure, Sir Richard? My memory fails me about specific details but was there not a death here eight months ago?'

Lady Isabella's face now paled and Sir Richard refused to look up.

'No!'

'Come, come, sir,' Cranston barked. 'There was something.'

'Yes,' Lady Isabella said softly, 'Sir Richard's memory fails him.' She looked at Sir John more guardedly, as if realising the coroner was not the fool he liked to appear. 'There was Eudo's death.'

'Ah, yes, Eudo,' Cranston repeated. 'Who was he?'

Sir Richard looked up. 'A young page boy. He fell from a window and broke his neck, out there in the courtyard. No explanation for the fall was ever given, though Sir Thomas believed he may have been involved in some stupid jape. The boy was killed outright, head smashed in, neck broken.'

Cranston drained his cup and beamed in self-congratulation, giving a sly grin at Athelstan, who glared back. He wished the coroner had told him about this!

'Yes, Eudo's death. I was ill at the time with the ague, but I remember the verdict being recorded. Poor boy!' Cranston murmured. 'This house has ill fortune.' He stood and took in his audience with one heavy-lidded stare. 'I urge you all to be most careful. There is a malignancy here, an evil curse. It may yet claim other lives! Lady Isabella, Sir Richard.' He bowed and stepped out of the chamber.

Athelstan stopped at the door and looked back. The group sat quite still as if bound by some secret.

'Sir Richard?' Athelstan asked.

'Yes, Brother?'

'May I have permission to visit the garret where Brampton died?'

'Of course! But, as I have said, his corpse has been sheeted and removed to St Mary Le Bow.'

Athelstan smiled. 'Yes. But there is something I must see.'

He asked Cranston to wait for him outside and went upstairs. On the first landing he stopped and stole a glance down the Nightingale Gallery, so engrossed he jumped when Allingham suddenly touched him on the shoulder.

'Brother Athelstan, can I help you?'

The merchant's long face was even more mournful and the friar was sure the man had been crying.

'No, no, Master Allingham, I thank you. You have heard of Vechey's death, no doubt?'

The merchant nodded sorrowfully.

'Poor man!' Athelstan muttered. 'You know of no reason why he should take his life?'

'His was a troubled soul,' Allingham replied. 'A troubled soul, vexed and tormented by his own lusts and pleasures.' He paused. 'The only puzzling thing was that he kept muttering, "There were only thirty-one, there were only thirty-one".'

'Do you know what he meant?'

'No. When we went into Sir Thomas's chamber yesterday, I heard him mutter.' Allingham screwed up his eyes. 'Vechey said, "Only thirty-one, I am sure there were only thirty-one." I remember it,' he continued, 'because Vechey was puzzled, upset.'

'Do you know to what he was referring?'

Allingham pursed his lips.

'No, I don't, Brother. But if I find out, I shall tell you. I bid you adieu.'

He proceeded down the wooden stairs and Athelstan went along the gallery and up to the garret. He pushed the door open and wished he had asked for a candle. The chamber was dark and dank. Athelstan shivered. There was a sinister atmosphere, a feeling of oppressive malevolence. Were the church fathers right, he wondered, when they claimed that the soul of a suicide was bound eternally to the place where he died? Did Brampton's soul hover here, as he would for eternity, between heaven and hell?

He stepped in and looked around. The table was now clear of its ghastly remains, and the floor had been swept clear of its litter. It looked tidier, neater than it had the previous day. What had he seen here that afterwards had jolted, pricked against his memory? Something which had been out of place?

He leaned against the wall desperately trying to clear his mind but the memory proved elusive. He sighed, looked round once more and went back to rejoin Sir John.

The coroner was fretting, hopping from foot to foot, standing close to the wall of the house, well away from the crowds which now thronged the entire thoroughfare of Cheapside. He pulled Athelstan closer.

'They are lying, aren't they, Brother? There's something wrong, but what?'

'I don't know, Sir John, but there may be many logical explanations. Something may be wrong, but they may not realise it. Something may be wrong but only one or two may know the truth. Or, finally, something may be wrong but known to someone outside the household.'

'Such as who?'

Athelstan looked round and lowered his voice. 'My Lord of Gaunt or even Chief Justice Fortescue. After all, he did lie; the Chief Justice said he left the house about curfew, but Sir Richard claims it was much later.'

Sir John rubbed the side of his face.

'Yes, Chief Justice Fortescue. We don't even have a good reason for his being there. Why should he be visiting a London merchant?' The coroner grinned evilly, biting his lower lip with his strong, white teeth. 'I look forward to putting that very question to our Lord Chief Justice, but now for refreshment. Oh!'

Cranston grinned and tapped his wallet. 'I've taken the small phial of poison Brampton's supposed to have used.' He tapped the side of his nose. 'I've an idea, but not now. What I need now is a drink!'

Chapter 4

Athelstan cringed. He had hoped Sir John's appetite had been curbed but he seemed both insatiable and unable to learn from previous experience. The friar followed him dolefully across the street as Sir John scampered direct as an arrow for the Holy Lamb of God. Cranston took to its dry, dark warmth as a duck to water. He waddled amongst the customers, using his not inconsiderable bulk to force a way through pedlars, tinkers, labourers and farmers fresh from the countryside, spending the profits of their produce on large stoups of ale.

Sir John commandeered a table in the corner, greeting the ale wife as if she was a long-lost sister. The lady looked like a female incarnation of Satan. She had a hooked, perpetually dripping nose, skin as rough as a sack and bleary, bloodshot eyes. She munched continuously on her lips and her fingers were dirty and greasy down to the knuckles. Her cloak of Lincoln green covered a red kirtle which hung a few inches above tallow-smeared shoes. Athelstan looked at her and prayed to God to forgive him for all he felt was disgust. She, with her wide hips, dirty grey hair and face as wrinkled as a pig's ear, looked as blowsy as any harridan from hell. Athelstan sat looking at her in wonderment, constantly marvelling at the difference in women, contrasting this hag to the beauty of Lady Isabella. He grimly reminded himself that his vow of celibacy had certain consolations.

Cranston, however, acted as if she was an old friend, flattered and fussed her. She winked wickedly back at him, slyly insinuating that she would satisfy all his wants.

'Enough of that, you wicked wench!' Cranston teased. 'Food and ale first, then other comforts perhaps.' He dropped one eyelid. 'Later.'

The ale wife went away cackling and came back to serve both of them huge tankards slopping over with ale and a shared platter of meat mixed with onions and leeks swimming in a sea of grease. Cranston stuffed his mouth. He downed one tankard and, when the friar nodded, helped himself to the second.

'You are not eating, Brother?'

Athelstan toyed with the food on the platter in front of him.

'I don't feel hungry. I am wondering what we do next.'

Cranston, his mouth full of food, stared up at the blackened ceiling, coveting the leg of ham hooked there to be cured in the smoke.

'There's nothing much to do,' he replied. 'We have our suspicions but no proof. Oh, there's something wrong, we all know there is. Two suicides, one murder... but no proof whatsoever, no evidence. We should file our record, send copies to the sheriff, go back and tell Chief Justice Fortescue that whatever secret Springall had died with him, and then return to our normal business.'

'There's something wrong,' Athelstan repeated. He peered across the tavern, watching a group of men busy baiting a relic-seller who claimed he had Aaron's beard in a sack and was prepared to sell it to them for a few coins.

'It's like grasping a slippery fish or a greasy pole. You think you have it, then it slips away.'

Cranston stuck his red, bulbous nose into a tankard, took one slurp and slammed it down on the table.

'Very well, Brother, what is wrong? What do you think?'

'I believe there were no suicides. I think all three deaths were murder, and I think the murderer still walks!'

'And your proof?'

'Nothing, just a feeling of unease.'

'Oh, for God's sake!' Cranston bellowed. 'What do we have here? A merchant who likes riddles is murdered by his servant, who later hangs himself; a small, fat, morose man who thinks he is a Hector with the ladies and, when he realises he is not, goes out and hangs himself. A few riddles written on paper. Let's face the truth. That group over there,' he nodded in the direction of the Springall mansion, 'do not mourn for anyone. I suspect they are glad Sir Thomas is dead! And Brampton! And Vechey! More money, less fingers in the pot and a larger portion of the spoils. All you can feel, Brother, is human greed. Look around, there's a whole sea of it lapping at us everywhere we walk, sit, eat, and pray!' He glared at the friar. 'Come, Brother,' he concluded wearily, 'let us tie the ends of this and call it suicide.'

'In a while,' Athelstan murmured.

He asked for a cup of water, finished it, and leaving Cranston to his drinking, went outside. It was now mid-afternoon. The stalls and booths along Cheapside were plying a busy trade, the shouts of their keepers and the bold imprecations of the apprentices creating an unbearable din. A knight broke through on his way to a local joust or tournament, his steel codpiece carved as large as a bull's whilst the helmet which swung from his saddle bow was fashioned in the macabre mask of a hangman. The helmet gave Athelstan an idea. He was curious and, shouldering his way through the crowd, made his way to St Mary Le Bow.

Father Matthew was resting. Athelstan suspected he was half drunk, but he welcomed the friar cheerily enough, trying to force a cup of Rhenish into his hand. Athelstan promptly refused, for the few mouthfuls of ale he had already drunk bit at his stomach. He also felt rather sick when he recalled how in the ale house he had just left he had seen a hen roosting on the brim of an uncovered beer tub. He just hoped the ale wife strained the ale before she served it to Sir John! Chicken dung would not do even the coroner's innards any good.

The priest listened to Athelstan carefully.

'Yes, yes,' he murmured. He knew the Springalls, a good but rather secretive family. They attended Mass on Sundays, they gave generously to the poor, and the chancery priest sometimes celebrated Mass at St Mary's. They were always generous at Christmas, Epiphany and Maundy.

'And the funeral of Sir Thomas?' Athelstan asked.

'It will take place tomorrow morning. Once the Requiem Mass is sung, the coffin will be buried here.'

'And Brampton, the suicide?'

The priest, lounging in his chair, shrugged, wiping his greasy hands on his gown.

'What can we do? Brampton has no relatives and he is a suicide. Canon Law has laid down...'

'I know what Canon Law says,' Athelstan snapped back. 'But for God's sake, man, Christ's mercy!'

The priest made a face. 'Oh, he will be given a burial.'

'Where is the body?'

'In the death house, a small hut behind the church near the graveyard.'

'May I have a look?'

'The man is sheeted already with a canvas cloth.'

Athelstan dug in his purse and took out a silver coin. 'If I rip the cloth open, you will have it resewn. Surely some old lady in the parish?'

Father Matthew nodded and the silver coin disappeared in the twinkling of an eye. 'Do what you want!' he muttered.

He leant over to where keys hung on hooks in the wall and took a huge, rusting one down. 'You will need this.' He went into the small scullery and came back with a pomander, a ball of cloth stuffed with cloves and herbs.

'Hold it to your nose. The stench will be terrible.'

Athelstan took the key and the pomander, left the priest's house and walked down the length of the church to the derelict hut beyond. The door was barred and bolted. The huge padlock seemed oddly out of place, for anyone could have broken in if they had wished. He inserted the key, released the padlock and the door creaked open. Inside it was dark and musty. A strange, sour smell pervaded the air. An ancient tallow candle stood fixed in its grease on one of the cross-beams, with a tinder beside it. Athelstan took it, lit the candle, and the room flared into life.

Brampton's corpse lay on the ground, covered in a dirty, yellowing canvas sheet, inexpertly sewed up. Athelstan carefully ripped the canvas open with the small knife he always carried. The stench was terrible. Putrefaction had already set in. Used to the sight and the smell of the dead, Athelstan did not feel queasy, though now and again he held the pomander to his nose for a welcome respite. Brampton now looked hideous. His face had turned a blueish-yellow and his stomach was swollen, straining against the thin linen shirt. The friar studied the body carefully; the shirt, the hose, but there were no boots. He looked at the soles of the feet, making careful note of what he saw. He then made the sign of the cross, said a Requiem for the poor steward's soul, re-locked the hut, returned the key to the priest and wandered back into Cheapside.

Athelstan stood there dreaming, wondering what was happening in St Erconwald's. Who would feed Godric? Would Bonaventure return or take offence at not being fed by him and disappear forever into the stinking alleyways? He wished he was free of Cranston and this matter; free of Cheapside, back at the top of his tower, staring up at the stars. He leaned against the wall and analysed his guilt-laden thoughts. He missed Benedicta the widow. Her face, innocent and angelic, was always with him. How long had he known her? Six months? He breathed a prayer. He had sinned. Yes, he wished he was back in his church with his beloved sky and charts, standing on the tower, letting the evening breeze cool him as he stared up, lost in the vastness. Was he breaking his vows by wanting that? Should he have become a friar or a student? An astrologer, one of those cowled, bent figures who haunted the halls of Oxford.

And what was the attraction of the planets in the sky? Athelstan bit his lip. There was order there. Order in time. Order in motion. Was Aristotle correct? he wondered. Did the planets and spheres give off music when they turned in the universe? A cart crashed by, its driver mouthing oaths. Athelstan stepped back, free from his dreams, and looked around.

There was no order here. A beggar, his face covered in sores, his legs cut off just beneath the knees, scampered about on wooden crutches. A whore tripped by, her eyes ringed with black paint, her thick painted lips lustrous and red like rotting fruit. She smirked and dismissed Athelstan with a flicker of her eyes. He walked across the thorough-fare. In the centre of Cheapside stood the stocks, empty except for one person, a large, fat man, his head securely clasped between the wooden slats. Beneath him were the charred remains of a small fire. Athelstan studied the notice posted above the prisoner's head and gathered that he was a butcher who had sold putrid meat. The friar stopped a water carrier, took his ladle and gave the fellow a drink. The prisoner slurped noisily, thanking him, bleary-eyed. A mounted soldier trotted by and Athelstan remembered the knight's helmet as well as something he had glimpsed in the garret and at the tower gate of London Bridge...

Athelstan made his way north to the Elms near Newgate where a great three-branched scaffold stood stark against the sky; each bore its grisly burden, a corpse swinging by its neck, head askew, hands and feet securely tied. The crowd had gone and a serjeant-at-arms, wearing the florid livery of the city, threw dice with his two companions, ignoring the grim carrion swaying just above their heads. The area around them was empty. Strange, Athelstan thought, how men liked to see their brothers die, yet feared the actual sight and stench of death. The serjeant looked up as he approached.

'What is it, Brother?'

Athelstan pointed to the three dangling figures, trying to ignore their empurpled faces, black protruding tongues, popping eyes and stained breeches.

'These men?'

'They were shriven this morning, Friar,' the soldier interrupted. 'Before we turned them off the ladder.'

'How long will they hang?' he asked.

The fellow shrugged and Athelstan tried not to concentrate on the great yellowing ulcer on the right side of his face, the pus now suppurating, bubbling out, staining his cheek. The soldier, his eyes dead and full of drink, shrugged and grinned at his two companions, sallow, pimply youths already much the worse for wine.

'They will hang, Father, till sunset. Why do you ask?'

'I want to look at them.'

'They are to hang until sunset,' the serjeant repeated.

'Their clothes and belongings are ours. There is a canvas sheet for each of them, a swift prayer, and then into some forsaken grave to meet their maker.' He tapped one of the swaying bodies. 'Don't feel sorry for any of them, Father. They murdered a woman and cut her throat, after they brutally sliced her breasts, raped and burnt her over a fire!'

'Sweet Jesus have mercy on them!' Athelstan whispered. 'But I am here on the orders of Sir John Cranston, coroner of the city. I want to see them.'

He felt in his purse and threw down a couple of copper coins. The serjeant rubbed his chin and looked at them and then at the friar, sucking in air noisily through his blackened teeth. At last he rose and barked an order at one of the young men who placed the ladder lying on the ground against the scaffold, then gestured dramatically at Athelstan.

'Brother, the ladder awaits. Do what you want!'

Athelstan climbed the ladder slowly. He studied each of the corpses, noting how the rope had been tied firmly behind one ear. He moved around, inspecting each body carefully, holding his breath against the sour smell of corruption. At last he came down. Another coin was thrown on the ground. The serjeant looked up.

'What now, Brother?'

'Who hanged these men?'

'Well, we all did.'

'No, I mean who tied the ropes around their necks?'

'I did!' One of the pimply youths got up. 'I did, Brother. I do it expertly.'

'Would you say,' Athelstan asked, trying to hide his distaste at the glee in the young man's face, 'that each hangman arranges the knot in his own way?'

'Of, of course!'

'And from the noose you could tell which man you'd hanged and which you had not?'

'Naturally. A goldsmith has his mark, leaves his insignia on a plate. An artist who sketches a painting can recognise his own work. The same with the hangman. My knots are unique. I place them carefully.' The young man beamed expansively. 'I am skilled in my trade, Brother. I always make sure they take a long time to die.'

'Why?'

The fellow shrugged. 'Why not?'

'Do you enjoy it?'

'Well, the bastards deserve to suffer long.'

'And how do they suffer?'

'Oh, they kick a lot. They always kick.'

Athelstan pointed to the feet of the corpses.

'So, you always hang them without their boots on?'

'Yes, of course. Otherwise they would kick them off and we'd lose them. Some thief from the crowd might steal them and we'd be all the poorer. Why do you ask, Brother?'

The friar smiled and sketched a sign of the cross in the air. 'Nothing, my son, nothing at all.'

Athelstan turned and left the grisly bodies and walked back up Cheapside towards the Holy Lamb of God. He was convinced that Brampton and Vechey had been brutally murdered, though by whom he could not say.

He found Cranston dozing, comfortably ensconced in the inglenook of the tavern, a number of large empty pewter tankards arranged on the table before him. The ale wife walked over. Athelstan tossed her a coin and asked her to bring a fresh tankard and some wine whilst he roused Sir John. The coroner woke like a child, mumbling to himself, wondering where he was. Athelstan told him of the visits to the death house and the gibbet. The coroner nodded off to sleep again so, crossing to a barrel of dirty water, Athelstan filled the ladle and splashed it over Cranston's face. This time Sir John woke, shaking himself like a dog, mouthing the most terrible curses. He was only placated by the ale wife placing a frothing tankard in front of him and throwing him the most longing and sly of glances, as if he was Paris and she Helen of Troy. In the presence of such flattery and with the taste of ale once more on his lips, Sir John regained his good temper and this time listened attentively as Athelstan spoke. He belched loudly when the account was finished and picked at his teeth with a sliver of wood. Athelstan thought he was going off to sleep again but the coroner took one further gulp from his tankard.

'Sir John,' Athelstan said testily, 'we must discuss matters!'

'Yes, yes,' the coroner bellowed. 'Buy me another one of these and I will listen to you again!'

Athelstan did so. Sir John, now fully awake but still in his cups, belched and gazed around the tavern, murmuring what an excellent place it was. Athelstan remembered the hen roosting over the beer barrel and kept his own counsel. He sipped slowly at a cup of watered wine and decided to return to his church. The roof might not have been repaired. Cecily the courtesan might still be plying her trade. And what would happen to Godric? Fleetingly, he wondered once again if Benedicta had missed him. He looked through the narrow tavern window. The sun was beginning to set. It was time he was gone. The Springall business was hidden by a tissue of lies. He was too tired to probe and Cranston too drunk.

Athelstan rose to his feet. 'Sir John, look!'

The coroner glanced up blearily.

'Sir John, I can do nothing with you. I must go back to my church. Tomorrow or the day after, when you are in a better frame of mind, join me there.'

Athelstan picked up his leather bag, marched out of the tavern, collected Philomel and made his way slowly through the empty streets to London Bridge.

Cranston watched him go, then leaned back against the wall.

'Christ!' he murmured. 'I wish you'd stay, Athelstan, just for once!'

He groaned and pushed the tankard away. He had drunk enough and wished he hadn't. But the friar was not the only one with secrets and Sir John drank to drown his. No one remembered, except Maude who kept her thoughts to herself, that seven years ago this week his little child, Matthew, died suddenly, the victim of the plague which stalked the alleyways and streets of London. Cranston tightened his lips, blinking his eyes furiously as he always did when the tears threatened to return. Every day he thought of Matthew, the small angelic face, the blue eyes shimmering with innocence. Christ could not blame him for drinking. He'd drink and drink until the memory was gone. And why not? Yet drink clouded his mind, and in his heart, Cranston knew that Athelstan was right to disapprove. His maudlin drunkenness was not helping matters. There had been murder, deliberate and malicious, perpetrated in the Springall household. But where was the proof? He vaguely tried to remember what the friar had told him. Something about neither Brampton nor Vechey killing themselves. But where was the proof? Cranston tried to clear his thoughts. He, too, knew there was something wrong. Something was bothering him, something he had seen this morning at the bridge... He looked at the half-empty tankard.

'Christ, Matthew, I miss you!' he murmured. 'Oh, let the world hang itself!'

He was about to order another when he thought of Maude and his promise to her. At least tonight he would return halfway sober. Cranston pushed the tankard away and waddled out of the tavern to collect his horse and return to his house in Poultry.

Two days after he returned from the city, Athelstan rose early and went to examine his small garden. Outside he glared angrily about. Someone's pig had been rooting amongst the cabbage patch. Athelstan cursed in some of the language Cranston used on such occasions. He felt angry, agitated. He had come back to find his church safe but Godric gone.

'You see, Father,' Watkin the dung-collector explained, 'the silly bastard thought he could slip out, so he did, through the sacristy door. Of course, they were waiting for him, the sheriff's men. They beat him up in the alleyway, tied his hands and led him off to the Marshalsea. He'll probably hang!'

'Yes, Watkin,' Athelstan replied, 'he'll probably hang.'

Apart from that, everything had been in order except for Bonaventure, who had slipped away and had not been seen since. Athelstan hoped he was safe and would come padding back when he was hungry, tail in the air, miaowing for food and comfort.

The friar looked up. The sky was still blue; the sun, growing in strength, promised a hot sweltering day.

He sighed. He'd said his prayers and celebrated Mass, Benedicta just slipping in at the door and kneeling next to the baptismal font instead of coming further up the nave. Athelstan wondered if there was anything wrong. He moved down the side of his church to see if Crim was waiting on the steps but they were empty. He went back, took a hoe from inside the door of his house and stabbed furiously at the cabbage patch, trying to rearrange the furrows in neat order. Once Crim had arrived, he would go and see Hob the grave-digger, dying they said after he had slipped and fallen under a cartwheel, which had crushed his ribs.

Athelstan tired of his task. He threw the hoe to the ground, hoped that at least the pig had had a good meal, and went back inside his church. He looked around and felt happier. Simon the tiler had done a good job. The roof was secure against the coming winter rains. Huddle the painter had scraped the wall and begun a new fresco, his first church painting. Athelstan had requested that Huddle should first draw charcoal sketches, from these giving the gifted young man scriptural advice to the effect that there was no evidence whatsoever that Herod had eventually stabbed Pilate in the back! So the charcoaled drawings had been wiped out and Huddle had begun again, a lovely vigorous painting of the Annunciation and birth of Christ. The church floor was swept and washed clean, thanks to Cecily the courtesan who had earned her pennies honestly by scrubbing every inch.

'Honestly, Father,' she confessed, leaning on her broom of brittle twigs, 'I've changed. I intend to change.'

Athelstan stared into her childlike eyes and wondered if the woman was a little simple. The friar was sure he had seen her lying in the graveyard amongst the tombs with Simon the tiler, and he a married man with three children.

'So, Father,' she had whispered, moving closer and swinging her hips suggestively, 'can I play the part of the Virgin Mary in the parish masque for Corpus Christi?'

Athelstan had hidden his smile beneath a stern look and said he would discuss it with the church council.

'Watkin the dung-collector,' he advised, 'takes his duties as church warden most seriously. He has his own thoughts in the matter.'

'I don't give a fig for what Watkin says!' Cecily had snapped. 'I could tell you a lot about Watkin, Father!'

'Thank you, Cecily,' Athelstan had said. 'Soon the church will look nicer.'

Cecily got on with her cleaning. Athelstan felt sorry. Perhaps he had been a little too harsh with her. Cecily was a good girl who meant to do well. He could see no objection to her playing the part of the Virgin. The only obstacle was Watkin the dung-collector, whose own ample wife also had her eye on the role.

On balance, decided Athelstan, he was pleased. All was well, apart from Godric, Bonaventure, and of course the pardoner. Huddle had told him about the rogue, turning up in his garish garments and standing on the church steps, offering to sell pardons to those who could afford them. Athelstan swore that if he got his hands on the fellow, Cranston would have another murder to investigate.

He leaned against the rood screen and stared up at his newly repaired roof. He wondered where Cranston was. Why had he allowed two days to go by? Was he sulking or just ill with drinking? Athelstan couldn't leave his parish and go into the city, but he wished he could speak to the coroner, apologise for leaving him so abruptly the night before last. He hadn't meant to, it was just that he had become so tired, so exhausted with the Springalls, the murders, the deceit and the lies. He felt Vechey and Brampton had not committed suicide. He also suspected that Sir Thomas Springall had not been murdered by Brampton. The real murderers now hid in the shadows, mocking both him and Cranston, believing they would never search out the truth. Athelstan smiled thinly. Cranston, when he gathered his wits, would soon prove the bastards wrong.

Athelstan heard a sound and looked round. The church door opened and Crim, the young urchin, scampered in. His mother had taken special care to remove the dirt from his face and hands at least.

'Good morning, Crim,' Athelstan called. 'Come!'

He took a taper and lit it from the large wax candle burning in front of the statue of the Madonna.

'Now hold that and, as I walk through the street, you go before me carrying the light. And here,' he went behind the altar and took a small bell, 'you ring this. Now, if the candle goes out, don't be afraid. Just keep on walking and ringing the bell. You know where we are going?'

The little boy, round-eyed, shook his head.

'To Hob the grave-digger.'

'Oh. He's dying, Father!'

'Yes, Crim, I know. And he must die with Christ, so it's important we get there. Do you understand?'

The little fellow nodded solemnly. Athelstan, taking the keys from his belt, went up beneath the winking red sanctuary lamp and opened the tabernacle door. He took out the Viaticum, placing it in a small leather pouch which he slung round his neck, then went into the sacristy to collect the church's one and only cope. A faded, red and gold garment, showing the Holy Spirit as a dove with one wing, sending faded rays down on an even more faded Christ. Athelstan wrapped the cope around him and, telling Crim to go forward, they left the church, processing down the steps and into the maze of Southwark streets. Athelstan was always surprised at the effect he caused; here he was in a place where men died for the price of a few coins, but at the sight of the lighted wax candle, the sound of the small tinkling bell and him swathed in a cope, the coarsest men and women stood aside as if they acknowledged the great mysteries he carried.

Hob's cottage was a dour, earth-floored building divided into three rooms; one a bedroom for Hob and his wife, the second for his four children, the third a scullery and eating-place. It was poor but swept clean, a few pewter pots and pans, scrubbed in boiling water, hanging from nails in the wall. Inside, at the far end of the hut, Hob lay on a bed, his face white, the red blood frothing at his lips. Athelstan blessed the man, holding his hand, reassuring his good wife that all would be well whilst trying not to look at the blood. He gave the man the Viaticum and blessed him, anointing him on the head, chest, hands and feet. Afterwards he had a few words with Hob's wife, the children cowering around her. Athelstan promised he would do something to help her and left quietly, the cope still round his shoulders, Crim jumping up and down in front of him all the way back to the church.

Ranulf the rat-catcher was waiting for him just outside the door, a sleek, well-fed Bonaventure in his hands. He waited until Athelstan had put the black pouch back into the tabernacle and Crim had taken his penny and fled like the wind, before putting the cat down and approaching Athelstan.

'I found him waiting, Father, but if you want to sell him?'

Athelstan smiled.

'If you want him, Ranulf, he's yours. But I doubt if he will leave.'

The friar knelt down and tickled the cat between his ears. He looked up at the lined, seamed face of the rat-catcher, framed by his black, tarry leather hood.

'He's a mercenary. If you took him away, he'd be back tonight!'

Bonaventure agreed, stretched, and walked back to his favourite place at the base of the pillar.

Once Ranulf had gone, Athelstan sat on the altar steps, his mind going back to the corpses he had seen: Vechey's lying cold amongst those dreadful heads on the tower gate of London Bridge; Brampton's sheathed in dirty canvas in the death house of St Mary Le Bow; Springall lying alone under its leather covering in the great four poster bed in his mansion. What eluded him still? He thought of Hob dying in his hovel, his wife frightened of the future. Surely he could get some money for her from somewhere? He lifted his hands to his face and smelt the chrism he had used on Hob's head, hands, chest and feet. The feet!

Athelstan jumped up. Of course, that was it, Brampton's feet! The manservant hadn't committed suicide. He couldn't have done. He had been murdered!

Athelstan looked around the church. He wished Cranston were here. The sun streamed through the horn-glazed windows and Bonaventure stretched out, relaxing after a good night's hunting. Athelstan turned from the familiar, domestic sight and knelt before the altar, his eyes fixed on the red light.

'Oh, God,' he prayed, 'help me now. Please!'

In his own private chamber at his house in Poultry, Sir John also was thinking as he leant over his writing desk, quill in hand. He was engaged in the great love of his life: writing a treatise on the maintenance of law in the city of London. Cranston had a love of the law and, ever since his appointment as coroner, had been engaged in drawing up his own proposals for law reform. He would put them forward in a specially written book, bound in the finest calf, to some powerful patron who, in Cranston's dreams, would see them as the solution to all of London's problems.

Sir John loved the city, knew every stone, every church, every highway, every alleyway. Immersed in London's history, he was constantly begging the monks of Westminster Abbey, or the clerks of the chancery in the Tower, to let him have access to manuscripts and documents. Some he would take home, copying them out most carefully before returning them in their leather cases to their proper places. In a sense, Cranston never wished to finish his labour. He believed that his survey would be of use, but privately thought of it as his escape. No one else knew. No one except Maude, of course.

Cranston put down the pen, a wave of self-pity suffusing his huge body. He looked out of the window and heard the cries from Cheapside, the clatter of carts, the rattle against the cobbles of iron-shod horses going towards Smithfield and the horse market. He drank too much, Cranston knew that. He must give it up. He must reform his life. Virtuously, he patted his great stomach. But not today. Perhaps tomorrow. He wondered what Athelstan was doing. He speculated whether he should speak to the friar, open his heart, tell him his secrets, get rid of the sea of misery he felt bathing his body, drowning his mind.

Maude came in and Cranston looked at her, hang-dog, for even in bed his tourney of love was failing. He watched his wife carefully out of the corner of his eye as she busied herself, stacking blankets, opening chests, replacing candles in their holders. He studied her comely figure, her small, full breasts, clear face, bright eyes, ready smile, the slight sway when she walked. Cranston got up. Perhaps there was some-thing wrong, but it was not that serious. He moved over and embraced his wife, pulling her close to him.

'Oh, Sir John!' she whispered, nestling against him.

'Bolt the door!' he murmured thickly. 'Bolt the door. I wish to show you something!'

She turned, her eyes round.

'I suspect I have seen it before.'

Nevertheless, the door was locked, the window casement shut, and Cranston proved to his own satisfaction, as well as his wife's, that perhaps age had not yet drained the juices of his body. As they lay on the great four poster bed, their bodies entwined, Maude almost lost in Cranston's great fat folds, Sir John stared up at the ceiling, brushing his wife's hair with his cheek, listening to her chattering about this and that.

'What was that?' He pushed her away sharply.

'Sir John, what is the matter?'

'What did you just say?'

Maude shrugged. 'I was talking about Agnes, the wife of David the waterman. You often hire him to take us across the river. Well, she says that the boatmen and wharfers are drawing up a petition which they would like you to look at. They wish some of the arches of the bridge to be widened, the starlings to be replaced. The water level is so high, it is dangerous and boats are dashed against the pier or the arches. Sir John, men have drowned. Children as well!'

Cranston sat up in bed, his fat body quivering with pleasure.

'That's what was wrong! Now I know what I saw on the bridge!' He turned and embraced his surprised wife, kissing her passionately on the forehead and cheeks.

'Maude, whatever would I do without you? You and your chatter. Of course! I wonder if Athelstan thought of that?'

Despite his huge bulk, Cranston leapt out of bed.

'Come, Maude! Come, wife, quickly! Fresh hose, a clean shirt, a cup of claret, a meat pie and a manchet loaf! I must be off! Come on!'

Lady Maude moved just as quickly, glaring at her husband. One minute he was embracing her, kissing her passionately, and now he was leaping around the bedroom like a young gallant, getting ready to get out. Nevertheless, she scurried around, putting on her dress and smock whilst muttering how, if other people had left her alone, she would have things ready anyway.

Sir John ignored her, dressing hastily; he now knew that Vechey had been murdered. Had to have been. The level of the river water would prove that. He would drag that bloody friar from his stars and they would go back to the Springall mansion and this time demand answers to their questions.

Chapter 5

As soon as Athelstan skirted the church, he saw the coroner standing beside Philomel. The old destrier was saddled and ready to depart. Cranston grinned.

'Good morning, Brother!' he bellowed, loud enough for half the parish to hear. 'Your horse is ready. Your saddlebags are packed.' He held them up. 'Quills, pens, writing tray, parchment, and I have ensured the inkhorn is well sealed, so if it spills, don't blame me.'

Athelstan, still feeling depressed after his visit to Hob's wife, ignored the coroner and pushed by him into his small, two-roomed house. Cranston followed like an unwelcome draught, sweeping in, filling the room with his broad girth.

'Really, Brother!' he boomed, as he looked around. 'You should live in a little more comfort. Do you have any wine?'

Athelstan gestured towards an earthenware jug and watched with delight as Cranston took a great gulp, then, his face puce as a plum, went to the door to spit it out.

'God's teeth, man! More water than wine!' he snapped.

'St Dominic and my Order,' Athelstan said tartly, 'have in their wisdom decreed that wine at full strength is not for monks.' He tapped Cranston's great girth. 'Perhaps not even for king's coroners!'

Cranston drew himself up to his full height and squinted at Athelstan.

'My orders, little friar, are that you are to accompany me into Cheapside to a tavern called the Bear and Ragged Staff. You have heard of it?'

Athelstan shook his head, his heart sinking. Cranston smirked.

'We are going to sit there. I shall remain sober and tell you how Vechey was murdered. He did not commit suicide.'

'And I shall tell you, my Lord Coroner, how Edmund Brampton, steward to Sir Thomas Springall, did not hang himself in the garret of that house in Cheapside!'

'So you have been thinking, Friar?'

'Coroner, I never stop.'

'Well, come on then!'

'Sir John, we could stay here and discuss our concerns.'

Cranston turned, shaking his head. 'Here? Where every little snot from Southwark can come knocking at your door, bothering you with their complaints. Oh, no, Brother. Our stop at the Bear and Ragged

Staff is only half our journey. We go then to Newgate, and perhaps elsewhere.'

So saying, he strode out of the house. Athelstan breathed a prayer for patience, made a sign of the cross over himself and followed suit. Cranston, now mounted, watched him.

'Aren't you going to lock your door?' he bellowed.

'What's the use?' Athelstan replied. 'If I do, thieves will break it down thinking there is something valuable to steal.'

Snorting at the friar's apparent stupidity, Cranston turned his horse and led them out of the main alleyways of Southwark. A group of urchins, recognising Sir John, followed from afar and, despite Athelstan's pleas, shouted insults about the coroner's ponderous girth. Garth the woodcutter, who also took the death carts round the streets, was drinking outside the tavern and joined in the noisy abuse.

'Sir John Cranston!' he bellowed, tapping his own round belly. 'You must be pregnant. What will it be, boy or girl?'

That was too much for the coroner. He reined in his horse and glared at his cheery-faced tormentor.

'If I was pregnant by you,' he shouted back, 'then it would be a bloody great Barbary ape!'

And, amidst the raucous laughter which greeted this repartee, Athelstan and Cranston continued on their way to London Bridge. They crossed over quietly enough, Athelstan smiling as he passed through the gateway at the far end on to Fish Street Hill. He wondered how the little man was coping, remembered the heads and concluded it was an acquaintance he would not wish to renew.

The fine day had brought the crowds pouring into London, varlets, squires, and men-at-arms accompanying knights north to the great horse fair at Smithfield, after which there would be tournaments and tourneys. The streets were packed with men, helmeted and armed, and great destriers caparisoned in all the colours and awesome regalia of war moved majestically along Fish Street Hill. High in the saddle rode the knights, resplendent in coloured surcoats, their slit-eyed helmets swinging from saddle bows, bannered lances carried before them by squires. Hordes of others followed on foot: retainers gaudy in the livery of great lords, and the bright French silks of young gallants who swarmed into the city like butterflies under the warm sun and blue skies. They thronged the taverns, their coloured garments a sharp contrast to the dirty leather aprons of the blacksmiths and the short jerkins and caps of the apprentices.

As Cranston and Athelstan turned into Cheapside, they saw the festive spirit had spread. Stalls were out and there were mummers performing miracle plays. Men shouted themselves hoarse proclaiming cock fights, dog battles, and savage contests never seen before between wild hogs and mangy bears. The crowds had impeded the dung carts, and the piles of rubbish and refuse were everywhere, the flies rising in thick black swarms.

'God's teeth!' Cranston said. 'Come, Athelstan.'

They had to dismount and force their way through, past the Conduit and the Tun and up a small alleyway which led into the Bear and Ragged Staff. They stabled their horses and did not enter the tavern but passed into a pleasant garden beyond. A private place with a chessboard garden, a square divided into four plots by small gravelled walks and paths. These were fringed by a hedge of varying shrubs and small trees – white-thorn, privet, sweetbriar and the occasional rose – all entwined together. They sat against the wall on turfed seats in the shade, looking out over raised herb banks of hyssop, lavender and other fragrant shrubs. A slattern brought a small table for Athelstan to rest his writing tray on, and of course a jug of wine and two goblets, though Athelstan shook his head and asked for water. They sat and enjoyed the fragrant smells and the coolness after their dusty ride through the city.

'I could stay here all day,' Athelstan said, leaning back against the wall. 'So quiet, so peaceful.'

'You would prefer to be back in your monastery?'

Athelstan smiled. 'I didn't say that!'

'But you do not like your work?'

'I did not say that either.' He turned and looked at Cranston, noting how the fat coroner's face was dewed with drops of sweat. 'Do you like yours, Sir

John? The murder, the lies, the deceits? Do you remember,' Athelstan asked, 'I once quoted Bartholomew the Englishman?'

Cranston looked expectant.

'He wrote a book entitled *The Nature of Things*,' Athelstan continued, 'in which he described the planet Saturn as cold as ice, dark as night, and malignant as Satan. He claims that the planet governs the murderous intent of men.' Athelstan squinted, watching the bees hover round a succulent rose. 'I often think it governs mine. You heard Fortescue refer to my own brother?' Cranston nodded. 'My father owned a prosperous farm to the south, in Sussex. I was intended for the religious life. My brother was destined to till the soil. Now there's a road which goes by our farm down to the coast. We used to see the men-at-arms, the crossbow men on their way to the ports for the crossing to France, then we'd watch them return laden with booty. We heard the legends and romantic stories about knights in shining armour, war horses moving majestically across green fields.

'One spring I left my noviciate and came back to the farm. The next party of soldiers which passed, my brother and I joined. We sailed from Dover, landing at Honfleur, joining one of the many bands plundering across France.' Athelstan stared up at the sky. 'We were under the command of the Black Prince with his general Walter de Manny and others. Our dreams soon died. No chivalrous knights, no majestic armies moving according to rules, but horrible deeds, towns gutted and burnt, women and children slain. Then one day my brother and I, serving as archers, were caught outside a town by a group of French horsemen. We took up our positions, driving stakes into the ground in the usual pattern. The French charged sooner than we thought. They were amongst us, hacking and killing.'

Athelstan stopped to compose himself before continuing: 'When it was over, my brother was dead and I had aged a hundred years. I might as well tell you, Cranston. I returned home. I'll never forget my father's face. I'd never seen him like that. He just stared at me. My mother? All she could do was crouch in a corner and sob. I think she cried till the day she died. My father soon followed her to the grave. I went back to my Order. Oh, they accepted me, but life was harsh. I had to do private and public penance, and take a solemn vow that, after I was ordained, I would accept whatever duties my superiors gave me.'

Athelstan snorted with laughter and leaned forward, his arms crossed, as if he was talking to himself and had forgotten the coroner sitting beside him. 'Whatever duties! Hard study and the most menial work the house could provide; cleaning sewers, digging ditches and, after ordination, I must go here, I must go there! Eventually I protested so Father Prior took me for a walk in the meadows and said I was to prove my worth with one final task.'

He leaned back against the wall. 'My final task was St Erconwald's in Southwark.' Athelstan stared across at Cranston. 'My father prior chose well. My parents accused me of the murder of my brother. Every day in Southwark someone dies. Men and women drenched with drink, quarrelling and violently fighting each other. In some alleyway or runnel, a man hacked to death for stealing ale. A woman slashed from jaw to groin found floating in a ditch. And then you, Sir John! Just in case I should forget, or withdraw, or hide behind my church walls, you are here, ready to lead me along the streets, remind me that there is no escape from murder, from witnessing the greatest sin of all – a man slaying his brother!'

Cranston drained his cup of wine and said, 'Perhaps your father prior is wiser than you think.'

'What do you mean?'

'I am writing a treatise, have been for years, on the maintenance of the king's peace in London. The most terrible crime is murder. The belief that a man can kill someone, walk away, and say, "I am not responsible". I am no theologian, Athelstan, nor a scripture scholar, but the first crime committed after Eden was one of murder: Cain plotting to slay his brother Abel and afterwards claiming he knew nothing about it.' Cranston grinned. 'The first great mystery – I mean murder. But nothing like what happened to your brother.' He turned and spat. 'That wasn't murder. That was young dreams and hot blood, minds crammed with stupid stories about Troy and Knights of the Round Table. No, murder is different. And why do men commit murder, Athelstan? For profit? And what will stop men murdering? Hanging, torture?' He shrugged. 'Go down to Newgate, as we will do later. The prison is packed with murderers, the gibbets are heavy like apple trees in the autumn, the branches bend with their rotten fruit.'

Cranston moved closer, his face more serious than Athelstan had ever seen it. 'What will prevent murder, robbery, arson, is when the perpetrator knows, believes, accepts in his heart, that he will be caught and he will be punished. The more vigilant we are, the fewer murders, the fewer deaths. The fewer women slashed from jaw to groin, the fewer men with their throats cut, hanging in a garret or swinging from some beam under a bridge. Your prior knows, Athelstan, that with your guilt and deep sense of justice, you are well suited to such a task.'

He laughed abruptly and went back to his wine cup. 'If your order produced more men like you, Athelstan, and fewer preachers and theologians, London would be a safer place. That's the reason I have brought you to this quiet garden, not to some tavern where I would drink myself senseless. No, I want to plot and catch an evil murderer. A man who has slain Thomas Springall and blamed it on poor Brampton, afterwards making his death look like suicide. I believe the same villain executed Vechey and strung his corpse up like carrion under London Bridge.'

Athelstan drank greedily from the water cup, refusing to look at Cranston. He had talked about his brother's death, and for the first time ever someone had not laid the blame at his door. Athelstan knew it would make no immediate difference, but a seed had been planted in his soul. The possibility that he had committed a sin but no murder. That he would atone for it and so the slate would be wiped clean. He put down the cup.

'You say Springall was murdered by someone else, not Brampton?' he asked abruptly.

'I do,' said Cranston. 'And so do you. And how can we prove that? The loose thread in this rotten tapestry is Vechey. Now, you may remember when we inspected his corpse, we noticed the water had soaked him up to his knees?'

'Yes,' Athelstan nodded.

'We also know that if Vechey committed suicide, he must have done it in the early hours, just before dawn. Correct?' Again Athelstan nodded.

'But that is impossible,' Cranston continued with a self-satisfied smirk. 'You see, after midnight, the Thames runs fast and full. The water rises and it would almost cover the arch. There would be, at the very most, a foot between the surface of the water and the beam Vechey used to hang himself.' He held up his stubby fingers. 'First, are we to accept that a man waded through water up to his neck to tie a noose to hang himself? Or that he hanged himself virtually under water? Yet when Vechey's corpse was found, somehow or other it had dried out except beneath the knees.'

Athelstan grinned. '*Mirabile dictu*, Sir John! Of course the river would be full. Vechey would have had to swim out to hang himself and that is a logical contradiction. So what do you think happened?'

'Vechey was drugged or knocked on the head, the corpse being strung up for others to find.'

'But why such contrivance?'

'I have been wondering about that,' Cranston replied. 'Remember, we know very little about the man. Vechey was promiscuous. He liked soft and perfumed flesh but, being a respectable citizen, he would hunt well away from his home in Cheapside. So I think he went down to the stews and bawdy houses along the river. Somehow or other he was trapped, knocked on the head or drugged, and his body taken down to London Bridge. The noose was tied around his neck and strung over the beam. The murderer was very clever, and the riverbank was deserted. The bridge, as the dwarf told us, was a favourite place for people to commit suicide. The murderer made one mistake. He probably inspected the area when the water had fallen well below the starlings. He forgot that when he came to hang up Vechey's corpse the river would have risen, covering any suitable platform for a suicide to stand on.'

'Yet he still went ahead. Why?'

'Because Vechey was probably dead, strangled before he ever reached that bridge, and what else could the murderer do with the corpse? Throw it in the river still bearing the noose-mark, or cart it round London and risk capture looking for a new gibbet!'

Athelstan smiled. 'Perfect, Sir John.'

'And Brampton?'

'You may remember, or perhaps not,' Athelstan replied, 'that Brampton's corpse was dressed in hose and a linen shirt. First, do we really accept that a man in the act of undressing suddenly decides halfway through that he will hang himself and goes up to the garret without his boots on to carry out the terrible act? Now, even if he had, the garret floor was covered with pieces of glass and dirt. However, when I examined the soles of Brampton's feet, there were no marks or cuts. Yet there should have been if he had walked across that floor without his boots on. In fact, there was very little dust on the soles of his hose. The only conclusion is that Brampton died like Vechey. He was carried up to that garret, probably in a state of stupor, drunk or drugged. The rope was tied round his neck. He fought for a while, hence the strands of cord found under the fingernails, but he was murdered and left there to hang so others would think he had taken his own life.'

Cranston pursed his lips and smiled. 'Most logical, Brother.'

'The other factor,' Athelstan continued, 'is that Vechey and Brampton supposedly hanged themselves. Now, I examined the bruise on each of the corpses. It is a remarkable coincidence that two men, relative strangers, put a noose knot in exactly the same place, Vechey copying Brampton in every particular when he hanged himself. I went down to the execution yard where I saw three corpses. The executioner himself said that each hangman has his own hallmark. The three corpses I studied there had the noose placed in the same spot. Vechey and Brampton also had the noose placed in the same spot. The only logical conclusion is that Brampton and Vechey were hanged by the same person.'

Athelstan picked up a quill with a modest flourish, uncapped the inkhorn and dipped in his pen. Cranston leant nearer. Athelstan found himself relishing the closeness. He felt as if he was back in time with his brother, plotting some mischief.

'As the good book says, let us start with the last. Vechey—' Athelstan wrote the name '—hanged by the neck under London Bridge. It appears he took his own life, but the truth is that he was murdered. By whom and how?' Athelstan drew a question mark and looked up at Cranston.

'Perhaps we will know soon,' Cranston observed. 'On my way down, I sent a message to the sheriff's office at the Guildhall and asked for two cursitors to make diligent inquiries amongst the taverns and stews along this side of the river. Perhaps they will discover something. Vechey was a fairly well-known man, a goldsmith. He would dress the part, even though he wore a cloak or hood. Such places tend to know their customers.'

'Secondly,' Athelstan continued writing, 'we have Brampton, steward of Sir Thomas Springall, who died apparently by his own hand in the garret of Springall's house.'

Cranston watched Athelstan's pen race across the page.

'We know it was murder not suicide, but how and by whom?'

Another question mark.

'Finally,' Athelstan concluded, 'Sir Thomas Springall was murdered in his own bed chamber by a cup of poisoned wine which was placed there by Brampton. But we have Dame Ermengilde's assurance that no one went up to Sir Thomas's chamber after Brampton had visited him. Nor did anyone enter the chamber after he retired. We know Sir Thomas drank the poisoned cup inside the room and not at the banquet, otherwise his death would have been public and in company.'

Athelstan wrote carefully. Cranston, craning his neck, followed the words forming quickly in the blue-green ink.

'So many questions, Sir John, so few answers. So where do we begin?'

Cranston jabbed one stubby finger at Athelstan's last few words.

'We will begin there. We have not fully scrutinised Springall's death. That is the key. If we solve that, the rest will unravel like a piece of cloth.'

'Easier said than done, Sir John, and you have only had one cup of refreshment!'

'Enough for the day is the evil thereof, friar. You should know that.'

Athelstan picked up his quill again. 'We have three riddles. First, Genesis, Chapter 3, Verse 1; secondly, the Book of the Apocalypse Chapter 6, Verse 8. And, thirdly, the shoemaker.'

'The shoemaker means nothing to me,' Cranston replied. 'But the verses... apparently Sir Thomas liked to tease his colleagues, and they would be curious. Vechey probably carried the verses around trying to solve the riddle. Oh,' the coroner grinned, 'my apologies for not telling you about Eudo the page boy but, according to my memory, there was nothing suspicious, just a fall from a window.'

The friar made a face. 'If Chief Justice Fortescue asked for a report, we could pose many questions and few solutions, Sir John.'

'That is why,' the coroner barked, getting up, 'we are off to Newgate to see Solper.' He grinned at Athelstan. 'Every morning the Guildhall send me a list of those indicted to hang. Young Solper was on this list, not before time. A rat from the sewer, but one of my best informants. Let us see if he wants to live!'

He strode away, leaving Athelstan scrambling to clear his writing tray, repack the leather bag and follow him out to the yard. Cranston had already ordered their horses to be brought out into Cheapside. They rode through the marketplace. The noise, clamour and dusty heat prevented any conversation. Cranston looked around him.

Yes, he would mention this in his treatise, he thought. There should be beadles placed at every corner, each covering his own section of the marketplace, and others mingling with the crowd. This would cut down on the number of naps, foists and pickpockets who plagued these places like the locusts of Egypt. His mind drifted and he let his horse find its path through the crowds. Athelstan pulled his hood over his head as he felt the heat of the sun on the back of his neck. He wondered what Sir John Cranston wanted at Newgate.

They moved out of Cheapside up towards the old city wall which housed the infamous gaol, past the small church of Nicholas Le Quern near Blow-Bladder Street and into the great open space before the prison. This was really no more than two huge towers linked by a high curtain wall. The area in front of Newgate, Athelstan thought, must be the nearest thing to hell on earth. There was a market down the centre, the stalls facing out, but the air and ground were polluted with the blood, dirt and ordure which ran down from the shambles where the animals were slaughtered and the gore allowed to find its own channel. Sometimes the blood oozed into great black puddles over which huge swarms of flies hovered. Athelstan was glad that Cranston had decided to ride.

The marketplace itself was full of people, jostling and fighting their way to the stalls, their tempers not helped by the heat, dust and flies. In front of the prison gate every type of disreputable under heaven was now thronging: pickpockets, knaves, and apple squires, as well as the relatives of debtors and other people trying to gain access to their loved ones. Cranston and Athelstan stabled their horses in a dingy tavern and walked back, forcing their way through to the great prison door. Outside, standing on a beer barrel, a member of the ward watch rang a hand bell which tolled like a death knell through the noisy clamour of the place.

'You prisoners,' the fellow was shouting, 'that are within for wickedness and sin, know now that after many mercies you are appointed to die just before noon tomorrow!'

On and on he went, shouting the usual rubbish about God's mercy and justice over all. Cranston and Athelstan pushed by him and hammered at the great gate. A grille was opened, revealing an evil, narrow-faced, yellow-featured man with eyes of watery blue and a mouth as thin as a vice.

'What do you want?' the fellow snapped, his lips curled back to reveal blackened stumps of teeth. Cranston pushed his face to the grille.

'I am Sir John Cranston, king's coroner in the city. Now open up!'

The grille slammed shut and they heard the noise of footsteps. A small postern door in the great gate opened. A guard stepped out with a club, forcing others back as Cranston and Athelstan were waved in. They shoved by, the stale odour of the gate-keeper's body making them choke. They stepped into the lodge or small chamber where the keeper always greeted new prisoners.

'I wish to see the keeper, Fitzosbert!' Cranston snapped.

The fellow grinned and took them along a dark, smelly passageway into another chamber where the keeper of Newgate, Fitzosbert, was squatting behind a great oak table like a king enthroned in his palace. Athelstan had heard about the fellow but this was the first time he had met him. Indeed, anyone who had any business with the law in London knew Fitzosbert's fearsome reputation. A very rich and therefore powerful man, as head keeper of Newgate, Fitzosbert had the pick of all the prisoners' possessions as well as the sale of concessions, be it beds, sheets, coals, drink, food, even a wench. Anyone who entered the prison had to pay a fee and Athelstan recollected that one of his parishioners, too poor to pay, had been beaten up for his poverty whilst Fitzosbert had stood by, smiling all the time. The keeper, Athelstan concluded, was not a pleasant man and on seeing him, the friar believed every story he had heard. He had a louse-ridden face, dirty blond hair and carmine-painted lips. Fitzosbert's sunken cheeks were liberally rouged and this made his bulbous grey eyes seem even more fish-like. The friar just stared at him and concluded that Fitzosbert would have liked to have been born a woman. Only that would explain his short lace-trimmed jerkin and the tight red hose. Athelstan smiled, revelling in fantasies of revenge, but Fitzosbert, however, had already dismissed him with a flicker of his eyes and was staring coolly at Sir John as if to prove he was not cowed by any show of authority.

'You have warrants, Sir?'

'I don't need warrants!' Cranston snapped. 'I am the king's coroner. I wish to see a prisoner.'

'Who?'

'Nathaniel Solper.'

Fitzosbert smiled. 'And your business with him?'

'My own.'

Again Fitzosbert smiled though Athelstan had seen more humour and warmth on the silver plate of a coffin lid.

'You must explain, Sir John.' The fellow placed two effete ring-bedecked hands on the desk before him. 'I cannot allow anyone, even the regent himself, to come wandering through my prison asking to see prisoners, especially such as Solper. He's a condemned man.'

'He's not yet hanged and I wish to speak with him, now!' Cranston leaned over the table, placing his hands over those of Fitzosbert and pressing down hard until the keeper's face paled and beads of sweat broke out on his brow.

'Now look, Master Fitzosbert,' Cranston continued slowly, 'if you wish, I will leave now. And tomorrow I will come back with warrants duly signed and sealed by the regent, and accompanied by a group of soldiers from the Tower. Then I will go through this prison, see Solper, and perhaps...' He smiled. 'We all have friends. Perhaps petitions could be presented in the Commons. Petitions demanding an investigation of your accounts. I am sure the Barons of the Exchequer would be interested in the profits to be made in the king's prison, and in what happens to money entrusted to you.'

Fitzosbert pursed his lips. 'I agree!' he muttered.

Cranston stood back. 'And now, sir, Solper!'

The keeper got up and minced out of the room. Athelstan and Cranston followed him, the friar fascinated by the man's swaying walk. He was about to nudge Cranston and congratulate him on his skills of persuasion, when he heard a sound and turned quickly. Two huge gaolers, with the bodies of apes and the faces of cruel mastiffs, padded silently behind them. Fitzosbert stopped and turned.

'Gog and Magog!' he sang out. 'They are my bodyguards, Sir John, my assistants in case I am attacked.'

Cranston's hand flew immediately to his sword. He pulled out the great blade, tapping the toe of his boot with it.

'This is my servant, Master Fitzosbert! May I remind you that I carry the king's warrant. If anything happens to me, it's treason!'

'Of course.' Fitzosbert's smile made him look more hideous than ever. They walked on, wandering through a warren of tortuous passageways where the noise and stench grasped Athelstan by the throat. He had heard that Newgate was a hellhole, but now he experienced it firsthand and understood why some prisoners went quickly insane. There were many who talked and sang incessantly, whilst others, particularly the women, who knew they were not there for too long, refused to clean themselves and lay about like sows in their own filth. Deeper into the prison they walked, past one open chamber where the limbs of quartered men lay like joints of meat on a butcher's stall, waiting to be soaked with salt and cumin seed before being tarred. Deeper into the hell, Athelstan shivered, folding his arms into the voluminous sleeves of his robe. Mad faces pushed against the grilles in the doors, tortured ones begging for mercy. The guilty baying their hatred, the innocent quietly pleading for a hearing. At last Fitzosbert stopped at one cell door and clicked his fingers. One of the giants shuffled forward, a ring of keys in his huge fist. A key was inserted in the lock and the door opened. Fitzosbert whispered something and the giant nodded and pushed his way into the cell. They heard screams, kicks, the sickening thud of a punch, and the ogre roaring Solper's name. He reappeared, grasping the unfortunate by the scruff of his shabby collar. Fitzosbert went up to the prisoner and tapped him gently on the cheek.

'Master Solper, you are fortunate. You have important visitors. Someone I believe you know, Sir John Cranston, and his—' he looked coyly at Athelstan '—companion.'

The friar ignored him, staring at Solper. The prisoner was nothing remarkable: young, white-faced, and so filthy it was difficult to tell where one garment ended and another began.

'We need a chamber to talk to this man,' demanded Cranston.

The head keeper shrugged and led them back up a passageway to a cleaner empty cell. The door was left open. Cranston waved Solper to a seat.

'Master keeper!' he called.

Fitzosbert came back into the room and Cranston laid some silver on the table.

'Some wine, bread, and two of your cleanest cups!'

The head keeper scooped up the coins as deftly as any tax collector. A few minutes later one of the giant gaolers pushed back into the cell, carrying a tray with all Cranston had asked for. He placed it on the table and left slamming the door behind him. The young prisoner just sat nervously on a stool watching Athelstan. Cranston took one of the cups and a small white loaf and thrust them into his hands.

'Well, Solper, we meet again.'

The man licked his lips nervously.

Cranston grinned wolfishly. 'You have been condemned?'

'Yesterday, before the Justices,' the young man squeaked in reply, his voice surprisingly high.

'On what charge?'

'Counterfeiting coins.'

'Ah, yes! Let me introduce you, Brother,' Cranston said. 'Master Solper, counterfeiter, thief, footpad and seller of relics. Two years ago, Master Solper could get you anything: a piece of cloth from the napkins used at the Last Supper, a hair from the beard of St Joseph, part of a toy once used by the Baby Christ. Master Solper has tried his hand at – well, God only knows! You are marked?'

The young man nodded and pulled down his dirty jerkin. Athelstan saw the huge 'F' branded into his right shoulder, proclaiming him a felon.

'Twice indicted, the third time caught,' Cranston intoned. 'You are due to hang, and yet you may evade justice.'

Athelstan saw the hope flare in the young man's eyes. He squirmed nervously on the stool.

'What do you want? What do I have to do?'

'The Sons of Dives, have you ever heard of them?'

The young man pulled a face.

'Have you or haven't you?'

'Yes, everybody has. In the Guilds,' the young man continued, 'there are always small groups or societies prepared to lend money at high interest rates to the nobles or to other merchants. They take names and titles: the Keepers of the Gate, the Guardians of the Coffers.' He shrugged. 'The Sons of Dives are another group.'

'And their leader?'

'Springall, Sir Thomas Springall. He's well known.'

'Now, another matter.'

Cranston delved into a small leather pouch he had taken from his saddlebag, undid the cord at the neck and drew out a small vase containing the poison he had taken from Springall's house. He unstoppered the jar and handed it over.

'Smell that!'

The young man gingerly lifted the rim to his nose, took one sniff, made a face and handed it back.

'Poison!'

'Good man, Solper, poison. This is the real reason I came. I half guessed who the Sons of Dives were. But if I wanted to buy poison, a rare exotic poison such as belladonna, crushed diamond or arsenic, where would I go?'

The young man looked across at Athelstan.

'Any monastery or friary has them. They are often used in the paints they mix for the illuminated manuscripts.'

'Ah, yes, but you can't very well knock on a monastery gate and say, "May I have some poison?" and expect the father abbot or prior to hand it over without a question. Without taking careful note of who you are, why you asked and what you want it for. So where else? The apothecary, Master Solper?'

Cranston eased his great bulk on the table. Athelstan watched nervously. The table, not being the strongest, creaked and groaned in protest under his weight.

'Master Solper,' Cranston continued conversationally, 'I have come here offering you your life. Not much perhaps, but if you answer my questions, I can arrange for a pardon to be sent down under the usual condition: that you abjure the realm. You know what that means? Straight as an arrow to the nearest port, secure a passage and go elsewhere. Anywhere – Outremer, France, Scythia, Persia – but not England, and certainly not London! You do understand?'

The young man licked his lips. 'Yes,' he muttered.

'And if you do not satisfy my curiosity,' Cranston continued, 'I am going to knock on the door, leave, and tomorrow you will hang. So, if I want to buy a poison in London, where would I go?'

'Nightshade House.'

'Where's that?'

'It's owned by Simon Foreman. It's in an alleyway.' The young man screwed up his eyes, concentrating on getting the facts right. 'That's right, a street called Piper Street, Nightshade House in Piper Street. Simon Foreman would sell anything for a great price and not ask any questions. It is probable the poison in that phial came from him. He could tell you.'

'One further question. Sir Thomas Springall – you knew of him?'

The young man nodded his head towards the door.

'Like Fitzosbert, he liked young boys, the softer and more pliant the better, or so the whisper says. He went to houses where such people meet. Springall was also a moneylender, a usurer. He had few friends and many enemies. There was gossip about him.' The young man drained his cup and sat cradling it, eyes fixed on the wine remaining in the jug. 'It was only a matter of time before someone used that information.' He shrugged. 'But Springall had powerful friends at court and in the church. No bailiff or constable would touch him. He and all his kind meet in a tavern outside the city on the Mile End Road – it's called the Gaveston. You can buy what you want there, as long as you pay in good gold. That's all I know.'

Fitzosbert banged on the door.

'Sir John, are you finished?'

'Yes,' Cranston called. 'Listen!' he said to Solper. 'You are sure you know nothing else?'

The young fellow shook his head. 'I have told you all I know. The pardon, you will keep your word?'

'Of course. God keep you, Solper,' he muttered and went towards the door just as Fitzosbert threw it open. The coroner gently pushed the keeper out before him, took out his purse and clinked a few coins into his hand.

'I thank you again for your hospitality, Fitzosbert,' he said. 'Look after our friend here. Some more wine, a better cell. Letters will come down from the Guildhall tomorrow. You will act accordingly. You understand?'

Fitzosbert smiled and winked. 'Of course, Sir John. No problem. I will carry out any order given to me by such an illustrious coroner of the city.'

Cranston pulled a face and he and the friar walked as fast as dignity would allow from that loathsome place. When the great gate of Newgate slammed behind them, Cranston leaned against it, gasping for clean air, his great body quivering like a beached whale's.

'Thank God!' he spluttered. 'Thank God to be out of there! Pray to your God and anyone else you know that you never land up in the power of Fitzosbert, in one of those Godforsaken cells!'

He looked up at the great tower soaring above him.

'If I had my way, I would burn the entire place to the ground and hang Fitzosbert on a scaffold as high as the sky. But, come, Whitefriars and the Springall mansion await.'

Chapter 6

They collected their horses and made their way down Fleet Street towards the high white chalk store building of Whitefriars. As the press of people was so great, they walked their horses.

'Do you think Solper was right about Springall?' asked Athelstan.

Sir John nodded. 'I suspected as much. Many men have such inclinations. Yet, you know the sentence for such crimes: boiled alive in a great vat over a roaring fire at Southwark. Not the usual end for a powerful London merchant! Hence the secrecy, and hence perhaps the vicious quarrel with Brampton, the rather effete manners of Master Buckingham, as well as the fact that Sir Thomas did not sleep with his wife.' He looked slyly at the friar. 'Such a woman, such a body! It fair makes your mouth water. Why should a real man lock himself away from such pleasures, eh?' He stopped momentarily to watch a juggler. 'Springall, like many a man,' he said, pushing forward again, 'had his public life and his private one. I suspect if the drapes were really pulled aside, we would find a stinking mess.' He lifted his hand and gestured to the great houses on either side, soaring four storeys above them, blocking out the hot afternoon sun. 'In any of these buildings scandal, sin, failings and weaknesses are to be found. They even say,' he nudged Athelstan playfully, 'that vices similar to Springall's are found in monasteries and amongst friars. What do you think of that, Brother, eh?'

'I would say that priests are like any other men, be they lawyer or coroner, Sir John, they have their weaknesses. And, but for the grace of God...' Athelstan let his voice trail away. 'But why are we here?' he asked angrily, realising they were entering the area around the great Carmelite monastery.

Cranston touched him on the arm and pointed to the far corner, just past the huge gateway. An emaciated fellow with jet black hair, thin lips and large brooding eyes caught the friar's eye. The man was dressed completely in black, his dark cloak covered with the most fantastic symbols: pentangles, stars, moons, suns, and on his head a pointed hat. He had laid out a great canvas sheet before him, bearing different phials and small bowls. Now he stood still, his very appearance drawing the people around him.

'Watch this!' Cranston whispered. 'The fellow's our guide.'

The man took out two small whistles and, pushing one into each corner of his mouth, began to play a strange, rhythmic, haunting tune. He then put down the instruments and held up powerful hands.

'Ladies and gentlemen, knights, courtiers, members of the Guild!' He caught Athelstan's eye. 'Friars, priests, citizens of London! I am Doctor Mirablis. I have studied in Byzantium and Trezibond, and travelled across the land to the great Cham of Tartary. I have seen battle fleets in the Black Sea and the great war galleons of the Caspian. I have supped with the Golden Horde of Genghis Khan. I have crossed deserts, visited fabulous cities, and in my journeys, I have amassed many secrets and mysteries!'

His claims were greeted with roars of laughter. Cranston and Athelstan drew closer. An apprentice from a nearby stall took out a bullock horn, scooped some dirty water from a rain barrel and began to sprinkle the magician with it. Dr Mirabilis just ignored him and held up his hands, calming the clamour and good-natured catcalls.

'I will show you I have power over matter. Over the very birds in the air.' He turned, pointing up to the top of the monastery wall. 'See that pigeon there!' Everyone's eyes followed the direction of his finger. 'Now, look,' the fellow continued, and taking a piece of black charcoal, painted a rough picture of the bird on the monastery wall. He then began to stab the drawing, uttering magical incantations. The clamour grew around him, Cranston and Athelstan moved closer, their hands on their wallets as the crowd was infested with naps, foists and pickpockets as a rick of hay with mice and rats. Mirabilis continued to stab the picture, muttering low-voiced curses, looking up at the walls where the pigeon was still standing. Suddenly the bird, as if influenced by the magical incantations against the picture below, twitched and dropped down dead. The 'oohs' and 'ahs' of reverence which greeted this would have been the envy of any priest or preacher. Cranston grinned and gripped Athelstan by the wrist.

'Wait awhile,' he said.

Doctor Mirabilis's reputation now enhanced by this miracle, he began to sell his jars and philtres of crushed diamond, skin of newt collected at midnight, batwing, marjoram, fennel and hyssop.

'Certain cures,' he said, 'for any agues, aches and rheums you suffer from.'

For a while business was brisk, then the crowd drifted away to watch an old man further down the lane who cavorted and danced in the most fantastical way. Cranston handed the reins of his horse to Athelstan and went over to the 'doctor.'

'Most Reverend Doctor Mirabilis, it is good to meet you again.'

The fellow looked up, his eyes milky blue like those of a cat. He studied Cranston then stared past him at Athelstan.

'Do I know you?' he asked. 'Do you wish to buy my physic?'

'Samuel Parrot,' continued Cranston, 'I would not buy green grass from you in the spring.'

The fellow's eyes shifted to right and left.

'Who are you?' he whispered.

'Surely you have not forgotten me, Mirabilis?' Cranston murmured. 'A certain case before the Justices in the Guildhall about physic which was supposed to cure. Instead, it made men and women sick for weeks.'

The famous Doctor Mirabilis stepped closer.

'Of course!' His face broke into a gap-toothed smile. 'Sir John Cranston, coroner!' The smile was hideously false. 'Is there anything I can do for you?'

'Not here,' Cranston said. 'But Piper Alley, Night-shade House. You can lead us there?'

The physician nodded and, scooping up his philtres and potions into a leather sheet, led Cranston and Athelstan from Whitefriars down a maze of streets so narrow they continued to lead their horses.

'How does he do it?' Athelstan whispered.

'Do what?'

'The bird, the pigeon?'

Cranston laughed and gestured to where Doctor Mirabilis was now walking ahead of them.

'If you went to his little garret, you would find baskets of trained pigeons – you know, the type which carries messages. Every so often our friend here drugs one of them with nox vomica, a slow acting poison. The pigeon is released and takes up a stance nearby. The poor bird will remain immobile because of the effects of the poison. After a while it

will drop down dead, and there you have his magic!'
He laughed. 'Sometimes, of course, it does not work.
Doctor Mirabilis here is always ready to run, fleet as
a deer, fast as any hare!'

The learned physician, as if he knew his name
was being mentioned, turned and gave a gap-toothed
grin, waving at them to follow a little faster.

Athelstan now saw why Cranston had hired
Mirabilis. Southwark was bad but this area around
Whitefriars was worse. Even though it was still
daylight, the alleyways and runnels were dark, closed
off by the houses built on either side. A silent,
evil place, becoming more ominous the deeper they
went. The houses around them, built hundreds of
years ago, now derelict and unkempt, huddled close
together, blocking out the summer sky. Underfoot
the track was dirty, caking their boots and sandals
with ordure and mud. Most of the doorways were
empty. Now and again a shadow would slip out but,
seeing Cranston's long sword, retreat again. Mirabilis
twisted and turned, Athelstan and Cranston finding it
hard to keep up. Abruptly he stopped and indicated
an alleyway with a long, dark passage ahead.

'Piper Alley,' he whispered. 'Goodbye, Sir!'

And, before Cranston could object, Doctor
Mirabilis slipped up another alleyway and disappeared
out of sight.

Athelstan and Cranston walked cautiously down
Piper Alley. The houses on either side were shuttered

and closed. At last they came to one fitting Doctor Mirabilis's description of Simon Foreman's house. It had a huge, battered sign at the end of a long ash pole.

Nightshade House was separated from the street by a flagged courtyard, the general approach defended by iron railings. Even in daylight it had a sombre, suspicious air as if it wished to slink back from the adjoining houses. More like a prison than a private residence, the windows were grated and the huge door barred and bound with iron bands. There was no answer to Cranston's knock, so he banged again. Behind them a dog howled and a door opened and shut. Looking down towards the mouth of the street, they saw shadows gathering. Again Cranston knocked. Athelstan joined him, hammering on the door with his fist. There was a sound of soft footsteps, of chains being loosened and bolts drawn back. The door was swung open by an unprepossessing man of middle stature, creamy-faced, and merry-eyed. He constantly scratched the bald dome of his head. Mirabilis looked like a magician, while Foreman had the appearance of some village parson in his dark fustian jacket, hose and soft felt slippers. Like a host in some cheerful tavern, he told them to tether their horses and ushered them in, asking them to sit at the table and wait while he finished his business in his own secret chamber. They sat and glanced around. The room was surprisingly neat, tidy and well kept. A fire burnt merrily in the hearth. Around the room were tables and chairs, some covered with quilted cushions, and on the walls shelves of jars which were neatly labelled. Athelstan studied the jars, dismissing them as nothing but mild cures for ague, aches and pains. They contained herbs such as hyssop, crushed sycamore leaves, moss – nothing that could not be bought at any apothecary's throughout the length and breadth of the city. At last Foreman came back, pulling up a chair beside them like some benevolent uncle ready to listen to a story or tell a merry tale.

'Well, sirs, who are you?'

'Sir John Cranston, coroner, and my clerk, Brother Athelstan.'

The man smiled with his lips, but his eyes became hard and watchful.

'You wish to purchase something?'

'Yes, red arsenic and belladonna. You do sell them?'

The transformation in Foreman was marvellous to behold. The merry mask slipped and his eyes became more vigilant. He straightened in his chair, looking nervously over his shoulder. Athelstan sensed that, if he had known who they were before he answered the door, he would never have let them inside, or else would have taken measures to hide whatever he had in the house.

'Well, sir?' Cranston asked. 'Do you have these poisons?'

Foreman shook his head, his eyes never leaving the coroner's.

'Sir, I am an apothecary. If you want a cure for the rheum in your knee, an ache in your head, or your stomach is churned up by bad humours, I can do it. But belladonna and red arsenic are deadly poisons.' He let out a deep sigh. 'Very few people sell them. They are costly and highly dangerous in the hands of those who might use them for the destruction of life.'

Cranston smiled and leaned closer, his face a few inches from that of the apothecary.

'Now, Master Foreman, I am going to begin again. You do sell red arsenic, nightshade, belladonna, and other deadly potions to those who are prepared to pay. Look,' he lied, 'I have in my wallet a warrant from the Chief Justice and I shall stay here whilst my clerk hurries back to the city and brings men from the under-sheriff to search this house. If one grain of poison, red arsenic, white arsenic, the juice of the poppy or any other damnable philtre is here, then you will answer for it, not at the Guildhall but before King's Bench! Come, surely somewhere in this house there are records, memoranda of what you sell?'

The apothecary's face paled and beads of sweat broke out on his brow.

'There would be many,' the fellow whispered, 'who would curse you, Cranston, for dragging me into court! I have powerful friends.' His eyes flickered towards Athelstan. 'Abbots, archdeacons, priests. Men only too willing to defend me and keep my secrets – and theirs – hidden from the light the law!'

'Good!' Cranston answered. 'Now we understand each other, Master Foreman. I have no desire to stop your evil trade in whatever you sell, buy and plot, or to search out your secrets, though one day perhaps I will.' He stared up at the shelves above him. 'What I want now is to know who in the last month has been here to buy arsenic and belladonna? Surely you recognise this?' He took out the small stoppered jar of poison and Foreman's eyes rounded in surprise. 'This is yours, sir,' Cranston probed gently. 'Look, on your shelves, there are similar ones. Who in the last few weeks purchased this poison?'

He held up the jar. Foreman sighed, rose, and wandered back into the chamber. Cranston took out his dagger and laid it on the floor beside him. A short while later the apothecary returned, looked at the dagger and smiled thinly.

'There is no need for that, Sir John. I will give you the information. Anything to have you gone!'

He sat down on the chair, a roll of parchment in his hands. He unrolled it slowly, muttering to himself.

'One person,' he said, looking up, 'bought both poisons in that jar about a week ago, as well as a rare odourless potion which can stop the heart but not be traced.'

'What did he look like?'

The apothecary smiled. 'Unlike any man! She was a lady, richly dressed. She wore a mask to conceal her face. You know the type ladies from the court wear when they go some place with a gallant who is usually not their husband? She came and paid me generously.'

'What kind of woman was she?'

'The woman kind,' the fellow replied sardonically, now realising he had very little information to give this snooping coroner.

'Describe her!'

Foreman rolled up the parchment and sat back in his chair.

'She was tall. As I said she wore a mask, and a rich black cloak with white lambswool trimmings. Her hood was well pulled forward but I glimpsed her hair, a reddish chestnut colour, like some beautiful leaf in autumn. Stately, she was.' He looked at Cranston and shrugged. 'Another lady, I thought, looking for poison to make her love life that little bit easier.' Foreman tapped the roll of parchment against his thigh. 'That, sirs, is all I can and will tell you.'

Once they had left the shop and collected their horses, Athelstan and Cranston rode as fast as they could up Piper Alley back into the main thoroughfare. Once or twice they lost their way, but Cranston still kept his dagger unsheathed and soon they had reached Whitefriars and were back into Fleet Street.

'You know who the woman was, Cranston, don't you?'

The coroner nodded. 'Lady Isabella Springall.' He stopped his horse and looked across at the friar. 'The description fits her, Brother. She also had the motive.'

'Which is?'

'A surmise but I think correct: Lady Isabella is an adulteress. She did not love her husband but instead her husband's brother. But now is not the time to speculate. Let's ask the lady herself.'

When they arrived at Springall's mansion in Cheapside, Cranston acted with the full majesty and force of the law. He told a surprised Buckingham, who greeted them in the hallway, that he wanted to see Sir Richard and Lady Isabella and other members of the household in the hall immediately. The young clerk pouted his lips as if he was going to object.

'I mean now, sir!' Cranston bellowed, not caring if his voice carried through the house, out into the enclosed courtyard where craftsmen were working. 'I want to see everybody!' He swept into the great hall. 'Here!'

He then marched up the hall, climbed on to the dais and sat down at the head of the table there, snapping his fingers for Athelstan to join him. The friar shrugged and got out his writing tray, parchment, ink horn and quills. Buckingham must have realised something was wrong for he was quickly joined in the hall, first by Sir Richard and then by Lady Isabella. The latter's looks were not impaired by grief today. Her eyes were not so red, her cheeks blooming like roses. She was dressed in a dark blue gown, the white veil hiding her beautiful chestnut hair.

Sir Richard, in hose and open cambric shirt, wiped dust from his hands, apologising that he had been out with the craftsmen who were putting the finishing touches to their pageant for the young king's coronation. Cranston just nodded, accepting his explanation as something irrelevant.

The priest also came hobbling in, his long hair swinging like a veil round his emaciated face. He threw a look of deep distaste at the coroner but called out civilly: 'You are well, Sir John?'

'I am well, Sir Priest,' answered Cranston. 'And much better for seeing you all here.'

The young priest must have caught the new note of authority in his voice. He stood still a moment and stared at Sir John through narrowed eyes. Then he smiled as if savouring some secret joke and slumped at the end of the table so he could stretch his leg. Dame Ermengilde swept in, unctuously escorted by Buckingham. Dressed completely in black, she moved down the hall like some silent spider and stood over the coroner.

'I will not be summoned,' she snapped, 'here in my own house!'

'Madam,' Cranston didn't even bother to look up, 'you will sit down and listen to what I say. You will obey me or I will take you to the Marshalsea Prison, and *there* you can sit and listen to what I say.' He looked up at Sir Richard and Lady Isabella. 'I mean no offence. I appreciate that yesterday the funeral ceremonies were carried out, but Masses were also sung for the souls of two other men, Brampton and Vechey, and I have news of them. They did not commit suicide. They were murdered!'

Cranston's words hung in the air like a noose. Dame Ermengilde tightened her thin little lips and sat down without further ado. Sir Richard looked nervously at Lady Isabella. Ermengilde, seated beside Athelstan, also looked frightened, trying hard to hide it behind her mask of arrogance. Further down the table the priest tapped the table gently, singing some hymn softly under his breath. Buckingham sat, hands together, staring down at the tabletop, his face registering surprise and shock at Sir John's words. Allingham was the last to join them. The tall, lanky merchant was nervous and ill at ease, his hand constantly fluttering to his mouth or patting his greasy hair. He mumbled some apology and sat next to the priest. He seemed unable to meet the coroner's eyes, not daring even to look in his direction.

'Sir John,' the merchant mumbled, 'you said Brampton and Vechey had been murdered? But how? Why? Brampton may have been a quiet man, but I cannot imagine him allowing anyone to hustle him upstairs in a house full of people, tie a noose round his neck and hang him. The same is true of Vechey.' He looked down the table at Allingham. 'Stephen, you would accept that, wouldn't you?'

The merchant never looked up but nodded and muttered something to himself.

'What are you saying?' Cranston leaned over the table. 'Master Allingham, you spoke. What did you say?'

The merchant rubbed his hands together as if trying to wash them.

'There's something evil in this house,' the merchant said slowly. 'Satan is here. He stands in the corners, in quiet places, and watches us. I believe the coroner is right.' He looked up, his lugubrious face pale, and Athelstan saw it was tear-stained. 'Vechey was murdered! I think he knew something.'

'Tush, man!' cried Sir Richard. 'Master Stephen, you worry too much. You have spent too many hours on your knees in church.'

'What?' Athelstan asked, putting his quill down. 'What did Vechey know?'

The lanky merchant leaned forward, his face screwed up, eyes pinpricks of hatred.

'I don't know,' he hissed. 'And, if I did, I would not tell you, Friar. What can you do?'

'On your allegiance,' Cranston bawled, 'I ask you, do you know anything about the deaths which have occurred in this household?'

'No!' Allingham grated. 'They are a mystery. But Sir Thomas liked riddles and his own private jokes. There must be something in this house which would explain it all.'

'What are you talking about, man?' asked Sir Richard.

But the merchant rubbed the side of his face uneasily. 'I have spoken enough,' he mumbled, and fell silent.

'In which case,' Cranston began, 'let us make a brief summary of what we do know. Correct me if I am wrong but Sir Thomas Springall was an alderman and a goldsmith. On the night he died he held a great banquet, a feast for his household, and invited Chief Justice Fortescue. He drank deeply, yes?'

Lady Isabella nodded, her beautiful eyes fixed on Cranston's face. Sir Richard, however, watched Athelstan's quill skim over the piece of vellum.

'The banquet ends,' Cranston continued. 'Sir Thomas retires. You, Sir Richard, wish him good night whilst Lady Isabella sends down a maidservant to ask if he wishes for anything.'

Both of them acknowledged this.

'You, Dame Ermengilde, heard Brampton take a cup of wine up to Sir Thomas's room during the feast?'

'I did not just hear!' she retorted. 'I opened my door and saw him. Then he went down.'

'And how was he dressed?'

'In a jerkin and doublet.'

'And his feet?'

'He had on the usual soft pair of boots which he always wore.'

'Why do you remember this?'

'Brampton was a quiet man,' Dame Ermengilde replied, a touch of softness in her voice. 'A good steward. He moved slowly, quietly, like a dutiful servant.'

'And how did he seem?'

'As normal. A little white-faced. He knew I opened the door but he never looked at me. He went down the stairs. No! He went along the other gallery up to the second floor and his own room.'

'Did you ever see him again?'

'No, I did not.'

'And you say that only Sir Thomas, then Sir Richard and Lady Isabella's maidservant, went along the Nightingale Gallery?'

'Yes, I am certain of that.'

'And you are sure that Sir Thomas was not disturbed during the night?'

'Yes, I told you, man!' she snapped. 'I am a light sleeper. I heard no one.'

'And you, Father Crispin?' Cranston leaned sideways to catch a glimpse of the young clerk's face. 'You went up the next morning. Dame Ermengilde heard you go along the Nightingale. When you failed to rouse Sir Thomas you went for Sir Richard whose chamber is on the adjoining passageway. Sir Richard came back with you. You were unable to arouse Sir Thomas, so you asked the servants to break down the door?'

'Yes.' The priest nodded, his eyes bright. 'That is exactly what I did.'

'When the room was broken into, all of you here were present? You went in. Sir Thomas was sprawled on his bed, a cup of poison on the table beside him. Nobody said anything...'

'Except Vechey!' Allingham broke in. 'He said, "There were only thirty-one!"'

'Do you know what he meant by that?' Cranston asked.

'No, I wish to God I did!'

'The physician was sent for,' Cranston continued. 'Master de Troyes. He came. He examined Sir Thomas's corpse, pronounced him to have been poisoned, and claimed the potion was placed in a half-drunk cup of wine beside Sir Thomas's bed. Now Brampton was last seen late in the evening taking a wine cup up to Sir Thomas's chamber and was not seen alive again. The next morning, after Sir Thomas had been discovered dead, Brampton's corpse was found swinging from a beam up in the garret. Master Vechey was here when Brother Athelstan and I came to the house for the first time. He went out late on the same evening, God knows where, and was found hanging from a beam under London Bridge. Now we have evidence which we will keep privy for the time being which will prove that neither Brampton nor Vechey committed suicide. Though, Lady Isabella, we are no further forward in resolving the mystery of your husband's death.'

'It could still have been Brampton!'

It was Buckingham who spoke. Cranston looked at him.

'What makes you say that?'

The clerk shrugged. 'I accept you have your own reasons for claiming Brampton did not commit suicide but that does not mean he is innocent of Sir Thomas's death.'

Cranston grinned.

'A good point, Master clerk. You would make a good lawyer. I shall remember that.' There was a sudden commotion at the door. A servant scurried in, leaned over Sir Richard's shoulder and whispered in his ear. The merchant looked up.

'Sir John, there is a messenger, a cursitor from the sheriff's office, who wishes to speak to you.'

'I will see him, Sir Richard, by your leave. Tell him to come in.'

The cursitor, a pompous young man, swaggered in. 'Sir John, a message from the under-sheriff.' He looked around him. 'It concerns Master Vechey.'

'Yes!' Cranston said. 'You may speak here.'

'He was seen in a tavern down near the riverside. The landlord of the Golden Keys said a man who fitted Vechey's description was there drinking late at night. He left with a young, red-haired whore whom he had never seen before.'

'Is that all?' Cranston asked.

'Yes, Sir John.'

Cranston dismissed the cursitor. Athelstan felt the mood of the company in the hall lift.

'See!' Dame Ermengilde cried exultantly. 'Vechey was seen with one of his whores. Master Buckingham

189

must be right. Brampton may still have killed my son, and Vechey's death be totally unconnected with this.'

Athelstan could see Cranston was not pleased by the news.

'Nevertheless,' he snapped, 'I have other questions. Lady Isabella and Sir Richard, I must ask you to stay. The others, I would prefer to leave.'

Dame Ermengilde was about to protest. Her son stretched across the table and touched her gently on the wrist, his eyes pleading with her. She rose, threw one withering look at Cranston and followed the others out. Sir John watched them go.

'Lady Isabella,' he said softly, 'have you ever been to Nightshade House in Piper Alley near Whitefriars?'

'Never!'

'And you have no knowledge of an apothecary called Simon Foreman?'

'I have heard of him but never met him.'

Athelstan saw the fear in Lady Isabella's eyes. Her face lost its golden hue, becoming pale and haggard.

'Sir Richard?'

'No!' As he leaned forward, he clapped his hand to his side, where his sword should have been. 'You come into this house!' he hissed. 'You insult both me and Lady Isabella, hinting we go amongst rogues and vagabonds. Don't be clever, Cranston! My brother was murdered by poison. I resent the inference in your questions that one of us visited that apothecary and secured the poison to carry the murder out.'

'Yet this afternoon,' Cranston said conversationally, 'both Brother Athelstan and myself went to that apothecary's shop. He claims he sold poison to a woman fitting your description, Lady Isabella. She was dressed in a black cloak lined with white fur, had chestnut hair, was of your height and colouring.'

'I have never been to Whitefriars! I have never visited an apothecary's shop!'

'You do have a black cloak lined with white fur?'

'Yes, like hundreds of women in the city!'

'Have you ever met Foreman?'

'I don't know. I could have done. My husband had many strange friends. Anyway, why should I kill him?' Lady Isabella cried, half rising from the chair. 'He was a good man. He gave me everything a woman could desire.'

'Lady Isabella,' Cranston said smoothly, 'it is well known that your husband had strange tastes and foibles. Did you love him?'

'That, sir, is enough!' Sir Richard grabbed Cranston by the wrist but the coroner shook him off.

'That will do!' Cranston was annoyed now by the arrogance of these people, thinking they could push him around whenever they wished. 'I am an officer of the king, and the crown is involved. These charges may involve treason, conspiracy as well as murder!'

Sir Richard sat down again, breathing heavily. Lady Isabella linked her arm through his. She looked at him and shook her head.

'My Lady,' Athelstan said softly, 'it is best if you tell the truth. You must! Your husband lies murdered. Two others have been brutally executed. The murderer may well strike again. Sir John and I go around London playing Blind Man's Buff in this deadly game. Your husband, Lady Isabella, had secrets – that is why he was murdered. Brampton was supposed to have been the culprit but, due to chance and circumstances, we have ascertained he was innocent, and he, too, was murdered, though it was made to look like suicide. Vechey saw or heard something so he, also, was silenced. Now, Lady Isabella, on your oath to the new king, have you ever visited the apothecary called Simon Foreman?'

'No!'

Athelstan stared back.

'Did you love your husband?'

'No! He was a gentle, kind man but he did not know me, not in the carnal sense. He had his own tastes...' her voice trailed away.

'A liking for young men?' Athelstan asked.

'He was a sodomite!' Cranston barked. 'He liked young men! He lusted after them!' Athelstan stared at him and shook his head. Lady Isabella put her face in her hands and sobbed bitterly. 'My Lady,' Athelstan pressed her, 'your husband?'

'He left me alone. I made no inquiry into what he thought or did.'

'You, Sir Richard, do you love the Lady Isabella?'

The crestfallen merchant pulled himself together. 'Yes. Yes, I do!'

'Are you lovers?'

'Yes, we are.'

'So you both had a motive?'

'For what?' Sir Richard had lost his usual ebullience. He slouched back in the chair, his face drawn as if he realised the mortal danger they were now in.

'For murder, sir.'

The merchant shook his head. 'I may have lusted after my brother's wife,' he muttered, 'but not his life!'

'In King's Bench,' Cranston barked, 'it would not appear like that. It would appear, Sir Richard, that you lusted after your brother's wife as well as his riches; that while he was alive you committed adultery with her and, with each other, you plotted together to carry out his murder and lay the blame on Brampton.'

'In which case,' Sir Richard replied meekly, 'I must also be responsible for the deaths of Vechey and Brampton. But I have witnesses. I stayed at the banquet with my brother the entire evening. I said good night to him, and the rest of the time I was with the Lady Isabella. We shared the same bed,' he confessed.

'And the night Vechey died?' Cranston asked abruptly.

'The same. We have servants here. Workmen in the yard. They will vouch that I stayed here, doing accounts, going out to look at the carvings which were being made for the pageant for the king's coronation.'

Lady Isabella drew herself up, resting her elbows on the arms of her chair.

'If we had murdered Sir Thomas,' she asked, 'how could we enter his chamber, force poison down his throat or into his wine cup, and leave the room, locking and bolting the door from inside? That, sir, is impossible.' Her eyes turned towards Athelstan, pleading with him. 'I beg you, sir, to believe us. If we were in bed together, how could we go down, seize Brampton, take him up to that garret and hang him? No, I did not go to Whitefriars. I did not visit Simon Foreman. I did not buy poisons. I am innocent, not of sin but of my husband's death and that of others. I swear before God I had nothing to do with them.'

'You sent wine up to Brampton?' Athelstan asked.

'Yes, as a peace offering.'

'And was Brampton in his room?'

'No, I found out later that he was busy taking the cup of claret to my husband's chamber.' She wiped her eyes. 'The servant left the wine in Brampton's chamber and came down. That is all, I swear!'

Despite the tears, Athelstan still wondered if her adultery made her an assassin or perhaps an accomplice to murder. The friar felt the frustration grow within him. How had Sir Thomas been murdered? And how had Brampton been hanged? And Vechey?

Athelstan dallied with the thought of tying each of the people in this house down to their exact movements during the night Sir Thomas died, as well as the following one when Vechey disappeared, but realised the futility of it. Moreover, there was no real proof linking the murderers with anyone in the house. Perhaps they had been carried out on the orders of someone else? But who? And how? Why?

Athelstan stood, walking up and down just beneath the dais, his fingers to his lips. Cranston watched him carefully. The clever friar would sift one fact from another. The coroner was quite prepared to let Athelstan use the advantage they had now gained.

'Lady Isabella, Sir Richard,' he began, 'I have no real proof to convict you. Nevertheless, we have enough evidence under the law to swear out warrants for your arrest and ask for your committal to Newgate, Marshalsea, even the Tower.' He held up his hand. 'However, we wish for your cooperation. We want the truth. The Sons of Dives… you belong to them, don't you, Sir Richard?'

The merchant nodded.

'Everyone in this household is a member, are they not?'

'Yes,' Sir Richard replied meekly. 'Yes, we are. The church condemns usury and the loaning of money at high interest. The Guilds also condemn it. However, in every guild, in every livery company in the city, groups of merchants get together in some society. They give themselves strange names. Ours is known as the Sons of Dives. We lend money secretly to whoever needs it but charge interest much higher than the Lombards or Venetians. The money is delivered quickly. Payment is over a number of years. We choose our customers carefully: only those who can underwrite the loan, give pledges that they are good for the money they have borrowed. A petty mystery, our guild is full of such covens.'

'And the riddles? The shoemaker?'

Both Sir Richard and Lady Isabella shook their heads.

'We don't know!' they murmured in unison.

'And the scriptural quotations from Genesis and the Book of the Apocalypse, you have no clue to their meaning?'

Again a chorus of denials. Athelstan returned to the table, rolled up the piece of parchment and put away his quills and inkhorn.

'Sir John, for the moment leave matters be. Sir Richard and Lady Isabella now know that perhaps we are not as stupid or as feckless as sometimes we may appear. You may rest assured, Sir Richard, that in the end we will discover the truth and the murderer, whoever he or she may be, will hang at the Elms for all London to see!'

Cranston pursed his lips and nodded as if Athelstan had said all there was to say. They bade both the merchant and his paramour adieu.

As they left the Springall mansion and waited in Cheapside for an ostler to bring their horses round from the stables, Athelstan sensed Cranston was furious with him, but the coroner waited until they had mounted and moved away from the house before stopping and giving full vent to his fury.

'Brother Athelstan,' he said testily, 'I would remind you that *I* am the king's coroner and those two,' he gestured in the direction of the Springall house, 'Sir Richard and that expensive paramour of his, are guilty of murder!'

'Sir John,' Athelstan began, 'I apologise.'

'You apologise!' Cranston mimicked. He leaned forward and grasped the horn of Athelstan's saddle. 'You apologise! If you had kept your mouth shut, Friar, we might perhaps have gained the truth. But, oh no! We established that Lady Isabella went to the apothecary's. We established that she and Sir Richard are lovers, adulterers, fornicators, and in only a matter of time we could have had a confession that they were guilty of Sir Thomas's death as well as the others!'

'I don't accept that, Sir John. There is no real proof of murder. Oh, they are guilty of adultery.' Athelstan felt his own anger rise. 'If that was the case, Sir John, we would hang half of Cheapside for adultery and still not discover who the real murderer is.'

'Now, look.' Sir John leaned closer, his face choleric. 'In future, Brother, I would be grateful if you would observe the courtesies and, before making any pronouncements, consult with me. As I said, I am the coroner!'

'Let me remind you, Sir John,' Athelstan retorted, leaning back in his saddle, 'that I am a clerk, a priest, and not your messenger boy, your little lap dog! In these matters I will say what I believe is best and if you find it so difficult to work with me, then write to my father prior. This is one burden I would be relieved of!' The friar's voice rose so loud that passersby stopped and looked curiously at him. 'Do you think I look forward to this, Sir John? Going around listening to the fat and the rich of the land confessing their secret sins, and secretly mocking us every time we reach a stone wall and can go no further? Do you?' Athelstan turned his horse. 'I suggest we both go back to our respective homes and reflect on what has happened. Perhaps tomorrow, or the day after we may continue our investigations?'

'You will go home when I say!' Sir John shouted.

'I will go when I wish!' Athelstan retorted.

And, without waiting for any reply, he urged Philomel down Cheapside, leaving the fuming coroner behind.

Chapter 7

By the time he reached St Erconwald's, Athelstan regretted his hasty words. Sir John was correct. He had pronounced on Lady Isabella and Sir Richard's guilt or innocence without any reference to the coroner. There might have been further questions Cranston would have liked to put. He wished he had taken Sir John aside, made his peace and offered some refreshment, some claret in one of the Cheapside taverns. After all there were other strands to the case, loose ends which needed to be tied up. Who was the red-haired whore who had lured Vechey to his death? Had it been Lady Isabella? But many whores wore red wigs.

After he had stabled Philomel, Athelstan remembered the verses from Scripture and studied the great leather-bound Bible that he kept chained in his house's one and only cupboard. Genesis 3, Verse 1: 'The serpent was the most subtle of all wild beasts in that garden God had made.' Athelstan translated as he read aloud: 'Did God really say you were not to eat any of this tree in the garden?' And the other text, the Book of the Apocalypse 6, Verse 8: 'I heard the voice,' Athelstan murmured, 'of the fourth animal shout "Come!" and immediately another horse appeared, deathly pale, and its rider was called Death and all Hell followed at its heels.'

What could they possibly mean? Somehow Athelstan knew these texts were the key to the mystery. And Sir John? Athelstan wondered whether he should eat a hasty evening meal and go back across the city and make his peace. But he felt tired, he'd had enough, and such matters would wait.

He went out and unlocked the church and checked that all was well. He took a pitcher of water for Philomel and a dish of creamy milk for Bonaventure. He'd bought the latter just after he had crossed London Bridge. Still feeling perturbed, he went back into his house, lay on his pallet bed and stared up at the flaking ceiling. He tried to compose himself, first with a psalm, '*Exsurge Domine, Exsurge et vindica causam meam* – Rise, oh Lord, rise and judge my cause.'

Athelstan let his mind drift, back to Cranston and the startled, frightened face of Lady Isabella. Athelstan shook his head free of such images. He wondered what the evening sky would be like and if Father Prior would send him a copy of the writings of Richard of Wallingford. Once Abbot of St Albans, Richard had invented the most wondrous instrument for measuring and fixing the stars. Athelstan had talked to another friar who had seen Wallingford's ingenious clock, the wheels within it fixed as if by magic, which not only measured the hours but indicated signs, the phases of the moon, the position of the sun, the planets and the heavens. Athelstan licked his lips. He would give a fortune for one of those. Everything he owned just to have it in his hands for a few hours. Perhaps Father Prior would help? He'd already asked for a copy of the calendars of the Carmelite, Nicholas of Lyn.

The ceiling reminded him about the church. The roof had been mended but really it was little more than a pig sty. He heard voices outside his door, rose in just his robe, peered out of the window and groaned quietly. Of course, he had forgotten, the meeting with his parishioners! They were to assemble in the nave and discuss the pageant for Corpus Christi.

Athelstan's premonitions about the occasion proved correct. The meeting was not a happy one. Foremost amongst his parishioners were Watkin the dung-collector and his wife, a woman built like a battering ram, hard-faced, with iron grey hair hanging down to her shoulders. Cecily the courtesan made constant barbed remarks, hinting she knew more about Watkin than his wife did. Ranulf the rat-catcher, Simon the tiler, and a host of others thronged the nave, sitting facing each other on the church's two and only benches with Athelstan sitting between them on the sanctuary chair.

The occasion was marred by bickering. Nothing was resolved and Athelstan felt he had failed to take a decisive role. The meeting ended with all his parishioners glaring up at him accusingly. He apologised, said he felt tired, and promised they would meet again when some decisions could be made. They all trooped out, mumbling and muttering, except Benedicta. She remained sitting on the end of one bench, her cloak wrapped about her.

Athelstan went to close the door behind his parishioners. When he returned, he thought Benedicta was crying, her shoulders were shaking so. But when she looked up, he realised she was laughing, the tears streaming down her face.

'You find our parish meetings amusing, Benedicta?'

'Yes.' He noticed how low and cultured her voice was.

'Yes, Father, I do. I mean—' She spread her hands and giggled again.

Athelstan just glared at her but still she could not control her mirth. Her shoulders shook with laughter, her alabaster cheeks flushed with warmth. Athelstan could not prevent his smile.

'I mean,' she said, 'Cecily the courtesan's ambition to act the role of the Virgin Mary! And the face of Watkin's wife!' She laughed so infectiously that Athelstan joined in and, for the first time since he had arrived at St Erconwald's, the nave of his church rang with laughter. At last Benedicta composed herself.

'Not seemly,' she observed, her eyes dancing with merriment, 'for a widow and her parish priest to be laughing so loudly in church at the expense of his parishioners! But I must say, never in my short life have I witnessed anything so funny. You must regard us as a cross to bear.'

'No,' Athelstan replied and sat down beside her. 'No cross.'

'Then what is it, Father? Why are you so sad?'

Athelstan stared across at the blue, red and gold painting now being formed on the wall. What is my cross? he thought. A large burden, a veritable mortal sin of the flesh, with balding head, shrewd brown eyes, and a face as red as a bloody rag. Sir John Cranston, lord of the stomach, master of the sturdy legs and an arse so huge that Athelstan secretly called it 'Horsecrusher'. But how could he explain Cranston to Benedicta?

'No crosses, Benedicta. Nothing, perhaps, except loneliness.'

He suddenly realised how close he was to her. She stared calmly back, her jet black hair escaping from underneath the wimple. Her face was so smooth. He was fascinated by her generous mouth and her eyes, beautiful and dark as the night. He coughed abruptly and got up.

'You stayed back, Benedicta! Do you wish to talk to me?'

'No.' She, too, rose as if sensing the sudden chill between them. 'But you should know that Hob has died. I visited his house before I came here and saw his widow.'

'God save him!' whispered Athelstan. 'God save us all, Benedicta! God save us all!'

–

The next day Athelstan refused to think about Sir John and the terrible murders in the Springall household. Instead, he busied himself about his parish duties. The new poor box was replaced and padlocked near the baptismal font. He tried to settle matters between Cecily and Watkin the dung-collector's wife and achieved some accord: Cecily would be the Madonna provided Watkin's wife could be the Virgin's cousin, Saint Elizabeth. Watkin would have pride of place as St George while Ranulf the rat-catcher eagerly agreed to put on a costume and act the role of the dragon.

There were other more serious matters. Hob the grave-digger was buried late in the afternoon and Athelstan organised a collection, giving what he could to the poor widow and promising her more as soon as circumstances allowed. He slept well that night, getting up early to climb the wet, mildewed stairs to the top of the church tower where he saw the stars clear in the skies, studying their alignment before they faded with the dawn.

Later in the morning he was down in the church preparing the corpse of Meg of Four Lanes for burial.

Meg of the flowing, black hair, white face and nose hooked like an eagle's beak. In life she had been no beauty, in death she looked ugly, her greasy locks falling in wisps to her dirty shoulders. Her face was mere bone over which the skin had been stretched tight and transparent like a piece of cloth. Her pale sea green eyes were now dull and sunken deep in their sockets.

Her mouth sagged open and her body, dirty white like the underbelly of a landed fish, was covered in marks and bruises. The corpse had been brought in just after the morning mass by members of the parish. Athelstan had borrowed a gown from an old lady who lived in one of the tenements behind the church and dressed Meg's corpse with as much dignity as circumstances would allow. The parish constable, a mournful little man, had informed him that Meg had been murdered.

'A tragic end,' he wailed, 'to a sad life!'

Athelstan had questioned him further. Apparently some villain, hot with his own juices, had bought Meg's body and used her carnally before plunging a knife between her ribs. Just after dawn that day her corpse, cold and hard, had been found in a rat-infested spinney. No one would come forward to claim the body and Athelstan knew the parish watch would bury it like the decaying corpse of a dog. However, the morning Mass had been well attended and the members of the parish had decided otherwise. Tab the tinker, who had come in to be shriven, had agreed to fashion a coffin of sorts out of thin planks of wood. He had built this out on the steps of the church and placed it on trestles before the rood screen. Athelstan blessed Meg, sprinkling the open coffin with holy water and praying that the sweet Christ would have mercy on her soul. Then with Tab's help he nailed down the lid, reciting the prayers for the dead, and entered her name amongst other deceased of the parish to be remembered at the weekly Requiem Mass.

After that, Athelstan gave Tab and his two apprentices some pennies to take the coffin from the church and out to the old cemetery. Athelstan walked behind, chanting verses from the psalms. Meg's coffin was lowered into a shallow grave packed in the dry, hard ground. Athelstan, distracted, vowed to remember to place a cross there and as soon as possible sing a Mass for her soul and that of poor Hob. He walked back to the church feeling guilty. He had spent time watching the stars whilst people like Meg of Four Lanes died horrible deaths, their bodies afterwards lowered into obscure graves. Athelstan felt angry and went to kneel before the statue of the Virgin, praying for Meg and the evil bastard who had sent her soul unshriven out into the darkness. He got up and was about to return to his house to wash the dirt from Meg's grave from his hands when Cranston swaggered in, throwing the door open as if he was announcing the Second Coming.

'It's murder, Athelstan!' he bawled. 'Bloody murder! Foul homicide!'

Athelstan knew Cranston loved to startle him, delighting in dramatic exits and entrances, and didn't know whether to laugh or cry. Cranston stood there, legs apart, hands on hips. The friar sat down on the sanctuary steps and stared into his fat, cheery face.

'What are you talking about, Sir John?' he said crossly.

The grinning tub of lard just stood there, smiling. 'The Springalls!' he bawled at last. 'It's happened again. This time poor Allingham's been found dead in his chamber, with not a mark on his body. Chief Justice Fortescue is hopping like a cat. By the way, where's yours?'

'Bonaventure probably left when he heard you coming!' Athelstan muttered. 'Why, what's wrong with the Chief Justice? What's he got to do with Bonaventure?'

'Fortescue is hopping like a cat on hot bricks, demanding something should be done, but he has no more idea than I what *can* be done. Anyway, we're off, Athelstan, back to the Springall house!'

'Sir John! I am busy with matters here. Two deaths, two burials.'

The coroner walked towards him, a wicked grin on his satyr-like face.

'Now, now, Athelstan. You know better than that.'

Of course, the friar did. He knew he had no choice in the matter but cursed and muttered as he filled his saddlebags, harnessed Philomel and joined Cranston who sat slouched on his horse on the track outside the church. They stopped for Athelstan to leave messages with Tab the tinker, now drinking away the profits of Meg's funeral at the nearest tavern, and began the slow journey down to London Bridge and across to Cheapside. Cranston was full of good cheer, aided and abetted by an apparently miraculous wineskin which never seemed to empty. Athelstan tried to apologise for his part in the quarrel at their last parting, but the coroner just waved his words aside.

'Not your fault, Brother!' he boomed. 'Not yours! The humours, the heat of the day. We all quarrel. It happens in the best of families.'

So, with Athelstan praying and cursing, and Cranston farting and swaying in his saddle, they cleared London Bridge and pressed on to Fish Street Hill. Of course, when the wine ran out, Cranston's mood darkened. He announced that he didn't give a rat's fart for mumbling monks.

'Orders were orders!' he roared, looking darkly at the friar, before going on to regale both him and the horses with an account of the meal his poor wife was preparing for the coming Sunday.

'A veritable banquet!' Cranston announced. 'Boar's head, cygnet, venison, quince tarts, junkets of apple-flavoured cream...'

Athelstan listened with half an ear. Allingham was dead. He remembered the merchant, long, lanky, and lugubrious of countenance. How unsettled and agitated he had been when they last had visited the Springall house. He glared darkly at Cranston and hoped the coroner was not too deeply in his cups.

On their arrival at the house in Cheapside, Athelstan was astonished to find how calm and collected Sir Richard and Lady Isabella were. The friar suddenly realised that Cranston's claim that Allingham was murdered was really a piece of pure guesswork on his part. Sir Richard greeted them courteously, Lady Isabella beside him. She was dressed in dark blue velvet, a high white lace wimple on her head. She recounted how they had gone up to Master Allingham's chamber and, finding the door locked, had ordered the workmen from the yard below to force the chamber.

'Allingham was found dead on the bed due to a stroke or apoplexy,' Sir Richard commented. 'We do not know which. We sent for Father Crispin.' He pointed to where the priest sat on a chair just within the hall door. 'He examined Allingham, held a piece of glass to his lips, but there was no sign of the breath of life. So he did what he has become accustomed to doing – gave the last rites. You wish to see the corpse?'

Athelstan turned and looked at Cranston, who just shrugged.

'So you think that Allingham's death was by natural causes?'

'Oh, of course! What else? There's no mark of violence. No sign of poison,' Sir Richard answered.

Athelstan remembered Foreman's words – how the lady who had visited his shop had bought a poison which could not be traced or smelt yet would stop the heart. He believed Sir Richard and Lady Isabella were speaking the truth, at least literally: in their eyes, and perhaps even those of a skilled physician, Allingham's death was from natural causes, but Athelstan thought differently. He agreed with Sir John. Allingham had been murdered.

The young clerk, Buckingham, now dressed more festively, the funerals being over, took them up to the first floor, then up more stairs to the second storey of the house. The middle chamber on that floor was Allingham's: the door had been forced off its leather hinges and a workman was busy replacing it. He pushed it open for them and they went inside.

The chamber was small but pleasant, with a window overlooking the garden. On the bed, a small four poster with the bolsters piled high, Allingham lay as if asleep. Athelstan looked round the room. There was a short, coloured tapestry on the wall depicting Simeon greeting the baby Jesus, two or three chests, a table, one high-backed chair, some stools and a cupboard with a heavy oak frontal pushed open. He caught the fragrant smell of herbs sprinkled across and stared down at Allingham's body. He said a short prayer. Cranston sat on the bed just staring at the corpse as if the man was alive and the coroner wished to draw him into friendly conversation.

Athelstan knew that Cranston, despite all his bluster and drunken ways, was quite capable of making a careful, perceptive study of the dead man. Athelstan leaned over to perform his own examination. The dead merchant's skin was like the cold scales of a fish. Rigor mortis had set in, but not totally. He pushed the mouth open and inhaled. A slight spicy smell but nothing unusual, and no discoloration of the skin, nails or face. He picked up the fingers. Again no smell except for chrism where the priest had anointed the dead man. Athelstan felt slightly ridiculous, he and Sir John sitting on the bed, Buckingham and Sir Richard looking down at them. Behind them, at the door, Lady Isabella peered on tiptoe over their shoulders, as if watching some masque or mummer's play. And then, behind her, the dull dragging footsteps of Father Crispin as he, too, came up to join them.

'Tell me,' Athelstan said, 'who found the corpse?'

'I did,' Sir Richard replied. 'We had all risen early this morning. Father Crispin here took one of the horses, a young one, out through Aldgate to gallop in the fields. He came back, stabled the horse and came in to break fast with us. We then noticed Allingham had not come down although he was generally an early riser. We sent up a manservant. He tried to rouse Stephen but, unable to, came down to tell us.

Father Crispin had unfortunately just knocked over a wine cup and was cleaning up the mess with a napkin. When the servant summoned me, I went up; Father Crispin, Master Buckingham and Lady Isabella followed me. Allingham could not be roused so we then sent for the workmen in the yard. They brought up a timber and forced the door.'

Athelstan went over to the door and looked carefully at it. Both the bolt and the lock were now broken beyond repair where the makeshift battering ram had forced a way in.

'Inside, Stephen Allingham was lying on the bed, as you see him now. Father Crispin examined him and said there was no sign of life.'

'What else happened?'

'Nothing. We arranged the body, which was lying half sprawled, legs on the floor, the rest on the bed.'

'Nothing suspicious?'

'No.'

'Except one thing,' Father Crispin spoke up, ignoring Sir Richard's warning glance. 'I could not understand why, if Allingham had been taken by a seizure, he had not tried to open the door, turn the key and call for help. I thought the lock might have stuck.' He shrugged. 'I went back and examined it. The handle of the door was jammed. I tried to free it, using the cloth I had brought up from the hall to gain a better purchase. I did not succeed, perhaps because of the way it had been forced. The lock itself seemed good, though wrenched away by the forced entry. The key was lying on the floor.'

'And how had Master Allingham been in recent days?'

'Morose!' Sir Richard snapped back. 'He kept to himself. On one occasion my mother, Lady Ermengilde, found him muttering to himself, something about the same number Vechey mentioned – thirty-one. And about shoemakers!'

'Yes, that's right,' Lady Isabella said. 'At table he would just glower at his food and refuse to talk. He said he must be more careful about what he ate and drank. He spent a great deal of time in the yard below with the carpenters and masons who were making the pageant cart for the coronation procession. He spent hours talking to them, especially the master carpenter, Andrew Bulkeley.'

'What was so important?' Cranston asked.

Lady Isabella shrugged her pretty shoulders, a movement which made even Athelstan's breath catch in his throat.

'I don't know,' she murmured. 'He used to go down there and stand and look at the frieze Bulkeley was carving; the one that will surmount the cart and later be hung in the chantry chapel at the other end of this house. Perhaps you should speak to him?'

Cranston looked across at Athelstan and nodded.

'Oh, one further question, Lady Isabella, and I ask it here in the presence of your household. Your husband's wealth – he made a will?'

'Yes, it's already with the Court of Probate in Chancery at Westminster Hall. Why do you ask?'

Athelstan noticed how her cheeks had become flushed and Sir Richard moved restlessly.

'Who were your husband's heirs?'

'Sir Richard and myself.'

'You are to receive all his wealth?'

'Yes, all.'

'And, Sir Richard,' Cranston continued, 'you have now been through all the memoranda, documents, household books and accounts in your brother's possession. Have you found anything suspicious? Loans made perhaps to powerful men who refused to pay?'

Sir Richard smiled. 'Nothing of the sort. Oh, the powerful lords owed my brother, and now me, monies but none of them would dare renege. Remember, they can only do it once. After that who else will loan them monies?'

Cranston patted his thigh and grinned. 'The world of finance, Sir Richard, escapes me – and of course Brother Athelstan here, with his vow of poverty. Come, Brother!' He rose and Athelstan followed him out.

'Where are you going?' Sir Richard hurried to catch up with them.

'Why, to see Master Bulkeley, of course! I would like to know what Master Allingham found so interesting in the yard.'

Sir Richard led them down through a flagstoned kitchen and scullery, out into the great yard around which the house was built. The place was a hive of activity. Dogs charged about like lunatics, scattering the chickens and geese, which pecked for food in the hard-packed soil. Grooms, farriers and ostlers were taking horses in and out of the stables, checking legs, hooves and coats for any injuries or blemishes. A few small boys, the children of servants, played hide and seek behind the carts, baskets and bales of straw. Servants hurried in and out of kitchens with pitchers of water while others sat in the shade whiling their time away with dice and other games of hazard. Outside the kitchen door scullions were bringing out steaming chunks of bloody red meat to throw into huge casks of pickle and salt to preserve them. At the other end of the yard, carpenters were busy around a huge, gaily decorated cart, the four sides now being covered with elaborate cloths and carvings. Sir Richard took Cranston and Athelstan over.

'Oh, by the way, Sir Richard. The Syrians, the beautiful chess set, what happened to them?' asked Cranston.

Sir Richard stood still, staring up at the blue sky, turning his face to feel the sun.

'Too precious to be left out on display. Master Buckingham has polished them and put them away, locked in a casket. They are safe. Why do you ask?'

Cranston shrugged. 'I wondered, that's all.'

The noise around the carts was terrible: the banging and the sawing and the moving of wood. The air was thick with sawdust and the sweet smell of freshly cut wood. The pageant prepared by Springall, which was only a small part of the vast coronation procession, looked even more magnificent at close quarters. The cart was huge, about nine feet high. The merchant explained there would be a tableau which would give honour to the king as well as reflect the glory of the Goldsmith's Guild, with huge screens on which the carpenters and masons had carved elaborate scenes.

'There are four,' Sir Richard explained, 'one for the front, one for the back and one for each side of the cart. These will be fastened on and above them a platform. On that will be set the tableau. Everything has to be correct,' he commented. 'We do not wish to bring any disgrace or dishonour on the guild from our cart collapsing as it rolls through the streets of Cheapside.'

No expense had been spared. Athelstan particularly examined each of the screens showing the four last things; Death, Judgement, Heaven and Hell. He admired the sheer complexity of the scenes as well as the genius of the craftsmen, in particular in their depiction of Hell. There was a representation of the devil carrying off the wicked to Hades. Each of the damned souls was guarded by a group of hideous demons. In the centre of the piece was a carving of a shoemaker resisting four shaggy devils who were dragging him from the embraces of what at first Athelstan thought was a young lady but, on looking closer, realised that with his tail and close-cropped hair, it was a depiction of a male prostitute. The profession of the Devil's captive, a shoemaker, was made apparent by the bag of tools clutched in one hand and the unfinished shoe in the other.

'Who carved this?' Athelstan asked Sir Richard.

'Andrew Bulkeley.'

'Where is he?'

Sir Richard turned and called the man's name and a small, bald-headed man wandered over. His vast form, more corpulent than that of Cranston, was swathed in a dirty white apron. He looked like one of the carefree devils he had carved, with his fat, cheery face, snub nose and large blue eyes which seemed to dance with wicked merriment.

'Master Bulkeley.' Athelstan smiled and shook the proffered hand. 'Your carvings are exquisite.'

'Thank you, Brother.' The voice betrayed a soft burr of warmer, fresher climes.

Athelstan pointed to the depiction of Hell. 'This particular carving, it's your work?'

'Yes, Brother.'

'And the idea is yours?'

'Oh, no, Brother. Sir Thomas himself laid down what we should do and how we should carve it.'

'But why the shoemaker and why the male prostitute?'

The craftsman wiped his mouth with the back of
his hand.

'I don't really know. I have done such scenes many
times. It's always the same. Someone being dragged
from the warm embraces of a group of young ladies.
But this time, I think Sir Thomas had some secret
joke. He insisted that it be a shoemaker and the prostitute be male. That's all I know. He paid the money;
I did what he asked. Have you seen the others?'

'Yes, thank you,' Athelstan said, and looked across
at Cranston.

'Master Allingham came out to look at these
carvings?' Cranston asked.

'Yes.'

'Do you know why?'

'No.'

'Any carving in particular?'

The craftsman shrugged.

'He'd look at them all, usually when we were not
there, but he constantly asked why Sir Thomas had
chosen certain themes. I gave him the same answer I
gave you.'

Athelstan turned to the merchant. 'Was your
brother fascinated by shoemakers?'

'I told you,' Sir Richard replied, exasperated, 'he
liked riddles. Perhaps a shoemaker had offended him.
I don't know!'

Athelstan touched Sir John gently on the elbow. 'I have seen enough. Perhaps we should go?'

The coroner looked puzzled but quietly agreed. They walked back through the kitchen and down the hallway to the front entrance of the house. They were about to leave when Sir Richard called out: 'Brother Athelstan! Sir John!'

They both spun round.

'You keep coming back here, yet you have not found any evidence linking the deaths, or the reasons for them. Is that not so?'

The merchant had regained some of his arrogance and Cranston could not stop himself.

'Yes, that's so, Sir Richard. So far, we have found nothing conclusive. But, I can tell you something fresh and you may tell the others.'

'Yes, Sir John?'

'Whatever the evidence, whatever you may think, Stephen Allingham was murdered. You should all take care!'

Before the startled merchant could think of a reply, Cranston had taken Athelstan by the elbow and steered him out into the sun-baked street.

'Last time we were here,' Athelstan quipped, 'you warned me, Sir John, not to open my mouth and say things I was not bidden to. Yet you have done so today. There is no evidence that Allingham was murdered.'

'Oh, I know that,' Sir John grunted. 'And so do you.' He stopped and tapped the friar gently on the temple. 'But up there, Athelstan, and here in your heart, what do you really think?'

Athelstan stared at the hubbub around them, the people oblivious to his dark thoughts of murder, fighting their way through the stalls, gossiping, talking, buying and selling, engaged in everyday matters.

'I think you are right, Sir John. Allingham's murder was well planned, and the murderer is in that house.' He pulled his cowl up against the hot midday sun. 'Shall we collect our horses?'

Sir John looked away sheepishly. 'Sir John,' Athelstan repeated, 'the horses, shall we collect them?'

Cranston let out a sigh, shook his head and gazed appealingly at Athelstan.

'I have bad news, Brother. We are summoned to Westminster. Chief Justice Fortescue believes that we have spent enough public money and time in the pursuit of what he calls will-o'-the-wisps. He wants us to account for our stewardship. But before I clap eyes on his miserable face, I intend to down as many cups of sack as I can! You are with me?'

For the first time ever, Athelstan fully agreed with Sir John's desire for refreshment. They walked quickly through Cheapside down to Fleet Street and into the Saracen's Head, a cool, dark place off the main thoroughfare. Athelstan was pleased to see that it was empty and insisted that this time he should be host. He ordered the taverner to bring two black-jacks of brimming ale and, since it was Friday, not meat but a dish of lampreys and fresh white bread for himself and Sir John. Cranston took to the food like a duck to water, smacking his lips, draining the black-jack, and shouting for the taverner's pot boy to come and fill it again. Once the first pangs of hunger had been satisfied, Cranston interrogated the friar.

'Come, Brother, what do you think? Is there a solution? You are the philosopher, Athelstan, though didn't one of your famous theologians say "From nothing comes nothing – *Nihil ex nihilo!*"'

'There must be an answer,' Athelstan said, reclining against the cool stone at his back. 'When I studied Logic, we learnt one central truth. If the problem exists, there must be a solution. If there's no solution, there's no problem. Consequently, if there is a problem, there must be a solution.'

Cranston belched and blinked at Athelstan. 'Where did you learn that?' he taunted.

'Logic will resolve this problem,' Athelstan persisted. 'That and evidence. The problem, Sir John, is that we have no evidence. We can build no premise without it. We are like two men on the edge of a cliff. A chasm separates us from the other side and now we are looking round for the bridge.' Athelstan paused before continuing. 'Our bridge will be evidence, the resolving of Sir Thomas's riddles about the biblical verses and the shoemaker.'

Cranston shook his head. 'We should have talked to Allingham.'

'We did try, Sir John, but he obstinately refused to confide in us though I agree that he knew something. I think he was either going to flee or perhaps blackmail the murderers, without telling us. He made one mistake. He underestimated the sheer malice of his opponents.'

'What makes you say that?'

Athelstan bit his lip, cradling the black-jack in his hands, enjoying its coolness.

'They relish what they are doing. They plot, they devise stratagems, they cause as much confusion as they can. They not only pursue a certain quarry, the mysteries and riddles of Sir Thomas, I think they enjoy the killing. They have insufferable arrogance. Satan has set up camp in their souls. In a word, Sir John, they enjoy what they do as much as you do a goblet of claret or a game of hazard or teasing me. To them murder is now part of their lives, a piece in the fabric of their souls. They will continue to murder for profit, to protect themselves but also because they want to. All the more to see us floundering around in the dark. The more we flounder, the more enjoyment we give them.'

Sir John shivered and looked around the tavern. He felt uneasy for the first time ever, a prickling at the back of his neck, a sense of personal danger. Had they been followed? He looked quickly across at Athelstan. The friar was right. Whoever had committed these murders planned them well. If Lady Isabella was not the woman who went to the apothecary's shop, then who was? And the harlot who had lured Vechey to his doom? And the secret poisoner of Sir Thomas and Master Allingham? Cranston suddenly blinked.

'You keep saying "they",' he said. 'Why?'

'There must be more than one. Either that or it's someone very clever. I did think that someone outside that house was using assassins, professional killers, but that would be too dangerous. You see, the more people you hire to carry out a plot, the greater the danger of betrayal; either through a mistake, or a bribe, or simply by one of your minions being caught red-handed.'

'And you have no suspects?'

'No. It could be Sir Richard, it could be Lady Isabella, Buckingham, Father Crispin, even Dame Ermengilde. Who knows? One of the murdered men may have been an assassin.'

Sir John drained his tankard and slammed it down on the table.

'You know, Athelstan, if it wasn't for you and your bloody logic, I'd put the entire mystery down to witchcraft. People moving about in the dead of night, poisons being administered in a locked room. How on earth can we resolve it?'

'As I said, Sir John, logic and a little evidence, some speculation, and perhaps some help from Mistress Fortune. In the end we will grasp the truth. I don't particularly mourn the four who died.

What bothers me, what's making me sour and evil-tempered, is that the murderers are here, laughing at us, watching us fumble. They shall pay for that enjoyment. We can all murder, Sir John.' He rose, dusting the crumbs from his habit. 'Cain is in each of us. We lose our temper, feel cornered and frightened, it can be the work of an instant. But to savour murder – that's not the prompting of Cain, that's Satan!'

Cranston, his mouth full of hot food, simply mumbled his reply. Athelstan felt the thick ale seep into his stomach, making him relaxed, even sleepy.

'Come on, Sir John. Chief Justice Fortescue awaits us and, as you know, justice waits for no man!'

Sir John glared, stuffed the rest of the food in his mouth and drained his tankard in one final gulp.

They hurried out into Fleet Street, Sir John wiping his mouth on the back of his hand, hitching his sword belt, shouting that he would revisit the tavern at his earliest convenience. They were halfway down Fleet Street when suddenly the Coroner's mood changed. He stopped abruptly and gazed round, staring back at the throng they had pushed through.

'What's wrong, Sir John?'

The coroner chewed his lip. 'We are being followed, Brother Athelstan, and I don't like that.'

He looked round and went over to a tinker's stall. Athelstan saw money change hands and Cranston came back with a thick broomstick.

'Here, Athelstan!'

The friar looked in surprise at the long, smoothly planed ash pole.

'I have no need of a staff, Sir John.'

Cranston grinned, his hands falling to the dagger and great broad sword he carried.

'You may have, Athelstan. Remember what your psalmist says: "The devil goes around like a lion seeking whom he would devour." I believe a lion or a devil, or both, are trailing us now!'

Chapter 8

As they hurried down Fleet Street Athelstan wondered if perhaps Sir John had drunk too deep. They turned abruptly into the long gardens of the Inner Temple, fenced off from sightseers. The gate-keeper, recognising Cranston, let them in without a word. They hurried through the tranquil, fragrant-smelling garden, past the Inner and Middle Temples, and down Temple Stairs where they hired a wherry to take them to Westminster. Cranston, despite his bulk, jumped into the boat, pulling a surprised Athelstan along with him. He tripped on his staff and nearly pitched head first into the water. The boatman cursed, telling them to sit down and keep still, and then, puffing and sweating, he pulled his craft out midstream through the flocks of swans who arched their wings in protest as if they owned the river.

They followed the Thames as it curved down past the Savoy Palace, Durham and York House, past the high-pooped ships scarred from long voyages which were crowding in for repairs. At Charing Cross the boatman began to pull in as the deep bend in the river became more pronounced. They passed

Scotland Yard; Westminster Abbey came into sight; then the tower of St Margaret's and the roofs, turrets and gables, shop-dwellings, houses and taverns, which made up the small city of Westminster.

The boatman pulled in, allowing Athelstan and Cranston to disembark at the Garden Stairs and go through the courts, corridors and passageways which linked the different buildings of Westminster Palace. The place was thronged: gaolers with their prisoners, attorneys, lawyers and clients, as well as vendors of paper, ink and food. The ne'er-do-wells and the many sightseers mixed with the army of law clerks carrying rolls of parchment up from the cellar known as Hell where, Sir John explained, the legal records were kept. The smell was terrible, despite the fresh breezes wafting in from the river. Some of the lawyers and justices, resplendent in their silken robes, held nosegays to their faces to fend off the odour.

Cranston led Athelstan into the Great Hall, pointing out the painted walls, though some of the frescoes were beginning to flake. The famous ceiling, where the wooden angels flew face down through the dusty air above the crowd, was so high it could scarcely be seen in the gloom. Cranston stopped a beadle in his blue cloak, the shield of office on his breast and long staff tapping the paving stones proclaiming his sense of importance. Yes, the fellow assured them, with a nod of his head to the far end of the hall, the Court of King's Bench was now in session and Chief Justice Fortescue attendant upon it.

The beady, little eyes softened as Cranston displayed his warrant, a silver coin lying on top of it. However, the court had finished its morning session. Perhaps Chief Justice Fortescue was in his chamber?

The beadle led them through the gloomy rooms off the main hall where the Court of Common Pleas, Court of Chancery and Court of Requests sat, and down a warren of lime-washed corridors until he stopped in front of a door and rapped noisily with his wand.

'Come in!' Chief Justice Fortescue, his scarlet, fur-trimmed robe tossed over a chair, was sitting behind a table. The angry look on the judge's sallow face showed that either his attendance in court that morning or Cranston's arrival had put him in an ill humour.

'Ah!' Fortescue dropped the manuscript he was reading on to the table. 'Our zealous city coroner and his clerk. Please sit down.' He gestured to a well-cushioned window seat.

Cranston glared back at him and waddled over. Athelstan sat next to the coroner and wondered what was to come. The Chief Justice threw them both another ill-favoured glance.

'What progress has been made?'

In short, clipped tones Cranston told him exactly what had happened, and their suspicions. How the four deaths were linked. How Brampton and Vechey had probably not committed suicide but been murdered and that Allingham's supposed death from natural causes was probably the murderer striking again.

'You have no idea who it is?'

'No, My Lord.'

'Or why?'

'No, My Lord.'

'You found no great mystery that Sir Thomas Springall was hiding? Nothing which could endanger either the crown or the safety of the realm?'

'Nothing,' Cranston retorted. 'Why should there be?'

Fortescue dropped his glance, fiddling with the great amethyst ring on one of his fingers.

'Sir John, you hold your office from the crown. You could be removed.'

Cranston's face sagged and Athelstan felt a tremor run through the great, corpulent body. He spoke up.

'My Lord Chief Justice?'

Fortescue looked surprised, as if he had expected Athelstan to keep his mouth shut for the entire interview.

'Yes, Brother? You have something to add, perhaps? Something Sir John does not know.'

'No, I have nothing to add,' replied Athelstan. 'Except that Sir John and I have been most zealous in this matter. We could ask further questions – such as, My Lord, what you yourself were doing at the banquet on the night Sir Thomas died? You said to us that you left early in the evening, but according to other witnesses you left just an hour before midnight. It would help us, My Lord,' he said, ignoring the look of deep annoyance on the Chief Justice's face. 'If everyone spoke the truth, we might avoid future dangers.'

'Is that why you carry the staff, Brother?' The Chief Justice retorted, totally ignoring Athelstan's jibe. 'You fear something, don't you? What?'

'I fear nothing, My Lord, except perhaps that those who do not wish us to find the truth may intervene in a way we least expect. And that, of course, would help no one.'

'Meaning?'

'I mean, My Lord,' continued Athelstan, warming to his task, 'Sir John is a well-known and well-beloved coroner in the city. If he was attacked in public, people would be scandalised. The king's chief peace officer in the capital prevented from walking the streets! And if he was removed from office, questions would be asked. People would look very carefully at what matters Sir John was involved in when he was removed. There would be questions. There are aldermen who sit in the Commons, in St Stephen's Chapel, just a stone's throw away, only too willing to use any ammunition against the regent.' He spread his hands. 'Now, My Lord, I ask you to think again before you threaten Sir John. Remember, this task was given to us by you. If you wish, we can let the matter drop and others, perhaps more fortunate, can dig amongst the scandals, the lies and the deceit and possibly search out the truth.'

Fortescue took a deep breath to control the fury raging within him. How dare this friar, this bare-arsed Dominican in his dusty black robe and shoddy leather sandals, sit and lecture him, Chief Justice of the realm! Yet Fortescue was no man's fool. He knew Athelstan spoke the truth. He smiled falsely.

'True, Brother,' he replied, 'but there seems no answer to this conundrum in sight and the regent is most pressing. Indeed, he has invited both of you to a special tournament to be held at Smithfield the day after next and, following that, later in the evening, a banquet in the Savoy Palace. I may as well be blunt: Sir Richard Springall and all his household have also been invited. The duke does not care whether you wish to attend or not – he orders it. He wishes to inspect at close quarters all the actors in this drama. I take it you will attend?'

'Of course, My Lord,' Sir John spoke up. 'It's our duty.' He grinned slyly at his assistant. 'And both Brother Athelstan and myself would like some sort of respite, a short rest from tramping the streets on your work.'

On that parting note, Cranston belched noisily and left Chief Justice Fortescue, with Athelstan behind him. They made their way back to the river steps.

During their journey upriver, Cranston sat morosely in the bows of the boat, staring into the water. Only when they reached Temple Stairs and disembarked did he put one podgy arm round Athelstan's shoulders and press his face closer to that of the friar. His breath smelt as rich as a wine press.

'Athelstan,' he slurred, 'I thank you for what you said there, in the presence of that mean-faced bastard! I'll not forget.'

Athelstan stepped back in mock annoyance. 'Sir John, remember the old adage? "The devil you know is better than the devil you don't." Moreover, I always think that working with you will lessen my spell in Purgatory when I die.'

Sir John turned and belched as loudly as he could.

'That, Brother,' he retorted, 'is the only answer I can and will make!'

They continued through the Temple Gates into the alleyway which would lead them into Fleet Street and a new cook shop. They were chatting about the tournament and John of Gaunt's invitation when Cranston stopped as he heard a sound behind them: a slithering across the cobbles.

'Athelstan,' he whispered, 'keep on walking.' His hand went to the hilt of his sword. 'But grip your staff and be ready!'

They walked a few steps further. Athelstan heard a sound close behind him and spun round as Cranston followed suit. Two men stood there, one tall and masked, the other a small, weasel-eyed individual dressed in a dirty leather jerkin, hose and boots which had seen better days. He wore a flat, battered cap on his head, pushed to one side to give him a jaunty air. Athelstan swallowed hard and felt a surge of panic. Both men were armed, each carrying a naked sword and dirk. What frightened him most was their absolute silence, the way they stared, unmoving, not issuing threats.

'Why do you follow us?' Cranston said, pushing Athelstan behind him.

'We do not follow, sir,' the weasel-eyed man replied. 'My companion and I merely walk the same path as you do.'

'I think you do follow us,' Cranston replied, 'and have been for some time. You followed us down to the river and waited until we returned. You have been expecting us.'

'I don't know what you are talking about!' The man took one step closer, sword and dagger now half raised. 'But you insult us, sir, and you must apologise.'

'I do not apologise to you, nor to the murderous bastard next to you! I am Sir John Cranston, coroner of the city.' He drew his sword and scrabbled behind his back to pull out the dirk. 'You, sirs, are footpads, which is a felony. You are attacking a king's officer and that is treason. This is Brother Athelstan, a member of the Dominican order, a priest of the church. Any attack on him would bring down excommunication on you. And that, sirs, is the least you can expect! I will count to three,' the coroner continued as if enjoying himself, 'and then, if you are not out of this alleyway and back whence you came, you will answer to me! One... two...'

That was as far as he got. The men rushed at them, swords and daggers raised. The coroner met both attackers, catching their weapons in a whirling arc of steel as he nimbly spun his own in self-defence. In those few seconds Athelstan realised the depth of his own arrogance. He had always considered Sir John a portly, self-indulgent toper, but at this moment the coroner seemed more at ease, sword and dagger in his hands, fighting for his life, than he had at any time since they had met. He moved with a grace and speed which surprised both Athelstan and his opponents. Sir John was a competent swordsman, moving only when he needed to, keeping both dagger and sword locked in constant play. Athelstan could only stand and watch, open-mouthed. The coroner was smiling, his eyes half closed, sweat running down his face. The friar could have sworn that Sir John was singing a hymn or a song under his breath. There seemed little danger. Whoever had sent these assassins had completely underestimated the fat knight. Sir John fenced on, parrying sideways, backwards and forwards, playing with his opponents. Cautiously, Athelstan joined the fray − not as expertly as Sir John, but the long ash pole came into play, creating as much confusion as it did harm. Athelstan now stood shoulder to shoulder with Cranston. Their two assailants drew back.

Cranston was loath to stop the fight. 'And again, my buckos!' he cried. 'Just once more and then a wound, an injury. If I don't kill you, the hangman will! Be sure of that.'

The small, weasel-eyed man looked at his companion, and before the coroner could advance another step, both men took to their heels and fled. Cranston leaned suddenly against the wall, wiping away the sweat now coursing down his face. His jerkin was stained with damp patches at the armpits and chest.

'You see that, Athelstan?' he gasped, resting his sword point on the ground. 'You saw me, didn't you? The sword play, the footwork. You will vouch for me with Lady Maude?'

Athelstan smiled. Sir John saw himself as a knight errant, a chevalier, and his little wife Maude as his princess.

'I saw it, Sir John,' he said. 'A born soldier. A true Saint George. You were in no danger?'

Cranston coughed and spat.

'From those? Alleymen, roaring boys, the dregs of some commissioner's levy! I tell you this, Athel-stan,' sheathing his sword and dagger, 'I fought in France against the cream of French chivalry for the Old King, bless him! We were raging lions then and

England's name was feared from the northern seas to the Straits of Gibraltar. In my younger days,' he bellowed, pulling his shoulders back martial fashion, 'I was keen as a greyhound, fast as a falcon swooping to the kill.'

Athelstan hid a smile, looking at the sweat still pouring down the fat coroner's face, the great, stout stomach wobbling with a mixture of pride and anger.

Of course they had to stop at the nearest tavern for Sir John to take refreshment and go over his sword play, step by step, blow by blow. Athelstan, concealing his amusement, listened as attentively as he could.

'Sir John,' he interrupted finally, 'those men, the footpads, they were sent, were they not? They were waiting for us.'

'Yes,' Cranston stuck his fiery red nose deeper into his tankard, slurping noisily, 'they were sent after us. Which means, Brother Athelstan, that our final remark to Sir Richard as we left the Springall house hit home. The murderer now knows that we are on his trail. Vechey, Brampton and Allingham are dead, and the number of suspects shrinks. We have a greater chance of being able to flush this assassin out. But we must remain vigilant, Brother, for he may strike again.'

He stood up and gazed round the tavern. Athelstan wondered if he was going to describe to all and sundry the recent fray in the alleyway.

'You will come back with me, Athelstan, to Lady Maude?'

He shook his head. If he went back the day would be done. Cranston would drink himself silly, celebrating his triumph, and make Athelstan recount time and time again his great victory.

'No, Sir John, I crave your pardon but not this time. We shall meet the day after next. We have an invitation to a tournament which we must accept.'

Cranston reluctantly conceded his point and they both left the tavern and walked back to collect their horses. The coroner stood and watched Athelstan mount the ancient but voracious Philomel.

'My Lady Maude will come to the tournament,' he said, then looking up at the friar, tapped the side of his fleshy nose. 'You can always bring the woman Benedicta.'

Athelstan blushed. He dare not ask how Cranston knew about Benedicta. The coroner laughed and was still bellowing with mirth as Athelstan urged his horse forward out into the street. He still retained the staff Cranston had bought him. On the journey home he felt slightly ridiculous, like some broken-down knight preparing for a tournament. He tried to ignore the murmured whispers and laughter as he made his way through the streets across London Bridge and back into Southwark. He thought over the attack but felt no fear. The danger from the footpad, the silent assassin, was always present, here in his church or across the river. Athelstan stopped his horse outside St Erconwald's and thought about that further. Suddenly he realised he had no fear of death. Why? Because of his brother? Because of his priesthood? Or because his conscience was clear? Then he thought of Benedicta and felt a twinge of doubt.

That night, whilst Sir John roistered in his house like Hector home from the wars, Athelstan fed Philomel and Bonaventure. He promised himself he would not go up to the tower to observe the stars. Instead he went into his own church, secured the door, lit candles and took them to his small carrel where he placed his writing tray. He chose a piece of smooth parchment and began to write down everything that had happened since he first went to the Springall mansion. He was sitting there, half dozing over what he had written, when there was a loud knocking on the door. At first he refused to answer, then realised that no assassin would make such a noise so went down to the door and called out: 'Who's there?'

'Rosamund, Brother!'

Athelstan recognised the voice of the eldest daughter of Pike the ditcher. He unlocked the door and peered out into the darkness. A fresh-faced young girl burbled out her news. How her mother had just given birth to another child, her fifth, this time a boy. Athelstan smiled and mumbled his congratulations. The little girl looked at him solemnly.

'Mother wishes you to choose a name.'

Athelstan smiled and acknowledged the great honour.

'She wants a saint's name, Brother.'

Athelstan promised he would do what he could and hoped to see her and her family as soon as possible. He heard the girl run back down the steps and her footsteps faded in the distance. He locked the door and went back to the carrel. Athelstan picked up the piece of parchment and the candle, scrutinising what he had written. He shook his head. He was too tired for work but felt he must continue, otherwise he would think back to Cranston's words about Benedicta. Idly, he wondered if the widow would accompany him. After all, there would be nothing wrong in a day out for both of them. 'Christ had his friends,' he kept murmuring to himself. He thought of little Rosamund and went to the high altar where the great missal lay. The friar opened the book, turning to the back where a previous incumbent had written the names of all the saints, listing in a neat hand which guild, craft or profession they were patrons of. Joseph, Athelstan grinned, patron saint of undertakers and mortuary men. The friar laughed. Joseph of Arimithea – the only man he ever buried was alive and well three days later! Perhaps not the best saint the church should have chosen for such a profession. His eyes ran down the list, looking for a suitable saint's name. Suddenly he saw one and stopped, his heart pounding with excitement. He was fully awake. He looked at the name again and the craft and guild of which he was patron. Was it possible? Was it really possible?

Athelstan closed the missal, all thoughts of Pike the ditcher and his family cleared from his head. He went back to the carrel, seized his pen and continued to write out everything he knew. He tried to extract every detail from his memory, quoting to himself what he had said to Cranston earlier in the day: 'If there's a problem, logically there must be a solution.' For the first time ever, Athelstan had a piece of evidence, something that would fit, something which might unlock the rest of the secrets.

He fell asleep for a few hours just before dawn and woke cold and cramped, his head on the small desk, his body somehow wedged on the stool. He stretched, cracking muscles, and looked up at the small window above the high altar, pleased to see it would be a fair day. He prepared the altar for Mass, opened the door and waited for the small trickle of his congregation to enter. At last, when he thought he could wait no longer, he glimpsed Benedicta slip silently up the nave to join the other two members of his congregation, kneeling between them at the entrance to the rood screen. The widow's ivory face, framed in its veil of luxurious black curls, seemed more exquisite than ever and Athelstan said a prayer of thanks to God for such beauty.

As usual, after Mass, Benedicta stayed to light a candle before the statue of the Virgin. She smiled as Athelstan approached and asked softly if all was well.

Athelstan took his courage in both hands and blurted out his invitation. Benedicta's eyes rounded in surprise, but she smiled and agreed so quickly that the friar wondered if she, too, felt the kinship between them. For the rest of the day he could hardly concentrate on any problem, caught between contrition that he had done something wrong in inviting Benedicta and pleasure that she had so readily accepted. He could not really account for what he did, moving from duty to duty like a sleepwalker, so buoyed up he didn't even bother to study the stars that night, in spite of the sky being cloud free. His mind was unwilling to rest. Sleep eluded him. Instead he tossed and turned, hoping Girth the bricklayer's son had delivered his message to Sir John Cranston indicating where they should meet the next day.

The friar was up just before dawn and celebrated his Mass, Bonaventure and Benedicta being his only congregation. Athelstan's pleasure increased when he saw that Benedicta, her hair now braided and hidden under a wimple, had a small basket by her side in preparation for their journey to Smithfield. After Mass they talked, chatting about this and that, as they walked from Southwark across London Bridge to meet Cranston and his wife at the Golden Pig, a comfortable tavern on the city side of the river.

Lady Maude, small and pert, was cheerful as a little sparrow, welcoming Benedicta like a long-lost sister. Cranston, with at least three flagons of wine down him already, was in good form, nudging Athelstan in the ribs and leering lecherously at Benedicta. After Sir

John had pronounced himself refreshed, they made their way up to Thames Street to the Kirtle tavern which stood on the edge of Smithfield, just under the forbidding walls of Newgate Prison.

Athelstan remembered what he had learnt from his study of the Index of Saints but decided not to confide in Sir John. The puzzle had other pieces and the friar decided to wait, although he felt guiltily that Benedicta's presence might have more to do with his tardiness than it should have.

The day had proved to be a fine one. The streets were hot and dusty, so Cranston and Athelstan's party welcomed the tavern's coolness. They sat in a corner watching the citizens of every class and station go noisily by, eager to reserve a good place from which to watch the day's events: merchants sweltering under beaver hats, their fat wives clothed in gaudy gowns, beggars, quacks, story-tellers, hordes of apprentices, and a man from the guilds. Athelstan groaned and hid his face as a crowd of parishioners led by Black Clem, Ranulf the rat-catcher and Pike the ditcher, passed the tavern door, roaring a filthy song at the top of their voices. At last Cranston finished his further refreshment and, with Benedicta so close beside him his heart kept skipping for joy, Athelstan led them out into the great cleared area of Smithfield. Three blackened crow-pecked corpses still hung from a gibbet, but the crowd ignored them. The food-sellers were doing a roaring trade in spiced sausages and, beside them, water-sellers with great buckets slung round their necks sold cooling drinks to soothe the mouths of those who chewed the hot, spicy meat. Athelstan looked away, his gorge rising, after seeing Ranulf the rat-catcher sidle up beside one of these water-sellers and quietly piss into one of the buckets.

Smithfield had been specially cleared for the joust. Even the customary dung heaps and piles of ordure had been taken away. A vast open space had been cordoned off for the day. At one side was the royal enclosure with row after row of wooden seats, all covered in purple or gold cloth. In the centre a huge canopy shielded the place where the king and his leading nobility would sit. The banners of John of Gaunt, resplendent with the gaudy device of the House of Lancaster, waved lazily in the breeze. Marshalls of the royal household in their colourful tabards, white wands of office held high, directed Cranston and his party to their reserved seats.

All around them benches were quickly filling with ladies in silk gowns, giggling and chattering, who clutched velvet cushions to their bosoms as they simpered past the young men eyeing them. These gallants, with hair long and curled, and jerkins dripping pearls, proved to be raucous and strident. Cranston was merry, but some of these young men were already far gone in their cups. Athelstan ignored the lustful glances directed at Benedicta, trying to curb the sparks of jealousy which flared in his heart.

Once they were seated, he looked round, studying the tournament area. The field, a great grassy plain, was divided down the centre by a huge tilt barrier covered in a black and white canvas. At the end of this barrier were the pavilions, gold, red, blue and scarlet, one for each of the jousters. Already the contestants were arriving and around each pavilion scuttled pages and squires. Armour glinted and dazzled in the sun; banners bearing the gules and lozenges, lions, wyverns and dragons of the noble houses, fluttered in the faint summer breeze. A bray of trumpets stilled the clamour, their shrill so angry the birds in the trees around Smithfield rose in noisy protesting flocks. The royal party had arrived.

Cranston pointed out John of Gaunt, Duke of Lancaster, his face cruel under blond hair, skin burnt dark from his campaigns in Castile. On either side of him stood his brothers and a collection of young lords. In the centre of the group, with one of John of Gaunt's hands on his shoulder, stood a young boy, his face white as snow under a mop of golden hair, a silver chaplet on his head. Cranston nudged and pointed again: beside the royal party Athelstan glimpsed Chief Justice Fortescue in scarlet, lined with pure white lamb's wool, Sir Richard, Lady Isabella, the priest Crispin, Master Buckingham, Dame Ermengilde, and others of their household. Athelstan was sure that they all looked his way but again came the shrill bray of the trumpets. Gaunt raised his hand as if welcoming the plaudits of the crowd. There was clapping from the claque of young courtiers around him but the London mob was silent and Athelstan remembered Cranston's mutterings about how the expensive tastes of the court, coupled with the military defeats against the French, had brought Gaunt and his party into disrepute.

'Our quarry's in sight!' Cranston whispered to the friar, though his voice carried for yards around them. Athelstan looked sideways at Benedicta and his heart lurched. She had turned slightly, staring coolly back at a young, dark-faced gallant, resplendent in red and white silks, who lounged in his seat with eyes for no one but Athelstan's fair companion. Cranston, sharp enough under his bluff, drunken exterior, caught the friar's pained glance. He leaned over and tapped Athelstan on the arm.

'The tournament is about to begin, Brother,' he said. 'Watch carefully. You may learn something about combat.'

Another shrill blast of the trumpets. Banners were lowered, and behind the pavilions came a procession led by pages in tight quilted jackets, multi-coloured hose and gaudy feathered hats. They carried huge canvas paintings depicting scenes from the Bible and classical times. Hercules fighting with the python; the slaying of Hector; the Siege of Troy; Samson amongst the Philistines; and the serpent entering Eden. Such a tableau always preceded tournaments. It was followed by musicians with tambour, fife and viol. Behind them came squires and further pages and, finally, the knights themselves, not yet armoured, their colours carried before them. The procession wound around the whole tournament area, knights and men-at-arms acknowledging the cheers and cries of the crowd.

Athelstan looked more closely at one of the paintings, a scene from the Book of Genesis, remembered something he had glimpsed in the Springall house, and he gasped. The sounds around him died away. All he could see was that crude canvas painting being carried by two pages. Of course! His stomach churned with excitement. He turned to Cranston, grabbing him by the arm.

'The paintings! The canvas paintings!' he whispered hoarsely.

Cranston looked at him blearily.

'The paintings, Sir John, in the Springall house? The canvas ones on the walls. When we first went there, they were covered in black drapes because of the mourning. Don't you remember? Genesis Chapter Three, Verse One, the serpent entering Eden! There was a painting like that in one of the galleries in Springall's house. Maybe that is what Sir Thomas was referring to?'

Cranston blinked. Making sure his wife did not see him, he pulled a wineskin from underneath his cloak and took a generous swig.

'I am here to enjoy myself, man,' he said hoarsely. As he put the stopper back, Athelstan's words sank in.

'My God, of course, you're right! The paintings, the three riddles. They may hold the secret!'

Athelstan dare not tell him that he had already resolved one of them.

'What shall we do?' murmured Cranston.

'Go now!' Athelstan said.

'But we are here as the guests of John of Gaunt. I know the duke. If we leave, he will send some busy body squire or serjeant-at-arms after us.'

'Now is the best time,' Athelstan replied, drawing closer, whispering into Sir John's ear, conscious that Lady Maude was totally absorbed in the pageant before her whilst Benedicta, distracted, was still staring back at the admiring gallant.

'Sir John, the Springall house is empty now. Let us strike whilst the iron is hot!'

Cranston looked as if he was going to refuse but thought again. 'Follow me,' he said.

Cranston whispered to his wife, then waddled off with Athelstan in tow, pushing through the crowd towards the royal enclosure. Knight bannerets of the king's household stopped them but Cranston muttered a few words and they let him by. Athelstan, however, had to stand outside the protective ring of steel watching Cranston bow at the foot of the steps and fall to one knee. Athelstan looked behind him. The procession was still circling the arena. John of Gaunt came down the steps, laughing. He tapped Cranston on the shoulder and raised him up, whispering in his ear. The coroner replied. Behind Gaunt,

Chief Justice Fortescue glowered like some angry hawk. John of Gaunt looked up abruptly and stared like a hungry cat at Athelstan, his eyes yellow, hard and unblinking. He nodded and muttered something over his shoulder to Fortescue, then to Cranston. The coroner bowed and backed away. Athelstan looked to his left to where the Springall household sat. Surprisingly, no one seemed interested in Sir John's meeting with the regent.

Cranston himself said nothing until they had walked away from the royal enclosure.

'Brother,' he whispered, 'we have the Regent's permission to go down to the Springall house now, to examine and take anything we wish. The regent has said, even if it takes all day, we are not to appear at the royal palace or the Savoy until we have something more to tell him!'

Athelstan's heart sank. On the one hand he wished to examine those paintings and resolve the mystery. But on the other, he wished to be with Benedicta. He looked up. Fitful clouds were beginning to obscure the sun. He glanced across to where the women sat. Cranston's wife was making herself comfortable on the bench whilst the gallant who had been eyeing Benedicta had now moved closer and was talking quietly with her. He was teasing her, but Benedicta did not seem to mind. She seemed absorbed in the young man's conversation. Athelstan barely listened to Cranston's muttering. He fought to control a sense of panic and reminded himself that he was a priest, a man ordained, sworn to God. Had he not taken a vow of celibacy? Although he might have a woman as a friend, he could not lust, he could not desire or covet any woman, whether she be free or not. Athelstan steeled himself. Benedicta was courteous to everyone, whether it be Hob's wife, Ranulf the rat-catcher, or now a court gallant. Nevertheless, Athelstan felt a growing rage at his condition; a sense of jealous hurt that Benedicta could find someone else so attractive and entertaining, even though he dismissed the emotion itself as both childish and dangerous.

Chapter 9

They left Smithfield, taking a different route back into the city, past the ditch which smelt so rank and fetid that even Cranston, filled to his gills with wine, stopped to gag and cover his nose. The coroner made a mental note to include in his treatise a special chapter on the cleaning of the ditch. They hurried past Cock Lane. The mouth of the street was thronged with whores in scarlet, red or violet dresses; one of them, swaying her hips and making her breasts dance, shouted: 'Sir John! Sir John! See us now!'

Cranston turned, a broad smile on his expansive face, not caring about Athelstan standing beside him, writhing in embarrassment.

'All my girls!' he muttered. 'All my lovely girls!'

Then, urged on by Athelstan, they continued past Newgate into the Shambles and Westchepe. The city was fairly silent, quieter than usual due to the great tournament at Smithfield. The city authorities had taken care to use the day to process certain cases in the court. A number of whores caught and convicted at their second offence were being taken, their heads shaved, a white wand in their hands, down towards

251

the Tun near Cornhill, the open gaol where they stood to be reviled by any passerby. They did not seem to mind, each patting her head and calling out that her hair would soon grow, which was more than could be said for the balding bailiffs escorting them. A liar or perjurer stood in the docks, a great whetstone round his neck, a placard proclaiming that he was a false perjurer and breaker of oaths; beside him a hapless youth who had stolen a leg of mutton and was standing there with the piece of meat, now well decaying and buzzing with flies, slung round his neck. Athelstan watched the scene around him and tried to keep his mind free of Benedicta and the petty jealousies which nagged him.

They found the Springall house deserted except for a few servants. By the looks of them, they had been playing whilst the cat was away. Most of them were well gone in their cups and offered no objection when Cranston knocked at the door and demanded entrance. The old retainer who had received them on their first visit tried to help but Cranston pushed him gently away, saying it was a holiday and besides he was here at Sir Richard's request to pursue his inquiries privately. Naturally, the fragrant smell of wine reminded Cranston of how long it had been since he had refreshed himself, so he ordered a large jug and the deepest goblet to be found in the kitchen.

He followed Athelstan as the friar went from one canvas painting to the next. Cranston showed himself surprisingly knowledgeable on the subject of the paintings they examined. He claimed that some were the work of Edward Prince, an artist who lived in the north of the city. Athelstan half listened to Cranston's chatter, trying to remember where he had seen the painting of Eve in the garden enchanted by the serpent. At last he recalled it was not in the Nightingale Gallery but in the one running to the left.

Followed by Cranston, who was now staggering, Athelstan went upstairs and removed the huge canvas painting from the wall. He cursed. It was apparent that someone else had realised the painting might hold the key to Sir Thomas's mystery. The wood at the back of the painting was deeply scored with a dagger as if someone had been searching for some secret crevice or compartment. Yet there was nothing.

'It is useless, Brother!' Cranston murmured, pouring himself another cup of claret. 'It is absolutely bloody useless! There is nothing here. And the other two? The reference to Death on a pale horse in the Apocalypse, and the shoemaker? We're wasting our time.'

Athelstan made him sit on the floor with his back to the wall and, crouching down beside him, told him quietly what he had learnt: how the wood carving being made for the coronation pageant might hold a clue to the killer's identity. Cranston, despite his befuddled wits, heard him out then bellowed in righteous indignation.

'Why didn't you tell me before? It makes sense. It's possible. But why didn't you tell me?'

Athelstan found nothing more amusing than Cranston portraying virtue outraged and let the coroner ramble on until he had exhausted his litany of complaint. Athelstan heaved the painting back on the wall. After that he went from chamber to chamber, from corridor to corridor, looking for other canvases which might fit the verse from the Apocalypse. Cranston staggered behind him, holding a wine cup in one hand and the jug in the other. They found nothing. Of course, certain chambers were locked: Sir Richard's and Lady Isabella's, for instance. With Cranston bouncing along the Nightingale Gallery, the whole house seemed to sing with noise. Sir Thomas's chamber, deserted except for a bed, table, and other sticks of furniture was, surprisingly, open. Cranston stared round. There was no painting here either. The walls were bare. Athelstan went over to the window and stared down at the chess table.

'You know, Sir John, if we find nothing this afternoon then I agree, we should record verdicts of suicide and murder and leave this matter alone for we are making little progress.'

He heard a loud crash behind him. Cranston had placed the wine cup and jug beside the bed, collapsed on to the mattress and was smiling beatifically at the ceiling, fast asleep. Athelstan sighed, went over, and with great difficulty arranged Sir John's huge body more comfortably on the bed. Then he sat beside him. He had not brought his writing tray or materials but mentally he went through each of the deaths he had investigated, trying to fix a pattern, with little success. Cranston snored gently like a child, muttering now and again and smacking his lips. Athelstan grinned as he heard the words 'Refreshment' and 'Some cups of sack!' Sir John burped noisily, rolled on one side and, if Athelstan had not been there, would have fallen completely off the bed. Athelstan let the coroner sleep. Why not? After all, there was only one painting which fitted the texts and that held nothing. His thoughts strayed to Benedicta. Was she missing him? Why had she talked so easily to that nobleman? Were all women like that? Had he done wrong in inviting her in the first place?

He picked up the wine cup and sipped from it and then sat on the bed next to Sir John, staring down at the great wooden bed posters. He dozed and was about to fall asleep when suddenly he woke with a start. The carvings! Especially the one on the right... He got off the bed and went around. Whoever had constructed the bed post had created a vivid scene. The serpent carved there seemed to writhe, its tongue darting, whilst its intended victim, Eve, stood like the personification of innocence with one hand covering her groin, the other raised to hold back her long flowing hair. In between them was the drooping branch of an apple tree. Even in wood the fruit seemed full and lush. Athelstan stood for a moment in disbelief, then he moved over to the other bed post: there, in the centre, the artist had etched a life-like horse. The dark brown of the wood made the creature seem real, one leg raised, head arched, and on its back a frightening, ghostly figure with a hood. Peeping out from beneath it was the skeletal face of Death itself. Athelstan gasped with excitement and went round to rouse the coroner.

'Sir John! Wake up!'

The coroner moved, snored and smacked his lips.

'Sir John!' Athelstan slapped him gently on the face. The coroner's eyes opened.

'My dear Maude...'

'I am not Maude!' Athelstan replied sharply. 'Sir John, I have discovered something.'

'A cup of sack?'

Athelstan refilled the goblet and held it to the coroner's lips. 'For God's sake, Sir John, wake up!'

The coroner sat up, shaking the sleep from his eyes, and stared blearily round.

'For God's sake, Friar, what has happened now?'

Athelstan showed him. At first, his mind dulled with sleep and wine, Cranston stared blankly but the significance of the friar's discovery gradually dawned on him. Without more ado, the coroner began to finger the carving of the figure of Death, probing and pressing it.

'There must be a secret compartment. I have heard of such in the Italian mode, built into chairs, tables and desks. I have even heard of hiding places in beds but never seen one.'

Their search was fruitless, so they moved to the other bed post. They pushed different parts of the carving but nothing moved. Suddenly Cranston looked up and nudged Athelstan.

'Look, Brother!'

Athelstan stared across at the bed post where a small block of wood on which the carving had rested had now opened outwards like a door.

'The mechanism must be in this bed post, with a spring that runs here under the boarding and up into the other.'

Again they pressed, watching the small door close when Athelstan pushed the apple between the serpent and Eve. He pushed and it re-opened. Slowly they approached the cavity, each trying to control his excitement. Athelstan put his hand gingerly into the small, dark space and brought out two rolls of parchment. He ignored Cranston's excited pleas to hurry and went over to the window, unrolling them carefully. The first was a love poem written in a rough hand in Norman French. At first Athelstan thought it was addressed to a woman but realised it was written to a young man. He handed it over to Cranston.

'Make of that what you wish!'

The second was a small indenture or agreement. The top was perforated, so someone else must have a copy. Athelstan read and knew why John of Gaunt,

Duke of Lancaster, was so indebted to Sir Thomas Springall, and why the merchant had possessed secrets which could have brought him even greater wealth. Cranston had already dismissed the poem, but when he read the indenture, he sat at the foot of the bed stupefied, the parchment held loosely between his fingers.

'This was written fourteen months ago,' he said quietly. 'As the Black Prince, father of the present king, lay dying. If the Lord Edward had known this, he would have had John of Gaunt's head on a pole on London Bridge. If it was revealed now there would be a public outcry.'

'So we know the reasons for Springall's death,' Athelstan said, 'but not the hows, the wherefores, and above all the culprit or culprits. Look, Sir John, let's follow the method of the Schools at Oxford. You sit on the bed, I'll sit beside you. You will recite everything you know about each of the four murders, beginning with Sir Thomas Springall's. Though in fact there was another killing, making five in all.' He pointed to the parchment poem. 'The young boy who died here must also be regarded as a victim.'

And so they began, Cranston occasionally pausing for refreshment as he recited in an almost sing-song voice what they knew about Springall's death, and then Brampton's, Vechey's and Allingham's. Athelstan would correct him and make Cranston repeat the list of facts time and again until the coroner, not famous for his patience, shouted: 'Hell's teeth! What are you doing, Brother? We are wasting time! All we are doing is repeating what we already know.'

'Be patient, Sir John,' Athelstan replied, 'Remember, we are looking for a pattern. In logic when you have a problem, the very words of the puzzle contain the answer. There must be a pattern in each of the murders.' He saw Sir John set his mouth and glare from beneath bushy grey eyebrows. 'Look, there is one murder we know very little about – Vechey's. But three, Allingham's, Brampton's and Springall's, we do. There must be common factors, things which link all three. We have already established one: poison. I also suspect Vechey and Brampton were drugged. They would not have allowed people to pluck them up, take them prisoner, tie a noose around their necks and kill them. So we have some matching strands. Let us see if there are more.'

Once again Sir John grudgingly recited the facts they knew. Outside the day drew to a close. Athelstan, now listening with half an ear to Sir John's recitation, looked out of the window and wondered what had happened to Benedicta and Lady Maude. Should they return to escort the ladies? He broke Sir John's concentration by asking but the coroner just glowered.

'The Ladies Benedicta and Maude are well able to look after themselves,' he said. 'You started this,

Brother, so we'll see it through to the bitter end. Moreover,' he smiled, 'I asked the young gallant who was sitting by Benedicta to take care of both ladies. I am sure he will.'

Athelstan ground his teeth and glared at the coroner, but Sir John smiled sweetly back as if innocent of any devious stratagem. Athelstan again made him repeat all they knew, though this time excluding Sir Thomas Springall's murder. Then he walked over to the window and stared down at the chess board. Absentmindedly he began to count the squares, and his heart quickened.

'There is a pattern, Sir John,' he said softly. 'Yes!' He turned, his lean face bright with excitement. 'There is a pattern!'

'You know who the murderer is, don't you? Come on, you bloody friar!' Cranston roared. 'Tell me! I haven't sat here on this bed like a boy in a schoolroom reciting lists of facts for nothing!'

'Tush, Sir John, patience,' Athelstan replied. 'Let me work it into a pattern. Let me get the proper sequence of events, then I shall tell you what I know and the problem will be resolved. But for now you stay here, examine the indenture, reflect on what you have said. I won't be long!'

Before a bemused Cranston could reply, Athelstan had slipped out of the room, walking gingerly across the noisy Nightingale Gallery, down the stairs and out into Cheapside. Just in case he met any of the

Springall household, he went down Friday Street, turning into Bread Street and back up St Mary Le Bow. The church was open. Athelstan went into the nave and sat at the base of a pillar, legs crossed, whilst he stared up at the high altar behind the rood screen. He looked round the cool, beautiful church, at the frescoes on the wall, lectern, and pulpit of exquisitely carved oak. From the stalls in the sanctuary he heard the master assembling the choir, rehearsing the hymns and canticles for the feast of Corpus Christi. Athelstan leaned back, letting his head rest against the coldness of the pillar whilst he stared into the darkness, trying to rearrange what he knew, to make the pattern complete and trap the murderer. This was one occasion when the sons of Cain, the killers, would not turn round and claim with mocking innocence, 'Are we our brother's keepers? We are not responsible because we are innocent,' while the blood of five human beings stained their hands and darkened their souls.

The choir began the beautiful hymn 'Pange Lingua'. Athelstan let his mind and soul be calmed, moved by the rhythmical chanting. At one point the youngest boys, the choir's sopranos, took up the refrain, pure and lucid, filling the entire church with angelic sound.

'*Respice. Respice Domine.* Look back, oh Lord, look back on us!'

Athelstan muttered the words under his breath. 'Look back, oh Lord,' he prayed. 'Give me wisdom and light. Let me plumb the darkness, root out the wickedness. Let those things that were done in the dark of night be revealed for your justice and that of the king in the full light of day.'

Athelstan meditated for an hour. He saw the irony that here he was in a church, the house of God and gate to heaven, thinking about murder. But gradually the pattern was resolved. The culprits were identified, their motives revealed, and he reluctantly admired their deviousness, the sheer wickedness of their plan. He built his own traps, hedging them about, and, when he was ready, returned to the Springall house.

He found Cranston still resting on Sir Thomas's bed, a cup of claret in his hand, softly singing a lullaby. Athelstan could have sworn he was acting as if there was someone else there. As if he was singing to someone he loved. The friar noticed the coroner's eyes were brimming with tears. He looked away, pretending to stare out of the window as he began to summarise his conclusions. Behind him, Cranston regained control of himself. He listened to the friar describe the motive and the identity of the murderers. At first, the coroner rejected everything his assistant said.

'Too ingenious!' he cried. 'Too clever! Too diabolic!'

Athelstan turned. 'Diabolic, yes. But these murders were crafted in the human soul and decided upon by the human mind even if carried out for malicious, devilish purposes. I think I speak the truth, Sir John.'

Cranston stared moodily down at the floorboards, scuffing his boots over the polished surface. Suddenly the Nightingale Gallery outside creaked and sang. Cranston's hand went towards his dagger and Athelstan rapidly approached the door. It was only the old servant, deeper in his cups than Cranston. He staggered and leaned on the door post.

'You have been here a long time, masters. Are you staying? Waiting for Sir Richard?'

'No,' Cranston replied, 'I have told you already. We are here on the regent's orders!' He lifted the wine cup and drained it. 'But I do thank you for your hospitality, sir. I shall remember it.'

'Oh,' Athelstan added, 'is it possible that I could speak to one of the laundresses?'

The servant looked surprised. He blinked but agreed, and some time later ushered a scared girl into the room. She became even more frightened as Athelstan outlined his request and asked her to bring the napkin as soon as possible. When she did, Athelstan poured the dregs of the wine over it, cleaned a dusty part of the room and put it beneath his cloak. The maid servant quickly left. Sir John looked bemused.

'What I have done is vital, Sir John,' Athelstan assured him. 'It may well trap the murderers.'

They left the deserted house, the old manservant locking the door behind them, and went down into a deserted Cheapside. Black rain clouds were scudding in over the Thames. It was dark and some of the merchants had lit the lantern-horns outside their doors, whilst Athelstan glimpsed the beacon light shining red and full in the steeple of St Mary Le Bow. They made their way down Friday Street, Old Fish Street and into the Vintry, and hired a wherry at Queenshithe Wharf to take them along the choppy river to the Savoy Palace. Viewed from the riverbank, John of Gaunt's palatial residence looked magnificent, and even more so tonight with the festivities going on. The windows were lit by the flames of thousands of beeswax candles and, as they approached the main entrance, they heard faint strains of music, chatter, and the sounds of merriment. A burly serjeant-of-arms stopped them, asked their business, and grudgingly let them through into the main courtyard where they were halted by a steward who took them up into the main hall.

Athelstan was dumbfounded by the magnificent spectacle awaiting them: the hall was long, the hammer-beam roof high, whilst every piece of wood-work and stone was covered in the most luxurious velvet and samite hangings, gorgeous banners and hangings of every hue. Down the hall on each side were long trestle tables covered in the costliest silk. Every few feet were huge eight-branched candelabra, each with its own beeswax candles. Above them in the loft the musicians played, though their music had to compete with the noise of the revellers sitting at table.

At the far end, on the dais, Athelstan glimpsed John of Gaunt. On the same table he saw the young king, Chief Justice Fortescue, and some of the leading nobility of the realm. At the table just beneath the dais, running parallel with it, they saw Sir Richard Springall, red-faced and deep in his cups. At his side was Lady Isabella who for that day had cast aside her mourning weeds and wore a pure gold dress with matching veil. Father Crispin and Master Buckingham were also visible, while at the other end of the table were Lady Maude and Benedicta, between them the young nobleman who had made his intentions so blatantly obvious earlier in the day. Lady Maude was looking down the hall, obviously looking out for her husband. Benedicta, cooler and more composed, was listening attentively to some story the nobleman was telling her, though now and again moving slightly away from him as if she had come to resent the young gallant's attentions. The steward was about to announce them, but Athelstan put a hand on his arm.

'No,' he muttered. 'Not now. The feast is in progress.' He looked down at the tablecloths splattered with grease and wine, the platters now cleared. The servants were bringing in bowls of fruit, junkets of cream, plates of thin pastries, sugar-filled doucettes, and jellies formed in exquisite shapes of castles, swans and horses. Soon the banquet would be over. He looked at Sir John. 'There's no point in joining the festivities. It is best if we have no dealings with Sir Richard and other members of his household.'

The coroner, gazing longingly at the jugs of claret, was about to protest.

'Sir John,' Athelstan reminded him, 'we have important business to attend to.'

Cranston sighed, nodded, and turned to the steward, asking him to take them to one of the duke's private chambers. The man looked askance but Cranston insisted.

'Yes, you will, sir,' he repeated. 'You will take us to one of the duke's private chambers here in the palace. Then you will tell your master and Chief Justice Fortescue that we have important matters to relate, matters affecting the crown. You will ask that Sir Richard and his household also join us as soon as the festivities are over.'

Cranston made the man repeat the message as he reluctantly took them out of the main hall and up the wide, spacious stairs to one of the duke's private chambers. Athelstan gazed around and nodded. Yes, this would do. A small fire had been lit in the hearth. The room, possibly used as a chancery by the duke, was dominated by a long table with chairs down either side and a high-backed, throne-like seat at the top. The steward left Cranston and Athelstan, who stood examining the exquisite hangings on the wall and a small cupboard full of manuscripts bound with the costliest leather and vellum. A servant brought them some wine and sugared pastries which Cranston immediately attacked. Another servant entered, a young page who announced in a high, shrill voice that the duke had received Sir John's message and would be with him as soon as dignity and circumstances would allow.

An hour candle placed on the table under the window had burnt a complete ring before Cranston heard footsteps outside. He and Athelstan rose as Gaunt swept into the room. Beside the duke was the young king, a silver chaplet around his head. Uncle and nephew were dressed identically in purple gowns edged with gold. The young king looked serene though Gaunt seemed angry and troubled, as if he resented Cranston's message. He slumped into the chair at the end of the table and ordered a servant to bring in a similar one for his nephew. Chief Justice Fortescue slid in like a spider, scuttling across to sit next to the Duke. He was followed by Sir Richard Springall and his household. The merchant was flushed with drink; he grinned at Cranston and Athelstan as if they were lifelong friends; Dame Ermengilde, her nose in the air, chose to ignore them. Father Crispin and Buckingham smiled wanly whilst Lady Isabella looked decidedly agitated.

'Are we all assembled?' Gaunt asked sardonically.

Chief Justice Fortescue glanced around and nodded. 'Yes, Your Grace, we are all here.'

Athelstan noticed that a burly serjeant-at-arms had just stepped into the room.

'I want this chamber guarded closely!' the regent ordered. 'No one is to leave or enter without my permission. Do you understand?'

The man nodded. Outside Athelstan could hear him shouting orders, the sound of running feet and the clash of arms. He gazed at the assembled company. Sir Richard Springall had sobered up surprisingly quickly. Lady Isabella was looking across at him, nervously twisting her fingers. Dame Ermengilde, even though she was in the presence of royalty, sat staring at the wall opposite her. The rest of them kept their eyes fastened on the duke, waiting to see what lay behind his summons.

Gaunt leaned forward, the jewels on his tanned hands flashing in the candlelight.

'Sir John, coroner of the city, I am pleased to see you. And even though you were not present at the banquet, it is obvious that you have drunk well. I hope your day was a fruitful one?'

Cranston caught the touch of menace in the duke's words and glanced at Athelstan.

The friar acknowledged the regent and the young king. 'My Lord of Gaunt, Your Grace, we were given a commission to investigate the true causes and purposes behind Sir Thomas Springall's death, and in consequence the truth behind other deaths equally unfortunate.' He rose to his feet. 'Your Grace, I ask your indulgence, but I would like us to perform a small mummer's play, a useful introduction to what we are about to declare.'

Gaunt gazed at the friar crossly. 'What is it, Brother?' he asked.

'A game, Uncle!' The young king suddenly spoke up, childish glee replacing the mask of royalty on his face. He clapped his hands.

'Your Grace,' Gaunt smiled thinly at his nephew, 'perhaps you should not be here?'

'Perhaps I should!' the young boy piped back. 'I want to be. It is my right!'

Athelstan was surprised at the precociousness of the child and, despite his tender years, the sway he held over his formidable uncle.

Gaunt sighed. 'Brother, we are in your hands. Though I warn you,' he gestured threateningly, 'don't waste my time or engage us in meddlesome, wasteful tricks. I am here for the truth!'

Chapter 10

Athelstan pointed to the chamber door.

'My Lord of Gaunt, let us pretend that behind that door lies someone you dearly love.'

Gaunt glared back at him.

'The door is locked and you are about to rouse them. What would you do?'

'A simple question! I would try the door, I would knock, I would hammer, I would shout!'

'Thank you, Your Grace. Lady Ermengilde, you heard Father Crispin come up to rouse Sir Thomas that fateful morning. What happened?'

The old dame had caught the drift of Athelstan's words, her face losing some of its haughty composure. She narrowed her eyes. 'I heard him come up. He tried the handle of the door of my son's bed chamber. Then he walked away. He went to find Sir Richard.'

'Now why was that, Father?' Athelstan asked. 'You went up to waken your master – he had asked to be roused early, remember? You went up as anyone would do, you tried the door, but then you went to get his brother. Why did you not try to rouse Sir Thomas Springall yourself? You tried the door but there was no sound from within. Anyone else would have pounded on the door, shouting Sir Thomas's name. You failed to do so. You immediately walked away to rouse Sir Richard. Why?'

'Because I thought that was the best thing to do.'

'It was not the logical thing to do,' Athelstan replied quickly. 'The logical thing was to pound on the door and shout Sir Thomas's name. You did not. It was as if you knew something was wrong.'

The priest swallowed quickly but gazed coolly around the room. 'What are you implying, Brother?'

'At the moment I am implying nothing. Let us proceed a little further. Sir Richard comes upstairs with other members of the household. The door is forced. And inside?'

'Why,' the priest replied, 'my master, Sir Thomas Springall, lying on the bed, poisoned.'

'And what happened then? Precisely?'

'I went across to look at Sir Thomas.'

'No, he did not!' Sir Richard thrust himself forward. 'I did that. You came into the room with me, but I did that!'

'So what *did* you do, Father?' Athelstan continued.

'I just stood there.'

'No, you did something else.'

'Oh, yes. I picked up the wine cup and smelt it. I took it over to the window to look at the contents because its odour was strange.'

'And when you went to the window, you passed the chess board. Then what?'

'I pronounced the cup was poisoned. The rest you know.'

'And how were you dressed?'

'I told you. I had been outside, visiting the stables.'

'You were wearing gloves? A cloak?'

'Yes, I was.'

'I will tell you this, priest,' Athelstan replied, 'you wore the gloves for a purpose. You see, you knew that Sir Thomas was already dead before you went into that chamber. You had arranged it that way. The wine cup was not poisoned. You took it to the window and poured in the potion which you had concealed in your glove. As you passed the chess board you took a piece from it, the bishop, the reason being that it was heavily coated with a certain poison.'

Father Crispin's face was marble white. He shook his head wordlessly.

'This is what happened,' Athelstan continued. 'On the afternoon of the banquet, you engaged Sir Thomas in a game of chess. You played with all your skill and finesse and managed to trap Sir Thomas. The game broke off just before the meal. You knew how Sir Thomas hated to be beaten, you admitted that yourself. He would be absorbed in the moves so that when the game recommenced, he could try to escape from the trap posed by your pieces. Now, I put this to you, sir. Just before the banquet, as people were coming down, you went up to Sir Thomas's room, unnoticed by anyone else and, choosing a chess piece, coated it thickly with poison. Some time later, Brampton took up the wine cup.

'After the feast was over, Sir Thomas retired to his chamber, locking the door behind him. Then he did what you intended him to do, what any good chess player would have done. He went across to the chess board, trying to work out the best method to escape the trap you had placed him in. He picked up the bishop, the piece under threat, moving it around the board, attempting to find a way out. Like anyone who is deeply puzzled, he would raise his fingers to his lips. Little did he know that every time he did so, he was poisoning himself. It would not have taken long. The poisons you had bought from the apothecary were potent. Sir Thomas may have felt strange from the first symptoms; he left the chess board and went to his bed where he later died.

'The next morning you came up to his chamber, gloved, because you knew you would have to touch the poison yourself. But you needed witnesses, you wanted to make it very clear that the blame lay with Brampton. Sir Richard entered the room with you, as did other members of the household. Like any people breaking into a room and finding someone unexpectedly dead, they gathered round the corpse. Meanwhile you had removed the chess piece, poisoned the wine cup and placed it back on the table.'

'The cup now seemed the bringer of death and the blame was placed on Brampton.'

The priest regained his wits. 'That's impossible!' he said. 'How could I know that Sir Thomas would touch the chess board after he had retired for that night?'

'Oh, but you did,' Cranston broke in. 'You did, you admitted as much yourself. You said that Sir Thomas could not leave the chess board alone. And the only people that touched the cup were Brampton, Sir Thomas and yourself. Only after that was the poison detected in it.'

'And I suppose that I am responsible for Brampton's murder?'

'Yes.' Cranston took up the tale. 'My good secretarius here, my faithful clerk, has established that Brampton probably went back to his room after the banquet had begun. He felt hurt by Sir Thomas's accusation that he had been meddling with his private papers. Now, of course, Brampton had not. *You* had. However, we will return to that. You probably drugged Brampton.'

'Drugged!' the priest snapped. 'Brampton wasn't drugged! That's nonsense!'

He looked around the room, appealing for support, but Athelstan noticed how the others were beginning to distance themselves from the priest. Chief Justice Fortescue looked steadily at the tabletop. Gaunt had a smile on his twisted lips. The young king seemed totally absorbed. Cranston shook his head.

'It's no use lying, murderer,' he snapped. 'You know Brampton had drunk deeply that day. A servant

275

told us as much. And you, Lady Isabella, didn't you say your husband had broached his best cask of Bordeaux and that you sent a cup to Brampton as a peace offering?'

'Yes, I did,' she murmured. 'No! I sent the cup up—' she pointed at the priest '—but you poured it, Father Crispin. Yes, it was *your* idea. It was drugged!' she exclaimed.

'That night,' Athelstan interrupted, 'after the rest of the household retired, Father Crispin went up to Brampton's room. You are a strong young man, Crispin. Brampton was small and light; he lived on the second storey of the house, very near the stairs to the garret. You took him off his bed and carried him up, half sat him on the table, fastened the waiting noose round his neck and left him to hang, God save his soul! But poor Brampton knew for a while that he was choking to death. He grabbed the rope, but it was useless. His breath was choked off and his unshriven soul fled into the darkness.'

Athelstan went and stood over the priest. 'You are steeped in mortal sin,' he murmured. 'Your soul is red, scarlet and wounded. You killed that man but you made a mistake! Why should Brampton walk up to the garret with his boots off. And, if he had worn them, he would have kicked them off in his death throes.' Athelstan bent down, his face only inches from Crispin's. 'But let us say he did go up without his boots. The garret was dirty, there was broken glass on the floor, yet the soles of Brampton's feet, even after his corpse had been cut down, were clean and unscarred. Why? Because his feet never touched the ground.'

'Vechey was murdered too, wasn't he?' Lady Isabella stammered.

'Yes,' Athelstan replied. 'And do you know why? When the door to your husband's chamber was forced, Vechey came in. At one point he must have looked at the chess board after Crispin had removed the poisoned piece to clean it.'

'Of course,' Dame Ermengilde trumpeted. 'That's why Vechey kept talking about there being only thirty-one. He noticed the missing piece. Vechey always coveted the Syrians!'

'And then the piece was returned,' Athelstan answered, 'which only perplexed him further. Nevertheless, Vechey's sharp eyes cost him his life and he, too, was marked down for murder lest he voice his doubts.'

'God knows how you managed that murder!' Cranston bawled. 'The red-haired whore may have been a lure in your pay. It may, cunning priest, even have been you in disguise. I wonder, a thorough search being made, if we wouldn't find a red wig and dress in your possession. But, there again, you made a mistake. Vechey was probably drugged or knocked on the head. You hung him up under an arch of London Bridge, but the water level would have made such a death impossible. You hoped no one would notice that.'

'Wait!' Crispin cried. 'You allege I had the poison, but you know a lady very similar to our Lady Isabella in dress and appearance bought the identical poison from the apothecary, Simon Foreman!'

'Yes,' Cranston said, 'and that's your third mistake. I did ask Lady Isabella about that, but you were not in the room. Remember, we asked you to withdraw? Lady Isabella, Sir Richard, is that correct?'

Both nodded their heads.

'And did you ever tell the priest about my question?'

Again, both shook their heads wordlessly.

'You couldn't have overhead!' Dame Ermengilde snapped. 'Because I stood near the door of the hall. I tried to listen but I couldn't hear anything.'

'The only way you could know,' Athelstan murmured, 'was because you dressed in clothes secretly borrowed from Lady Isabella's wardrobe. Your head was hidden by a red wig as well as a hood. You went to Nightshade House and bought the poison.' Athelstan sipped from his wine cup.

'You would enjoy that, wouldn't you?'

The priest refused to answer.

'But such subterfuge!' Lady Isabella cried.

'Oh, Crispin planned well. One of Brampton's buttons was placed near your husband's manuscripts to start the tragedy. However, in case something went wrong and the poison was traced...'

'What better person than you to implicate, Lady Isabella?' Cranston observed. 'After all, you were playing the two-backed beast with your husband's brother!'

Lady Isabella looked away whilst Crispin placed his head in his hands. Dame Ermengilde turned to Cranston, her eyes full of malice.

'You are not such a fool, Master Coroner. But haven't you forgotten a few things? If my son had touched the poisoned chess pieces, his hands would have been stained. And how do you explain Allingham's death?'

Athelstan looked down at the priest. Father Crispin raised his head and stared unblinkingly back.

'Remember, our murderer also bestowed the rites of the Church. He made sure that the hands of both Sir Thomas Springall and Master Allingham were washed before he anointed them with holy oils.'

'That's right,' Sir Richard whispered. 'And the anointing took place immediately!'

'So there was no stain,' Athelstan continued conversationally, 'as in all his murders, no real evidence. You are a killer, Father. An assassin. And we know why. You remember the young page boy who fell from the window? Sir Thomas lusted after him, and found you wrote a love poem to him. We have seen it. I suspect you tried to seduce the boy. God knows what happened. Tell us, Father, did he jump because he was frightened or did you push him?'

The priest glared back at him but made no answer.

'I think Sir Thomas knew the truth but dared not accuse you openly. After all, he was guilty of the same sin of sodomy as you. Of course, being a chaplain, you were privy to the secrets of others. So what Sir Thomas did was take his revenge through the carving, the panel he was going to use in the coronation pageant and later hang in the chapel.' Athelstan glanced at Sir Richard. 'Do you remember the carving? What was it of?'

'A shoemaker being dragged away by devils.'

'Did you ever look at the shoemaker's feet?'

'No.'

Cranston banged the heel of his boot on the floor.

'Poor Father Crispin, always hobbling around, using his injury as a banner. But when he so chooses, he puts on his boots with their raised heel – and, behold, he can walk like any of us. That's true, isn't it, Priest? You were out riding the day Allingham died?'

Father Crispin dismissed Cranston's accusation with a flicker of his eyes.

'Sir John is correct,' Athelstan took up the story. 'A priest can go anywhere, be it in his master's chamber to poison a chess piece, around the house at the dead of night to comfort poor Brampton, to say prayers at St Mary Le Bow... whereas in fact on the night Vechey died, Father Crispin disguised himself as the red-haired whore and went hunting his prey amongst the riverside stews.' Athelstan paused and looked quickly at Fortescue. 'I told Sir John that there was more than one murderer. In a sense I was correct. You are two people, Father, the hobbling priest and the cunning assassin.'

Athelstan noticed how the Chief Justice's face had become so pale it looked as if he was going to vomit.

'Of course, Crispin,' Athelstan continued, 'you had your accomplice. Someone you had met at your master's table. Someone who could tell you where we went so you could have assassins lying in waiting. You remember the gospel, Father, and the man who claimed his name was Legion, so many devils possessed him? He would recognise you, Priest. You murdered for revenge, for profit, but also for the sheer malicious delight of plot and counter-plot.'

'What has that got to do with the carving in the Springall yard?' Gaunt sharply interrupted.

Athelstan looked at Sir Richard.

'You should have examined that carving,' he remarked. 'Especially the shoemaker. He is very like our Father Crispin. He has a clubbed foot.'

Athelstan ignored Lady Isabella's gasp. Instead he looked up at young King Richard, who seemed fascinated by the priest, whilst Gaunt was now staring at Fortescue out of the corner of his eye.

'And Father, who is the patron saint of shoe-makers?'

Athelstan admired the priest's composure. Not a muscle twitched in that gaunt, haunted face.

'Come, Father, you know. Crispin Crispianus! We celebrate his feast in October. Sir Thomas was mocking you. The insult would be carried throughout the length and breadth of London and afterwards it would ridicule you every time you entered the small chapel in Sir Thomas's house. Perhaps one day a more astute person might notice it. Allingham certainly did, didn't he, Father? He began to wonder, as well as to remember Vechey's absorption with the number thirty-one!'

Cranston belched and rose to his feet unbidden, as if he had forgotten he was in the presence of royalty.

'My clerk,' he announced grandly, 'is correct. So you, Father, the master poisoner, struck again. You bought your poisons from Foreman, mixing them deliberately so the wine cup smelt rank and offensive, to ensure Brampton got the blame. But Allingham was different. He took a poison which was more difficult to trace. After his mid-day meal, Allingham went back to his chamber and fell asleep. What he did not know was that the handle of his door had been smeared with poison. The same trick you had played on Sir Thomas, but you were sure it would work again.'

Cranston stopped to refill his cup, rather shakily so the wine spilled over on the table. But the coroner, in full flow and bent on refreshment, didn't give a fig.

'Brother Athelstan,' he announced expansively, 'will summarise my conclusions.'

Athelstan hid his smile. Cranston was amusing but the hard-faced priest, the wolf in sheep's clothing, was not.

'You see, first, Allingham had a nervous gesture. Do you remember? His hands were constantly at his lips, fluttering up and down like a butterfly. During his final sleep, Father Crispin here probably locked him in his chamber. Allingham wakes, and finds there is no key. Nervous and agitated, he tries the door; all the time his death-bearing fingers are going to his mouth. He feels ill, goes back to the bed where he collapses and dies. The door is forced, the priest makes sure he is there, the key is dropped on the ground. Naturally, people would think it fell due to the door's being forced. Of course, Crispin here acts the perplexed innocent. He poses the question, if Allingham had a seizure, why did he not try and open the door? Strangely enough, while trying the lock, our murderer holds a napkin which he had been using to mop up some wine he had spilt. He examines the handle, using the napkin to gain a better grip. Of course, what he is really doing is cleaning the poison off.' Athelstan dug beneath his robe and brought out the soiled cloth he had begged from the laundress. 'This is the cloth.'

'It can't be!' Fortescue suddenly shouted.

'Shut up!' the priest yelled at him, his eyes and face full of hatred. 'Shut up, you idiot!'

'Why can't it be?' Cranston asked softly. 'Isn't it strange that you should remember what happened to an innocent napkin?'

Athelstan held his breath. Would a confession come?

'I only did what he asked,' Crispin whispered.

'Who?' Cranston asked softly.

'Fortescue, of course!'

The Chief Justice looked up, his face white with terror.

'I asked the priest to get the secrets Sir Thomas held. I did not plan murder.'

'Perhaps not,' Athelstan replied. 'But your accomplice, Father Crispin, did. On your orders, Chief Justice Fortescue, he tried to find out Sir Thomas Springall's secrets. Sir Thomas, a canny man, knew his private accounts had been scrutinised and the blame was put on Brampton. However, Sir Thomas and Brampton may have reached an accord and questions been asked, so Father Crispin plotted Springall's death. Brampton would be blamed after his supposed suicide and the way left clear for you to search for Sir Thomas's secret.'

John of Gaunt suddenly stood up. 'Sir Coroner, do your duty!' he ordered.

Cranston waddled round the table. 'Father Crispin, I arrest you in the name of the king for the dreadful crimes of treason, homicide and sedition!'

The priest gazed stonily back and continued to do so when the burly serjeant-at-arms, summoned by Gaunt, tied his thumbs together behind his back.

'Wait!'

Athelstan walked over to Fortescue. He noticed how Buckingham was quivering with fright, his face drenched in sweat. The effete young secretarius would never forget this day.

'Chief Justice Fortescue,' Athelstan murmured, 'you are the king's highest law officer. Why did you act as you did? Was it the lust for power, wealth, or the desire to control the regent? You knew Springall held some great secret and, in one of your visits to his household, made a pact with this priest, this limb of Satan.'

Fortescue tried to reply but the words stuck in his throat.

'Don't you realise, my Lord Chief Justice, that when you make a pact with the devil, you lose your soul?'

'I am no murderer,' he muttered.

Athelstan turned back to the priest. 'You murdered the page boy, Eudo, didn't you? You sent the assassins after Sir John and myself. You were the red-haired woman, as well as the scarlet whore.'

Father Crispin laughed and, bringing his head back, spat full in Athelstan's face.

'Ask me in hell, Brother!' he shrieked. 'When we both dance with the devil!'

He was still laughing like a madman when the door closed behind him.

'I did not plan murder. I was curious but I am no murderer,' Fortescue proclaimed, half rising from his chair.

'In forty-eight hours,' Gaunt snapped, 'I shall send soldiers to your house. If you haven't abjured the realm by then, I will arrest you, Fortescue, for treason! You may well rot a long time before I gather the evidence to try you!'

Fortescue fled from the room.

Athelstan studied the duke, noting the beads of sweat on his face, the agitation in his eyes. He looked almost pleadingly at Cranston.

'Sir Richard Springall,' the coroner barked, 'and Lady Isabella, you had best leave now, together with your household. If you still wonder about the Bible texts Sir Thomas quoted, examine the posts of his bed which you desecrated!'

The merchant, Lady Isabella, a nervous Buckingham and the now not so proud Dame Ermengilde hastily left the room, cowed by the dreadful things they had seen and heard. Cranston followed them out and muttered a command to the guard there. He had no sooner re-entered than the young king rose to his feet.

'What was Sir Thomas's secret?' he asked.

'Nephew!' Gaunt's voice was harsh and brittle. 'Your Grace,' he stammered, 'I think you should leave. These matters are not for tender minds.'

King Richard turned, a stubborn look on his thin, pale face.

'Your Grace,' Gaunt repeated, 'these matters do not concern you. I must insist. Sir John, Brother Athelstan, you are to say no word!'

The young king walked towards the door. With his gloved fingers on the handle, he stopped and beckoned Athelstan over. The friar went and bent so that the king could whisper in his ear.

'Brother,' he hissed, 'when I grow up, I will make you an abbot! And you will take my side when…' The young king's voice trailed off.

'When what, Your Grace?' he murmured.

Richard put his lips closer against the friar's ears. 'When I murder my uncle!' he whispered.

Athelstan stared into those childlike yet totally chilling blue eyes. The young king smiled and kissed him on both cheeks before disappearing through the half-open door, a boy going out to play. Athelstan rose and closed the door.

'What did he say, Brother?'

'Nothing, My Lord, some childish game.'

Gaunt grinned to himself as if savouring some private joke and stretched out his hand.

'The indenture. You have it?'

'Yes, My Lord.'

Gaunt snapped his fingers. 'Give it to me!'

Cranston handed both it and the love poem over. Gaunt scrutinised them carefully, crumpled them up in his hand and watched the flames of the fire burn them to black feathery ash.

'You know what it said?'

Cranston chewed his lip, not replying.

'Yes, My Lord, we do.' Athelstan sat down uninvited, not caring for idle ceremony. 'My Lord, we are tired. We know what the document says, but it does not concern us. Fourteen months ago, your brother, the Black Prince, the young king's father, was dying. You drew up an indenture with Sir Thomas Springall in which he promised you vast sums of money to raise troops. As surety you offered the crown jewels, the ring, the orb, the sceptre, and the crown of Edward the Confessor. They were not yours to offer. If your brother had known, if your father, the old king, had even suspected, you might well have lost your head. If the Commons found out now, they would suspect you of plotting against the king. If your noble brothers and the other great lords, Gloucester and Arundel, even glimpsed that document, they would tear you to pieces!'

'I was worried,' Gaunt haltingly replied. 'My brother was dying, my father senile, young Richard sickly. This realm needs strong government. Yes, if necessary, I would have seized the crown.'

'And now, My Lord?' Cranston asked.

'I am the king's most loyal servant,' Gaunt answered glibly. 'I am indebted to you, Sir John. I will not forget it.'

'Then, My Lord, we bid you goodnight.'

'Sir John,' Gaunt called after them, 'I will see you later on this matter. Brother Athelstan, ask any favour you wish.'

'Yes, My Lord. I would like some silver for my church and, secondly, a pension for a poor woman, widow of Hob the grave-digger.'

Gaunt grinned. 'So little for so much! See my clerks. It will be done.'

Athelstan and Cranston strode out along the now emptying corridors of the Savoy Palace, down through the heavily perfumed garden and on to the riverside.

Athelstan rubbed his eyes wearily. 'The murderer made one mistake and so did we, Sir John. First, I suspect Father Crispin waited until the tide fell before stringing the hapless corpse up.'

'But he told us he was gone on errands?'

'And that's where we made our mistake, Lord Coroner. We didn't ask when he returned, not that it would have made any difference in the Springall house where Sir Richard and Lady Isabella were lost in themselves and Allingham led his own lonely exist-ence. Moreover, I am sure the priest had ways of sneaking in and out of such a large mansion without being noticed.'

'Do you think Crispin will hang?' asked Cranston.

Athelstan shook his head.

'Fortescue asked him to get the information but then, as we know, matters got out of hand. Fortescue will go abroad and gain employment in some foreign court. Father Crispin, being a priest, will probably be immured in a monastery for the rest of his life and eat the bitter bread of repentance.' He crossed himself. 'Gaunt would never dare bring either of them to trial. But I suspect, within a year, Fortescue and our evil priest will both suffer some "accident" and answer for their crimes before God's tribunal.' Suddenly he remembered Benedicta. 'Sir John!' he cried. 'Your lady wife? Benedicta?'

Cranston turned and looked slyly at him.

'I asked the captain,' he said, 'to have two of his men escort the Lady Maude home. Benedicta was invited to go with her, but whether she did or not...' His voice trailed off.

Athelstan stared up at the sky, now blood red as the sun began to set. He felt the evening breeze cool his face. He hardly spared a thought for assassins steeped in murder and ambition. How crimson was his own soul? Had not he too committed a secret sin?

'What shall we do, Brother?' Cranston interrupted.

Athelstan looked at that fat, friendly face, the good-humoured smile, the compassion in the bleary, drink-sodden eyes.

'You are a good man, Sir John.'

The coroner looked away.

'And I shall tell you what we shall do,' Athelstan continued, taking him by the elbow. 'We shall celebrate!'

He led Sir John along the waterside into the nearest tavern where he secured the best seats near the window. Athelstan raised a hand and called the landlord over.

'I want a jug of your best Bordeaux and two deep cups. My friend and I are going to get drunk!'

Sir John clapped his hands like a child, crowing with excitement. They drank like parched men. They heard the chimes of midnight and saw the stars come out before reeling back into the city and the warm security of Cranston's house. The Lady Maude screeched how she had heard of good seed falling amongst briars but never of good men falling from grace amongst friars! Cranston told her to shut up, announced he was going to give up ale and become a Dominican. He was still grinning beatifically when he passed out. Lady Maude knelt near her husband's porpoise-like body and made him comfortable for the night. She talked softly, keening over him as if he was Abelard and she Heloise. Love is strange, Athelstan thought, and has so many forms!

Late the next morning, thick-headed and a little wiser, Athelstan went back to his church. He said Mass with no congregation present and sang his matins, wondering what had happened to Benedicta. He had lacked the courage to question Lady Maude. He was just finishing a psalm when the door opened behind him. He knew Benedicta was standing there as she always did, leaning against the pillar at the back of the church. She called his name softly, once, twice, but Athelstan did not turn. He heard her footsteps and the door close behind her. The friar remembered the words of the poet: 'When a heart breaks, worlds shatter without a sound.'

–

Father Prior came to visit Athelstan, appearing suddenly like a thief in the night. He was courteous enough, for he had also visited Sir John Cranston to inquire how Athelstan was progressing, and the good coroner had escorted him across London Bridge to Southwark to see. Of course, Athelstan had had some warning: Cranston sent ahead Walt, son of Lionel the hangman, to advise him of the prior's intended arrival. Athelstan hastily rounded up some of his parishioners, a not too difficult task as they constantly loitered around the steps of the church, each involved in his or her own nefarious activities.

Cecily the courtesan brushed and scrubbed the porch, while Watkin did his best to clean some of the dirt from the nave and refilled the holy water stoups which the children always drank from. Athelstan had just preached a sermon on how men and women were all God's flowers, some being roses, others bluebells. He'd hoped to convince his parishioners that God loved their differences and that a garden full of roses might be very pleasant but also very boring. The sermon was difficult to give as Benedicta persisted in kneeling in front of him, staring up with those beautiful eyes. She would have resembled the holy Agatha had it not been for the laughter lines round her mouth.

At last Father Prior arrived with his clerks, secretarius, sacristan and other officials. Cranston was stone sober, sitting on his horse like a Solomon come to judgement. Athelstan's parishioners thronged round; Orme, one of the many sons of Watkin, thought Father Prior was the Pope but Cecily the courtesan loudly proclaimed he was the bishop. Athelstan shooed them away and brought his guests into the church whilst Crim and Dyke guarded the horses. Father Prior's retainers amused themselves by looking round. It didn't take them long and Athelstan saw the snotty-nosed sacristan laughing at his pathetic attempts to turn this church into a house of God. But who cared for his opinion? thought Athelstan. Perhaps someone should remind him that it all began in a manger, and the stable in Bethlehem had no fine paintings. Father Prior, however, was kind; he sat opposite Athelstan on the other of the church's two benches and gently questioned him on his doings over the last few months. Cranston sat beside him, staring up at the ceiling. Father Prior heard the friar out before taking him by the hand.

'Brother Athelstan,' he said, 'if you wish, you may come back to the Mother House. Your work and your penance are over.' He turned to the coroner. 'What do you think, Sir John?'

Cranston smiled and shrugged. 'He's a better priest,' he quipped, 'than he is a coroner's clerk! I think it best he should return.'

His eyes refused to meet Athelstan's.

The prior nodded, rose, and patted Athelstan on the shoulder.

'I have to go somewhere else,' he said. 'Sir John has kindly agreed to escort me. It's only a short distance. We shall return within the hour and receive your answer then.'

He walked out of the church, his black and white robe billowing behind him. Cranston did not spare Athelstan a second glance as he waddled out. A moment later Athelstan heard him roaring to Cecily the courtesan that he didn't care how pretty her arse was, she was to get out of his saddle! Father Prior's retainers, eager to leave, needed no second invitation. Athelstan heard their horses clatter off and told Watkin to guard the church door and leave him alone.

'Are you leaving us, Father?' the man asked anxiously.

Athelstan couldn't answer. He shut the door, barred it, and went to sit on the sanctuary steps. What should he do? On the one hand, he was glad Father Prior had come to take him back, but on the other, what would happen to his parishioners? Watkin's bevy of children? The youngest, Edmund, seemed a clever boy. If schooled properly, he might become a clerk. And Cecily the courtesan? What would happen if he no longer gave her pennies for cleaning the church? And Benedicta? He shut his eyes and tried to expunge her face from his mind. He prayed for a sign. The good Lord would surely guide him. He opened his eyes, got up and noticed the candle, the one Benedicta always lit in front of the Madonna. Athelstan went across and stared down at it. Only then did he notice the rose, a small white one, placed at the foot of the statue. He had his answer.

Athelstan was waiting for Father Prior when he and his party came up the lane and stopped outside the church. Athelstan took his superior's horse by the bridle and looked up into the prior's kindly face. He ignored Cranston's glare.

'Do I have your answer, Brother Athelstan?'

'Yes, Father Prior,' he replied. 'I would like to stay here until I am as good a coroner's clerk as I am a priest!'

'You are sure, Brother?'

'Yes, Father, I am sure.'

The prior smiled.

'So be it,' he murmured. He sketched the sign of the cross in the air above Athelstan's head, bade him adieu and urged his horse forward. Athelstan waited till the sound of the horses faded before staring at Cranston, who was surreptitiously wiping his eyes on the cuff of his jerkin.

'God's bones, Athelstan!' he bellowed. 'I have never been so sober for so long in my life! Now I am so hot, even my eyes are sweating.'

He looked at Athelstan mischievously. 'Perhaps a little refreshment?'

'God save us all!' Athelstan muttered, and walked back up the steps of his church, leaving Cranston bellowing after him.

The House
of the
Red Slayer

To Jeffrey Norwood of Tower Books, Chico, California, USA.
A good and loyal friend.

Prologue

June 1362

Murder had been planned, foul and bloody, by a soul as dark as midnight. Only the searing sun and the glassy, wind-free waves of the Middle Sea would bear silent witness to Murder's impending approach.

The day had started hot and by noon the heat hung like a blanket around the three-master-carrack out of Famagusta in Cyprus. The sails drooped limp, the pitch and tar melted between the mildewed planks. On board, the passengers – pilgrims, merchants, travellers and tinkers – sheltered in whatever shade they could find. Some told their rosary beads; others, their red-rimmed eyes shaded against the sunlight, searched the skies for the faintest whisper of wind. The decks of the *Saint Mark* were hot to the touch; even the crew hid from the glare and heat of the sun. A look-out dozed high in the cross yard. Above his head a silver St Christopher medal nailed to the mast caught the dazzling sunlight and sent it back like a prayer for shade and a strong, cooling breeze.

Beneath the look-out, at the foot of the mast, dozed a knight clad in a white linen shirt and sweat-stained hose pushed into leather boots, which he moved restlessly. The knight wiped the sweat from his brow and scratched his black beard which ran from ear to ear. He looked towards a young boy, sheltering in the shadows of the bulwarks, who gazed in round-eyed wonderment at the armour piled there: mailed shirt, gauntlets, breastplate and hauberk. What caught the boy's attention was the livery of white cotton surcoat with a crude but huge red cross painted in the middle. The boy peered at the knight, his hands going out to touch the wire-coiled handle of the great, two-edged sword.

'Touch it, boy,' the knight murmured, white teeth flashing in his sunburned face. 'Go on, touch it if you want.'

The boy did so, his face wreathed in smiles.

'You want to be a knight, boy?'

'Yes, sir, a crusader though I am an orphan now,' the child replied seriously.

The knight grinned but his face grew sombre when he glanced at the poop. He had seen the helmsman call the captain; now both were staring out to sea. The captain looked anxious. Doffing his great, broad-brimmed hat, he stamped the deck and the knight heard his murmured curses. Above him the look-out suddenly yelled: 'I see ships, no sails, fast approaching!'

His cry roused the vessel. Boats with no sails skimming across the sea could only be a Moorish corsair. The people on the deck stirred, children cried, men and women shouted. There was a patter of hardened feet on ladders as both soldiers and sailors roused themselves. The chorus of groans grew louder.

'No sails!' a soldier cried. 'They must be galleys!'

The clamour stilled as fear of death replaced resentment against the hot searing rays of the sun. The day would die, darkness would come and the air would cool, but the green-bannered, rakish-oared galleys of the corsairs

2

would not disappear. They slunk round the Greek Islands like ravenous wolves and, if they closed, there would be no escape.

Genoese crossbowmen began to appear, heads covered in white woollen scarves, their huge arbalests bobbing on their backs; behind them ran boys with quivers full of jagged-edged bolts.

'One galley!' the look-out screamed. 'No, two! No, four! Bearing north by north-east!'

Sailors, passengers and soldiers ran to the rails, making the ship dip like a hawk.

'Back to your posts!' The puce-faced captain scampered down the ladder of the poop. 'Boson!' he roared. 'Armaments out! Crossbowmen to the poop!'

Again there was a rush; huge buckets of seawater were quickly placed round the deck alongside barrels of hard grey sand. Sailors and soldiers roared oaths at the frightened passengers, ordering them down into the stinking, fetid darkness below decks. The knight stirred as the captain approached.

'Galleys,' the seaman murmured. 'Lord help us – so many!' He looked up at the blue sky. 'We cannot escape. One might not attack, but four...'

'Will you fight?' the knight asked.

The captain spread his hands. 'They may not challenge us,' he replied despairingly. 'They could stand off and just take a levy.'

The knight nodded. He knew the sailor was lying. He turned to the small boy now sidling up beside him.

'A good day to die,' the knight whispered. 'Help me arm.'

The lad ran to the bulwarks and staggered back under the load of the heavy mailed shirt. The knight looked around as he dressed for battle. The crew had done everything they could. Now there was a deathly hush, broken only by the slap of water against the ship's sides and the growing murmur from the approaching, dark-shaped galleys.

'Bearers of death,' the knight murmured.

The captain heard him and spun round. 'Why so many?' he asked, perplexed. 'It's as if they knew we were here.'

The knight struggled into the mailed shirt and clasped the leather sword belt around his waist. 'Your cargo?'

The captain shrugged. 'Passengers,' he replied. 'Barrels of fruit, some pipes of wine, a few ells of cloth.'

'No treasure?'

The captain sneered and went back to search the sky for a breath of wind but the golden dazzle of the sun only mocked his anxious scrutiny. The knight studied the galleys, long, black and hawkish. On their decks he glimpsed the massed troops in their yellow cotton robes and white turbans. He stiffened and narrowed his eyes.

'Janissaries!'

The boy looked up. 'What, Master?'

'By the Bones!' the knight replied. 'What are elite troops, the cream of the Muslim Horde, doing packed in galleys hunting a ship which bears nothing but wine and fruit?'

The boy looked up mutely and the knight patted his head.

'Stay with me, lad,' he whispered. 'Stay beside me, and if I fall, show no fear. It's your best chance of life.'

The galleys swept in and the knight smelt the foul stench from the hundreds of sweating slaves who manned the oars. He heard the Moorish captain's commands, the

4

harsh Arabic syllables carrying clear across the water. The oars flashed up, white and dripping, like hundreds of spears as the galleys surrounded the becalmed ship. One took up position on the stem, another on the prow, with a third and fourth huge galley to either side. The captain of the *Saint Mark* wiped his sweating face with the cuff of his jerkin.

'They might not attack,' he whispered. He turned and the knight saw the relief in his eyes. 'They wish to talk.'

Agile as a monkey, the captain scrambled back on to the poop. The galley to starboard moved closer and the knight saw the brilliant liveries of a group of Moorish officers. One of these climbed on to the side of the galley.

'You are the *Saint Mark* from Famagusta?' he shouted.

'Yes,' the captain answered. 'We carry nothing but passengers and dried fruit. There is a truce,' he pleaded. 'Your Caliph has sworn oaths.'

The Moorish officer clasped two of the upraised oars to steady himself.

'You lie!' he screamed back. 'You carry treasure – treasure plundered from our Caliph! Hand it over, and let us search your ship for the culprit who stole it.'

'We have no treasure,' the captain whined back.

The Moorish officer jumped down. One beringed hand sliced the air, a guttural order was issued. The captain of the *Saint Mark* turned and looked despairingly at the knight and, as he did so, both he and the helmsman dropped under the hail of arrows which poured in from the galleys. The knight smiled, closed the visor of his helmet and pulled the young boy closer beside him. He grasped his great two-edged sword and placed his back against the mast.

'Yes,' he whispered, 'it's a good day to die.'

The kettledrums in the galleys beat out the glamour of war, cymbals clashed, gongs sounded. The Genoese archers on the merchantman did their best but the galleys closed in and the yellow-robed, drug-emboldened Janissaries poured across the decks of the *Saint Mark*. Here and there, pilgrims and merchants fought and died in small groups. Individuals tried to escape into the darkness below; the Janissaries followed and the blood poured like water through the tar-edged planks of the ship. But the real struggle swirled around the mast where the knight stood, feet planted slightly apart. His great sword scythed the air until the gore swilled ankle-deep, causing further assailants to slip and slide as they tried to close for the kill. Beside the knight, the young boy, his face alive with the excitement of battle, screamed encouragement but no man could resist such a force forever. Soon the fighting died and the galleys drew off, their sterns packed with prisoners and plunder. The *Saint Mark*, fire licking at its timbers, drifted gently on a strengthening breeze until it became one blazing funeral pyre. When darkness fell, it had sunk. Here and there a body still bobbed on the surface, the only trace that Murder had passed that way.

December 1377

A murderously cold wind swept the snow across London with dagger-like gusts of ice and hail. At first it fell in a few white flakes, then thick and heavy, like God's grace pouring from heaven to cover the wounds of that sombre city. The chroniclers in the monasteries on the outskirts of London tried to warm their cold fingers as they squatted in freezing carrels, writing that the terrible weather was God's judgment on the city.

The snow continued to fall, God's judgment or not, to carpet the stinking streets, and the mounds of shit in the lay stalls near the Thames where river pirates, hanging from the low scaffolds, turned hard and black as the river water froze. In savagely cold December, the heavy frost slipped into the city like an assassin to slay the beggars huddled in their rags. The lepers crouching in their filth outside Smithfield cried and moaned as the frost bit their open wounds. Aged, raddled whores were found frosty-faced, cold and dead on the corner of Cock Lane. The streets were empty, and even the rats could not forage; the huge piles of refuse and the open sewers which ran down the middle of every street, usually full and wet with human slime, froze to rock-hard ice.

The blizzards hid the sky and made the nights as black as hell. No God-fearing soul went abroad, especially in Petty Wales and East Smithfield, the area around the Great Tower whose snow-capped turrets thrust defiantly up into the dark night sky. Guards on the ice-covered parapets of the fortress gave up their watch and crouched behind the walls. No sentry stood near the portcullis because the locks and chains had frozen iron hard, and who could open them?

Yet even on a balmy summer's day, the Tower would be avoided. Old hags whispered that the place was the devil's work, and the black ravens, which swooped around its grim turrets, flocks of devils seeking human souls. The crones claimed human blood had been mixed in the mortar of its walls and that beneath its rocky foundations lay the skeletons of human sacrifices murdered by the great Caesar when he first built the fortress. Others, the few who could read, dismissed such stories as nonsense: the Tower and its great White Keep had been built by William the Conqueror to overawe London, and they scoffed at stories told to frighten the children.

Nevertheless, the old hags were correct: the Tower had its macabre secrets. Beneath one of its walls ran cold, green-slimed passageways. Torches, old and blackening, hung listlessly from sconces rusting on the walls. No one had been down there for years, a mysterious warren of tunnels even the soldiers never frequented. Three dungeons were there but only two doors and in the central cell, a square black box of a room, sprawled a decaying skeleton. There was no witness to what it had been when the flesh hung plump on the bones and the blood ran like hot wine through heart and brain. The skeleton was yellowing now; a rat scurried through the rib cage and poked fruitlessly at the empty eye-sockets before scampering along the bony arm which rested against one wall, just beneath the crudely drawn figure of a three-master ship.

The assassin hiding in the shadows on the frozen parapet of the great Bell Tower knew nothing of such secret places, though he realized the Tower held great mysteries. He drew deeper into his cloak.

'"The time has come",' he muttered to himself, quoting the Gospels, '"when all those things hidden in the dark shall be revealed in the light of day".' He squinted up at the sky. 'Blood can only be avenged,' he whispered, 'by blood being spilt!'

Yes, he liked that thought: justice and death walking hand-in-hand. He gazed across at the dark mass of the Chapel of St Peter ad Vincula. Surely God would understand? Did he not brand Cain for slaying Abel, and why should murderers walk free? The assassin did not mind the biting wind, the steadily falling flakes of snow or the lonely, haunting call of the night birds down near the icy river.

'There are things colder than the wind,' he whispered as he turned inwards and meditated on his own bleak soul and the great open sore festering there. Soon it would be Yuletide and Childermass. A time of innocence and warmth, of food roasting slowly on turning spits. Green boughs would decorate rooms; there would be mummers, revelries, games, hot cakes and mulled wine. The assassin smiled. And, like every Christmas, the murderers would gather here in the Tower. He rocked himself gently to and fro. The trial would begin. The warnings were already prepared. He stretched his hands up against the night sky.

'Let the blood flow,' he murmured. 'Let Murder be my weapon!'

The cross of St Peter ad Vincula caught his eye. 'Let God be my judge,' he whispered, thrusting his hands beneath his cloak, his eyes staring into the black night. He remembered the past and rocked himself gently, crooning a song only he understood. Now he felt warm. He would bathe his soul's wounds in the blood of his victims.

Chapter 1

Brother Athelstan stood on the tower of St Erconwald's Church in Southwark and stared up at the sky. He chewed on his lip and quietly cursed. He'd thought the clouds would have broken up by now; they had for a while, and the stars had glittered down like jewels against a velvet cushion. Athelstan had wanted to study the constellations as the longest night of the year approached and see if the writer of the *Equatorie of the Planets* was correct. However, the wind had drawn the snow clouds like a thick veil across the sky.

The friar stamped his sandalled feet and blew on his freezing fingers. He picked up his ink horn, quill, astrolabe and roll of parchment, lifted the trap door and cautiously went down the steps. The church was freezing and dark. He took a tinder and lit the tapers in front of Our Lady's statue, the sconce torches down the nave and the fat, white beeswax candles on the altar. Athelstan went back down the sanctuary steps and under the newly carved chancel screen, freshly painted by Huddle with a tableau depicting Christ leading souls from Limbo. Athelstan admired the painter's vigorous brush strokes in green, red, blue and gold colours.

'The young man has a genius,' he muttered to himself, standing back to scrutinise the figures delineated there. He just wished Huddle had been a little more delicate in his depiction of a young lady with rounded juicy breasts whom Cecily the courtesan claimed was a fair representation of her.

'Well, let's see!' Tab the tinker had shouted out before Ursula the pig woman jabbed a sharp elbow in his ribs.

Athelstan shook his head and went across to warm his hands over the small charcoal brazier, which glowingly offered some heat against the freezing night air. He looked down the nave of the church, noticing the boughs of evergreens, the holly and ivy which Watkin the dung-collector's wife had wound round the great broad pillars. Athelstan was pleased. The roof was mended, the windows glazed with horn. 'More like a church now,' he muttered, 'than a long, dark tunnel with holes in the walls.' Soon Advent would be over. The greenery had been placed there to welcome the newborn Christ. 'Evergreen,' the friar murmured. 'For the evergreen Lord.' A small shadow, deeper than the rest, slunk from the darkened aisle.

'You always know when to appear, Bonaventura.'

The great tom cat padded across, stopped and stretched in front of Athelstan, then brushed imploringly against the friar's black robe. Athelstan glanced down.

'No mice here,' he whispered. 'Thank God!'

He'd never forget how Ranulf the rat-catcher had secreted traps in the rushes and Cecily had caught her toe in one of them as she cleaned the church one morning. Athelstan had lived for thirty years and served with soldiers, but never had he heard such a litany of ripe oaths as those which had poured from Cecily's pretty mouth.

The friar crouched and picked up the cat, studying the great black and white face, the tattered ears. 'Bonaventura the Great Mouser,' he murmured. 'So you have come for your reward.' Athelstan went into one of the darkened transepts and took a bowl of freezing milk and sliced pilchard from the windowsill. 'Whose life is more rewarding, Bonaventura,' he murmured as he crouched to feed the animal, 'a torn cat's in Southwark or that of a Dominican monk who likes the stars but has to work in the mud?'

The cat blinked back, squatted down and gobbled the food from a pewter platter, one eye alert on a small flurry where the rushes lay thick against a pillar. Athelstan returned to the bottom of the sanctuary steps, knelt, crossed himself and began the first prayer of Divine Office.

'*Veni, veni, Emmanuel!*' Come, O come, Emmanuel!

When would Christ come again? Athelstan idly wondered. To heal the wounds and enforce justice... No. He closed his eyes. He'd sworn an oath he wouldn't think of Cranston; he wouldn't dwell on that fat red face and balding head, those mischievous blue eyes, and the great girth which would drain a vineyard dry. He remembered the old story about the devil collecting all the half-hearted prayers of priests, gathering every missing word in a bag for Judgment Day. Athelstan closed his eyes and breathed deeply to calm himself.

He finished his psalms then went into the small, freezing cold sacristy. Washing his hands at the lavarium, he looked round. 'Not purple vestments today,' he murmured, and opened the great missal. 'Today is the Feast of St Lucy.' He unlocked the battered cupboard door and plucked out the gold-covered chasuble with a scarlet cross embroidered in the centre. Unlike the musty cupboard, the chasuble was new and fragrant-smelling. He marvelled at the handiwork and thought of its maker, the widow Benedicta. 'As beautiful as she is,' he murmured. 'Sorry,

sorry!' He whispered an apology for his own distraction and said the prayers which every priest must recite as he dresses for Mass.

Athelstan had trained himself. He knew the dark shadows in his soul threatened to rise and interrupt his morning routine. He must not think of them. The small window in the sacristy clattered as its shutter banged against it. Athelstan started. It was still black as night outside in the cemetery, God's Acre, with its broken wooden crosses guarding the mounds of soil where the ancestors of the good people of the parish slept their eternal dream, waiting for Christ to come again. Yet Athelstan knew there was something else out there. Some dark evil thing which committed terrible blasphemies by dragging corpses from the soil.

The friar shook himself free from his morbid reverie. He opened the strong box and took out the chalice and paten. He placed the white communion wafers on a plate and half filled the goblet with altar wine. Afterwards he picked up the jar and gazed suspiciously at the contents.

'It looks,' he announced to the empty darkness, 'as if our sexton, Watkin the dung-collector, is sampling the wine!' He filled the water bowl for the Lavabo, that part of the Mass when the priest cleanses himself of his sins, and gazed down at the water where thin slivers of ice bobbed. 'What sins?' he whispered. The alabaster-skinned face of Benedicta, veiled by her blue-black hair, sprang to mind. Athelstan felt Bonaventure brush against his leg. 'No sin,' he whispered to the cat. 'Surely it is no sin? She's a friend and I am lonely.' He took a deep breath. 'You're a fool, Athelstan,' he muttered to himself. 'You are a priest, what do you expect?' He continued this line of thought as he finished robing. He had confessed as much to the Father Prior, yet why was he lonely? Despite his moans, Athelstan sought to be loved by the parish and the people he served. But it was his other office, as clerk to Sir John Cranston the coroner, which depressed him. And why? Athelstan absent-mindedly picked up Bonaventura and began to stroke him. He could cope with the violent deaths, the gore and the bloody wounds. It was the others which chilled him – the planned murders, coolly calculated by souls steeped in the black night of mortal sin. Athelstan felt he was on the verge of another such mystery. Something warned him, a sixth sense, as if the evil lurking in the lonely cemetery was waiting to confront him. He stirred himself and kissed Bonaventure on the top of his head.

'There's Mass to be said.'

Athelstan went back into the church, glanced up and saw the first light of dawn through the horn-glazed window. He shivered. Despite the braziers, the church was deathly cold. He reached the altar and stared towards the Pyx holding the Blessed Sacrament, Christ under the appearance of bread, swinging under its golden canopy with only a lonely taper on the altar beneath as a sign that God was present. Behind him the door crashed open and Mugwort the bell cleric waddled in, his bald head and quivering red cheeks concealed beneath woollen rags.

'Good morrow, Father!' he bellowed in a voice Athelstan believed could be heard the length and breadth of the parish.

The friar closed his eyes and prayed for patience as Mugwort began to pull on the bell – more like a tocsin than a summons to prayer. At last the clatter stopped. Benedicta, shrouded in a brown cloak, slipped into the church. She smiled sheepishly at the friar who stood waiting patiently at the foot of the steps. Cecily the courtesan followed. Athelstan knew it was she by the gale of cheap perfume which always preceded her. He closed his eyes and prayed that the only tasks Cecily performed now were to work as a seamstress for Benedicta and to clean the church. He remembered the parish joke: how Cecily had lain down in the cemetery more often than the parish coffin. Pernel, the old Flemish lady, came next; her hair dyed red, her face painted white, a woman of indeterminate background and even more uncertain morals. Athelstan quietly vowed to watch her. He'd heard a story that Pernel did not swallow the host but took it home and placed it in her beehive to keep the bees healthy. If he caught her, he would not offer the Eucharist or accept her silly answer that the honeycombs from her hives were always in the shape of a church! At last Watkin the dung-collector, sexton, warden of St Erconwald's and leader of the parish council, arrived. His ever-growing brood of children clattered down the aisle in their wooden clogs; one of them, Crim, with at least his hands washed, slipped next to Athelstan to serve as altar boy. The friar felt slightly ridiculous, a duty-faced Crim on one side and Bonaventura the cat on the other. Manyer the hangman came last and slammed the door shut.

Athelstan took a deep breath and made the sign of the cross, vowing he would concentrate on the mysteries of the Mass and not on the evils in the cemetery outside.

–

Sir John Cranston, Coroner of the City of London, was standing in Blind Basket Alley off Poor Jewry. The runnel cut like a sliver of ice between the backs of the overhanging houses. The good coroner stamped his feet and blew on his mittened fingers in a futile attempt to warm them.

'Hold that torch higher!' he snapped at the alderman's clerk. Cranston stared at the men around him, dark shapes in the poor light, and then up at the shuttered window of the sombre, desolate house. He saved his most venomous glance for Luke Venables, Alderman of the Ward, who had roused him from a warm bed. Sir John liked his sleep at the best of times, particularly after a strenuous week's work. Two days ago, he had gone to the church of St Stephen in Walbrook to examine the corpse of William Clarke, who had climbed the belfry to look for a pigeon's nest. As the idiot crawled from beam to beam, he'd slipped and fallen, being killed instantly. Cranston had adjudged that the beam was to blame and imposed a fine of fourpence on the angry vicar. Yesterday Cranston had been to West Chepe to examine the corpse of William Pannar, a skinner, found lying near the Conduit. Pannar had been stupid enough to go to a physician with some ailment or other. Of course he had been leeched of blood, so much so that the poor bastard had collapsed on the way home and died on the spot.

Cranston chewed his lip as he banged on the door again. Yet it was not just his work which bothered him. There was something else: his beloved wife Maude was not being honest with him and Cranston suspected she was hiding a dreadful secret. Sir John was infatuated with his wife and could not resist the pleasures of the bed chamber, yet recently, last night included, he had snuggled up next to her only to have his advances rejected. She had whimpered her protests softly in the darkness, would not tell him the reason and refused to be comforted. Now, in the early hours, this idiot Venables had brought him out into the cold in order to force entry into this mysterious house. Cranston hammered on the door again but there was no reply, only the muttered oaths and shuffling feet of his companions.

'So!' Cranston turned to the alderman. 'Tell me again what the problem is.'

Venables knew Sir John and stared anxiously at the be-whiskered red face, the icy-blue eyes and furrowed brow under the great, woollen beaver hat. Sir John was a good man, Venables reflected, but when he lost his temper, he could be the devil incarnate. Venables pointed to the broken ale-stake jutting out just above the door.

'The facts are these, Sir John. The householder here is Simon de Wyxford. This is his ale-house. He had no family, only a servant, Roger Droxford. Eight days ago, master and servant had a violent quarrel which continued all day. On December the sixth the servant, Roger, opened the ale-house as usual, set out the benches and sold wine, but nothing was seen of Simon. The next day neighbours asked Roger where his master was. He replied that Simon had gone to Westminster to recover some debts.' Venables blew out his cheeks and turned to one of the shadowed figures beside him. 'Tell Sir John the rest.'

'Four days ago—' began the neighbour, a small man swathed in robes.

Cranston could see only a pair of timid eyes and a dripping nose above the muffler.

'Speak up!' Cranston roared. 'Remove the muffler from your mouth.'

'Four days ago,' the fellow continued, obeying Sir John with alacrity, 'Roger was seen leaving here, a bundle of possessions slung across his back. We thought he was fleeing but he went to one of our neighbours, Hammo the cook, telling him he was going to seek out Simon, his master, and gave Hammo the key should de Wyxford suddenly return. Last night,' he continued, clearing his throat, 'Francis Boggett, a taverner, came here to recover a debt Master Simon owed him.'

'Come on! Come on!' Cranston interrupted.

'Boggett entered the house,' the alderman intervened smoothly, 'to find no trace of Simon or his servant, so he seized three tuns of wine as recompense for his debt.'

'How did he get in?' Cranston snapped.

'Hammo the cook gave him the key.'

Sir John pursed his lips. 'Boggett is to be fined fivepence for trespass and the cook twopence as his accomplice.' He glared at the alderman. 'You have the key on you?'

Venables nodded. Cranston snapped his fingers and the alderman handed it over. The coroner drew himself up to his full height.

'As coroner of this city,' he grandly announced, 'in view of the mysterious events reported to me, I now authorise our entry to this house to search out the truth. Master Alderman, you will accompany me.'

There was further confusion as Venables asked for a tinder from one of his companions. Sir John unlocked the door and entered the cold darkness of the tavern. The place smelt dirty and musty. They crashed against barrels, stools and tables until Venables struck a tinder and lit two cresset torches, one of which he handed to Cranston. They went from room to room and then upstairs where they found the two chambers ransacked, and coffers and chests with their lids broken or thrown aside, but no trace of any body.

'You know what we are looking for?' Cranston murmured.

Venables nodded. 'But so far nothing, Sir John.'

'There is a cellar?'

The alderman led Cranston downstairs. They searched the darkened taproom until they found a trap door, which Venables pulled back. Both men descended gingerly by wooden ladders. The cellar was a long, oblong box with a trap door at the far end for the carts to unload their barrels through. Cranston told Venables to stand still and walked carefully through the cellar, his great bulk made grotesque by the dim light of the flickering torches. At the far end he stopped, lowered the torch and looked behind three great wine tuns. The light made the spiders' webs which clung to the barrels shimmer like cloth of gold. Cranston leaned over and felt the sticky mess he had spotted. He brought his hand up into the light and looked at the blood which coated his fingers like paste. He forced his arm back further behind the barrels, and scrabbled around.

'Sir John!' the alderman called out. 'All is well?'

'As well as can be expected, Master Venables. I have found the taverner, or at least part of him!' Cranston picked up the decapitated head from behind the barrels and held it aloft as if he was the Tower headsman. The alderman took one look at the blue-white face, the half-closed eyes, sagging blood-stained mouth and the jagged remains of the neck, and sat down heavily on a stone plinth, retching violently. Cranston put down the head and walked back, wiping his fingers on the mildewed wall. As he passed, he patted Venables gently on the shoulder.

'Have some claret, my good alderman, it steadies the stomach and fortifies the heart.' He stopped and took a step back. 'After that, swear out warrants for the arrest of

Roger Droxford. Declare him a wolfshead, and place...'
Cranston screwed up his eyes. 'Yes, place ten pounds'
reward on his head, dead or alive. Have this house sealed,
and in the event of no will or self-proclaimed heir appearing, the city council might find itself a little richer.'

He climbed the ladder and the taproom steps and
emerged on to the bitterly cold street.

'We've found the taverner,' he announced. 'Murdered.
I think the good alderman will need your help to assemble
the corpse.'

Then, hand on his long Welsh dagger, Sir John trudged
back along the ice-packed runnels and alleyways. He
turned into the Mercery and gasped as the icy wind tore
away his breath. 'Oh, for summer!' he wailed to himself.
'For weeds in clumps, for grass lovely and lush.'

He slithered on the icy cobbles and leaned against the
wooden frame of a house, grinning.

'Athelstan should be here helping,' he murmured. 'If
not with headless corpses, then at least by keeping me
steady on the ice.'

He walked on up Cheapside. A dark shape slid from
the shadows to meet him. Cranston half drew his dagger.

'Sir John, for the love of Christ!'

Cranston peered closer at the raw-boned face of the
one-legged beggar who always sold trinkets from his rickety stall on the corner of Milk Street.

'Not in bed, Leif? Looking for a lady, are we?'

'Sir John, I've been robbed!'

'See the sheriff!'

'Sir John, I have no money and no food.'

'Then stay in bed!'

Leif steadied himself against the wall. 'I paid no rent,
so I lost my garret,' he wailed.

'Well, go and beg at St Bartholomew's!' Cranston barked back, and trudged on. He heard Leif hopping behind him.

'Sir John, help me.'

'Bugger off, Leif.'

'Thank you, Sir John,' the beggar answered as coins tinkled to the ground. Leif knew enough about the fat coroner to understand Sir John hated to be seen giving charity.

Cranston stopped before his own house and looked up at the candlelit windows. Leif nearly crashed into him and Cranston shrugged him off. What is the matter with Maude? he wondered. He had always considered marriage similar to dipping one's hand into a bag of eels – it depended on luck what you drew out. Yet he had been so fortunate. He adored Maude, from the mousey hair of her head to the soles of her tiny feet.

As he mused, a figure suddenly emerged from the alleyway which ran alongside Cranston's house.

'By the sod!' he exclaimed. 'Doesn't anyone in this benighted city sleep?'

The fellow approached and Cranston recognised the livery of the Lord Mayor.

'By the sod,' he repeated, 'more trouble!'

The young pursuivant, teeth chattering, hoarsely delivered his message.

'Sir John, the Lord Mayor and his sheriffs wish to see you now at the Guildhall.'

'Go to hell!'

'Thank you, Sir John. The Lord Mayor said your reply would be something like that. Shall I wait for you?' The young man clapped his hands together. 'Sir John, I am cold.'

Still bellowing 'By the sod!' Cranston banged on the door of his house. A thin-faced maid opened it. Behind her stood Maude, now fully dressed, her sweet face tear-stained. Sir John grinned at her to hide his own disquiet.

'Lady wife, I am off to the Guildhall – but not before I break fast.' He dragged the young pursuivant in with him. 'He'll eat too. He looks as if he needs it.'

Cranston spun on his heel, went back outside and re-entered, dragging in Leif by the scruff of his neck. 'This idle bugger will also be joining us. After which, find him a job. He will be spending Yuletide here.' He tapped his broad girth. 'For all of us, hot oatmeal and spiced cakes!' The coroner sniffed the air. 'And some of that white manchet, freshly baked.' He looked slyly at his wife. 'And claret, hot and spiced. Then tell the groom I need a horse!' He grinned broadly, but despite his bluster Cranston noticed how pale and ill his wife looked. He glanced away. Oh God! he thought. Am I to lose Maude? He tossed off his cloak and strode past his wife, touching her gently on the shoulder as he passed.

-

Athelstan was distributing communion, placing the thin white wafers on the tongues of his parishioners. Crim held the silver plate under their chins to catch any crumbs which might fall. Most of the parish council had turned up, some wandering in when Mass was half over.

The friar was about to return to the altar when he heard a tapping on the outside wall of the far aisle. Of course! He had forgotten the lepers, two unfortunates whom he'd allowed to shelter in the musty charnel house in the cemetery. Athelstan provided them with food and drink and a bowl of water infused with mulberry to wash in, but never once had he glimpsed their scabrous white faces, though from his clothes one was definitely a male. He wished he could do more for them but Canon Law was most insistent – a leper was not allowed to take communion with the rest of the congregation but could only receive it through the leper squint, a small hole in the wall of the church.

Crim remembered his duties and, picking up a thin twig of ash, handed it to the friar who placed a host on the end and pushed it through the leper squint. He repeated the action, whispered a prayer, and went back to finish the Mass.

Afterwards Athelstan disrobed in the sacristy, closing his ears to the crashing sounds from the nave as Watkin the dung-collector rearranged the benches for the meeting of the parish council. Athelstan knelt on his *prie dieu*, asked for guidance, and hoped to God his parishioners would overlook the dreadful events happening outside.

As soon as he stepped into the nave, he knew his prayers had been fruitless. Watkin was sitting in pride of place, with the other members on benches on either side of him. Crim had placed Athelstan's chair out of the sanctuary ready for him and, as he took it, Athelstan caught Watkin's self-important look, the ominous flickering of the eyes and the mouth pursed as if on the brink of announcing something very important.

Ursula the pig woman had joined them, bringing her large fat sow into church with her in spite of the protests of the rest. The creature waddled around grunting with pleasure. Athelstan was sure the annoying beast was grinning at him. He did not object to its presence. Better here than outside. Ursula was a garrulous but kindly old woman. Nevertheless, the friar hid a blind hatred for her large, fat-bellied sow which periodically plundered his garden of any vegetables he tried to plant there.

Athelstan said a prayer to the Holy Ghost and leaned back in his chair.

'Brothers and sisters,' he began, 'welcome to this meeting on our holiday feast of St Lucy.' He ignored Watkin's eye. 'We have certain matters to discuss.' He smiled at Benedicta then noticed with alarm how Watkin's wife was glaring at Cecily the courtesan. A mutual antipathy existed between these two women, Watkin's wife in the past loudly wondering why it was necessary for her husband to confer so often with Cecily on the cleaning of the church. Huddle the painter stared vacantly at a blank wall, probably dreaming of the mural he would like to put there if Athelstan gave him the monies.

Most of the parish business was a long litany of mundane items. Pike the ditcher's daughter wished to marry Amisias the fuller's eldest boy. The great Blood Book was consulted to ensure there were no lines of consanguinity. Athelstan was pleased to announce there were not and matters turned to the approaching Yuletide: the Ceremony of the Star, which would take place in the church, the timing of the three Masses for Christmas Day, the non-payment of burial dues, and the children using the holy water stoup as a drinking fountain. Tab the tinker offered to fashion new candlesticks, two large ones, fronted with lions. Gamelyn the clerk volunteered to sing a pleasant carol at the end of each Mass at Yuletide. Athelstan agreed to a mummers' play in the nave on St Stephen's Day, and some discussion was held about who would play the role of the boy bishop at Childermass, the feast of the Holy Innocents, on the twenty-eighth of December.

Athelstan, however, noticed despairingly how Watkin just slumped on his bench, glaring impatiently as he clawed his codpiece and shuffled his muddy boots. Benedicta caught Athelstan's concern and gazed anxiously at this man she loved but could not attain because he was an ordained priest. At last Athelstan ran out of things to say.

'Well, Watkin,' he commented drily. 'You have a matter of great urgency?'

Watkin drew himself up to his full height. His greasy brow was furrowed under a shock of bright red hair, receding fast to leave a bushy fringe. His pale blue eyes, which seemed to fight each other for space next to a bulbous nose, glared around at his colleagues.

'The cemetery has been looted!' he blurted out.

Athelstan groaned and lowered his head.

'What do you mean?' shouted Ranulf the rat-catcher, his face sharp and pointed under a black, tarry hood.

'In the last few days,' Watkin announced, 'corpses have been exhumed!'

Consternation broke out. Athelstan rose and clapped his hands for silence, and kept doing so until the clamour ceased. 'You know,' he began, 'how our cemetery of St Erconwald's is often used for the burial of corpses of strangers – beggars on whom no claim is made. No grave of any parishioner's relative has been disturbed.' He breathed deeply. 'Nevertheless, Watkin is correct. Three graves have been robbed of their bodies. Each had been freshly interred. A young beggar woman, a Brabantine mercenary found dead after a tavern brawl, and an old man seen begging outside the hospital of St Thomas, who was found in the courtyard of the Tabard Inn, frozen

26

dead.' Athelstan licked his lips. 'The ground is hard,' he continued. 'Watkin knows how difficult it is to dig with mattock and hoe to furnish a grave deep enough, so the very shallowness of the graves has assisted these blasphemous robbers.'

'A guard should be placed,' Pike the ditcher called out.

'Will you do it?' Benedicta asked softly. 'Will you spend all night in the cemetery, Pike, and wait for the grave robbers?' Her dark eyes took in the rest of the council. 'Who will stand guard? And who knows,' she continued, 'if the robberies are committed at night? Perhaps they take place in the afternoon or eventide.'

Athelstan glanced at her gratefully. 'I could watch,' he interrupted. 'Indeed, I have done so when I – er...' he faltered.

'When you study the stars, Brother,' Ursula the pig woman broke in, provoking a soft chorus of laughter, for all the parishioners knew of their priest's strange occupation.

Huddle the painter stirred himself. 'You could ask Sir John Cranston to help us. Perhaps he could send soldiers to guard the graves?'

Athelstan shook his head. 'My Lord Coroner,' he replied, 'has no authority to order the King's soldiers hither and thither.'

'What about the beadles?' Watkin's wife bellowed. 'What about the ward watch?'

Yes, what about them? Athelstan bleakly thought. The alderman and officials of the ward scarcely bothered about St Erconwald's, still less about its cemetery, and wouldn't give a fig for the graves of the three unknowns being pillaged.

'Who are they?' Benedicta asked softly. 'Why do they do it? What do they want?'

Her words created a pool of silence. All faces turned to their priest for an answer. This was the moment Athelstan feared. The cemetery was God's Acre. When he had first come to the parish nine months ago, he had been very strict about those who tried to set up market there or with the young boys who played games with the bones dug up by marauding dogs or pigs. 'The cemetery,' he had announced, 'is God's own land where the faithful wait for Christ to come again.' Even then Athelstan had not given the full reason for his strictures; secretly he shared the Church's fears of those who worshipped Satan, the Lord of the Crossroads and Master of the Gibbet, and often practised their black arts in cemeteries. Indeed, he had heard of a case in the parish of St Peter Cornhill where a black magician had used the blood drained from such corpses to raise demons and scorpions.

Athelstan coughed. How could he answer? Then the door was flung open and Cranston, his saviour, swept grandly into the church.

Chapter 2

Sir John pulled back his cloak and tipped his beaver hat to the back of his head.

'Come on, Brother!' he bawled, winking at Benedicta. 'We are needed at the Tower. Apparently Murder does not wait upon the weather.'

For once Athelstan was pleased by Cranston's dramatic style of entry. The friar peered closely at him.

'You have been at the claret, Sir John?'

Cranston tapped the side of his fleshy nose. 'A little,' he slurred.

'What about the cemetery?' Watkin wailed. 'Sir John, our priest has to see to that!'

'Sod off, you smelly little man!'

Watkin's wife rose and looked balefully at Cranston.

'My Lord Coroner, I shall be with you presently,' Athelstan smoothly intervened. 'Watkin, I shall attend to this business on my return. In the meantime, make sure that Bonaventura is fed and the torches doused. Cecily, you will put out food for the lepers?'

The girl stared vacuously and nodded.

'Mind you,' Athelstan muttered, 'they tend to wander and look after themselves during the day.'

He smiled beatifically around his favourite group of parishioners and made a quick departure down the icy steps of the church and across to the priest's house. He cut himself a slice of bread but spat it out as it tasted sour and stale. 'I'll eat on my journey,' he murmured, and packed his saddlebags with vellum, pen cases and ink horns. Philomel, his old war horse, snickered and nudged him, a real nuisance as Athelstan tried to fasten the girths beneath the aged destrier's ponderous belly.

'You're getting more like Cranston every day!' Athelstan muttered.

He led Philomel back to the front of the church and ran up the porch steps. Cranston was leaning against the pillar, leering at Cecily whilst trying to keep Bonaventura from brushing against his leg. The coroner couldn't stand cats ever since his campaigns in France when the French had catapulted their corpses into a small castle he was holding, in an attempt to spread contagious diseases. Bonaventura, however, adored the coroner. The cat seemed to know when he was in the vicinity and always put in an appearance.

Athelstan murmured a few words to Benedicta, and smiled apologetically at Watkin and the rest; he collected his deep-hooded cloak from the sanctuary and returned just in the nick of time to prevent Cranston from toppling head over heels over Ursula's fat-bellied sow. The coroner stormed out, glaring at Athelstan and daring him to laugh. Cranston mounted his horse, roaring oaths about pigs in church and how he would like nothing better than a succulent piece of roast pork. Athelstan swung his saddlebags across Philomel, mounted and, before Cranston could do further damage, led him away from the church into Fennel Alleyway.

'Why the Tower, Sir John?' he asked quickly, trying to divert the coroner's rage.

'In a while, monk!' Cranston rasped back.

'I'm a friar, not a monk,' Athelstan muttered.

Cranston belched and took another swig from his wineskin. 'What was going on back there?' he asked.

'A parish council meeting.'

'No, I mean about the cemetery.'

Athelstan informed him and the coroner's face grew serious.

'Do you think it's Satanists? The Black Lords of the graveyard?' he whispered, reining his horse closer to Athelstan's.

The friar grimaced. 'It may well be.'

'It must be!' Cranston snapped back. 'Who else would be interested in decaying corpses?'

The coroner steadied his horse as Philomel, conscious of the narrowing alleyway, tossed his head angrily at Cranston's mount.

'I'd like to root the lot out!' the coroner slurred. 'In my treatise on the governance of London…' Two blue eyes glared at Athelstan, scrutinising the friar's face for any trace of boredom as the coroner expounded on his favourite theme. 'In my treatise,' he continued, 'anyone practising the black arts would suffer heavy fines for the first offence and death for the second.' He shrugged. 'But perhaps it's just some petty nastiness.'

Athelstan shook his head. 'Such matters are never petty,' he replied. 'I attended an exorcism once at a little church near Blackfriars. A young boy possessed by demons was speaking in strange tongues and levitating himself from the ground. He claimed the demons entered him after a ceremony in which the corpse of a hanged man was the altar.'

Cranston shuddered. 'If you need any help…' the coroner tentatively offered.

Athelstan smiled. 'That's most kind of you, My Lord Coroner. As usual your generosity of spirit takes my breath away.'

'Any friend of the Good Lord is a friend of mine,' Cranston quipped. 'Even if he is a monk.'

'I'm a friar,' Athelstan replied. '*Not* a monk.' He glared at Cranston, but the coroner threw back his head and roared with laughter at his perennial joke against Athelstan.

At last they left the congested alleyways, taking care to avoid the snow which slid from the high, sloped roofs, and turned on to the main thoroughfare down to London Bridge. The cobbled area was sheeted with ice, coated with a thin layer of snow, which a biting wind stirred into sudden, sharp flurries. A few stalls were out, but their keepers hid behind tattered canvas awnings against the biting wind now packing the sky with deep, dark snow clouds.

'A time to keep secret house,' Cranston murmured.

A relic-seller stood outside the Abbot of Hyde's inn trying to sell a staff which, he claimed, had once belonged to Moses. Two prisoners, manacled together and released from the Marshalsea where debtors were held, begged for alms for themselves and other poor unfortunates. Athelstan threw them some pennies, moved to compassion by their ice-blue feet. Both Cranston's and Athelstan's horses were well shod but the few people who were about slipped and slithered on the treacherous black ice. These hardy walkers made their way gingerly along, grasping the frames of the houses they passed. Nevertheless, as Cranston remarked, justice was active; outside the hospital of St Thomas a baker had been fastened on a hurdle as punishment for selling mouldy bread. Athelstan remembered the stale food he had spat out earlier and watched as the unfortunate was pulled along by a donkey. A drunken bagpipe player slipped and slid along behind, playing a raucous tune to hide the baker's groans. In the stocks a taverner, wry-mouthed, was being made to drink sour wine, whilst a whore, fastened to the thews, was whipped by a sweating bailiff who lashed the poor woman's back with long thick twigs of holly.

'Sir John,' Athelstan whispered, 'the poor woman has had enough.'

'Sod her!' Cranston snarled back. 'She probably deserved it!'

Athelstan looked closer at the coroner's round red face.

'Sir John, for pity's sake, what is the matter?'

Beneath the false bonhomie and wine-guzzling, Athelstan sensed the coroner was either very angry or very anxious. Cranston blinked and smiled falsely. He drew his sword and, turning his horse aside, moved over to the whipping post and slashed at the ropes which held the whore. The woman collapsed in a bloody heap on the ice. The bailiff, a snarl making his ugly face more grotesque, walked threateningly towards Cranston. Sir John waved his sword and pulled the muffler from his face.

'I am Cranston the City Coroner!' he yelled.

The man backed off hastily. Sir John delved under his cloak, brought out a few pennies and tossed them to the whore.

'Earn an honest crust!' he snapped.

He glared at his companion, daring him to comment before continuing down past the stews and on to the wide expanse of London Bridge. The entire trackway of the bridge was coated with ice and shrouded in mist. Athelstan stopped, his hand on Cranston's arm.

'Sir John, something is wrong! It's so quiet!'

Cranston grinned. 'Haven't you realised, Brother? Look down, the river is frozen.'

Athelstan stared in disbelief over the railings of the bridge. Usually the water beneath surged and boiled. Now it seemed the river had been replaced by a field of white ice which stretched as far as the eye could see. Athelstan craned his neck and heard the shouts of boys skating there, using the shin bones of an ox for skates. Someone had even opened a stall and Athelstan's stomach clenched with hunger as he caught the fragrant smell of hot beef pies. They continued past the Chapel of St Thomas on to Bridge Street, into Billingsgate and up Botolph's Lane to Eastcheap. The city seemed to be caught under the spell of an ice witch. Few stalls were out and the usual roar of apprentices and merchants had been silenced by winter's vice-like grip. They stopped at a pie shop. Athelstan bought and bit deeply into a hot mince pie, savouring the juices which swirled there and the delightful fragrance of freshly baked pastry and highly spiced meat. Cranston watched him eat.

'You are enjoying that, Brother?'

'Yes, My Lord. Why don't you join me?'

Cranston smiled wickedly. 'I would love to,' he replied. 'But have you not forgotten, friar? It's Advent. You are supposed to abstain from meat!'

Athelstan looked longingly at the half-eaten pie, then smiled, finished his meal and licked his fingers. Cranston shook his head.

'What are we to do?' he wailed mockingly. 'When friars ignore Canon Law.'

Athelstan licked his lips and leaned closer. 'You're wrong, Sir John. Today is the thirteenth of December, a holy day, the feast of St Lucy, virgin and martyr. So I am allowed to eat meat.' He sketched a sign of the cross in the air. 'And you can drink twice as much claret as you usually do!' The friar gathered the reins of the horse in his hands. 'So, Sir John, what takes us to the Tower?'

Cranston pulled aside as a broad-wheeled cart stacked high with sour green apples trundled by.

'Sir Ralph Whitton, Constable of the Tower. You have heard of him?'

Athelstan nodded. 'Who hasn't? He's a redoubtable soldier, a brave crusader, and a personal friend of the Regent, John of Gaunt.'

'Was,' Cranston intervened. 'Early this morning Whitton was found in his chamber in the North Bastion of the Tower, his throat slit from ear to ear and more blood on his chest than you would get from a gutted pig.'

'Any sign of the murderer or the weapon?'

Cranston shook his head, blowing on his ice-edged fingers. 'Nothing,' he grated. 'Whitton had a daughter, Philippa. She was betrothed to Geoffrey Parchmeiner. Apparently Sir Ralph liked the young man and trusted him. Early this morning Geoffrey went to wake his prospective father-in-law and found him murdered.' He took a deep breath. 'More curious still, before his death Sir Ralph, suspected someone had evil designs on his life. Four days prior to his death he received a written warning.'

'What was this?'

'I don't know but apparently the constable became a frightened man. He left his usual chambers in the turret of the White Tower and for security reasons moved to the North Bastion. The stairway to his chamber was guarded by two trusted retainers. The door between the steps and the passageway was locked. Sir Ralph kept a key and so

35

did the guards. The same is true of Sir Ralph's chamber. He locked it from the inside, whilst the two guards had another key.'

Cranston suddenly leaned over and grabbed the bridle of Athelstan's horse, pulling him clear as a huge lump of snow slipped from the sloping roofs above and crashed on to the ice.

'We should move on,' the friar remarked drily. 'Otherwise, Sir John, you may have another corpse on your hands and this time *you* will be the suspect.'

Cranston belched and took a deep swig from his wine-skin.

'Is young Geoffrey one of the suspects?' Athelstan enquired.

Cranston shook his head. 'I don't think so. Both doors were still locked; the guards unlocked one, let him through and then locked it again. Apparently, Geoffrey went down the passageway, knocked and tried to rouse Sir Ralph. He failed to do this so came back for the guards who opened Sir Ralph's room. Inside they found the constable sprawled on his bed, his throat cut and the wooden shutters of his window flung wide open.' Cranston turned and spat, clearing his throat. 'One other thing – the guards would never allow anyone through without a rigorous body search, and that included young Geoffrey. No dagger was found on him nor any knife in the room.'

'What was Sir Ralph so fearful of?'

Cranston shook his head. 'God knows! But there's a fine array of suspects. His lieutenant, Gilbert Colebrooke, was on bad terms and wanted Sir Ralph's post for himself. There's the chaplain, William Hammond, whom Sir Ralph caught selling food stocks from the Tower stores. Two friends of Sir Ralph's, hospitaller knights, came as

36

they usually did to spend Christmas with him. Finally, there's a pagan, a mute body servant, a Saracen whom Sir Ralph picked up whilst crusading in Outremer.'

Athelstan pulled his hood closer as the cold wind nipped the corners of his ears. '*Cui bono?*' he asked.

'What does that mean?'

'Cicero's famous question: "Who profits?"'

Cranston pursed his lips. 'A good question, my dear friar. Which brings us to Sir Ralph's brother, Sir Fulke Whitton. He stands to inherit some of his brother's estate.'

Cranston fell silent, half closing his eyes and gently burping after the good breakfast he had eaten. Athelstan, however, prided himself on knowing the fat coroner as well as the palm of his own hand.

'Well, Sir John,' he needled, 'there is more, is there not?'

Cranston opened his eyes. 'Of course there is. Whitton was not liked by the court, nor by the Londoners, nor by the peasants.'

Athelstan felt his heart sink. They had been down this road on numerous occasions.

'You think it may be the Great Community?' he asked.

Cranston nodded. 'It could be. And, remember, Brother, some of your parishioners may be part of it. If the Great Community acts and revolt spreads, the rebels will try to seize the Tower. Whoever controls it controls the river, the city, Westminster and the crown.'

Athelstan pulled the reins closer to him and reflected on what Cranston had said. Matters were not going well in London. The king was a child; John of Gaunt, his uncle, a highly unpopular Regent. The court was dissolute, whilst the peasants were taxed to the hilt and tied to the soil by cruel laws. For some time there had been whispers, rumours carried like leaves on a strong breeze, of how peasants in Kent, Middlesex and Essex had formed a secret society called the Great Community. How its leaders were plotting rebellion and a march on London. Athelstan even vaguely knew one of these leaders – John Ball, a wandering priest; the man was so eloquent he could turn the most placid of peasants into an outright rebel by mouthing phrases such as: 'When Adam delved and Eve span, who was then the gentleman?' Was Whitton's death a preamble to all this? Athelstan wondered. Were any of his parishioners involved? He knew they met in the ale-houses and taverns and, God knew, had legitimate grievances. Harsh taxes and savage laws were cruel enough to provoke a saint to rebellion. And if the revolt came, what should he do? Side with the authorities or, like many priests, join the rebels? He looked sidelong at Cranston. The coroner seemed lost in his own thoughts and once again the friar detected an air of sadness about him.

'Sir John, is there anything wrong?'

'No, no,' the coroner mumbled.

Athelstan left him alone. Perhaps, he concluded, Sir John had drunk too deeply the night before.

They moved down a snow-covered Tower Street past the church where a poor beadsman knelt, making atonement for some sin; the hands clutching his rosary beads were frost-hardened and Athelstan winced at some of the penances his fellow priests imposed on their parishioners. Sir John blew his breath out so it hung like incense in the cold air.

'By the sod!' he muttered. 'When will the sun come again?'

They had turned into Petty Wales when suddenly a woman's voice, clear and lilting, broke into one of Athelstan's favourite carols. They stopped for a moment to listen then crossed the ice-glazed square. Above them soared the Tower's sheer snow-capped walls, turrets, bastions, bulwarks and crenellations. A mass of carved stone, the huge fortress seemed shaped not to defend London but to overawe it.

'A very narrow place,' Cranston muttered. 'The House of the Red Slayer.' He looked quizzically at Athelstan. 'Our old friends Death and Murder lurk here.'

Athelstan shivered and not just from the cold. They crossed the drawbridge. Beneath them the moat, its water and the dirty green slime which always covered it, were frozen hard. They went through the black arch of Middle Tower. The huge gateway stood like an open mouth, its teeth the half-lowered iron portcullis. Above them the severed heads of two pirates taken in the Channel grinned down. Athelstan breathed a prayer.

'God defend us,' he muttered, 'from all devils, demons, scorpions, and those malignant spirits who dwell here!'

'God defend me against the living!' Cranston quipped back. 'I suspect Satan himself weeps at the evil we get up to!'

The gateway was guarded by sentries who stood under the narrow vaulted archway, wrapped in brown serge cloaks.

'Sir John Cranston, Coroner!' he bellowed. 'I hold the King's writ. And this is my clerk, Brother Athelstan, who for his manifest sins is also parish priest of St Erconwald's in Southwark. A place,' the coroner grinned at the outrage in Athelstan's face, 'where virtue and vice rub shoulders and shake hands.'

The sentries nodded, reluctant to move because of the intense cold. Athelstan and Cranston continued past

By-ward Tower and up a cobbled causeway where their horses slithered and slipped on the icy stones. They turned left at Wakefield Tower, going through another of the concentric circles of defences, on to Tower Green. This was now carpeted by a thick white layer of snow which also covered the great machines of war lying there – catapults, battering rams, mangonels and huge iron-ringed carts. On their right stood a massive half-timbered great hall with other rooms built on to it. A sentry half dozed on the steps and didn't even bother to look up as Cranston roared for assistance. A snivelling, red-nosed groom hurried down to take their horses whilst another led them up the steps and into the great hall. Two rough-haired hunting dogs snuffled amongst the mucky rushes. One of them almost cocked a leg against Sir John but growled as the coroner lashed out with his boot.

The hall itself was a large sombre room with a dirty stone floor and brooding, heavy beams. Against the far wall was a fireplace wide enough to roast an ox. The grate was piled high with logs but the chimney must have needed cleaning for some of the smoke had escaped back into the hall to swirl beneath the rafters like a mist. The early morning meal had just been finished; scullions were clearing the table of pewter and wooden platters. In one corner, two men were idly baiting a badger with a dog and other groups were huddled round the fire. Athelstan gazed around. The heavy pall of death hung over the room. He recognised its stench, the suspicion and unspoken terrors which always followed a violent, mysterious slaying. One of the figures near the fire rose and hurried across as Cranston bellowed his title once again. The fellow was tall and lanky, red-haired, with eyes pink-lidded and devoid of lashes. An aquiline nose dominated his half-shaven, lantern-shaped face.

'I am Gilbert Colebrooke, the lieutenant. Sir John, you are most welcome.' His bleary eyes swung to Athelstan.

'My clerk,' Cranston blandly announced. The coroner nodded to the group round the fire. 'The constable's household, I suspect?'

'Yes,' Colebrooke snapped.

'Well, man, introduce us!'

As they moved across, the people crouching on stools near the fire rose to greet them. Introductions were made, and inevitably Cranston immediately dominated the proceedings. As usual Athelstan hung back, studying the people he would soon interrogate. He would dig out their secrets, perhaps even reveal scandals best left hidden. First the chaplain, Master William Hammond, thin and sombre in his dark black robes. He moved with a birdlike stoop, his face sallow with an unhealthy colour, balding head covered with greasy grey wisps of hair. A bitter man, Athelstan concluded, with a nose as sharp as a dagger point, small black eyes and lips thin as a miser's purse.

On the chaplain's right stood Sir Fulke Whitton, the dead man's brother, sleek and fat, with a pleasant face and corn-coloured hair. His handshake was firm and the man curved his considerable girth with the grace and speed of an athlete.

Beside him was the dead constable's daughter, Philippa. No great beauty, she was broad-featured with pleasant brown eyes and neat auburn hair. She was rather plump and reminded Athelstan of an over-fed capon. Next to her stood, or rather swayed, her betrothed, Geoffrey Parchmeiner, hair black as night though oiled and dressed like that of a woman. He seemed a pleasant enough fellow, strong-featured though his smooth-shaven face was slightly flushed with the blood-red claret he slopped around in a deep-bowled goblet. A merry fellow, Athelstan thought, and gazed with amusement at Geoffrey's tight hose and protuberant codpiece: the shin beneath the tawny cloak dripped with frills under the sarcenet doublet, and the toes of the shoes were so long and pointed they were tied up by a scarlet cord wound around the knees. God knows how he walks on ice, Athelstan thought. He recognized the type – a young man who aped the dandies of the court. A parchment-seller with a shop in some London street, Geoffrey would have the money to act like a courtier.

The two hospitaller knights whom Cranston had mentioned, Sir Gerard Mowbray and Sir Brian Fitzormonde, could have been brothers, each dressed in the grey garb of their Order, cloaks emblazoned with broad white pointed crosses. Athelstan knew the fearsome reputation of these knight monks and had on occasion even acted as confessor at their stronghold in Clerkenwell. Both Gerard and Brian were middle-aged, and every inch soldiers with their neat clipped beards, sharp eyes and close-cropped hair. They moved like cats, men conscious of their own prowess. Warriors, Athelstan mused, men who would kill if they thought the cause just.

Between them stood a lithe-figured dark man, his hair and beard liberally oiled. He was dressed in blue loose-fitting trousers and a heavy military cloak over his doublet. His eyes moved constantly and he watched Cranston and Athelstan as if they were enemies. The coroner barked a question at him, but the fellow just looked dumbly back, opened his mouth and pointed with his finger. Athelstan looked away in pity from the black space where the man's tongue should have been.

'Rastani is a mute.' The girl, Philippa, spoke up, her voice surprisingly deep and husky. 'He was a Muslim, though now converted to our faith. He is…' She bit her lip. 'He was my father's servant.' Her eyes filled with tears and she clutched the arm of her betrothed, though the young man was more unsteady on his feet than she.

Once the introductions were made, Colebrook shouted for more stools and, catching the greedy gaze of Sir John directed towards the young man's wine cup, goblets of hot posset. Cranston and Athelstan sat in the middle of the group. Sir John had no inhibitions but threw back his cloak, stretched out his log-like legs and revelled in the warmth from the fire. The posset he drained in one gulp, held out his cup to be refilled and slurped noisily from it, smacking his lips and staring around as if all his companions were close bosom friends. Athelstan muttered a silent prayer, as he rearranged the writing tray on his lap, that the Good Lord would keep Cranston both sober and awake. Geoffrey sniggered whilst the two knights stared in utter disbelief.

'You are the King's Coroner?' Sir Fulke loudly asked.

'Yes, he is,' Athelstan intervened. 'And Sir John is not always as he appears.'

Cranston smacked his lips again.

'No, no, I am not,' he murmured. 'And I suspect the same is true of everyone here. Always remember a useful dictum: every man born of woman is three persons: what he appears to be, what he claims to be and,' he beamed round, 'what he really is.' He grinned lecherously at Philippa. 'The same is true of the fairer sex.' He suddenly remembered Maude and the thought sobered him quicker than a douche of cold water. 'The same,' he continued crossly, 'is true of the murderer of Sir Ralph Whitton, Constable of this Tower.'

'You suspect someone here?' Sir Fulke said, his face now drained of good humour.

'Yes, I do!' Cranston snapped.

'That's an insult!' the chaplain blurted out. 'My Lord Coroner, you are in your cups! You swagger in here, you know us not...'

Athelstan placed his hand on the coroner's arm. He sensed Sir John was in a dangerous mood and noticed how the hospitallers had both opened their cloaks to display the daggers hooked in their belts. Cranston heeded the warning.

'I make no accusations,' he replied softly. 'But it usually transpires that murder, like charity, begins at home.'

'We face three problems,' Athelstan diplomatically intervened. 'Who killed Sir Ralph, why, and how?'

The lieutenant made a rude sound with his tongue. Cranston leaned forward.

'You wish to say something, sir?'

'Yes, I do. Sir Ralph could have been killed by any rebel from London, by a peasant from the hundreds of villages around us, or by some secret assassin sent in to perform the ghastly deed.'

Cranston nodded and smiled at him.

'Perhaps,' he replied sweetly, 'but I shall return to your theory later. In the meantime, none of you will leave the Tower.' He looked around the sombre hall. 'After I have viewed the corpse, I wish to see all of you, though in more suitable surroundings.'

The lieutenant agreed. 'St John's Chapel in the White Tower,' he announced. 'It is warm, secure, and affords some privacy.'

'Good! Good!' Cranston replied. He smiled falsely at the group. 'In a while, I shall see you all there. Now I wish to inspect Sir Ralph's body.'

'In the North Bastion,' Colebrooke retorted and, rising abruptly, led them out of the hall.

Sir John swayed like a galleon behind him whilst Athelstan hastily packed pen, inkhorn and parchment. The friar was pleased; he had names, first impressions, and Cranston had played his usual favourite trick of alienating everyone. The coroner was as crafty as a fox.

'If you handle suspects roughly,' he had once proclaimed, 'they are less likely to waste time on lies. And, as you know, Brother, most murderers are liars.'

Colebrook waited at the bottom of the steps of the great hall and silently led them past the soaring White Tower which shimmered in the thick snow packed around its base, traces of frost and slush on every shelf, cornice and windowsill. Athelstan stopped and looked up.

'Magnificent!' he murmured. 'How great are the works of man!'

'And how terrible,' Cranston added.

They both stood for a few seconds admiring the sheer white stone of the great tower. They were about to move on when a door at the foot of the keep, built under a flight of outside steps, was flung open. A fantastical hunchbacked creature with a shock of white hair appeared before them. For a moment, he stood as if frozen. His face was pallid, his body covered in a gaudy mass of dirty rags with oversized boots on his feet. Finally he scampered towards them on all fours like a dog, sending flurries of snow flying up on either side. The lieutenant cursed and turned away.

'Welcome to the Tower!' the creature shrieked. 'Welcome to my kingdom! Welcome to the Valley of the Shadow of Death!'

Athelstan looked down at the twisted white face and milky eyes of the albino crouching before him.

'Good morrow, sir,' he replied. 'And you are?'

'Red Hand. Red Hand,' the fellow muttered. He parted his blue-tinged lips, dirty yellow teeth chattering with the cold. 'My name is Red Hand.'

'Well, you're a funny bugger, Red Hand!' Cranston barked.

The mad eyes slyly studied the coroner.

'Madness is as madness does!' Red Hand muttered. 'Twice as mad as some and half as mad as others.' He brought his hand from behind his back and shook a stick with a dirty, inflated pig's bladder tied on the end. 'So, my darlings, you want to play with Red Hand?'

'Piss off, Red Hand!' the lieutenant growled, taking a threatening step towards him.

The albino just glared at Colebrooke.

'Old Red Hand knows things,' he said. 'Old Red Hand is not as stupid as he appears.' Grimy, claw-like fingers stretched out towards Athelstan. 'Red Hand can be your friend, for a price.'

Athelstan unloosed his purse and put two coins in the madman's hands. 'There,' he said softly. 'Now you can be both Sir John's friend and mine.'

'What do you know?' Cranston asked.

The albino jumped up and down. 'Sir Ralph is dead. Executed by God's finger. The Dark Shadows are here. A man's past is always with him. Sir Ralph should have heeded that.' The madman glared at the lieutenant. 'So should others! So should others!' he exclaimed. 'But Red Hand is busy, Red Hand must go.'

'My Lord Coroner, Brother Athelstan,' the lieutenant interrupted, 'Sir Ralph's corpse awaits us.'

'Off to see the gore and blood, are we?' Red Hand cried, jumping up and down. 'An evil man, Sir Ralph. He deserved what he got!'

The lieutenant lashed out with his boot, but Red Hand scampered away, shrieking with laughter.

'Who is he?' Athelstan whispered.

'A former mason here. His wife and child were killed in an accident many years ago.'

'And Sir Ralph let him stay here?'

'Sir Ralph hated the sight of him but could do very little about it. Red Hand is a royal beneficiary. He was a master mason to the old king and has a pension and the right to live here in the Tower.'

'Why Red Hand?' Athelstan asked.

'He lives in the dungeons, and scrubs the torture instruments and the killing block after executions.'

Athelstan shivered and wrapped his cloak more firmly about him. Truly, he thought, this was the Valley of Shadows, a place of violence and sudden death. The lieutenant was about to walk on, but Cranston caught him by the arm.

'What did Red Hand mean about Sir Ralph being an evil man who got his just deserts?'

Colebrooke's bleary eyes looked away. 'Sir Ralph was a strange man,' he muttered. 'Sometimes I think he had demons lurking in his soul.'

Chapter 3

Athelstan and Cranston followed Colebrooke around the half-timbered sheds and outbuildings, under the archway of the inner curtain wall and across the frozen yard to a huge tower which bulged out over the moat. He stopped and pointed.

'There are dungeons beneath ground level, and above them steps leading to the upper tier which has one chamber.' He shrugged. 'That's where Sir Ralph died.'

'Was murdered!' Cranston interrupted.

'Are there other chambers?' Athelstan asked.

'There used to be a second tier, but the doorway was sealed off.'

Athelstan looked up at the snow-capped crenellations and drew in his breath quickly.

'A tower of silence,' he murmured. 'A bleak place to die.'

They walked up the steps. Inside two guards squatted on stools round a brazier. Colebrooke nodded at them. They climbed another steep staircase, pulled back the half-open door, and a dark, musty passageway stretched before them. Quietly cursing to himself, Colebrooke took a tinder from a stone shelf and the sconce torches flared into life. They walked along the cold corridor. Athelstan noticed the pile of fallen masonry, loose bricks and shale which sealed off the former entrance to the upper storey.

Colebrooke searched amongst some keys he had brought out from beneath his cloak, opened the door and, with a half-mocking gesture, waved Athelstan and Cranston inside.

The chamber was a stone-vaulted room. The first impression was one of brooding greyness. No hangings or tapestries on the walls, nothing except the gaunt figure of a dying Christ on a black, wooden crucifix. Pride of place was given to a huge four-poster bed, its begrimed, tawny curtains tightly closed. There was a table, stools and three or four wooden pegs driven into the wall next to the bed. A cloak, heavy jerkin and broad leather sword belt still hung there. On the other side of the bed stood a wooden lavarium with a cracked pewter bowl and jug over which a soiled napkin had been placed. A small hooded fireplace would have afforded some warmth, but only cold powdery ash lay there. A brazier full of half-burnt charcoal stood forlornly in the centre of the room. Athelstan was sure it was colder in here than outside. Cranston snapped his fingers at the open shutters.

'By the Devil's tits, man!' he exclaimed. 'It's freezing!'

'We left things as we found them, My Lord Coroner,' Colebrooke snapped back.

Athelstan nodded towards the window. 'Is that where the assassin is supposed to have climbed in?'

He stared at the huge diamond-shaped opening.

'It could have been the only way,' Colebrooke muttered, going across and slamming the shutters firmly together. Athelstan stared round the room. He recognized the fetid stench of death and noticed with distaste the soiled rushes on the floor and the cracked chamber pot full of night stools and urine.

'By the sod!' Cranston barked, tapping it with his boot. 'Get that removed or the place will stink like a plague pit!'

The coroner crossed to the bed and pulled the curtains back. Athelstan took one look and stepped away in horror. The corpse sprawled there, white and bloodless against the grimy bolsters and sheets; rigid hands still clutched the blood-soaked bedcovers and the man's head was thrust back, face contorted in the rictus of death. The heavy-lidded eyes of the corpse were half-open and seemed to be staring down at the terrible slash which ran from one ear to the other. The blood had poured out like wine from a cracked barrel and lay in a thick congealed mess across the dead man's chest and bedclothes. Athelstan pulled the sheets back and gazed at the half-naked, white body.

'The cause of death,' he muttered, 'is obvious. No other wounds or bruise marks.' He silently made the sign of the cross over the corpse and stepped back.

Colebrooke wisely stood well away. 'Sir Ralph feared such a death,' he murmured.

'When did this fear begin?' Athelstan asked.

'Oh, three to four days ago.'

'Why?' Cranston queried. 'What did Sir Ralph fear?'

Colebrooke shrugged. 'God knows! Perhaps his daughter or kinsman will tell you that. All I know is that before he died, Sir Ralph believed the Angel of Death stood at his elbow.'

Cranston walked across to the window, pulled back the shutters and leaned out into the chill air.

'A sheer drop,' he commented, drawing himself back, much to Athelstan's relief. He alone realized how much the good coroner had drunk. Cranston slammed the shutters closed.

'Who would make such a climb at the dead of night and in the depths of winter?'

'Oh, there are steps cut in the wall,' Colebrooke answered smugly. 'Although few people know they are there.'

'Why?' Athelstan asked.

'They're really just footholds,' Colebrooke answered. 'A precaution of the mason who built the tower. If anyone fell in the moat, they could climb out.'

'So,' Cranston mumbled, slumping down on to the stool and wiping his forehead, 'you are saying someone, probably a soldier or paid assassin, used these footholds and climbed to the window.' He turned and looked at the shutters. 'According to you,' the coroner continued, 'the killer prized a dagger through the crack to lift the catch, got in, and slashed Sir Ralph's throat.'

Colebrooke nodded slowly. 'I suppose so, Sir John.'

'And I suppose,' Cranston added sarcastically, 'Sir Ralph just allowed his assassin entry, didn't even get out of his bed but lay back like a lamb and allowed his throat to be cut?'

Colebrooke went across to the shutters, and, pushing the wooden clasp back into place, locked them shut. He then took out his dagger, slid it into the crack between the shutters and gently levered the clasp open. He drew the shutters wide, turned and smiled at Cranston.

'It can be done, My Lord Coroner,' he observed gaily. 'The assassin, quiet-footed, crossed the chamber. It only takes seconds to cut a man's throat, especially someone who has drunk deeply.'

Athelstan reflected on what the lieutenant had said. It did make sense. Both he and Cranston knew about the Nightshades, robbers who could enter a house under cover of darkness and plunder it beneath the sleeping noses of burgesses, wives, children, and even dogs. Why should this be any different? Athelstan studied the chamber carefully: the heavy granite walls, the stone-vaulted ceiling and cold rag stone floor beneath the rushes.

'No, Brother!' Colebrooke called out as if reading the friar's thoughts. 'No secret passageways exist. There are two ways to enter this chamber – by the window or by the door. However, there were guards in the lower chamber, we passed them as we came up, and the upper storey is blocked off by a fall of masonry.'

'Were any traces of blood found?' Athelstan asked. He saw the lieutenant smirk and glance sideways at the gory corpse sprawled on the bed. 'No,' Athelstan continued crossly, 'I mean elsewhere. Near the window or the door. When the assassin walked away, his knife or sword must have been coated with blood.'

Colebrooke shook his head. 'Look for yourself, Brother. I found no trace.'

Athelstan glanced despairingly at Cranston who now sat like a sagging sack on the stool, eyes half-closed after his morning's heavy drinking and vigorous exertions in the cold. The friar conducted his search thoroughly: the bedclothes and corpse were soaked in dried blood but he found no traces near the window, in the rushes or around the door.

'Did you find anything else disturbed?'

Colebrooke shook his head. Cranston suddenly stirred himself.

'Why did Sir Ralph come here?' he asked abruptly. 'These were not his usual chambers.'

'He thought he would be safe. The North Bastion is one of the most inaccessible in the fortress. The constable's

53

usual lodgings are in the royal apartments in the White Tower.'

'And he was safe,' Athelstan concluded, 'until the moat froze over.'

'Yes,' Colebrooke replied. 'Neither I nor anyone else thought of that.'

'Wouldn't an assassin be seen?' Cranston interrupted.

'I doubt it, Sir John. At the dead of night, the Tower is shrouded in darkness. There were no guards on the North Bastion, whilst those on the curtain wall would spend most of their time trying to keep warm.'

'So,' Cranston narrowed his eyes, 'before we meet the others, let's establish the sequence of events.'

'Sir Ralph dined in the great hall and drank deeply. Geoffrey Parchmeiner and the two guards escorted him over here. The latter searched this chamber, the passage-way and the room below. All was in good order.'

'Then what?'

'Sir Ralph secured the door behind him. The guards outside heard that. They escorted Geoffrey out of the passageway, locked the door at the far end and began their vigil. They were at their posts all night and noticed nothing untoward. Neither did I on my usual nightly rounds.'

Athelstan held up his hand. 'This business of the keys?'

'Sir Ralph had a key to his own chamber, as did the guards, on a key ring below.'

'And the door at the end of that passage?'

'Again, both Sir Ralph and the guard had a key. You will see them when you go below, hanging from pegs driven into the wall.'

'Go on, Lieutenant, what happened then?'

'Just after Prime this morning, Geoffrey Parch-meiner...' The lieutenant looked slyly at Athelstan. 'You have met him? The beloved prospective son-in-law? Well, he came across to waken Sir Ralph.'

'Why Geoffrey?'

'Sir Ralph trusted him.'

'Did he bring food or drink?'

'No. He wanted to, but because of the cold weather Sir Ralph said he wished to be aroused with Geoffrey in attendance. They would plan the day, and breakfast with the rest of the company in the hall.'

'Continue,' Cranston blurted crossly, stamping his feet against the cold.

'Well, the guards led Geoffrey up the stairs, let him through the passageway door and locked it behind him. They heard him go down the corridor, knock on the door and shout, but Sir Ralph could not be roused. After a while Geoffrey came back. "Sir Ralph cannot be woken," he proclaimed.' Colebrooke stopped, scratched his head and closed his eyes in an attempt to recall events. 'Geoffrey took the key to Sir Ralph's chamber from the peg but changed his mind and came for me. I was in the great hall. I hurried here, collected the keys and unlocked the door.' The lieutenant gestured towards the bed. 'We found Sir Ralph as you did.'

'And the shutters were open?' Cranston asked.

'Yes.'

'How long has the moat been frozen solid?' Athelstan queried.

'About three days.' Colebrooke rubbed his hands together vigorously. 'Surely, Sir John, we need not stay here?' he pleaded. 'There are warmer places to ask such questions.'

Cranston stood and stretched.

'In a little while,' he murmured. 'How long had Sir Ralph been constable?'

'Oh, about four years.'

'Did you like him?'

'No, I did not. He was a martinet, a stickler for discipline – except where his daughter or her lover were concerned.'

Cranston nodded and went back to look at the corpse. 'I suppose,' he muttered, 'there's no sign of any murder weapon? Perhaps, Athelstan, you could check again?'

The friar groaned, but with Colebrooke's help carried out a quick survey of the room, raking back the rushes with their feet, and sifting amongst the cold ash in the fireplace.

'Nothing,' Colebrooke declared. 'It would be hard to hide a pin here.'

Athelstan went across and pulled the sword from Sir Ralph's sword belt. 'There are no blood stains here,' he commented. 'Not a jot, not a speck. Sir John, we should go.'

Outside, they stopped to examine a stain on the passage floor but it was only oil. They were halfway down the stairs when Athelstan suddenly pulled the lieutenant back. 'The two guards?' he whispered. 'They are the same sentries as last night?'

'Yes. Professional mercenaries who served Sir Ralph when he was in the household of His Grace the Regent.'

'They would be loyal?'

Colebrooke made a face. 'I should think so. They took a personal oath. More importantly, Sir Ralph had doubled their wages. They had nothing to gain from his death and a great deal to lose.'

'Do *you* have anything to gain?' Cranston asked thickly.

Colebrooke's hand fell to his dagger hilt. 'Sir John, I resent that, though I confess I did not like Whitton, notwithstanding His Grace the Regent did.'

'Did you want Whitton's post?'

'Of course. I believe I am the better man.'

'But the Regent disagreed?'

'John of Gaunt kept his own private counsel,' Colebrooke sourly observed. 'Though I hope he will now appoint me as Whitton's successor.'

'Why?' Athelstan asked softly.

Colebrooke looked surprised. 'I am loyal, and if trouble comes, I shall hold the Tower to my dying breath!'

Cranston grinned and tapped him gently on the chest. 'Now, my good lieutenant, you have it. We think the same on this. Sir Ralph's death may be linked to the conspiracies which flourish like weeds in the villages and hamlets around London.'

Colebrooke nodded. 'Whitton was a hard taskmaster,' he replied, 'and the Great Community's paid assassin would have found such a task fairly easy to accomplish.'

Athelstan too smiled and patted Colebrooke on the shoulder. 'You may be right, Master Colebrooke, but there is only one thing wrong with such a theory.'

The lieutenant gazed dumbly back.

'Can't you see?' Athelstan murmured. 'Someone in the Tower must have told such an assassin where, when and how Sir Ralph could be found!'

A now crestfallen lieutenant led them down the stairs. The two burly, thick-set guards still squatted with hands outstretched towards the fiery red brazier. They hardly moved as Colebrooke approached and Athelstan sensed their disdain for a junior officer suddenly thrust into authority.

'You were on guard last night?'

The soldiers nodded.

'You saw nothing untoward?'

Again the nods, accompanied by supercilious smiles as if they found Athelstan slightly amusing and rather boring.

'Stand up!' Cranston roared. 'Stand up. You whore-begotten sons of bitches! By the sod, I've had better men tied to trees and whipped till their backs were red!'

The two soldiers jumped up at the steely menace in Cranston's voice.

'That's better,' the coroner purred. 'Now, my buckos, answer my clerk's questions properly and all will be well.' He grasped one by the shoulder. 'Otherwise, I may put it about that in the dead of night you killed your master.'

'That's not true!' the fellow grated. 'We were loyal to Sir Ralph. We saw nothing, knew nothing, until the popinjay—' the guard shrugged '—the constable's prospective son-in-law, comes rushing down, exclaiming he can't rouse Sir Ralph. He grabs the key and is about to return, but the coward thinks better of it and sends for the lieutenant here.'

'You heard him knock on the door and call Sir Ralph?' Athelstan asked.

'Of course we did.'

'But he did not enter?'

'The key was down here,' the guard replied, pointing to a peg driven into the wall. 'It was hanging before our eyes. There were only two. One here, and Sir Ralph had the other.'

'You are certain of that?' Cranston asked.

'Yes, yes,' the fellow confirmed. 'I found the other key on the table next to the constable's bed as soon as I opened the door. I have it now.'

Cranston nodded. 'Ah, well,' he breathed, 'enough is enough. Let us see the tower from the outside.'

As they left the North Bastion, they suddenly heard an awesome din from the inner bailey. They followed the lieutenant as he hurried under the arch, staring across the snow-capped green. The noise came from a building in between the great hall and the White Tower. At first Athelstan couldn't distinguish what was happening. He saw figures running about, dogs leaping and yelping in the snow. Colebrooke breathed deeply and relaxed.

'It's only him,' he murmured. 'Look!'

Athelstan and Cranston watched in stupefaction as a great brown shaggy-haired bear lurched into full view. The beast stood on its hind legs, its paws pummelling the air.

'I have seen bears before,' Cranston murmured, 'rough-haired little beasts attacked by dogs, but nothing as majestic as that.'

The bear roared and Athelstan saw the great chains which swung from the iron collar round its neck, each held by a keeper as the lunatic Red Hand led the animal across the bailey to be fastened to a huge stake at the far side of the great hall.

'It's magnificent!' Athelstan murmured.

'A present,' the lieutenant replied, 'from a Norwegian prince to the present king's grandfather, God bless him! It is called Ursus Magnus.'

'Ah!' Athelstan smiled. 'After the constellation.'

Colebrooke looked dumb.

'The stars,' Athelstan persisted. 'A constellation in the heavens.'

Colebrooke smiled thinly and led them back to a postern gate in the outer curtain wall. He pulled back bolts and the hinges shrieked in protest as he threw open the solid, creaking gate.

No one, Athelstan thought, has gone through this gate for months.

They stepped gingerly on to the frozen moat, the very quietness and heavy mist creating an eerie, unreal feeling.

'The only time you'll ever walk on water, Priest!' Cranston muttered.

Athelstan grinned. 'A strange feeling,' he replied, then looked at the drawn face of Colebrooke. 'Why is the gate here?'

The lieutenant shrugged. 'It's used very rarely. Sometimes a spy or a secret messenger slips across the moat, or someone who wishes to leave the Tower unnoticed. Now,' he tapped his boot on the thick, heavy ice, 'it makes no difference.'

Athelstan stared around. Behind him the great soaring curtain wall stretched up to the snow-laden clouds, whilst the far side of the moat was hidden in a thick mist. Nothing stirred. There was no sound except their own breathing and the scraping noise of their boots on the ice. They walked gingerly, carefully, as if expecting the ice to crack and the water to reappear. They followed the sheer curtain wall round to the North Bastion.

'Where are these footholds?' Cranston asked.

Colebrooke beckoned them forward and pointed to the brickwork. At first the holds in the wall could hardly be detected, but at last they saw them, like the claw marks of a huge bird embedded deeply in the stonework. Cranston pushed his hand into one of them.

'Yes,' he muttered, 'someone has been here. Look, the ice is broken.'

Athelstan inspected the icy apertures and agreed. He followed the trail of the footholds up until they, like the top of the tower, were lost in the clinging mist.

'A hard climb,' he observed. 'Most dangerous in the dead of night.' He looked at the frost-covered snow and, stooping down, picked up something, hiding it in the palm of his hand until Colebrooke turned to go back.

'What is it?' Cranston slurred. 'What did you find there?'

The friar opened his hand and Cranston smiled at the silver-gilt buckle glinting in his palm.

'So,' Cranston mumbled, 'someone was here. All we have to do is match the buckle with its wearer, then it's heigh-ho to King's Bench, a swift trial, and a more prolonged execution.'

Athelstan shook his head. 'Oh, Sir John,' he whispered, 'if things were only so simple.' They went back through the postern gate and into the inner bailey. The Tower had now come to life even though the frost still held and there was still no sign of any break in the weather. Farriers had fired the forges and the bailey rang with the clang of the hammer and the whoosh of bellows as ragged apprentices worked hard to fan the forge fires to life. A butcher was slicing up a gutted pig and scullions ran, shaking the blood from the meat, to stick it into fat-bellied tubs of salt and brine so it would last through to the spring. A groom trotted a lame horse, roaring at his companions to look for any defect, whilst scullions and maids soaked piles of grease-stained pewter plates in vats of scalding water. The lieutenant watched the scene and grinned.

'Soon be Christmas!' he announced. 'All must be clean and ready.'

Athelstan nodded, watching three boys drag holly and other evergreen shrubs across the snow to the steps of the great keep.

'You will celebrate Christmas?' Athelstan asked, nodding to a high-wheeled cart from which soldiers were now unloading huge tuns of wine.

'Of course,' Colebrooke replied. 'Death is no stranger to the Tower, and Sir Ralph will be buried before Christmas Eve.' He walked on as if tired of their questions.

Athelstan winked at Cranston, stood his ground and called out: 'Master Colebrooke?'

The lieutenant turned, trying hard to hide his irritation. 'Yes, Brother?'

'Why are so many people here? I mean the hospitallers, Master Geoffrey, Sir Fulke?'

Colebrooke shrugged. 'The constable's kinsman always stay here.'

'And young Geoffrey?'

Colebrooke smirked. 'I think he's as hot for Mistress Philippa as she is for him. Sir Ralph invited him to the Tower for Christmas, and why not? This great frost has stopped all business in the city and Sir Ralph insisted, especially when he grew strangely fearful, that his daughter's betrothed stay with him.'

'The two hospitallers?' Cranston asked.

'Old friends,' Colebrooke replied. 'They come here each Christmas and go through the same ritual. They arrive two weeks before Yuletide, and every Christmas Eve go to sup at the Golden Mitre tavern outside the

Tower. They always stay till Twelfth Night and leave after the Feast of the Epiphany. Three times they've done so, though God knows why!' He turned and spat a globule of yellow phlegm on to the white snow. 'As I have said, Sir Ralph had his secrets and I never pried.'

Cranston fidgeted, a sign he was growing bored as well as tired of the cold, so Athelstan allowed Colebrooke to take them back into the White Tower, up a stone spiral staircase, through an antechamber and into the Chapel of St John.

Athelstan immediately relaxed as he caught the fragrant scent of incense. He walked into the nave with its soaring hammer-beamed roof and wide aisles, each flanked by twelve circular pillars around which thick green and scarlet velvet ribbons had been tied. The floor was polished, the strange red flagstones seeming to give off their own warmth, whilst the delicate paintings on the walls and the huge glazed windows caught the blinding white light of the snow and bathed both sanctuary and nave in a warm, glowing hue. Braziers, sprinkled with herbs, stood next to each pillar, making the air thick with the cloying sweetness of summer. Athelstan felt warm, comfortable and at peace, even though he studied the church enviously. If only, he thought, he had such decorations at St Erconwald! He saw the great silver star pinned above the chancel screen and, muttering with delight, walked into the silent sanctuary, marvelling at the marble steps and magnificent altar carved out of pure white alabaster.

'So serene,' he murmured, coming back to join his companions.

Colebrooke smiled self-consciously. 'Before we left the hall, I ordered servants to prepare the place,' he announced, and looked around. 'By some trick or artifice of the architects, whether it be the thickness of the stone or its location in the Tower, this chapel is always warm.'

'I need refreshment,' Cranston solemnly announced. 'I have walked up many stairs, studied a ghastly corpse, balanced on freezing ice, and now I've had enough! Master Lieutenant, you seem a goodly man. You will gather the rest here and, seeing it's the Yuletide season, bring a jug of claret for myself and my clerk.'

Colebrooke agreed and hurried off, but not before he and Athelstan had rearranged the chapel stools into a wide semicircle. Once he'd gone, Athelstan brought a polished table from the sanctuary and laid out pen, inkhorn and parchment. He took care to warm the ink over the brazier so it would run smooth and clear from his quill. Cranston just squatted on his chair, throwing back his cloak and revelling in the fragrant warmth. Athelstan studied him carefully.

'Sir John,' he murmured, 'take care with the wine. You have drunk enough and are tired.'

'Sod off, Athelstan!' Cranston slurred angrily. 'I'll drink what I damned well like!'

Athelstan closed his eyes and breathed a prayer for help. So far Sir John had behaved himself, but the wine in his belly might rouse the devil in his heart and only the Good Lord knew what mischief might then occur. Colebrooke hurried back. Behind him, much to Athelstan's despair, a servant carried a huge jug of claret and two deep-bowled goblets. Cranston seized the jug like a thirsty man and downed two cupfuls as the rest of the constable's household entered the chapel and sat on the stools before him. At last Cranston closed his eyes, gave a deep rich belch and pronounced himself satisfied. His reluctant guests stared in disbelief at the red face of the King's Coroner as he sprawled slack-limbed on the chair before them. Athelstan was torn between anger and admiration. Something had upset Cranston, though God only knew what. Nevertheless, the coroner's ability to drink a vineyard dry and still keep his wits about him always fascinated Athelstan.

The Dominican quickly scanned the assembled people. The two hospitallers looked aloof and disdainful. Philippa clung more closely to her now tipsy betrothed who grinned benevolently back at Cranston. Rastani, the servant, looked ill at ease, fearful of the huge cross which hung from one of the beams above him, and Athelstan wondered if the Muslim's conversion to the true faith was genuine. Sir Fulke looked bored, as if he wished to be free of such tiresome proceedings, whilst the chaplain's exasperation at being so abruptly summoned was barely suppressed.

'I do thank you,' Athelstan began smoothly, 'for coming here. Mistress Philippa, please accept our condolences on the sudden and ghastly loss of your father.' Athelstan toyed with the stem of his goose-quilled pen. 'We now know the details surrounding your father's death.'

'Murder!' Philippa strained forward, her ample bosom heaving under her thick taffeta dress. 'Murder, Brother! My father was murdered!'

'Yes, yes, so he was,' Cranston slurred. 'But by whom, eh? Why and how?' He sat up straight and drunkenly tapped the side of his fiery red nose. 'Do not worry, Mistress! The murderer will be found and do his last final dance on Tyburn scaffold.'

'Your father,' Athelstan interrupted, 'seemed most fearful, Mistress Philippa. He moved from his usual quarters and shut himself up in the North Bastion. Why? What frightened him?'

The group fell strangely silent, tensing at this intrusion into the very heart of their secrets.

'I asked a question,' Athelstan repeated softly. 'What was Sir Ralph so frightened of that he locked himself up in a chamber, doubled the wages of his guards, and insisted that visitors be searched? Who was it,' he continued, 'that wanted Sir Ralph's death so much he crossed an icy moat in the dead of night, climbed the sheer wall of a tower, and entered a guarded chamber to commit foul, midnight murder?'

'The rebels!' Colebrooke broke in. 'Traitors who wanted to remove a man who would protect the young King to the last drop of his blood!'

'Nonsense!' snapped Athelstan. 'His Grace the Regent, John of Gaunt, will as you said yourself, Master Colebrooke, appoint a successor no less fervent in his loyalty.'

'My father was special,' Philippa blurted out.

'Mistress,' Athelstan caught and held her tearful glance, 'God knows your father was special, both in his life and in his secrets. You know about those, so why not tell us?'

The girl's eyes fell away. She brought her hand from beneath her cloak and tossed a yellowing piece of parchment on to the table. 'That changed my father's life,' she stammered. 'Though God knows why!'

Athelstan picked up the parchment and quickly gazed at the people sitting around him. He noticed the hospitallers were suddenly tense. The friar smiled secretly to himself. Good, he thought. Now the mystery unfolds.

Chapter 4

The parchment was greasy and finger-stained, a six-inch square with a three-masted ship crudely drawn in the centre and a large black cross in each corner.

'Is that all?' Athelstan asked, passing the parchment back.

The girl tensed. Her lower lip trembled, tears pricked her eyes.

'There was something else,' Athelstan continued. 'Wasn't there?'

Philippa nodded. Geoffrey took her hand and held it, stroking it gently as if she was a child.

'There was a sesame seed cake.'

'What?' Cranston barked.

'A seed cake like a biscuit, a dirty yellow colour.'

'What happened to it?' Cranston asked.

'I saw my father walk along the parapet. He seemed very agitated. He brought his arm back and threw the cake into the moat. After that he was a changed man, keeping everyone away from him and insisting on moving to the North Bastion tower.'

'Is that correct?' Cranston asked the rest of the group.

'Of course it is!' the chaplain snapped. 'Mistress Philippa is not a liar.'

'Then, Father,' Cranston asked silkily, 'did Sir Ralph share his secrets with you?' He held up a podgy hand. 'I know about the seal of confession. All I'm asking is, did he confide in you?'

'I think not,' Colebrooke sniggered. 'Sir Ralph had certain questions to ask the chaplain about stores and provisions which appear to have gone missing.'

The priest turned on him, his lip curling like that of an angry dog.

'Watch your tongue, Lieutenant!' he rasped. 'True, things have gone missing, but that does not mean that I am the thief. There are others,' he added meaningfully, 'with access to the Wardrobe Tower.'

'Meaning?' Colebrooke shouted.

'Oh, shut up!' Cranston ordered. 'We are not here about stores but about a man's life. I ask all of you, on your allegiance to the King – for this could be a matter of treason – did Sir Ralph confide in one of you? Does this parchment mean anything to any of you?'

A chorus of 'No's' greeted the coroner's demands though Athelstan noticed that the hospitallers looked away as they mumbled their responses.

'I hope you are telling the truth,' Cranston tartly observed. 'Sir Ralph may have been slain by peasant leaders plotting rebellion. Your father, Mistress Philippa, was a close friend and trusted ally of the court.'

Athelstan intervened, trying to calm the situation. 'Mistress Philippa, tell me about your father.'

The girl laced her fingers together nervously and looked at the floor.

'He was always a soldier,' she began. 'He served in Prussia against the Latvians, on the Caspian, and then travelled to Outremer, Egypt, Palestine and Cyprus.' She blinked and nodded at the hospitallers. 'They can tell you more about that than I.' She took a deep breath. 'Fifteen years ago,' she continued, 'he was in Egypt in the army of the Caliph and then he came home covered in glory, a rich man. I was three years old. My mother died a year later and we entered the household of John of Gaunt. My father became one of his principal retainers; four years ago, he was appointed Constable of the Tower.'

Athelstan smiled understandingly. He knew Sir Ralph's type: a professional soldier, a mercenary who would crusade for the faith but was not averse to serving in the armies of the infidel. Athelstan stared round the group. How quiet and calm they appeared, though he sensed something was wrong. They were hiding mutual dislikes and rivalries in their over-eagerness to answer his questions.

'I suppose,' he remarked drily, 'you have already been through Sir Ralph's papers?'

Athelstan looked at Sir Fulke, who nodded.

'Of course I have been through my brother's documents, household accounts, memoranda and letters. I found nothing untoward. I am, after all,' he added, glaring round the room as if expecting a challenge, 'the executor of Sir Ralph's will.'

'Of course, of course,' Cranston assured him.

Athelstan groaned to himself. Yes, he thought, and if there was anything damaging, it will have been removed. He stared at the young man next to Philippa.

'How long, sir, have you known your betrothed?'

Geoffrey's wine-flushed face was wreathed in smiles as he gripped her hand more firmly. 'Two years.'

Athelstan noticed the conspiratorial smiles the two lovers exchanged.

Cranston leered at the girl whilst he considered the incongruous couple. Geoffrey was outstandingly handsome and probably quite wealthy, yet Philippa was almost plain. Moreover, Sir Ralph had been a soldier and Geoffrey was not, at first glance, the sort of man likely to be welcomed into such a family. Cranston then remembered Maude and his own passionate courting of her. Love was strange, as Athelstan kept reminding him, and opposites were often attracted to each other.

'Tell me, Geoffrey, why did you stay in the Tower?'

The young man belched and blinked his eyes as if he was on the point of falling asleep. 'Well,' he mumbled, 'the great frost has killed all trade in the city. Sir Ralph wished me to stay during the Yuletide season – even more so after he became distraught and upset.'

'Did you know the reason for his anxiety?'

'No,' Geoffrey slurred. 'Why should I?'

'Did you like Sir Ralph?'

'I loved him as a son does a father.'

Cranston switched his attention to Sir Fulke, who was beginning openly to fidget.

'Sir Fulke, you say you are the executor of Sir Ralph's will?'

'Yes, I am. And, before you ask, I am also a beneficiary, after the will is approved in the Court of Probate.'

'What does the will provide?'

'Well, Sir Ralph had property next to the Charterhouse in St Giles. This and all of the monies banked with the Lombards in Cornhill will go to Philippa.'

'And to you?'

'Meadows and pastures in the Manor of Holywell outside Oxford.'

'A rich holding?'

'Yes, Sir John, a rich holding, but not rich enough to murder for.'

'I didn't say that.'

'You implied it.'

'Sir Ralph,' Athelstan hurriedly interrupted, 'was a wealthy man?'

'He amassed wealth in his travels,' Sir Fulke snapped back. 'And he was careful with his monies.' Athelstan noticed the sour smile on the chaplain's face. Sir Ralph, he thought, was probably a miser. The friar looked sideways at Cranston and quietly groaned. The good coroner was taking one of his short naps, his great belly sagging, mouth half-open. Oh, Lord, Athelstan quietly prayed, please make sure he doesn't snore!

'Why do you live in the Tower, a bleak dwelling place for any man?' Athelstan abruptly asked.

Sir Fulke shrugged. 'My brother paid me to help him in an unofficial capacity.'

Both he and Athelstan chose to ignore the snorting laughter of Colebrooke. Cranston was now quietly nodding, belching softly and smacking his lips. Mistress Philippa tightened her mouth and Athelstan cursed; he did not wish his interrogation to end in mocking laughter.

'Sir Gerard, Sir Brian,' he almost shouted in an attempt to rouse Cranston, 'how long have you been in the Tower?'

'Two weeks,' Fitzormonde replied. 'We come every year.'

'It's a ritual,' Mowbray added, 'ever since we served with Sir Ralph in Egypt. We met to discuss old times.'

'So you were close friends of Sir Ralph?'

'In a sense. Colleagues, veterans from old wars.' Mowbray stroked his evenly clipped beard. 'But, I'll be honest with you, Sir Ralph was a man more feared and respected than loved.'

Athelstan picked up the yellowing piece of parchment and thrust it at them.

'Do you know what this drawing means or the significance of the seed cake?'

Both knights shook their heads, but Athelstan was sure they were lying. He leaned forward. 'Why?' he whispered. 'Why should Sir Ralph be so terrified of this?' He stared slowly round the rest of the group.

'A cup of sack!' Cranston muttered thickly.

'Who found this?' Athelstan quickly asked.

Sir Fulke pointed to Rastani, who sat with his dark face fearful and anxious. Athelstan leaned forward. 'What does this mean, Rastani?'

The eyes stared blankly back.

'Where did you find it?'

The fellow suddenly made strange gestures with his fingers.

'He can hear but not speak,' Philippa reminded the friar.

Fascinated, Athelstan watched the strange hand signs which Philippa translated for him.

'He found it on a table in my father's chamber,' she announced. 'Four days ago. Early on the morning of the ninth of December – that and the hard-baked seed cake.'

Athelstan caught and held Rastani's glance.

'You were a faithful servant to Sir Ralph?'

The man nodded in response.

'Why didn't you move with your master to the North Bastion?' Athelstan continued.

The fellow's mouth opened and shut like a landed carp's.

'I can answer that,' Philippa said. 'When the message was received, my father distanced himself from Rastani, though God knows why.' She gently stroked the man's hand. 'As I have said, Father became strange. Even I did not recognise him from his actions.'

Cranston smacked his lips and suddenly stirred.

'Yes, yes, very good!' he bawled. 'But did any of you approach the North Bastion tower the night Sir Ralph was killed?'

A series of firm denials greeted his question.

'So you can all account for your movements?'

'I can,' the kinsman spoke up. 'Rastani and I were out of the Tower. We were sent to buy stores from a merchant in Cripplegate. Or, at least, that's where the warehouse is. You can ask Master Christopher Manley in Heyward Lane near All Hallows.'

'That's near the Tower?'

'Yes, it is, Sir John.'

'And when did you leave?'

'Before dinner, and did not return until after Prime this morning when we heard of Sir Ralph's death. Rastani and I can vouch for each other. If you doubt that, speak to Master Manley. He saw us take lodgings at a tavern in Muswell Street.'

Sir John rose and stretched.

'Well, well! Now my clerk and I,' he trumpeted, 'would like to question each of you alone. Though,' he smiled at the girl, 'Mistress Philippa and Geoffrey had best stay together. Master Colebrooke, there's a chamber below. Perhaps our guests could wait there?'

There were mumbled protests and groans but Cranston, refreshed after his nap, glared round beneath thick furrowed brows. Led by Colebrooke, all left except for Philippa and Geoffrey.

'Your chamber, Master Geoffrey?' Athelstan asked. 'Where is it?'

'Above the gatehouse.'

'And you stayed there all night?'

The young man smiled weakly. 'You're a perceptive man, Sir John. That's why you asked me to stay, I suppose? I spent the night with Philippa.'

The girl looked away, blushing. Cranston smiled and tapped the man gently on the shoulder. 'Why did you not rouse Sir Ralph yourself?'

The young man rubbed his eyes. 'As I have said before, I didn't have a key and, God be my witness, I knew there was something wrong. The corridor was cold, with no sound from Sir Ralph's chamber.' He smiled bleakly at Athelstan. 'I am not the bravest of men, I'll be honest. I did not like Sir Ralph using me as a page boy but he distrusted the others.'

'You mean Colebrooke and the rest?'

'Yes, I think so.'

Cranston stared at Philippa. 'Had your father been in such dark spirits before?'

'Yes, about three years ago, just before Christmas. But it passed when he met his companions, as was their custom, and supped at the Golden Mitre.'

'Who were your father's companions?' Athelstan asked.

'Well, the two hospitallers, Sir Gerard Mowbray and Sir Brian Fitzormonde, and Sir Adam Home – he's a merchant in the city.'

'Did these include all your father's comrades-in-arms?'

'Oh, there was someone called Bartholomew. Bartholomew...' the girl repeated, biting her lip '...Burghgesh, I believe. But he never came.'

'Why?'

'I don't know.' She half laughed. 'I think he's dead.'

'Why did your father insist on meeting his friends every year just before Christmas?'

'I don't know. Some pact they made a long time ago.'

Athelstan scrutinised the girl carefully. He was sure she was hiding something. 'Tell me,' he said, changing tack, 'is there more than one postern gate on to the moat?'

'Oh, yes,' Philippa replied. 'Quite a number.'

Athelstan glanced at Cranston. 'My Lord Coroner, do you have any questions?'

'No,' Sir John replied. 'Enough is enough! Ask Master William Hammond to come in.'

The priest entered in a surly, disgruntled way, biting his thumb nail to the quick as he gave curt answers to Athelstan's questions. Yes, he had been in the fortress that evening, but in his chamber in the Beauchamp Tower near the Church of St Peter ad Vincula.

The two hospitaller knights were more courteous but equally adamant. They had chambers in Martin Tower and spent most of the evening drinking or trying their hand at chess.

'I assure you, Sir John,' Mowbray rasped, 'we can hardly find our way around the Tower in the full light of day, never mind on a freezing winter's night.'

'But you know what this means, don't you?' Athelstan accused, picking up the piece of yellow parchment.

'By heaven, we do not!' Fitzormonde replied.

'Sir,' Athelstan retorted, 'I think you do, as you also know about the seed cake.'

The two hospitallers shook their heads.

'Oh, come,' Athelstan continued. 'Let's not be coy. You are monks and knights. Your Order fights for the cross in Outremer. My Order, too, has brothers who serve there.

75

They bring back tales which they relate over the dinner table at Blackfriars.'

'What tales?' Mowbray challenged.

'How in the mountains of Palestine live a secret sect of infidels called the Assassins, ruled by a chieftain called the Old Man of the Mountain. This coven deals in secret assassination. They are fed on drugs and despatched by their master with golden daggers to kill whomever he has marked down for destruction.'

Cranston watched the two knights tense and, for the first time, show a flicker of nervousness, Fitzormonde particularly.

'Now these assassins,' Athelstan continued, 'always give their victim fair warning. They do not leave a picture but a flat seed cake as a sign that violent death will soon be upon them.' Athelstan stood up and stretched to ease the cramp in his thighs and legs. 'I ask myself, why is this secret sect which flourishes in the Middle Sea, carrying out murder in the cold and sombre chambers of the Tower of London?'

'Are you accusing us?' Mowbray shouted. 'If so, do it!'

'I am not accusing anyone, just remarking on a strange coincidence.'

'Rastani is from Palestine!' Mowbray cried. 'Sir Ralph did distance himself from his so-called faithful servant.'

'Why do you say "so-called"?' Cranston quickly asked.

'Because I do not believe Rastani's conversion to our faith was genuine. Such men bear grudges. They wait years to settle accounts.'

'But Rastani was absent from the Tower?'

'He could have slipped back.'

'No, no, no!' Athelstan sat down and shook his head. 'Sir Ralph's death is more complex than that. You served with him?'

'Yes, we did. The Caliph of Cairo hired us to crush revolts in the city of Alexandria.'

'And after that?'

'Sir Ralph came home. We stayed a while longer before returning to our house in Clerkenwell.'

'Have you ever returned across the seas?' Cranston asked.

Mowbray shook his head. 'No, Fitzormonde is slightly wrong. When we served with Sir Ralph, we were not hospitallers. We joined after we left him. The Order sent us back to England. I am at Clerkenwell, Fitzormonde in our house at Rievaulx near York.'

Athelstan stared at the closed, set faces of both knights. 'Forgive me,' Athelstan said quietly, 'I do not wish to call you liars, but there is a great mystery here and you are party to it.' He leaned over and suddenly pulled back Mowbray's cloak. 'You wear chained mail? And you, too, Sir Brian. Why? Do you also fear the assassin's dagger? How well do you sleep at night? What secrets did you share with Sir Ralph?'

'By the Rood!' Sir Brian suddenly stood up. 'I have heard enough. We have told you what we can. Leave it at that!'

Both hospitallers swept out of the room. Cranston slumped on the stool and stretched out his legs.

'A pretty mess, eh, Friar? What have we here? Treason by persons unknown or foul midnight murder?'

'I don't know.' Athelstan replaced the stopper in the ink horn as he rearranged his writing materials. 'But we do have the buckle we found on the icy moat, and I know who it belongs to.'

'By the sod!' Cranston cried. 'For a monk you are sharp-eyed, Athelstan.'

'For a friar I am very quick, My Lord Coroner, and so would you be if you drank less claret!'

'I drink to drown my sorrows.' Cranston looked away. What would Maude be doing now? he fretted. What was she hiding? Why wouldn't she just tell him instead of giving those long, mournful glances? Cranston glared at the small statue in a niche, the Virgin and Child; secretly, the coroner hated Christmas. Yuletide always brought back the memories of little Matthew, taken by the plague, but not before the mite had shown Sir John the wonder with which every child greeted Christmas. Did Maude also have her memories?

'Sir John!'

Cranston blinked to hide his tears and grinned over at Athelstan.

'I have a need of refreshment, monk!'

Athelstan saw the pain in his friend's face and looked away.

'In a while, Sir John. First, let us see Sir Fulke. I wish to search Sir Ralph's bed chamber here in the White Tower.'

Cranston nodded and lumbered off whilst Athelstan packed his writing tray away. The friar sat for a while admiring the beauty of St John's Chapel, comparing it to the grimness of St Erconwald's. He thought of Benedicta. How lovely she had looked at the early morning Mass. He wondered if Huddle would use her in the painting of the Visitation he was planning for one of the aisles. What, Athelstan wondered, would she do at Christmas? She had mentioned a brother in Colchester. Perhaps she might stay in Southwark and agree to go for a walk, or at least sit and share a goblet of wine with him and gossip about the past. Christmas could be so lonely... Athelstan's eye caught a crucifix and he suddenly remembered the horrors being perpetrated in the cemetery at St Erconwald's. He must get to the bottom of that matter. Who could it be, and why?

'Brother Athelstan! Brother Athelstan!' Cranston stood, leering down at him. 'You drink too much claret, priest,' the coroner mockingly announced. 'Come, we must visit the late constable's chamber. Colebrooke and Sir Fulke are on their way.'

Sir Ralph's quarters were up a polished wooden staircase in one of the turrets of the White Tower, a pleasant, sweet-smelling chamber in sharp contrast to the grim cell over in the North Bastion. Two small bay windows with cushioned seats below and an oriel window, glazed with stained glass depicting the Agnus Dei, provided light. The walls were of plaster, painted soft green and decorated with silver and gold lozenges. A thick tapestry hung just above the small canopied fireplace, the floor had been polished smooth, and the great bed was covered by a gold-tasselled counterpane. At the foot of the four-poster, with its lid thrown back, stood Sir Ralph's huge personal coffer.

'It's luxurious,' Cranston whispered. 'What terrified Sir Ralph so much he had to move from here to that bleak prison cell?'

Cranston and Athelstan squatted down before the coffer and began to go through Sir Ralph's personal papers, but they found nothing about his years in Outremer. Every document concerned his office as constable or his service in the retinue of John of Gaunt. They must have spent an hour sifting through letters, indentures and memoranda. Only a Book of Hours caught Athelstan's attention. Each page was decorated with delicate filigree-like scrollwork in a range of dazzling colours: on one page lightly drawn angel figures, on another a priest sprinkling a shrouded corpse with holy water as he committed it to the grave. The Nativity, with Mary and Joseph bowing over a sleeping child; Christ's walk through Limbo, driving away black-faced demons with the power of his golden eye. Athelstan became engrossed, fascinated by its beauty. He looked inside the cover and noticed how Sir Ralph had scrawled prayer after prayer to St Julian. 'St Julian, pray for me! St Julian, avert God's anger! St Julian, intercede for me with Christ's mother!' Each of the blank pages at the back of the book was filled with similar phrases. Athelstan read them all, ignoring Cranston's mutterings and the angry boot-tapping of Sir Fulke. Finally Athelstan closed the coffer and stood up.

'You are finished, friar?' the kinsman snapped.

Athelstan looked sharply at him: Sir Fulke was apparently a man who hid behind a veil of bonhomie and good humour but now he looked angry, suspicious, and resentful of their intrusion.

'Am I finished?' Athelstan echoed. 'Yes and no, Sir Fulke.'

The knight blew out his cheeks. 'The day is passing, friar,' he observed tartly, glaring out of the window. 'I am a busy man with matters to attend to. What more do you want?'

'You wear boots, Sir Fulke?'

'Yes, I wear boots!' came the mimicking reply.

'And there are buckles on your boots?'

The colour drained from Sir Fulke's face.

'Yes,' he mumbled.

'Well,' Athelstan pulled from his wallet the buckle he had found on the frozen moat, 'I believe this is yours. We found it on the ice outside the North Bastion tower, yet you said you were in the city all night.'

Sir Ralph's kinsman paled, the arrogance draining from his face. 'I lost the buckle yesterday.'

'Were you on the ice?'

Sir Fulke suddenly smiled. 'Yes, I was. I went there early this morning. You are not the only one, Brother, to think the assassins scaled the tower at dead of night to murder Sir Ralph.'

Athelstan tossed the buckle at him and Sir Fulke caught it clumsily.

'Then, Sir John, we are finished here. Perhaps some refreshment?'

They met Colebrooke in the passageway outside, thanked him for his attentions and went down the outside steps into the Tower bailey. Athelstan gauged it to be about two o'clock in the afternoon and this was confirmed by a servant who bumped into them as they passed the great hall. They were on the point of going under the Archway of Wakefield when Athelstan caught sight of the great brown bear chained to the wall in the corner near Bell Tower.

'I have never seen a bear so huge, Sir John!' he exclaimed.

Cranston clapped him on the shoulder. 'Then, my lad, it's time you did!'

The friar was fascinated by Ursus. The bear scarcely repaid the compliment but sat on his hindquarters, hungrily stuffing his great muzzle from a pile of scraps thrown around him. Cranston clapped his hands and the beast raised his huge, dark head. One paw came up and

81

Athelstan stood, riveted by the great, slavering jaws, the teeth – long, white and pointed like a row of daggers – and the insane ferocity blazing in those red-brown eyes. The bear lurched slightly towards them, growling softly in his throat. Cranston grabbed Athelstan's arm and pulled him back. The animal, alarmed by such rapid movement, now sprang to his full height, his great unsheathed paws beating the air as he strained at the massive steel collar around his neck. Both the coroner and his companion saw the chain fastened to the wall strain at its clasps.

'That chain,' Athelstan murmured, 'is not as secure as it should be.'

'Goodbye, Ursus,' Cranston whispered. 'Let's go, Athelstan. Very softly!'

They collected their horses and made their way out of the Tower into Petty Wales. A few stalls stood uncovered and some brave souls made their way through the ankle-deep, mucky slush. Two beggar children, arms and legs as thin as sticks, stood beside a brazier singing a carol. Cranston tossed them a penny, and turned to watch as a woman condemned as a scold was led by a beadle up to the stocks in Tower Street, a steel brank fastened tightly around her head. Down the dirt-filled alleyways business was thriving for the red-wigged whores and their constant stream of clients from the Tower garrison.

Cranston asked directions from a one-eyed beggar man and came back beaming from ear to ear.

'I have found it!' he announced. 'The Golden Mitre tavern! You know, the one Sir Ralph and the hospitallers went to every year for their banquet.'

The tavern was just near the Custom House on the corner of Thames Street, a grand, spacious affair with a green-leaved ale-stake pushed under the eaves from which hung a huge, gaudily painted sign. A red-nosed ostler took their horses. Inside, the tap room was airy and warmed by a fire. The rushes on the floor were clean and sprinkled with rosemary and thyme. The walls were lime-washed to keep off insects, and the hams which hung from the blackened beams gave off a sweet crisp smell which made Cranston smack his lips. They hired a table between the fire and the great polished wine butts. The landlord, a small, red-faced, balding fellow with a surprisingly clean apron draped across his expansive front, took one look at Sir John and brought across a deep bowl brimming with blood-red claret.

'Sir John!' he exclaimed. 'You remember me?'

Cranston seized the bowl by its two silver handles and half drained it at a gulp. 'Yes, I do,' he replied, smacking his lips and glaring over the rim. 'You are Miles Talbot who once worked as an ale-conner in the taverns round St Paul's.' Cranston put down the bowl and shook the landlord's hand. 'Let me introduce an honest man, Brother Athelstan. Talbot always knew when a blackjack of ale had been watered down. Well, well, well!' Cranston unclasped his cloak and basked in the sweet odours and warmth of the tavern. 'What can you serve us, Master Talbot? And don't give me fish. We know the river is frozen and the roads blocked, so anything from the water must be weeks old!'

The landlord grinned, listed the contents of his larder, and within the half-hour served a couple of pullets stuffed with herbs and covered with a piquant sauce of sweet butter and wild berries, a skillet pasty, an apple tansy, and a prodigious marrow pudding. Athelstan sat in complete stupefaction, drinking his beer, as Cranston cleared every platter, washing it all down with another bowl of claret.

At last Cranston belched, stretched, and beamed round the tavern, snapping his fingers to call Talbot over.

'Master Miles, a favour!'

'Anything you wish, Sir John.'

'Your house is frequented, or rather was frequented, by the late Constable of the Tower, Sir Ralph Whitton?'

Talbot's face became guarded. 'Now and again,' he mumbled. 'He used to meet here every Yuletide – he, two hospitallers, and others.'

'Oh, come, Miles. I'm not your enemy, you can trust me. What did they talk about?'

Talbot tapped the table with his stubby fingers. 'They sat here like you do, Sir John, well away from the rest. When I or any of the servants came near, they always fell silent.'

'And their demeanour? Were they sad or happy?'

'Sometimes they would laugh but they were generally very secretive. Often the two hospitallers would be locked in argument with Sir Ralph, and he would become quite hostile and snap back at them.'

'Anything else?'

Talbot shook his head and turned away. Cranston made a face at Athelstan and shrugged. Suddenly the taverner came back to the table.

'One thing,' he announced. 'Only one strange thing: about three years ago, around Christmas, a stranger came here.'

'What did he look like?'

'Oh, I can't remember his appearance but there was something about him. He was cowled and hooded, but he spoke like a soldier. He wanted to know if Sir Ralph drank here. I told him I knew nothing. He went on his way and

I never saw him again.' Talbot smiled apologetically. 'Sir John, on my oath, that's all I know.'

The coroner sat with lips pursed, staring down at the empty platters and dishes as if wishing the food he had devoured would magically reappear. Athelstan studied him carefully, rather concerned, for by now Sir John would usually have been shouting for more claret or sack.

'My Lord Coroner?'

'Yes, Brother Athelstan.'

'We must formulate some conclusions about Sir Ralph's death.'

Cranston blew noisily through his lips. 'What can we say?'

'First, you will agree that Sir Ralph was not murdered because he was Constable of the Tower. I mean, by peasant knaves plotting treason and rebellion?'

'I agree, Brother, but the assassin might have come from outside. He could have been a professional. There are plenty of ex-soldiers for hire in the city who would cut their mothers' throats if the price was right.'

Athelstan skimmed the rim of the wine goblet with his finger.

'I would like to believe that, Sir John, but it strikes me as false.' He shrugged. 'Yet, for the sake of argument, we will accept that the assassin crossed the frozen moat, climbed the North Bastion, undid the wooden shutters and quietly slashed Sir Ralph's throat.'

'It can and has been done, my good priest.'

'Of course,' Athelstan continued, 'the assassin may have been someone in the Tower who knew where Sir Ralph lay, and seized the opportunity of the moat freezing over to gain access to the footholds on the North Bastion.

Accordingly, either the murderer did this himself or paid someone else to do it.'

Cranston took a deep gulp from the wine bowl. 'Let us put the two together,' he said, cracking his knuckles softly. 'Let us say, for the sake of argument, that the plotter and the assassin are one and the same person. Virtually everyone we questioned, including Mistress Philippa, who may be plump but is very light on her feet, young and agile, could have climbed that tower.'

'Yet, in the main, they all have stories to explain their whereabouts.'

Cranston nodded. 'So they have. And it would be the devil's own job to prove any of them a liar. Moreover, have you noticed how each, apart from the chaplain, has someone to confirm their tale? Which means,' Cranston concluded, 'we could be hunting two murderers, not one: the two hospitallers, Sir Fulke and Rastani, Philippa and her young swain, Colebrooke and one of the guards.'

Athelstan stared idly up at one of the hams turning on its skewer from one of the rafters. 'In reality, we know nothing,' the friar concluded. 'We have no idea who the murderer is or how he or she gained access to Sir Ralph, though we did find Sir Fulke's buckle.'

'And yet he claims he walked on the frozen moat this morning before our arrival.'

'I believe him,' Athelstan answered. 'But remember how he said he lost the buckle the previous day.'

'What are you saying, friar?'

'Either he lost it as he crept across the moat to kill Sir Ralph or else someone put it there. I believe the latter. Sir Fulke's honesty in admitting he walked on the frozen moat saved him from suspicion. If he had denied it, and we later proved he had been on the moat, then it would have been a different matter.'

'How do we know he's honest?' Cranston barked. 'Did you notice the postern gate we used to gain access to the moat? Its hinges were rusty. Before we did, no one had used that door for years. Sir Fulke could be lying.'

'Or he could have used another postern gate.'

'An interesting thought, Brother, but let's look at motives.'

Athelstan spread his hands. 'There are as many motives as there are people in the Tower, Sir John. Was Sir Fulke greedy? Was the chaplain angry at being called a thief? Did Colebrooke want Sir Ralph's post? Did Philippa and her lover see Sir Ralph as an obstacle to their marriage or to Mistress Philippa's inheritance?'

'Which brings us,' Cranston concluded, 'to the two hospitallers. Now we know they are not telling the truth. Somehow or other that piece of parchment and the seed cake lie at the very heart of the murder and they must know something about both. Sir Ralph's death note bore the impression of a three-masted ship, the type often used in the Middle Sea, whilst the seed cake is the mark of the Assassins. Ergo, Sir Ralph's death must be linked to some mystery in his past, something connected with his days as a warrior in Outremer.'

Athelstan put his blackjack down on the table. He opened and shut his mouth.

'What's the matter, friar?'

'There's only one conclusion we can reach, Master Coroner – Sir Ralph might not be the first person to die in the Tower before Yuletide comes.'

Chapter 5

They stayed in the tavern a little longer. Athelstan expected Cranston to mount his horse and ride back to Cheapside but the coroner shook his head.

'I want to go back to your damned graveyard,' he snorted. 'You need a keen brain to plumb the mysteries there.'

'But Lady Maude will be waiting.'

'Let her!'

'Sir John, tell me, is there anything wrong?'

Cranston scowled and looked away.

'Is it Matthew?' Athelstan asked gently. 'Is it the anniversary of his death?'

Cranston stood up and linked his arm through Athelstan's as they went out to stand at the door whilst the ostler saddled their horses. 'Tell me. Brother, when you ran away from your order as a novice and took your younger brother to the wars in France, were you happy?'

Athelstan felt his own heart lurch. 'Of course.' He smiled thinly. 'I was young then. The blood boiled in my veins for some great adventure.'

'And when you found your brother dead, cold as ice in that battlefield, and trailed back to England to confess your deeds to your parents, what then?'

Athelstan looked across the darkening yard. 'In the Gospels, Sir John, Christ says that at the end of the world the very heavens will rock and the planets fall to earth in a fiery blaze.' Athelstan closed his eyes. He sensed Francis's ghost very close to him now. 'When I found my brother dead,' he continued, 'my heaven fell to earth.' He shrugged. 'I suppose it was the end of my world.'

'And what did you think of life then?'

Athelstan rubbed his mouth with his thumb and gazed directly at Cranston's sorrowful face. 'I felt betrayed by it,' he whispered.

Cranston tapped him gently on the shoulder. 'Aye, Brother, always remember the carmined kiss of the traitor is ever the sweetest. You remember that, as I shall.'

Athelstan gazed speechlessly back. He had never seen Cranston like this before. By now the coroner should have been singing some lewd song at the top of his voice, bellowing abuse at the landlord, or urging Athelstan to come back to his house in Cheapside.

They mounted their horses and made their way quietly up snow-packed Billingsgate, turning left into the approaches to London Bridge. A large crowd milled there despite the cold wind which lashed face and hand. Under a sky shrouded by deep snow clouds, some boys threw snowballs at each other, shrieking with laughter as they hit their target. A legless beggar pulled himself along through the slush on wooden slats. A group of tattered watermen muttered abuse at the frozen river and cursed the great frost which had taken their livelihood from them. Others, hooded and cowled, pushed forward into the city or joined Athelstan and Cranston in crossing the narrow frozen bridge to Southwark.

The coroner suddenly reined in his horse, staring back at a group of dark figures who had just slipped by. Were they a group, he wondered, or just individuals travelling together for comfort and security? He was sure he had glimpsed Lady Maude amongst them, her pale face peering out from beneath her hood. But what would she have been doing in Southwark? Apart from Athelstan she knew no one there, and Southwark was a dangerous place to visit on a dark winter's day.

'Sir John, is all well?'

Cranston stared once more at the group receding into the darkness. Should he go back? But then a great metal-rimmed cart came crashing by, and the people behind Cranston began to mutter and moan, so the coroner nodded at his companion that they should continue on their way. They crossed the bridge, passing the Priory of St Mary Overy at the far end, and took the main highway into Southwark. The two men rode down the narrow alleyways where the great four-storey houses were interspaced with the ramshackle cottages and lean-tos of the workmen and artisans. The coroner caught the acrid tang of dog urine.

'The snow doesn't hide the stench!' he muttered, twitching his nose.

Athelstan agreed, pulling the cowl of his hood closer against the sight of rotting refuse, and discarded food and human excrement tossed out in night pots, mixed with the sweepings from the houses as the citizens prepared for a festive season. Southwark, of course, never rested. The artisans and cottagers continually plied their trades: chandlers making tallow from pig fat; skinners, cheesemongers, capmakers, blacksmiths, and at night, when the stalls came down, the raw-boned villains of the underworld who scrounged for easy pickings amongst the brothels and stew sides of the Thames. No one, however, approached

Cranston or Athelstan. The friar was well respected whilst Cranston was more feared than the Chief Justice himself.

They found St Erconwald's in darkness. Athelstan was pleased that Watkin had doused the lights. He was about to lead Sir John through the wicket gate to the priest's house when a dark shape jumped from the shadows and grabbed Philomel by the bridle. Athelstan stared down at the long, white face under its tarry black hood.

'Ranulf, for God's sake, what's the matter?'

'Father, I have been waiting for you all afternoon.'

'Tell him to bugger off, Athelstan! I'm cold!'

'Never mind Sir John,' Athelstan replied soothingly. 'What do you want, Ranulf?'

The rat-catcher licked bloodless lips. 'I have an idea, Father. You know how the great Guilds across the river have their own churches? St Mary Le Bow for the mercers, St Paul's for the parchment-makers?'

'Yes. So?'

The rat-catcher looked up pleadingly.

'Go on, Ranulf, what do you want?'

'Well, Father, I and the other rat-catchers wondered whether St Erconwald's could be the church for our guild fraternity?'

Athelstan hid a smile, glanced at Cranston's glowering face and bunched the reins in his hands. 'A guild of rat-catchers, Ranulf? With St Erconwald's as your chancery church and I your chaplain?'

'Yes, Father.'

Athelstan dismounted. 'Of course.'

'We would pay our tithes.'

'In what?' Cranston bellowed. 'A tenth of the rats you catch?'

Ranulf flashed the coroner a dagger glance but Cranston was already rocking to and fro in the saddle, laughing uproariously at his own joke.

'I think it an excellent idea,' Athelstan murmured. 'And we shall talk about it again. You have my agreement in principle, Ranulf, but for the moment Sir John and I are both busily engaged on other matters. If you could stable our horses, give them some hay?'

The rat-catcher nodded vigorously and, gathering the reins of Sir John's horse, trotted into the darkness. Philomel followed, moving a little faster as he sensed feeding time was very close. Athelstan led Cranston round the church, stopped, and told the coroner to wait until he fetched a sconce torch. He hurried back to the priest's house, plucked one from the wall, lit it with a tinder and ran back before Cranston's litany of curses became too audible.

They crossed into the cemetery. Even in summertime it was a sombre place. Now, under a carpet of white snow, the branches of the yew trees spread like huge white claws over the forlorn mounds of earth, crude crosses and decaying headstones. Athelstan felt a deep sense of isolation. An eerie stillness hung like a cloud and even the breeze seemed softer. The trees were motionless. No night bird sounded. In places, the shadows seemed oppressively dark, sinister hiding-places where some demon or evil sprite might lurk. Athelstan held up his torch and Cranston looked around this most benighted of God's acres.

'By the sod, Athelstan!' he whispered. 'Who would come here in the dead of night, never mind pluck corpses from their final resting place? Where are the graves?'

Athelstan showed him the forlorn, shallow holes in the ground, the mud piled high on either side as if some demented creature had clawed the corpses out. Cranston knelt down next to them and whistled softly through his teeth. He looked up, his fat face distorted by the torchlight.

'Brother, you said that only the corpses of beggars and strangers have been stolen?'

'Yes, Sir John.'

'And how were they buried?'

'The corpse, wrapped in canvas, is placed on a piece of wickerwork in the parish coffin. During the funeral ceremony this is covered by a purple canopy and removed when the body is lowered into the soil.'

'And you found no trace of the grave robbers?'

'None whatsoever.'

Cranston stood up, wiping the slushy mud from his hands. 'We have three possibilities, Brother. First, it could be a macabre joke. Some of our idle rich young fops think it funny to place such a corpse in the bed of a friend, but there's no rumour of such an evil prank recently. Secondly, it could be animals, either four-footed or human. Oh, yes,' he murmured at Athelstan's shocked expression. 'When I served in France, I witnessed such abominations outside Poitou. However,' he stamped his feet and looked up at the darkened mass of the church, 'no one, not even in Southwark, can be *that* degenerate. Finally, there are Satanists, the Astrasoi, those born under an evil star.' He shrugged. 'You know more about such people than I do, Brother. The corpse may be used as an altar or the blood drained to raise a demon or they may need one of the limbs. You have heard of the hand of glory?'

Athelstan shook his head.

'The hand of the corpse is hacked off; the name of the person whom the witch or warlock wishes to hurt is placed between its fingers and then it's buried at the foot of a gibbet on the first stroke of midnight.'

Athelstan rubbed his face. 'But how can I stop such desecration, Sir John? The ward bailiffs and beadles are not interested. No citizen will guard our cemetery.'

'I will see what I can do,' Cranston murmured. He turned quickly. 'There's someone here.' He pointed to two dark shapes over near the charnel house at the far side of the cemetery. 'Look there!' He strode across the snow-covered grass like a charging bullock, Athelstan hurrying behind him.

'Stop!' Sir John bellowed. 'In the King's name, stop!'

Two cloaked figures turned and slowly walked towards them. At the sound of the clatter of wooden sticks and the soft tinkle of a bell, Cranston hurriedly stepped back.

'Lepers!' he whispered, and grabbing Athelstan's torch, held it up before him. 'By the sod!' Cranston breathed, and stared pityingly at the white-hooded faces. He looked round at Athelstan. 'You let them stay here?'

He nodded. 'During the day. At night it is easier for them to wander unmolested.'

'Have they seen anything?'

Athelstan shook his head. 'They are mutes, but I doubt if they would become involved. It would be a brave man, Sir John, never mind a healthy one, who would confront grave robbers.'

'You are sure they are lepers?' Cranston whispered.

Athelstan grinned in the darkness. 'They have letters from the bishops. Look at their wrists and hands. However, if you wish to examine them...?'

Cranston cursed and tossed a coin at one of the creatures then strode back to the house, bellowing that he had seen enough. Ranulf the rat-catcher had apparently disappeared, as indeed did any of Athelstan's parishioners when the coroner appeared.

'You will stay for a bowl of soup, Sir John? I have some fine claret.'

Cranston, huffing and puffing, checked the saddle girths of his horse. 'I would like to, Brother,' he replied over his shoulder, 'but I must return.'

Cranston did not wish Athelstan to probe his anxieties about the Lady Maude. 'I need to reflect upon what we saw at the Tower.' He pointed to the graveyard. 'I'll see what I can do to help you there.' He swung himself on to his horse, and with an airy wave clattered into the darkness.

Athelstan sighed and went round to unlock the church. It was cold inside, but the friar was pleased that it had lost its musty smell. He revelled in the fragrance of the green boughs so lovingly placed along the nave and sanctuary steps. He remembered the Chapel of St John and wondered what lies he had been told there. Athelstan was sure the murderer was in the Tower and equally certain that some evil deed from the past had finally caught up with Sir Ralph.

He took a tinder from his pouch, lit two sconce torches in the nave and collected his battered prayer book from the sacristy. He knelt on the sanctuary steps and began the Divine Office. He reached the line in the psalm 'My God, my God, why have you forsaken me?' and stopped. He stared into the flickering light of the candle, leaning back on his heels. Had God forsaken him? Why did things such as the desecration of the cemetery, Sir Ralph's murder or

Cranston's sadness happen? Oh, Athelstan knew about the problem of evil but sometimes he wondered, especially when he stared into the darkness, was there really anyone listening to him? What if there was not? What if Christ had not risen from the dead, and religion was mere hocus-pocus?

Painfully, Athelstan drew back from the precipice of doubt and depression. He finished his prayers, made the sign of the cross, and crouched with his back against the chancel screen. He took deep breaths, trying to calm his mind and soul so he could concentrate on the recent events in the Tower.

'What happens,' he asked the darkness, 'if Sir Ralph has been killed by secret peasant leaders? And if the revolt comes…?'

–

He dozed for an hour until a warm, furry body slid under his hand. 'Good evening, Bonaventura!' he whispered. 'A cold day for a gentleman of leisure.'

He sat up and stroked the cat gently, scratching between the backs of its ears, making Bonaventura purr with pleasure. 'So, you have been visiting all your ladies in the neighbourhood?' Athelstan knew about Bonaventure's sexual prowess. Sometimes the cat even brought his 'ladies' back to the church steps to sing their own eerie vespers to a cold silver moon. 'What will happen, Bonaventura, when the rebellion comes? Will we side with Pike the ditcher and the other dispossessed?'

Bonaventura grinned in a fine display of pink gums and sharp ivory teeth. Pike the ditcher! Strange, Athelstan thought, but there it was. He had no proof but he was certain the ditcher was a member of the Great Community and carried secret messages to its leaders. Athelstan tensed as the church door opened.

'Brother Athelstan? Brother Athelstan?'

The friar smiled. Benedicta. Perhaps she would share his supper? They could exchange gossip about the parish; anything to distract his mind. He put Bonaventura down, stood, and broadened his smile, to hide his disappointment. Beside Benedicta stood a tall man, his features quite clear in the torchlight. His face was burnt dark by the sun, his raven-black hair tied in a knot at the back of his head. He was dressed in a long blue robe which reached down to snow-flecked boots. Athelstan went along the nave to meet him. The man was strikingly good-looking, he thought, with the sharp features of a hunting peregrine, vivid cherry-brown eyes, a hooked nose and neatly clipped moustache and beard. Athelstan saw the pearl pendant which hung on a gold chain from one ear lobe.

'This is Doctor Vincentius,' Benedicta exclaimed.

Athelstan clasped a strong, brown hand. 'Good evening, sir. I have heard of you.'

And who hadn't? Athelstan wondered. The physician lived in Duckets Lane off Windmill Street, on the other side of the Tabard Inn. He had recently bought a huge house there with a garden which bordered on the river, directly opposite Botolph's Wharf. Vincentius had won himself a name as a reputable physician. His fees were petty and he didn't bleed his patients with leeches or use strange zodiac charts and stupid incantations. Instead he preferred to emphasise cleanliness, the importance of a sensible diet, the efficacy of boiled water, and the need to keep wounds clean. Cecily the courtesan had even intimated that he used an ointment which was most effective in curing certain sores on the most delicate parts of the body.

Athelstan studied the extraordinarily handsome face and the beaming smile on Benedicta's. The friar felt a twinge of jealousy.

'I have heard of you, Father,' the doctor smiled.

Athelstan shrugged. 'I am a priest, a friar, one amongst thousands.'

The doctor spread his hands and the rings on his fingers sparkled. 'But there again, it is written on many tombstones... "I was a healthy man until I met a physician".'

Athelstan laughed, immediately liking the man. 'I don't see you in church,' he teased.

'Perhaps one day, Father.'

'Doctor Vincentius so wanted to meet you.' Benedicta spoke as coyly as a young girl. 'I wonder, Father, if you could join us for supper?'

Athelstan felt like refusing, but that would have been churlish. He clapped his hands briskly. 'I would love to.' He doused the lights in the church and locked the door, leaving Bonaventure to hunt in the darkness. He went across to the house whilst Benedicta and her strange visitor waited on the church steps. Philomel was still munching noisily on his oats. Athelstan patted him gently, took his cloak from the house and rejoined Benedicta and Vincentius.

They walked through the silent, icy streets into Flete Lane, near Holyrood Walk, where the widow lived. This was the first time Athelstan had been to Benedicta's house, a two-storeyed building which stood alone, an alleyway on either side and a garden beyond. On the ground floor was a huge kitchen, parlour and storeroom. The kitchen had no rushes on the floor but the flagstones were scrubbed and wiped clean. Two box-chairs were pushed near the roaring log fire. Above the hearth ran a broad oaken shelf containing silver and pewter cups which shimmered by the light of two multi-branched candelabra; woollen rugs of dark murrey hung against the white-washed walls. A warm, homely place, Athelstan thought. Indeed, very much as he had imagined it. They both helped Benedicta prepare and serve the meal. First jussell, composed of eggs and spiced bread. Then succulent hare cooked in wine, a jelly moulded in the form of a castle, and a jug of chilled white wine and claret which Cranston would have downed in a trice.

Vincentius quietly dominated the conversation. Athelstan found his courtly manners and soft, well-modulated voice fascinating. Perhaps Vincentius realised he talked too much and, changing the conversation, asked about the friar's day. Athelstan described his journey to the Tower and Sir Ralph Whitton's death.

'He will not be missed,' Vincentius observed. 'A dour, war-like man.'

'You met him?'

The physician smiled. 'I know of him, though it's the Tower I find more interesting. I went there yesterday. A wonderful testimony to the subtlety of the human mind, especially when it comes to engines and places of war.' Vincentius sipped from his goblet. 'You say Sir Ralph's throat was slashed?'

'Yes,' Athelstan replied. 'Why?'

'How was the body when it was found?'

'What do you mean?'

'Was it cold? Was the blood congealed?'

'Yes, it was,' Athelstan replied, though he remembered he had not asked that question himself at the time. 'Where are you from, Doctor?' he deftly turned the conversation. The physician carefully put his wine cup back on the table.

'I was born in Greece, of Frankish parents. They later returned to England. I studied at Cambridge, then Santiago and Salerno.' He grinned. 'At Salerno,' he continued, 'I spent most of my time trying to forget what I had learnt at Cambridge. The Arabs have a more thorough grasp of medicine than we. They know more about the human body and have proper Greek translations of Galen's *Art of Medicine* and Hippocrates' *Book of Symptoms*.'

'What brought you back to Southwark?' Benedicta asked.

The physician smiled as if relishing some private jest.

'Why not?' he joked. 'Wealth? I have enough. And as you know, Brother, the poor need any help they can get.' He leaned across the table and studied Athelstan's face carefully.

'What are you going to recommend, Physician?' Athelstan teased. 'The eagle's remedy for bad eyesight?'

'What's that?' Benedicta asked.

'Brother Athelstan jokes,' Vincentius replied. 'The charlatans say the eagle gets its keen eyesight by eating raw lettuce. So they claim rubbing the eyes with the juice of the lettuce will clear up any eye infection.'

'And will it?'

'A bag of nonsense!' Vincentius snapped. 'Warm water and a clean cloth will do more! No, Brother,' he tapped Athelstan lightly on the fingers, 'what you need is more sleep. And if you have any lettuce, eat it. It will do you good.'

Athelstan laughed. 'If I can find it! The frost has killed everything in my garden, and Ursula's pig scoffs the rest.'

Whilst Benedicta described Ursula and her malevolent sow, Athelstan felt tempted to talk to Vincentius about the desecration of the cemetery but concluded it was not a topic suitable for the table. He looked across at the hour candle and saw it was growing late. He rose and made his farewells, politely refusing Benedicta's invitation to stay longer. He had enjoyed the meal but was glad to be gone, reminding himself that he was a priest and Benedicta was the mistress of her own life. He left her house and trudged wearily through the snow. The night was cold and black but when he stopped and looked up between the black overhanging gables of the houses, he was pleased to see the clouds beginning to break up. He would have gone straight home but made a short diversion when he found Pike the ditcher drunk as a bishop on the corner of the trackway leading down to the church. Athelstan helped his errant parishioner to his feet.

'Good evening, Father.'

Athelstan flinched at the ale fumes which billowed towards him.

'Pike! Pike!' he hissed. 'You great fool. You should be home in your bed with your wife.'

Pike staggered away from him, tapping his nose drunk-enly. 'I have been seeing people, Father.'

'I know you have, Pike.' Athelstan grasped him by the arm. 'For God's sake, man, be careful! Do you want to end your life swinging on the end of some gibbet as the crows come to peck your eyes out?'

'We'll rule like kings,' Pike slurred. He struggled free of the friar's grip and danced a quick jig. 'When Adam delved and Eve span,' he chanted, 'who was then the gentleman?' Pike smiled drunkenly at Athelstan. 'But you'll be safe, Father. You, your cat, and your bloody stars!' He laughed. 'You're a jewel. You charge no tithes. I just wish you'd bloody well laugh sometimes!'

'I'll bloody well laugh,' Athelstan hissed, seizing the drunken man by the arm, 'when you're sober!'

And he hustled the ditcher back to his angry wife waiting in their tenement in Crooked Lane.

Athelstan thankfully reached St Erconwald's, made sure everything was locked up and walked over to his house. It was only when he was lying on his pallet bed trying to pray and not be distracted by Benedicta's fair face, that Athelstan suddenly remembered what Vincentius had said. What had the good physician been doing at the Tower? Moreover, Vincentius admitted he had been educated in the area around the Middle Sea where Sir Ralph and the others had also served. Was there any connection? Athelstan wondered. He was still pondering on the problem when he drifted into a deep and dreamless sleep.

Cranston, too, was thinking about events in the Tower but was too anxious to concentrate on the problems they posed. The coroner sat forlornly at the desk in his chamber, his little chancery or writing office as he called it, a place he loved, at the back of the house away from noisy Cheapside. He stared around. The floor had been specially tiled with small red and white lozenge-shaped stones and covered with woollen rugs. The windows were glazed and tightly shuttered against piercing draughts. Pine logs crackled and snapped in the small fireplace and warming dishes stood on stands at either end of the great writing desk. Sir John loved to spend time here, concentrating on his great treatise on the governance of the city. Yet tonight he could not relax; he was too distracted, ill at ease with the atmosphere in his own household. Oh, he had found Maude a little happier, they had exchanged the usual pleasantries, but Cranston still sensed that she was hiding something. He stirred as below stairs the maid tinkled a bell, the sign for dinner. Sir John groaned as he eased his bulk up and sorrowfully waddled down to the aroma-filled kitchen. Leif, the beggar, was crouched in the inglenook, stuffing his mouth full of richly sauced venison. He grinned at Sir John, then stared in surprise as Cranston mournfully passed by. Leif was astonished. Usually Sir John would greet him with a stream of good-natured abuse.

The beggar shrugged and went back to his meal. He was enjoying himself. Lady Maude had given him a few pennies and tomorrow he planned to see his friend in Crabbe Street. They'd dine in an eating-house and go to Moorfields where foaming bears, huge-tusked hogs and fat bulls were baited by bloody-mouthed mastiffs.

In the linen-panelled dining chamber, the table had been specially laid, covered by a white cloth of lawn with gold embossed candlesticks placed at either end. Cranston looked suspiciously at his wife. She seemed too happy. He noticed the colour high in her cheeks whilst her eyes danced with pleasure. Sir John grew more mournful. Had Lady Maude found someone else? he wondered. A young swain more virile and lusty than he? Oh, he knew such practices were common. The bored wives of old men and burgesses often found happiness in the arms of some court dandy or noble fop.

Sir John eased himself into his great chair at the top of the table and gloomily reflected on the past. Yes, his marriage had been an arranged one. Maude Philpott, daughter of a cutler, solemnly betrothed to the young Cranston. Young? He had been fifteen years her senior when they met at the church door but he had been slimmer then, fleet as a greyhound, a veritable Hector on the battlefield and a Paris in the bedchamber. Sir John looked soulfully at his wife, who smiled back. Should he raise the matter? Sir John gulped. He dare not. Cranston was frightened of no one; he had the body of a bullock and the heart of a lion. Yet, secretly, he was wary of his miniature, doll-like wife. Oh, she never shouted or threw things at him. Just the opposite. She would sit and answer back, stripping away his pomposity as she would the layers of an onion, before going into a sulk which could last for days.

'Sir John, all is well?'

'Yes, My Lady,' Cranston mumbled.

The maid served dinner: beef stew pie, the pastry crisp and golden. The meat within was garnished with herbs and cooked in a rich onion sauce. Cranston's mood receded, aided and abetted by two generous cups of claret.

'You were at the Tower today, Sir John?'

'Yes, and all the fault of Sir Ralph Whitton, the constable. Last night he had a throat, tonight both throat and life have gone.'

Lady Maude nodded, remarking how she had heard that Sir Ralph was a hard, cruel man.

'And you, My Lady?'

'Oh, this morning I did the accounts, and later went to take the air.'

'Where?'

'In Cheapside. Why?'

'You didn't go to Southwark?'

'By the Mass, Sir John, no! Why do you ask?' Cranston shook his head and looked away. He had caught the tremor in her voice. His heart lurched and he splashed his goblet full to the brim with dark red claret.

—

In the darkness of the Tower, the hospitaller, Gerard Mowbray, walked along the high parapet which stretched between Broad Arrow Tower and Salt Tower on the inner curtain wall. The night wind whipped his grey cropped hair, bit at his ears and cheeks and clawed at the grey robe wrapped round his body. Sir Gerard ignored the cold. He always came here. This was his favourite walk. He would stand and stare into the darkness trying to see the old ruins of Caesar's time, but not tonight, as the mist was too thick. To the north he could glimpse the beacon light in the Tower of St Mary Grace's, and to the south the fires and torch flames from the Hospital of St Katherine. Sir Gerard looked up at the sky. The clouds were beginning to break, revealing a storm of stars across the heavens. Strange, he thought. In Outremer the stars seemed closer, the velvet darkness of the heavens so near you felt you could stand on tiptoe and pluck the lights from the sky.

Mowbray leaned against the crenellated wall. Oh, they had been happier times! He remembered the hot burning sands outside Alexandria where he, Sir Brian, Sir Ralph, and the others had been a band of carefree knights only too happy to take the gold of the enemy. Mowbray recalled the climax of their campaign. There had been a revolt in Alexandria and the Caliph's army, Mowbray's group amongst them, had massed outside the city: the air thick with the beat of their kettledrums, the wind snapping at the huge green banners, and the silver crescents on the standards dazzling in the scorching sunlight. The city had been besieged for months but at last a breach had been forced in one of the walls. He and Sir Brian had gone in first to stand shoulder to shoulder, their comrades around them, a fighting circle of steel slowly edging into the city. Behind them the massed troops of the Caliph, their battle cries rising and falling like a demoniac chorus. The knights had forced their way through the gap and along the wall to the steps leading to the parapet above the main gate.

Sir Gerard's mind slipped eagerly back into the past. He remembered the intense heat, the sunlight dancing off sword and dagger points, the roar of battle, and the blood which pumped like a thousand fountains as men fell screaming from horrible wounds in head, body or thigh. Slowly he and his companions had edged up the steps, hacking their way through flesh until they reached a point above the main gate. Now who had it been? Of course! As always, Bartholomew. He'd jumped down, engaging in combat with a huge Mameluke. Bartholomew had moved with the grace of a dancer, his sword a silver hissing snake. One false feint to the groin, then up and round in a semi-arc to slice the enemy between helmet and hauberk. Ralph had followed. He had been an honourable knight then.

The great bar to the gate was lifted and the Caliph's men had poured into the city. What a bloodletting! No quarter was asked and none was given. The narrow, hot streets dinned with the silver bray of trumpets and the shrieks of dying men and women. At least the knights had not been party to the massacre; they had achieved their task and now looked for suitable reward. They eventually found themselves in a huge square where a white marble fountain played in the centre. Nearby stood the banker's empty house. Oh, the treasure they had found there! Adam had run knee-deep in silver ducats and jewelled goblets full of pearls!

Mowbray suddenly shook himself free from his memories. He thought he'd heard a sound, there towards the end of the parapet at the top of the steps. No, he concluded, it was only the wind. He went back to his memories. Strange, Mowbray pondered, that Adam had not come to see them this Christmas. Perhaps he was too frightened. Had the dead Sir Ralph and the now wealthy burgess Adam known something he did not? What had happened three years ago to frighten the Constable so much?

'We are all frightened,' Mowbray whispered to himself. This fear had changed them all. That's what evil did to you, he thought. It corroded the will, rotted the soul, and fouled the chambers and passageways of the mind. What had been done in Outremer so many years ago had been evil! Bartholomew had been their leader. Half the treasure was rightfully his, and he had trusted them – a terrible mistake. Betrayal! Treachery! The words shrieked like tormented ghosts in the dark recesses of Mowbray's soul. Ralph had planned it but they had all been party to his evil. Mowbray stirred against the cold. Oh, he had confessed his sins, walked barefoot to the shrine of St James at Compostela and both he and Fitzormonde had become hospitallers to make reparation. He stared out into the darkness.

'Oh, sweet Christ!' he murmured. 'Wasn't that enough?' The hospitaller felt the black demons of Hell closing in around him. What terrors did the pit hold for traitors? To be basted with pitch in a dark pen full of brimstone where adders would suck at his eyes and snakes curl round his lying tongue! What could he do to break free of such phantasms? Tell Cranston? No! Perhaps Brother Athelstan? Mowbray remembered the dark eyes and closed face of the Dominican monk. Mowbray had met such men before; some of his commanders in the knights hospitaller had the same gift as Athelstan of sensing every thought. The friar knew there was something wrong, something evil and rotten, behind Sir Ralph's death.

Mowbray jumped as a night bird shrieked beyond the Tower walls. A dog howled in protest. Was it a dog? he wondered. Or one of Satan's scouts calling up the legions of the damned from the abyss of Hell? A bell clanged. Mowbray moaned in fear, caught now in his own fancies. The bell boomed as though it came from the bowels of the earth. He cursed and calmed himself.

The bell was the tocsin in the Tower! Mowbray's hand fell to his sword hilt as he realised that great brass tongue only tolled when the Tower was under attack. He gripped the hilt of his sword tightly. Perhaps he had been wrong? Perhaps Sir Ralph's death had been the work of rebels and now they were back? He ran along the gravel-strewn parapet. He wanted to fight. He wanted to kill, give vent to the fury boiling within him. Suddenly he stumbled. His arms flailed out like the wings of a bird, black against the sky, then he tipped and fell, his mind still gripped by delirium. He was a boy again, leaping from a rock into one of the sweet rivers of Yorkshire. He was the brave young knight storming the parapet of Alexandria, crying out for the rest to join him. Then, darkness.

Mowbray's body crashed against the earth, his brains spattering as the sharp, icy cobbles crushed his skull. His body twitched then lay still, even as the dying hand edged towards the wallet containing a yellow piece of parchment depicting a crudely etched ship with dark crosses drawn in each corner.

Chapter 6

Athelstan stood outside his church and stared in pleasant disbelief at the blue-washed sky and the early morning sun as its rays danced and shimmered over the snow-covered roofs of his parish. The friar took a deep breath and sighed. He had slept well, woken early, said Office, celebrated Mass, broken fast and then swept both his house and Philomel's stable. He had been to the cemetery. The lepers had gone and none of the graves had been disturbed. Athelstan felt pleased, even more so as the great frost had been broken by this sudden bright snap as if Christ himself wanted the weather to improve for his great feast day. He looked over his shoulder and smiled at Cecily the courtesan as she swept the porch of the church. She simpered back before looking, sloe-eyed, towards a dreamy-faced Huddle, now sketching in charcoal the outlines of one of his vigorous paintings on the wall of the nave.

'Keep your mind on the task in hand, Cecily,' Athelstan murmured. He stretched, turning his face up to the sun. 'Praise to thee, Lord,' he muttered, 'for Brother Day. Praise to thee, Lord,' he continued St Francis of Assisi's Canticle of the Sun, 'for our sister, Mother Earth.' Athelstan sniffed and wrinkled his nose. 'Even though,' he whispered, 'in Southwark she smells of sour vegetables and putrid refuse!' He suddenly remembered other beautiful mornings at his father's farm in Sussex and the sun seemed to lose some of its brightness.

'You are happy, Father?'

Athelstan grinned at Benedicta. 'Yes, I am. You left Mass early?' he queried.

'I had to, Father, have you forgotten?'

Athelstan remembered the date and winced. No, he hadn't forgotten Simon the carpenter, one of his more errant parishioners, a florid-faced, thick-set man with an evil temper and a long Welsh dagger. Two weeks ago, Simon had raped a girl whilst carousing in Old Fish Street then compounded his crime by brutally beating her. He had been tried for his life at the Guildhall and tomorrow would hang. Simon had neither family nor friends and three days ago the parish council had begged Athelstan and Benedicta to visit the unfortunate. The friar had even made a vain plea to Cranston to have the sentence commuted but the coroner had sorrowfully shaken his head.

'Brother,' he had replied, 'I can do very little, even if I wanted to. The girl was only twelve and she'll never walk again. The fellow has to die.'

Athelstan stared up at the sky. 'God have mercy on Simon,' he whispered. 'And God help his poor victim!'

'What was that, Father?'

'Nothing, Benedicta, nothing.' Athelstan turned to go back into his church just as a young pursuivant turned the corner of the alley, slipping and sliding on the ice as he bellowed the friar's name. Athelstan groaned. 'What is it, man?' As if he didn't know already.

'Sir John Cranston awaits you, Father, at the Golden Lamb tavern near the Guildhall. Father, he says it is urgent. You must go there now!'

Athelstan fished in his purse and flicked a penny at the young man. 'Go tell Sir John to stay where he is and not to drink too much. I'll be there shortly!'

Athelstan took the keys of the church, tied by a piece of string to the cord round his waist, and pressed them into Benedicta's soft, warm hand.

'Look after the church,' he pleaded.

Her eyes rounded with mock wonderment. 'A woman in charge of the church, Father? Next you'll be saying that God favours women more than men because he created Eve in Paradise, rather than before, as He did Adam.'

'They also say the serpent had a woman's face.'

'Aye, and a man's lying heart!'

'You'll lock the church?'

'Such trust, Father.'

Athelstan smiled. 'I believe you would do a better job than any of the men. Seriously, Benedicta, make sure Ranulf the rat-catcher doesn't take Bonaventure. The children are not to play snowballs in the porch. Try to keep Ursula's pig away from what is left of my garden, and above all watch Cecily! I think she is about to fall in love again.' He ran down the steps and turned. 'Oh, Benedicta?'

'Yes, Father.'

'Last night – the delicious meal, thank you. A strange man, Doctor Vincentius.'

Benedicta grinned. 'Not as strange as some priests I have met!'

Athelstan glowered back in mock anger whilst she turned and skipped like a young girl into the church.

He roused and saddled a snoring Philomel and took the road to London Bridge. He found the stews around the riverside as busy as an overturned ant heap in summer as boatmen, sailors and fishermen flocked down to the riverbank to watch the ice thaw. Athelstan gently nudged Philomel through the press around the bridge. He refused to look to either side; crossing the bridge on the pleasantest of days could be a frightening experience and more so now as the ice below split and cracked. Instead Athelstan looked across the river at the ships plying along the quays of Billingsgate and Queenhithe in a scene of frenetic activity. Galleys from Gascony laden with casks of wine, woad ships for Picardy, the whelk boats of Essex, and the great vessels of Alamein and Norway making ready for sea. Fishing boats, barges and lighters were busy around the ships, full of men smashing the ice with picks, hammers and mallets. From the high-stemmed poop of a Genoese cog, a boy sang a hymn to the Virgin in thanksgiving for the change in the weather whilst sailors in a Greek galley chanted their prayer for mercy: '*Kyrie Eleison, Christe Eleison, Kyrie Eleison.*' Lord, have mercy, Christ have mercy, Lord have mercy. The chant was so beautiful Athelstan stopped, closing his eyes to listen, until a rough-mouthed carter flicked his whip, bellowing how some men had to work and couldn't laze around like stupid priests. Athelstan sketched a blessing in the air at his tormentor, dismounted and led Philomel past the church of St Magnus on the corner of Bridge Street.

They turned into Candlewick, now thronged with carts, pack horses and wagons as virtually every tradesman in the city seized the opportunity afforded by the break in the weather. Athelstan continued into Walbrook. On one side of the street ran a sluggish stream in a deep channel cut through the earth. The water was black, ice-filled, and two youths were fighting with quarter-staffs on one of the shit-strewn footbridges. Athelstan and Philomel pressed forward though, for a while, both were forced into the shadows of the overhanging houses as a group of aldermen rode pompously down the street. A herald went before them, a silver trumpet to his lips, whilst two serjeants-at-arms cleared the way with sharp knocks from their staffs. Above the aldermen the city banner snapped in a glorious splash of bright vermilion, whilst the figure of St Paul, embroidered in gold, seemed to glow with its own special light. At the corner of Walbrook the rakers were out, their great wooden rods moving piles of slush and refuse into high, stinking heaps. A bailiff had found a pig wandering where it shouldn't and, according to city regulations, had promptly cut the animal's throat. The blood gushed out in hot, scarlet streams whilst its owner, a little balding man, threatened the official with a stream of horrible oaths. Athelstan remembered Ursula and her great, fat sow and wondered if the bailiff would cross to Southwark. The city parasites were also massing as thick as flies over a turd: smooth-skinned lads, cloak-twitchers, quacks, night wanderers, mimes and petty sorcerers.

At last Athelstan found the Golden Lamb, a little tavern on the corner of an alleyway. The dark taproom was dominated by a morose Cranston, who sat slumped on a bench with his back against the wall. The empty ale-jacks scattered on the table before him made the coroner look like an angry Bacchus surrounded by votive offerings. Athelstan walked across and Cranston's eyes swivelled to meet him.

'Where have you been?' the coroner snapped.

'I came as fast as I could.'

'It wasn't fast enough!'

Athelstan silently prayed for patience and sat down on the stool opposite Sir John. He didn't like the appearance of the coroner one bit. Cranston was a drinker but was usually a jovial soul, conscious of his own sins, faults and failings, and so tolerant of those of others. Now he looked positively sinister, his eyes continually flashing around as if seeking a challenge. His lips moved wordlessly and even the white whiskers bristled with some inner fury.

'Do you want some wine, Priest?'

'No, Sir John, I don't, and I think you've drunk enough.'

'Sod off!'

Athelstan leaned forward. 'Sir John, please, what is wrong? Perhaps I could help?'

'Mind your own business!'

Athelstan coughed and backed away. 'This,' he murmured, 'is going to be a very trying day. You said the mayor and the sheriffs wished to see us?'

'They have seen me. They got tired of waiting for you!'

'And what did they say, Sir John?' Athelstan asked sweetly.

The coroner shook himself, sat up and smiled shamefacedly at Athelstan. 'Forgive me, Brother,' he mumbled. 'A bad night, and I've got an aching head.'

And a filthy temper to boot, Athelstan thought, but decided to keep his own counsel. Sir John would talk soon enough.

Cranston chewed his lip and glared into a corner where a huge rat gnawed at a bloody globule of fat glistening amongst the dirty rushes. 'Is it the black or brown rat which carries infection?' he suddenly asked.

Athelstan followed Cranston's gaze and shuddered in disgust.

'Both, I think, so I'm not eating here, Sir John, and I suggest that neither should you. Anyway, tell me what's happened.'

'There's been more bloodshed in the Tower. Sir Gerard Mowbray, who also received a death warning, slipped from a parapet and fell.'

'Anything else?'

'About the same time that Mowbray died, the great tocsin of the Tower sounded, convincing the garrison it was under attack.'

'But there was no attack?' Athelstan replied. 'And, I am sure, no sign of a bell ringer?'

'Apparently.'

'And the business of the Mayor?'

Athelstan jumped as a fierce tom cat slunk out of the shadows, grasped the rat by its leg and pulled it squealing into the centre of the room.

'For God's sake!' Cranston bellowed at the taverner.

The fellow wandered over waving a broomstick and the cat, its quarry still swinging from his mouth, fled up the spiral, wooden staircase. Cranston lifted the ale-jack, remembered the rat, and slammed it back on the table.

'The business of the Mayor, my dear Athelstan, is that Sir Adam Horne, burgess, alderman and close friend of the late Sir Ralph, has received a drawing of a three-masted cog, together with a flat sesame seed cake.'

'And where is Horne now?'

'At his warehouse along the Thames. Horne did not tell the mayor about this, his wife did. Both message and cake were delivered anonymously to her. She handed them over to her husband and was terrified by his reaction. He became pale and ill as if taken by a sudden seizure.'

'When was this?'

'Earlier today. The wife immediately went to see one of the sheriffs. The rest you know.'

'Lady Horne acted very quickly?'

'Yes, the mayor himself is suspicious. He still believes Lady Horne knows more than she claims.'

Athelstan stared towards the door as a group of pedlars, battered trays slung round their necks, bustled in, raucously shouting for ale. A one-eyed beggar followed and, for a penny, agreed to do a dance. His skeletal body clothed in dirty rags looked grotesque as he hopped from foot to foot, to the mocking laughter of the tinkers.

'Isn't it strange, Sir John,' Athelstan murmured, 'how we men take such a delight in the humiliation of others?'

Cranston remembered Lady Maude, blinked and looked away.

Athelstan stirred. 'So, Sir John, do we question Horne or go to the Tower?'

Cranston rose. 'My office is to enquire as to the cause of death,' he announced pompously. 'Not to run errands for the powerful ones of this city. So we go to the Tower. After all, as the good book says, "Where the body lies, the vultures will gather".'

'Sir John?' Athelstan scratched his head. 'This warning – the seed cake and the ship, still troubles me.'

'What do you mean?' Cranston slurred, swaying dangerously against the table.

'Well, apparently Horne, for example, recognised the seed cake as a death threat, but why does the crude drawing of a ship hold such terrors for him and others?'

'All men are fearful because they're liars!' Cranston snapped. 'No one tells the truth!' He glared at Athelstan under bristling brows.

'What's wrong, Sir John?' Athelstan insisted. 'I can feel the fury and the hurt seething within you. You must tell me.'

'In a while,' the coroner muttered. 'Let's go!'

They collected their horses from the stables and led them through the cold, bustling streets. Every Londoner seemed to be out of doors: the stall-holders were busy making up for lost trade and the air was thick with savoury smells from taverns and cookshops. They went to Cornhill, past Leadenhall and into Aldgate, pausing where a crowd had gathered round a speaker on the corner of Poor Jewry. He was a striking figure with a long, dour face, the head completely shaven, his thin body clothed from head to toe in a black gown and cloak. The speaker paused as he glimpsed Cranston, and his mouth and jaw tensed with fury. The anger in his face made his eyes glow, reminding Athelstan of the figure of St John the Baptist in a mummer's play. The man's eyes never left Cranston's as he drew a deep breath, one bony finger pointing upwards to the clear blue sky.

'Woe to this city!' the preacher rasped. 'Woe to its corrupt officials! Woe to those they serve who are clad in silk, loll on couches, and fill their bellies with the best of food and the richness of wine. They will not escape the fury which is coming! How can we eat and drink when our poor brothers starve? What will their answer be then?'

Cranston angrily stepped forward, but Athelstan caught him by the sleeve.

'Not now, Sir John!'

'Who is it?' Cranston rasped.

'The hedge priest, John Ball. A great preacher,' Athelstan muttered. 'Sir John,' he advised, 'the man is well liked. This is neither the time nor the place!'

Cranston took a deep breath, spun on his heel and walked on. The preacher's fiery words pursued them as they passed the house of Crutched Friars and turned left down an alleyway towards the Tower.

'One day,' Cranston grated, 'I'll see that bastard hang!'

'Sir John, he speaks the truth.'

The coroner turned. His face and body sagged as the fury drained from him.

'What can I do, Athelstan? How can I feed the poor of Kent? I may eat too much, I know I drink too much, but I pursue justice and do the best I can.' Cranston's great fat hands flapped like the wings of a wounded bird and Athelstan saw the hurt in his eyes. 'By the sod, Brother, I can't even govern my own house.'

'Lady Maude?' Athelstan queried.

Cranston nodded. 'I fear she has met someone else,' he blurted out. 'Perhaps a fop from the court.'

Athelstan stared back in disbelief. 'Lady Maude? Never! Sir John, you are a fool!'

'If any other man said that, I'd kill him!'

'Well, I say it, Sir John. Lady Maude is an honourable woman, she loves you deeply. Though,' Athelstan snarled in genuine anger, 'sometimes I wonder how she can!' He grasped the fat coroner by his cloak. 'What proof do you have?'

'Last night I saw her coming across London Bridge from Southwark, yet when I asked her where she had been, she replied no further than Cheapside.'

Athelstan was about to snarl a further retort when the coroner's words suddenly quickened his own memories. Sir John might be right. A week ago, just before the feast of the Virgin, Athelstan had seen the Lady Maude near the

Tabard in Southwark. At the time he'd thought it strange but then forgot about it. Cranston narrowed his eyes.

'You know something, don't you, you bloody monk?'

Athelstan looked away. 'I'm a friar,' he replied softly. 'Sir John, I know nothing except that I honour you and the Lady Maude. I also know she would never betray you.'

Cranston brushed by him. 'Come on!' he barked. 'We have business to do.'

They reached the bottom of the alleyway, went up the hill and into the Tower through a rear postern gate. One of the sentries took their horses and led them across Tower Green, now ankle-deep in icy slush, to where a depressed-looking Colebrooke was waiting.

'More deaths,' the lieutenant announced mournfully. 'Sir John, I wish I could say you were welcome.' He took them out, stopped and stared up at the ravens cawing raucously against the blue sky. He pointed up at them. 'You have heard the legends, Sir John? While the ravens are here the Tower will never fall. And that when they caw so stridently, it's always a sign of impending death.' Colebrooke blew on the tips of his fingers. 'Unfortunately, the ravens' song is turning into a constant hymn.'

'Did anyone know that Mowbray had received the same warning as Sir Ralph?' Cranston abruptly asked.

Colebrooke shook his head. 'No. Mowbray was uneasy but, following Sir Ralph's death, so were we all. He and Sir Brian kept to themselves. Last night Mowbray went for his usual walk on the parapet between the Salt and Broad Arrow Towers. He was still there when the tocsin sounded. Mowbray apparently heard the alarm, ran, slipped and fell to his death.'

'There was no one else on the parapet with him?'

'No. Indeed, if it wasn't for the warning we found in his pouch, we would have assumed it was a simple accident.'

'Was the parapet slippery?'

'No, of course not, Sir John. You are a soldier. Sir Ralph was most strict on such matters. As soon as the weather worsens, sand and gravel are strewn on every step.'

'Then who rang the bell?' Athelstan asked.

'Ah, that's the mystery. Come, I'll show you.'

They walked into the centre of Tower Green. The snow was relatively unmarked here, packed high around a great wooden post with a beam jutting out like a scaffold. The tocsin bell was balanced on an iron ring and from its great brass tongue hung a long piece of cord.

'You see,' Colebrooke said, pointing up to the bell, 'this is only sounded when the Tower is under direct attack. If you touch the rope even, the bell is angled so as to sound continuously.'

Sir John looked up and nodded wisely. 'Of course,' he said. 'I have seen such a mechanism before. If the guard is wounded, once he starts the bell, it will swing and toll until someone stops it.'

'Exactly!' Colebrooke exclaimed. 'And that's the real mystery. I stopped the bell myself. No one else was about.'

'But someone could have rung it and run off?' Cranston queried.

Colebrooke shook his head. 'Impossible. I came out here with a sconce torch. I stopped the bell but, when I examined the snow, found no other footprints around.'

'What?' Cranston barked. 'None at all?'

'None, Sir John.' Colebrooke pointed to the surrounding carpet of snow. 'Because this bell is so important,' he explained, 'no one is allowed anywhere near it. Even the soldiers, when they are drunk, keep clear of the area in case they stumble and start the bell tolling.'

'And nothing else was found?'

'Nothing except the claw marks of the ravens.'

'But that's impossible,' Athelstan said.

Colebrooke sighed. 'I agree, Father, and what makes it even more mysterious is that we also had guards patrolling the green. They saw no one approach the bell. They found no footprints.' Colebrooke turned away and spat. 'A time of death,' he mourned. 'The ravens' song is the only one we hear.'

'And where was everyone?' Cranston snapped.

'Oh, Mistress Philippa had invited us all for supper in Beauchamp Tower.'

'All of you?' Athelstan asked.

'Well, the two hospitallers demurred. Rastani did not come, and I left occasionally to make my rounds. I'd just returned to Mistress Philippa's when the bell began to sound.'

'And you found no one?' Cranston repeated.

'No one at all,' Colebrooke muttered. 'Now the soldiers are uneasy. They talk darkly of demons and ghosts and the Tower is not a popular garrison. You know soldiers, Sir John, they're worse than sailors. They repeat stories of how the Tower was built on a place used for ancient sacrifice. How blood is mixed with the mortar, and men were nailed to the earth in its foundation.'

'Nonsense!' Cranston barked. 'What do you think, Brother?'

Athelstan shrugged. 'The lieutenant may be right, Sir John. There are more forces under heaven than we know.'

'So you believe the nonsense about ghosts?'

'Of course not! But the Tower is a bloody place. Men and women have died horrible deaths here.'

Athelstan stared round the green and shivered despite the bright sunshine.

'Fear is the real ghost,' he continued. 'It saps harmony of the mind and disturbs the soul. It creates an air of danger, of threatening menace. Our murderer is highly skilled and intelligent. He is achieving exactly what he wants.'

'Who found the corpse?' Cranston queried.

'Fitzormonde did. When the bell was sounded, people were running around all over the place, checking gates and doors. Fitzormonde went looking for Mowbray and found his corpse.'

'We'll check the parapet walk,' Athelstan muttered.

'Master Lieutenant, I would be grateful if you could gather everyone in Mistress Philippa's chamber. Please give my apologies and excuses to the lady, but it's important to meet where you all were last night when the tocsin was sounded.'

Cranston and Athelstan watched Colebrooke stride away.

'Do you think there's any connection?' Cranston asked.

'Between what?'

'Between the bell chiming and Mowbray's fall.'

'Of course, Sir John.' Athelstan tugged him by the sleeve and they made their way across the deserted bailey to the steps leading up to the parapet walk. They stopped at the foot and stared up at the curtain wall rising above them.

'A terrible fall,' Athelstan whispered.

'You said there was a connection?' Cranston replied testily, 'between the bell sounding and Mowbray falling.'

'A mere hypothesis, Sir John. Mowbray went on to the parapet walk. Like many old soldiers he liked to be by himself, to reflect well away from others. He stands there staring into the darkness. He has already received warnings of his own impending doom so is lost in his own thoughts, fears and anxieties. Suddenly the tocsin sounds, proclaiming the greatest fortress in the realm to be under attack.' Athelstan stared into Sir John's soulful eyes. 'If you had been Mowbray, what would you have done? Remember, Sir John,' Athelstan added slyly, 'you too are a warrior, a soldier.'

Cranston pushed back the beaverskin hat on his head, scratched his balding pate and pursed his lips as if he was a veritable Alexander. 'I'd run to find the cause,' he replied ponderously. 'Yes, that's what I'd do.' He stared at Athelstan. 'Of course, Mowbray would have done the same, but then what happened? Did he slip? Or was he pushed?'

'I don't think he slipped. Mowbray would have been too careful, and I doubt he would have let someone push him off the parapet walk without a struggle.'

'So how?'

'I don't know, Sir John. Let's study the evidence first.'

They were about to climb the steps when a voice suddenly sang out: 'Good morrow, friends!' Red Hand, his gaudy rags fluttering around him, jumped through the slush towards them. 'Good morrow, Master Coroner. Good morrow, Sir Priest,' he repeated. 'Do you like old Red Hand?'

Athelstan saw the chicken struggling in Red Hand's grip. The poor bird squawked and scrabbled, its claws beating the madman's stomach, ripping his rags still further, but Red Hand held it firmly by the neck.

'Death has come again!' he chanted, his colourless eyes dancing with mischievous glee. 'The old Red Slayer has returned and more will die. You wait and see. Death will come, snap, like this.'

And before Athelstan or Cranston could do anything, the madman bit into the hen's neck and tore its throat out. The bird squawked, struggled and lay limp. Red Hand stared up, his mouth ringed with blood, gore and feathers.

'Slay! Slay! Slay!' he chanted.

'Go away!' Cranston barked. 'Sod off, you little bugger!'

Red Hand turned and ran, the blood from the freshly killed chicken spraying the greying slush on every side. Cranston watched him disappear behind a wall.

'In my treatise, Brother,' he said softly, 'I will suggest houses for such men. Though I do wonder...'

'What, Sir John?'

'Well, if Red Hand is as mad as he claims to be.'

Athelstan shrugged. 'Who decides who is mad, Sir John? Red Hand may think he is the only sane man around here.'

They climbed the steep steps, Athelstan going first. Behind him followed Sir John, breathing heavily and muttering a litany of dark curses. The wind whipped their faces; halfway up Athelstan stopped and, stooping, picked up the thick sand mixed with gravel which carpeted every step.

'This would stop anyone from slipping, Sir John.'

'Unless he was drunk or careless,' Cranston replied.

'Aye, Sir John. A sober soldier is a rarity indeed.'

'Aye, monk, very rare, but not as rare as a holy priest.'

Athelstan grinned and continued climbing. They reached the parapet walk. It was about four feet wide and as carefully coated with sand and pebbles as the step. They leaned against the curtain wall. Cranston, breathing heavily, looked down, curiously watching the figures below as they scurried around like black ants on the various tasks of the garrison. He then stared up at the blue sky. The clouds were now only faint wisps lit by the strong mid-day sun. The coroner suddenly felt rather giddy and quietly cursed himself for drinking so much.

'Old age,' he murmured.

'Sir John?'

'*In media vitae, sumus in morte*,' Cranston replied. 'In the midst of life, we are in death, Brother. I do not feel too safe here, yet in France when I was younger but not so wise, I held one of these parapet walks against the best the French could send.' Cranston felt self-pity seep through him. Did Maude also think him old? he wondered. Was that it? Sir John breathed deeply, trying to control the spasm of rage and fear which shot through him. 'Go on, Athelstan,' he muttered. 'Make your careful, bloody study.'

'Stay there, Sir John,' Athelstan replied softly. The friar glanced despondently down at the sand and gravel. 'I suppose so many have been up here since Mowbray's fall, I doubt we will find anything.'

Athelstan walked gingerly along the parapet, using the crenellated wall as his guide. He walked slowly, not daring to look at the drop on his right and becoming ever more aware of the cold, biting wind and eerie sense of loneliness, as if he hung halfway between heaven and earth. On either side of the parapet walk were two towers. Near the Salt Tower he found the gravel-strewn slush had been disturbed, indicating someone had stood there for some time. Athelstan studied this spot for a while.

'What have you found, Brother?' Cranston bellowed.

Athelstan walked carefully back. 'Mowbray stood where I stopped. Now, Sir John, if you go first?'

Cranston went back to the top of the steps. Athelstan followed behind.

'Go on, Sir John. Stand on the top step.'

Cranston obliged, closing his eyes for he had begun to feel rather dizzy.

'What is it, Brother?' he rasped.

Athelstan crouched and stared closely where the sand and gravel had been scattered. 'I suspect Mowbray fell from here,' he replied. 'But why, and how?' The friar examined the crenellations from which an archer would shoot if the wall was under attack. 'Strange,' he murmured. 'There's a fresh mark in the wall as if an axe has been swung against it. And look, Sir John.' Athelstan carefully picked up some splinters of wood. 'These are fresh.'

Cranston opened his eyes. 'Yes, Brother, but what do they mean?'

'I don't know, but it would appear that someone took an axe and drove it hard against the wall, with such force the stone was marked and the wooden handle of the axe shattered.'

Cranston shook his head in disbelief.

'What it all means,' Athelstan murmured, 'I don't know. I cannot make the connection between Mowbray's fall and these fragments of evidence.' The Dominican looked suspiciously at the white, haggard face of Cranston, the bleary red eyes, and the way he was swaying rather dangerously on the top step. 'Come on, Sir John,' he said gently. 'We are finished here and others await.'

They made their way gingerly down the steps. At the bottom Cranston immediately felt better, turned and beamed at Athelstan.

'Thank God!' he bellowed. 'You don't do that every day, eh, Brother?'

Thank God, Athelstan thought, you are not in such a mood every day. The friar looked around. The Tower garrison was now busy: soldiers in half-armour lounged on benches. Despite the cold they wished to revel in the sunshine. A few played dice, others shared a wineskin. A scullion ran across with a basket of fresh-cooked meat, taking it to one of the kitchens where it would hang to be cured, diced, salted and stored for the duration of the winter. The clanging from the blacksmith's rang like a bell through the air, as somewhere a child cried, the son or daughter of one of the garrison. In the outer bailey an officer was shouting orders about a gate being oiled. A dog barked and they heard laughter from the kitchens. Athelstan smiled and relaxed.

He must not forget the small things of life, he concluded. They kept you sane. He linked his arm through Sir John's and they ambled across Tower Green, making their way carefully through the soft, dirty slush, alert for the icy patches which hadn't thawed. A guard ushered them into the Beauchamp Tower and up into Mistress Philippa's chamber on the second floor. It was a spacious room with a deep bay window overlooking Tower Green. The seats were cushioned and quilted, the windows glazed with fragments of stained glass. As soon as he entered, Athelstan sensed it was a woman's chamber – hand-woven tapestries hung on the walls, with one depicting a golden dragon locked in combat with a silver wyvern. Another portrayed the Infant Jesus smiling, arms outstretched, in the manger at Bethlehem where Christ's mother stood in a dress of gold and a mantle of deep sky blue. The bricks in the wall had been painted alternately white and red; large cupboards stood with doors half-open displaying gowns, dresses, hoods and mantles, of various colours and different fabrics. A small pine log fire blazed in the canopied hearth. In one corner stood a spinning wheel, the threads still pulled tight. In the other, curtained off from the rest of the room, was the bed chamber. A long, polished table stood in the centre of the room. On it were placed chafing dishes full of glowing charcoal, spices and herbs. Their perfume reminded Athelstan of a fresh spring morning on his father's farm in Sussex. He also noticed the other door in the far side wall, peeping out from behind the thick red arras. Athelstan grinned and winked at Sir John.

'A lady's bower, My Lord Coroner,' he whispered.

Cranston smiled, then remembered Lady Maude and his face grew long.

Mistress Philippa rose as they entered. In temperament, though not in looks, she reminded Athelstan of Benedicta; she had the same quiet composure and he had glimpsed the steely look in her eyes. Was Philippa strong and ruthless enough, he wondered, to commit murder? Athelstan stared round at the rest mumbling quietly like people who wanted to maintain appearances, though he sensed their tension. The conversation died abruptly as Cranston lurched across the room. Perhaps Philippa or the femininity of her chamber had reminded Cranston of Maude, for the coroner suddenly became bellicose with the girl.

'Another bloody murder!' he roared. 'What now, eh?'

Geoffrey Parchmeiner, Philippa's betrothed, stood up and walked out of the darkness near the wall. He looked anxious, more white-faced and sober than the last time Athelstan had seen him.

'Murder, My Lord Coroner?' he stammered. 'What proof do you have? You swagger in here, into my lady's chamber, and shout allegations yet show no evidence. What can we make of that?'

Athelstan looked around. Sir Fulke seemed subdued and remained slouched in his chair. The chaplain, crouched on a stool near the fireplace, stared into the flames wringing his hands whilst Rastani, the silent, dark servant, sat with his back to the wall as if he wished the very stones would open and swallow him. The other hospitaller, Fitzormonde, stood near the window, his hands folded, staring at the floor as if totally unaware of Cranston's presence. Colebrooke looked embarrassed, tapping his foot and whistling softly under his breath.

'My betrothed asked a question,' Philippa demanded. 'How do you know the knight was murdered? And what difference does it make, Sir Coroner? So was my father, and are you any nearer to finding his killer?'

'Your father's murder will be avenged,' Cranston snapped. 'As for Mowbray, he had that bloody parchment on him and the fragments of a seed cake. What further proof do you need?'

Philippa stared coolly back.

'Well!' Cranston shouted. 'I have answered one of your bloody questions!'

'Sir John,' she replied icily, 'moderate your language. My father,' her voice nearly broke, 'now lies sheeted in a coffin in the Chapel of St Peter ad Vincula. I, his daughter, grieve and demand justice, but all I get is the offensive language of the alleys and runnels of Southwark. Sir, I am a lady.'

Cranston's eyes narrowed evilly.

'So bloody what?' he answered before Athelstan could intervene. 'Show me a lady and I'll show you a whore!'

The girl gasped. Her betrothed leapt back to his feet, his hand going to the knife at his belt, but Cranston just dismissed him with a contemptuous flicker of his eyes. Athelstan watched the hospitaller suddenly stir and noticed with alarm how the knight now grasped one of his gloves in his hand.

Good Lord, the friar thought, not here, not now! The last thing Sir John needs is a challenge to the death.

'Sir John!' he snapped. 'Mistress Philippa is correct. You are the King's Coroner. She is a lady of high birth who has lost her father and now sees one of his friends meet a similar terrible death.' He grasped the coroner's arm and swung him round, keeping an eye on the hospitaller now standing behind them.

'Sir John! Control yourself, please,' he murmured. 'For my sake.'

Cranston stared at Athelstan with red-rimmed eyes. He reminded the friar of the great, shaggy bear squatting in the courtyard below. The friar touched Cranston's hand gently.

'Sir John,' he whispered, 'please. You are a gentleman and a knight.'

The coroner closed his eyes, took a deep breath, opened them and grinned.

'When you are around, monk,' he muttered, 'I don't need a bloody conscience.' He turned to Philippa. 'My lady,' he said, 'before Sir Brian or Sir Fulke,' he glanced contemptuously at the girl's uncle who still sat slumped in his chair, 'challenge me to a duel, I apologise profusely.' He gave her a dazzling smile. 'There are old men, Mistress,' he continued, 'and there are fools. But there's nothing worse than an old fool.' He stretched out his hand, took the girl's unresisting fingers and kissed them in a way the most professional courtier would have envied.

'I was most discourteous,' he bellowed. 'You must forgive me, especially at this time when your father's body is not yet buried.'

Chapter 7

The atmosphere in the room relaxed. Athelstan closed his eyes. Good God, he prayed, oh thank you! The hospitaller had been on the verge of striking Sir John and, once that happened, well, Athelstan knew Cranston. It would be a duel *à outrance*, to the death! Mistress Philippa smiled and stepped forward into the light and Athelstan realised just how boorish Cranston had been.

The girl's face was white as snow, her eyes red-rimmed and circled with deep shadows, but she sensed Cranston's insult had not been intended. She leaned over and kissed Sir John gently on the cheek. This only discomfited the coroner further. He stared down at the floor and shuffled his feet like some clumsy schoolboy. Philippa went across to a tray of goblets, filled two and brought them back. She gave one to Athelstan and pressed the other into Sir John's great paw. The coroner smiled at the wine, lifted the cup and downed it in one gulp. He smacked his lips, winked at the girl and held out the goblet to be refilled. Philippa smilingly obliged and Athelstan groaned. He didn't know what was worse, Cranston sulking or Cranston in his cups.

Sir John took the goblet and went over to the window, staring out at the sun dazzling the snow on Tower Green. Athelstan busied himself arranging his writing tray on the table. The rest of the group hardly moved, as if absorbed in everything the coroner said or did. They watched him intently, like a group of schoolboys would a fearsome master. Cranston watched the sunlight shimmer on the great tocsin bell then turned around abruptly.

'Mowbray,' he announced, 'was murdered. Well, at least I believe he was. He received the same message as Sir Ralph. I think he went on to the parapet and the tocsin was sounded to make him run. Now, I have examined the parapet most carefully...'

Athelstan remembered how Cranston had slouched against the wall and hid his smile.

'I have examined the parapet most carefully,' Cranston continued, glaring at Athelstan. 'Mowbray did not slip accidentally. The sand and gravel there are at least an inch thick. Someone planned his fall.'

'Did Mowbray drink?' Athelstan asked.

Cranston turned and glanced at the other hospitaller. Sir Brian shook his head.

'He was a seasoned warrior,' the knight replied. 'He could run along such a parapet in a blinding snowstorm.'

'Tell me,' Cranston said, 'what happened yesterday evening? I mean, before Mowbray fell?'

'We were all here,' Sir Fulke spoke up. He smiled. 'Mistress Philippa had invited us for supper.'

'I wasn't!' snapped Fitzormonde. 'I was in my own chamber, awaiting poor Mowbray's return.'

'And, of course, Rastani,' the chaplain stuttered, squirming on his stool.

'Yes,' Fitzormonde murmured. 'The Morisco wasn't here.' Athelstan left his desk and squatted in front of Rastani. He stared into the silent, fear-filled face.

'My Lady Philippa,' Athelstan murmured over his shoulder, 'I wish to talk to Rastani though I think he knows what I am going to ask.'

'So do I!' Sir Fulke shouted. 'I will answer for him.'

'No, sir, you won't!' Cranston barked.

Athelstan touched Rastani's hand, which was as cold as ice. The friar gazed into his liquid dark eyes. The man was terrified, but of what? Detection? Discovery?

'Where were you, Rastani?' Athelstan asked.

Beside him, Philippa made strange gestures with her fingers and Rastani replied in the same sign language.

'He says he was freezing cold,' Philippa explained. 'And stayed in my father's old chamber in the White Tower.'

'He's silent-footed as a cat,' Cranston observed. 'He could creep round this fortress and no one would notice.'

'What are you implying, Sir John?' Philippa snapped.

'Rastani could have rung the bell.'

'How on earth could he have done that when there were no footprints?' Geoffrey mocked, moving to stand beside Philippa.

Cranston smiled. 'A snowball?'

Colebrooke snorted with laughter. 'I have told you, Sir John, the area around the bell could be seen by sentries. They saw no one approach.'

Cranston sniffed loudly and looked longingly at his now empty wine goblet.

'Before you continue, Sir John,' Fitzormonde spoke up, 'and you start speculating on where I was, all I can say is that I was in my own chamber but no one saw me there.' He glared fiercely at Cranston. 'However, I am a priest, a knight and a gentleman. I am not a liar!'

'Why did you stay there, Sir Brian?' Athelstan tactfully interrupted.

Sir Brian shrugged. 'I was frightened. I, too, have received a letter of death.' He drew out a piece of parchment from beneath his cloak and Cranston almost snatched it from his hand.

The hospitaller was right. The same sketch Sir Ralph Whitton and Mowbray had received: a crudely drawn ship in full sail and, in each corner, a small black cross.

'I also had the seed cake,' Fitzormonde murmured. 'But I threw it away.'

'When Mowbray fell,' Cranston suddenly asked, 'did anyone else inspect the parapet?'

'I, Fitzormonde and Colebrooke did,' Fulke replied. 'When the tocsin sounded, we all left this room. The hospitaller was with us when Mowbray's body was found. Our young gallant here,' he waved his hand contemptuously at Geoffrey, 'was asked to accompany us to the parapet but it's well known he's terrified of heights.'

Geoffrey flushed with embarrassment and looked away.

'Uncle!' Philippa murmured. 'That's not fair.'

'What's not fair,' Cranston interrupted, 'is that we know so little about last night Mistress Philippa. What time did your guests assemble?'

'Oh, just after Vespers, about eight o'clock.'

'And all except Rastani and the hospitaller came?'

'Yes, yes, that's correct.'

Cranston turned to the hospitaller. 'And where did you say you were?'

'In my chamber.'

'And Mowbray?'

'On the parapet walk.'

'So,' Cranston heaved a sigh, 'as Mowbray brooded, the rest of you except Fitzormonde gathered here?'

'Yes.'

'And how long till the tocsin sounded?'

'About two to three hours.'

'And no one left?'

'Only Colebrooke on his round and others to the privy, but that's along the passageway.' The girl smiled wanly.

'We all drank deep.'

Athelstan raised a hand. 'Never mind that.' The friar, snatching the parchment from Cranston's hand, went and stood over the hospitaller. Athelstan pushed the drawing under the knight's face. 'Sir Brian, what does this mean?'

The knight looked away.

'Sir Brian Fitzormonde,' Athelstan repeated, 'soon you will appear before God's tribunal. I ask you, on your oath as a knight, what does this parchment signify?'

The hospitaller glanced up with his red-rimmed eyes in a drawn, pale face. Athelstan felt he was looking at a man already under the shadow of Death's soft, black wing. The friar leaned closer until he could see the small red veins in the knight's eyes and the grey, dusty pallor of his cheeks. Fitzormonde was probably a brave man but Athelstan could almost taste the stench of fear which emanated from him.

'On your oath to Christ,' Athelstan whispered, 'tell me the truth.'

Sir Brian suddenly lifted his face and whispered in Athelstan's ear. The Dominican stood back in surprise but then nodded.

'What did he say?' Cranston barked.

'Later, Sir John.' Athelstan turned to the rest of the group. 'What did happen here last night?' he asked, trying to divert the conversation.

Sir Fulke, his face now suffused with his usual false bonhomie, leaned forward. 'My niece,' he said, 'wished to thank us for our kindness following the death of Sir

Ralph. We sat and dined like a group of friends. We talked of old times and what might happen in the future.'

'And no one left?'

'Not until the tocsin sounded.'

'No, Sir Fulke,' Geoffrey interrupted. 'Remember, you drank deeply.' He smiled falsely. 'Perhaps too deeply to remember. The priest left.' Geoffrey pointed to where the chaplain, William Hammond, dressed like a crow, sat perched on his stool near the fire. 'Don't you remember, Father, you left?'

'I went back to my room,' the chaplain announced. 'I had a gift of some wine.' He glared maliciously at Geoffrey and then at Colebrooke. 'A parishioner gave it to me. It's not from the Tower stores if that's what you're thinking.' He shrugged. 'Yes, I too drank deeply and I was unsteady and slow in returning. I was about to re-enter Beauchamp Tower when the bell began to toll.'

'What happened then?' Athelstan asked. He glanced at Colebrooke and realised the lieutenant had told them little of his own movements. 'Well, Lieutenant?' Athelstan repeated. 'What did happen?'

'Well, the bell tolled. I and the others left Mistress Philippa. The garrison was roused and all gates were checked. We then scattered, trying to find what was wrong. Fitzormonde discovered Mowbray's body. We joined him then Master Parchmeiner came. We examined the corpse and I went up on to the parapet.'

'And?' Cranston barked.

'I found nothing. We were more concerned that the tocsin had been sounded.'

'But you found no trace of the bell ringer?' Athelstan asked.

'No, I have told you that.'

Athelstan gazed round in desperation. How, he wondered, could a bell ring and no one be seen pulling it? Or, indeed, any trace of someone being near the bell? What did happen? And how could the bell ringer run undetected across the Tower to arrange Mowbray's fall? Athelstan drew a deep breath.

'Where is Mowbray's body now?'

'It's already sheeted,' Philippa replied. 'It lies in its coffin before the chancel screen in the Chapel of St Peter ad Vincula.'

'And I will join him there,' Fitzormonde murmured. He looked up and smiled wanly. 'Oh, yes, I have the mark of death upon me.'

His statement hung like an arrow in the air, just before it turns and begins its fatal descent.

Athelstan whirled round as a loud snore from Cranston broke the silence. He heard Geoffrey giggle, even white-faced Philippa smiled, and the chaplain grinned sourly whilst Fulke snorted with laughter.

'Sir John has many problems to exhaust him,' Athelstan announced. 'Mistress Philippa, may we be your guests for a while?' He looked at Colebrooke. 'Master Lieutenant, I need words with Sir Brian. Is there a chamber here?'

Philippa pointed to the door in the far wall. 'There's a small one at the end of the corridor.' She blushed slightly. 'Just past the privy. The chamber will be warm. I had a brazier put there this morning.'

Athelstan bowed, smiled thinly at the rest of the group, glanced despairingly at the snoring Cranston and led Sir Brian down the corridor. On the left was the privy, covered by a curtain which hung from a metal rod. Athelstan pulled the curtain back and wrinkled his nose at the smell. The privy was crude, a small recess in the wall with a latrine seat, just under a tiny, open, oval-shaped window which looked down over the green.

'It drains down to the moat,' Sir Brian mumbled.

Athelstan nodded, let the curtain fall and walked on. The chamber at the end of the passage was more fragrant and clean. The walls were lime-washed, the windows closely shuttered. Athelstan sat down on a stool and gestured to a bench which ran along the wall.

'Sit down, Sir Brian. Now, tell me, what do you want?'

Sir Brian suddenly knelt at Athelstan's feet and sketched the sign of the cross in the air. Athelstan glanced around despairingly. He suspected what was coming.

'Bless me, Father,' Fitzormonde murmured, 'for I have sinned. And this is my confession.'

Athelstan drew back, the legs of the stool scraping the hard stone floor. 'I cannot,' he whispered. 'Sir Brian, you have tricked me! Whatever you tell me now will be covered by the seal of Confession.'

'I know!' Fitzormonde hissed. 'But my soul is steeped in the blackest sin.'

Athelstan shook his head and made to rise. 'I cannot,' the friar repeated. 'Whatever you tell me, I can only reveal on the orders of the Holy Father, the Pope in Avignon. Sir Brian, you are most unfair. Why this trickery?'

Fitzormonde glanced up, his eyes gleaming. 'No mummery,' he said. 'Father, I wish to confess. You must shrive me. I am a sinner *in periculo mortis!*'

Athelstan sighed. Sir Brian was right. Canon Law was most strict on this: a priest was bound to hear the confession of any man who believed he was in danger of death. To refuse would be a terrible sin. 'I agree,' Athelstan whispered.

Sir Brian made the sign of the cross again.

'Bless me, Father, for I have sinned. It is many years since my last confession and I confess in the face of God and in the hope of his divine mercy at the imminent approach of death.'

Athelstan closed his eyes and leaned back. He listened to the litany of sins: impure thoughts and actions, the lusts of the flesh, avarice, bad temper, foul language, as well as the petty bickerings which take place in any community. Sir Brian confessed about his fight against sin, his will to do good and his constant failures to carry this through. Athelstan, a skilled confessor, perceived Sir Brian was a good but deeply troubled man. At last the hospitaller finished and leaned back on his heels though he kept his head bowed.

'I am a sinner, Father,' he whispered.

'God knows,' Athelstan replied, 'we are all sinners, Sir Brian. There are those who know they are sinners, confess and try to pursue the good. You are one of these. There are others like the Pharisees who cannot be forgiven, for they believe they never do wrong!' Athelstan leaned closer. 'Now you wish absolution?' The friar raised his hand. '*Absolvo te*,' he intoned. 'I absolve you.'

'Stop!' Sir Brian lifted his head and Athelstan saw the tears on the white, haggard cheeks.

'Sir Brian, there is more?' he asked gently.

'Of course there is!' Fitzormonde hissed. 'I am a murderer, Father. An assassin. I took my friend's life. No! No!' He shook his head as if talking to himself. 'I was party to a murder. I turned my face the other way.'

Athelstan tensed, trying to hide that inner tingle of excitement, the deep curiosity aroused in a priest who, in confession, has the unique opportunity to see a soul bare itself.

'Whose murder?' he asked softly.

Sir Brian shook his head, sobbing like a child.

'Sir Brian.' Athelstan tapped him gently on the shoulder. 'Sit down, man! Come, sit down!'

Sir Brian slumped on the bench. Athelstan looked round the chamber and saw the wine jug and goblets on the chest. He got up, filled one of these and thrust it into Fitzormonde's hand.

'There's nothing in Canon Law,' Athelstan smiled, 'which says a man cannot have a drink during confession.' He wiped his sweat-stained hands on his robe. 'Or,' he continued, 'as St Paul says, "Take a little wine for the stomach's sake".'

Sir Brian sipped from the goblet and smiled. 'Aye, Father,' he replied. 'And, as the Romans put it, "*In vino veritas*". In wine there is truth.'

Athelstan nodded, pushed the stool nearer and sat down. 'Tell me, Sir Brian, in your own words and at your own time, the truth about this murder.'

'Many years ago,' Fitzormonde began, 'I was a wild, young man, a knight with visions of becoming a crusader. My friends were of a similar disposition. We all served in London or hereabouts: Ralph Whitton, Gerard Mowbray, Adam Horne, and...' The man's voice trailed off.

'And who?'

'Our leader, Bartholomew Burghgesh, of Woodforde in Essex.' Fitzormonde took a deep breath. 'The war in France was finished. Du Guesclin was reorganising the French armies, our old king was doddering and there was no need for English swords in France, so we sailed for Outremer. We offered our swords to the King of Cyprus. We spent two years there, becoming steeped in blood. Eventually, the Cypriot king dispensed with our services and we had nothing to show for it but our clothes, horses, armour, and the wounds of battle. So we became mercenaries in the armies of the Caliph of Egypt.'

'All of you?' Athelstan asked.

'Yes, yes. We were still a band of brothers. David and Jonathan to each other.' Fitzormonde smiled to himself. 'We feared nothing. We had each other and we always shared. Now there was a revolt in Alexandria. Our leader, Bartholomew, was hired by the Caliph to join his satraps in suppressing the uprising.' Fitzormonde stopped and gulped from the cup. 'It was a bloody business but eventually a breach was forced in the defences and Bartholomew led us through.' The hospitaller's eyes caught Athelstan's. 'We hacked our way through a wall of living flesh. Do you know, the cobblestones couldn't be seen for the blood which swilled like water? The Caliph's armies followed us in and the real killing began. Men, women and children were put to the sword.' Fitzormonde paused and wiped his mouth on the back of his hand. 'That, too, Father, I confess, though we were not party to it. Bartholomew led us away. We found a merchant's house full of treasure.' Fitzormonde licked his lips and closed his eyes tightly, trying to remember events in that sun-drenched city so many years ago. 'Now the Caliph's rules were strict,' he continued. 'As mercenaries we were allowed no plunder, so most of the treasure was useless to us, but Bartholomew found a heavy purse of gold.' The knight stopped speaking and pointed to the cord tied round Athelstan's waist. 'Think of that ten times thicker, Father. Two heavy pieces of leather sewn together and stuffed with money. Every coin was of pure gold. A king's ransom in a leather belt. There must have been thousands.'

Fitzormonde paused again. He was back in time, standing battered and blood-stained, gazing open-mouthed at the belt Bartholomew had found hidden beneath the tiled floor.

'What happened?' Athelstan asked.

Fitzormonde smiled. 'Bartholomew did a brave thing. He said he would wait to see if the Caliph would reward us for forcing the breach. He didn't, so Bartholomew kept the purse.'

'Why was that brave?'

'Well, if he had been caught, Bartholomew would have been sliced from neck to crotch, his genitals ripped off and stuffed into his mouth, and his decapitated head placed on a spike above the city gates. Now Bartholomew agreed to conceal the purse on condition that he had half the treasure whilst we shared the rest. We agreed, and by night fled the Caliph's armies and crossed the sea to Cyprus.'

'Is that the connection with the ship?' Athelstan asked.

'Oh, no. We reached Cyprus safely but the Caliph sent assassins after us. These were the Hashishoni, the followers of the Old Man of the Mountain, skilled killers who came by night. They were so confident they even sent us fair warning of their arrival.'

'A flat sesame seed cake?' Athelstan interrupted.

'Yes, but Bartholomew was waiting for them. One night they crept into our house but he had arranged for us to sleep on the roof whilst through a crack he could watch our sleeping chamber. Do you know,' Fitzormonde said in a dream-like voice, 'Bartholomew showed no fear? He trapped all three in that room and killed them.' Sir Brian's voice broke. 'He was the best – Bartholomew, I mean – honourable and fair. I have never met a more redoubtable fighter, yet we murdered him!'

Athelstan rose, took the wine jug and refilled the man's cup.

'Continue, Sir Brian.'

'Bartholomew wanted to go home, return to his manor at Woodforde. His wife was sickly and he also feared for his young son's life. At the same time, he had difficulties with Sir Ralph Whitton.' Fitzormonde glared into his wine cup. 'Ralph was the canker in the rose. I think he was secretly jealous of Bartholomew. He began to object to the way the treasure was being shared out, but Bartholomew failed to take him seriously. He said a bargain was a bargain; he had found the treasure, he had risked the Caliph's wrath, and he had killed the three assassins. However, he said he trusted his blood brothers and left the treasure with us when he took ship from Cyprus.' Fitzormonde stared at Athelstan and the friar began to suspect the true reason behind the drawing on the pieces of parchment.

'What happened to that ship, Sir Brian?'

The knight emptied the wine goblet in one gulp. 'A few days later we learnt Whitton had sent a secret message to the Caliph.' He shrugged. 'The rest is obvious. The ship Bartholomew was travelling on was intercepted and sunk.'

Athelstan whirled round as the door crashed open. Cranston stood there, foul-faced and bleary-eyed.

'What's the bloody matter, monk?' he boomed. 'Where the...?' Cranston used an obscene word and glared at the knight. 'You still wish to challenge me, Sir Brian?'

Athelstan rose, grabbed Cranston by the arm and hustled him out of the room, closing the door behind him.

'Sir John,' he rasped, 'I am hearing this man's confession!'

Cranston tried to push Athelstan aside. 'By the sod!' he roared. 'I don't give a shit!'

'Sir John, this is nothing to do with you.'

Athelstan, using all his weight, pushed Sir John back and sent him tottering down the corridor. Cranston steadied himself, pulled his long, wicked-looking dagger from its sheath and walked slowly back, his red-rimmed eyes fixed on Athelstan. The friar leaned against the door.

'What are you going to do, John?' Athelstan asked softly. 'Are you, the Lord Coroner, going to slay a priest, a colleague and a friend?'

Sir John stopped and slouched against the wall, staring upwards at the great beams resting on their corbels of stone.

'God forgive me, Athelstan,' he whispered. 'My apologies to Sir Brian. I shall wait for you downstairs.'

The friar re-entered the room. Fitzormonde still sat, cradling his head in his hands. Athelstan touched him gently on the shoulder.

'Forget Cranston.' He smiled. 'A man whose bark is much worse than his bite. Sir Brian, you wanted me to hear your confession? So Burghgesh was murdered. Surely the blame rests squarely with Sir Ralph?'

Fitzormonde shook his head and looked up. 'Don't patronise me, Father. Ralph told us what he had done. We could have stopped it. We could have brought Sir Ralph to justice. We could have searched the seas to see if Bartholomew had survived.'

'Was that possible?'

'Perhaps. Sometimes the Moors sell prisoners in the slave markets. But we didn't look there for him. We could have looked after Bartholomew's widow and his little son, but we failed to do that.' Fitzormonde drove one of his fists into the palm of his hand. 'We should have executed Sir Ralph. Instead, we became his accomplices and shared out his ill-gotten wealth.'

'What happened to Bartholomew's widow?'

'I don't know. We went our separate ways. Eventually guilt caught up with Mowbray and myself, so we joined the hospitallers, handing over what wealth we had left to the Order. Horne came back to the city and grew powerful on his riches. Whitton entered the service of John of Gaunt.' Fitzormonde placed the goblet on the ground before him. 'Do you know, Father, it wasn't until Whitton was dead that I realised how he had held us in his evil thrall.' Fitzormonde paused. 'You have seen the great bear in the Tower bailey?'

'Yes.'

'Every afternoon I am here,' Fitzormonde continued, 'I go to stare at it. The beast is a killer, but I'm fascinated by it. Whitton was like that. Sir Ralph made his guilt a bond between us all. As the years passed, we became more confident that our crime had been forgotten and began the custom of every year meeting to celebrate Christmas. We never discussed Bartholomew.'

Athelstan nodded. 'That's the terrible thing about sin, Sir Brian. We let it become part of us, like a rotting tooth which we tolerate and forget.'

Fitzormonde rubbed his face with his hands.

'But what happened,' Athelstan asked, 'three years ago?'

'I don't know. We came to the Tower as Ralph's guests for Yuletide, supping as usual at the Golden Mitre in Petty Wales, but when we met Sir Ralph that particular time, he looked as if he had seen a ghost. In fact, he said he had, and that's all he would say.'

149

Athelstan seized the man's wrist and forced him to look up. 'Have you confessed all, Sir Brian?'

'Everything I know.'

'And the piece of parchment?'

'A reminder of the ship Bartholomew was sailing on.'

'And the four crosses?'

'They represent Bartholomew's four companions.'

'And the seed cake?'

Fitzormonde sighed and blew his cheeks out. 'A reminder of how Bartholomew saved us from the assassins, and a warning of our own deaths.'

'Do you know who murdered Sir Ralph and Sir Gerard?'

'Before God, I do not!'

'Could Bartholomew have survived?'

'He may have.'

Athelstan stared at the lime-washed walls. 'What about Bartholomew's son? He would be a young man now.'

Fitzormonde shrugged. 'I thought of that, but I have made some enquiries. Young Burghgesh was killed in France. Now, Father, my penance?'

Athelstan raised his hand and pronounced absolution, making the broad sweep of the sign of the cross above Fitzormonde's bowed head. Sir Brian looked up.

'My penance, Father?' he repeated.

'Your penance is the guilt you have borne. You are to pray for Burghgesh's soul and for those of Sir Gerard and Sir Ralph. And one more thing!'

'Yes, Father?'

'You are to go downstairs and repeat your confession to Sir John.'

'He'll arrest me for murder.'

Athelstan grinned. 'Sir John is an old soldier and, when sober, a keen student of the human heart. He has more compassion in his little finger than many a priest. He'll hear you out and probably roar for a cup of sack.'

Chapter 8

Fitzormonde left, closing the door quietly behind him. Athelstan went to gaze out of the window, staring absent-mindedly at the great tocsin bell which hung so silently on its icy rope above the snow-covered green. The sun, now beginning to set, made the bell shimmer like a piece of silver. Athelstan turned and glimpsed Fitzormonde talking quietly to Cranston. The coroner was nodding, listening intently to the hospitaller's confession.

Athelstan wandered back to Philippa's chamber but it was deserted. He stayed for a while reflecting on what Fitzormonde had told him. First, both Sir Ralph and Mowbray's murders were connected to that terrible act of betrayal in Cyprus so many years earlier. Secondly, and Athelstan shivered, there would be other murders. He packed his writing tray away whilst speculating on other possibilities. First, Burghgesh could have survived and come back to wreak vengeance. Secondly, someone else, possibly Burghgesh's son, had returned to make his father's murderers atone for the death. But, if it had been either of these, how would they get into the Tower, mysteriously ring a tocsin bell and then arrange for Mowbray's fall? Athelstan sighed. Sir Ralph Whitton's murder was simple compared to the complexities surrounding Mowbray's.

Athelstan rubbed his chin with the palm of his hand and remembered he'd promised Benedicta to meet her at the Fleet prison where Simon the carpenter would spend his last evening on earth. The thought of Benedicta made him smile. Their relationship had become calmer, more gentle. Then he remembered Doctor Vincentius and hoped the physician would not ensnare her with his subtle charm. Athelstan's smile broadened. Here he was, a friar, a priest, a man sworn to chastity, feeling twinges of jealousy about someone he could only claim as a friend.

He shook himself free from his reverie and looked around the chamber. The murders... what other possibilities existed? Was it one of the group? Not Fitzormonde, but perhaps Horne the merchant? Or could it be Colebrooke, who had discovered Sir Ralph's murky past and was promoting his own ambitions under the guise of revenge for past misdeeds? Athelstan swung his cloak around him, picked up his writing tray and examined the beautiful embroidery of the dorsar draped over the back of one of the chairs. Of course, terrible though it might be to imagine, Mistress Philippa had the cool nerve and composure to be a murderess, and Parchmeiner might well be her accomplice. Hammond the chaplain had the spite, whilst Sir Fulke had everything to gain.

Athelstan heard Cranston bellowing his name so left the chamber and went downstairs where the coroner stood kicking absentmindedly at the snow.

'You feel better, Sir John?'

Cranston grunted.

'And Fitzormonde told you all?'

The coroner glanced up.

'Yes, I believe he did, Athelstan. You think the same as I do?'

He nodded. 'Our sins,' he murmured, 'always catch up with us. The Greeks call them the Furies. We Christians call it God's anger.'

Cranston was about to reply when Colebrooke came striding across the green. The lieutenant looked white-faced and tense.

'My Lord Coroner!' he called out. 'You are finished here?'

'In other words,' Cranston half whispered to Athelstan, 'the fellow is asking us when we are going to bugger off!'

'We will leave soon, Master Lieutenant, but may I ask one favour first?'

Colebrooke hid his distaste behind a false smile. 'Of course, Brother.'

'You have messengers here. Will you send one to the widow Benedicta at St Erconwald's in Southwark? Ask her to meet Sir John and me at the Three Cranes tavern in Cheapside. And, Master Lieutenant?'

'Yes!'

'Sir Ralph's corpse – was it cold and the blood congealing?'

'I'm a soldier, Brother, not a physician. But, yes, I think it was. Why?'

'Nothing,' Athelstan murmured. 'I thank you.'

Colebrooke nodded and strode off. Cranston stretched lazily.

'A pretty mess, Brother.'

'Hush, Sir John, not here. I think these walls do have ears, and our boon companion Red Hand wishes an audience.'

Cranston turned and quietly cursed as the madman scampered across the snow to greet them, yelping like an affectionate dog.

'Lots of blood! Lots of blood!' he screamed. 'Many deaths, dark secrets! Three dungeons but only two doors. Dark passages. Red Hand sees them all! Red Hand sees the shadows creak!' The madman danced in the snow before them. 'Up and down! Up and down, the body falls! What do you think? What do you think?'

'Sod off, Red Hand!' Cranston muttered and, taking Athelstan by the arm, guided him past the great hall towards the gateway under Wakefield Tower. Athelstan suddenly remembered the bear, stopped and walked back to where the animal sat chained in the corner where curtain wall met Bell Tower. The friar was fascinated. He stared and hid a smile, hoping Sir John would not notice, for there was a close affinity between the shaggy beast and the corpulent coroner.

'It smells like a death house,' Cranston moaned.

The bear turned and Athelstan glimpsed the fury in its small, red eyes. The great beast lumbered to his feet, straining at the chain around its neck.

'I don't know which is the madder,' Cranston muttered, 'the bear or Red Hand!'

The animal seemed to understand Sir John's words for it lunged towards him with a strangled growl; its top lip curled, showing teeth as sharp as a row of daggers.

'I think you are right, Sir John,' Athelstan observed.

'Perhaps we should go.'

The friar watched with alarm the way the chain around the bear's neck creaked and shook the iron clasp nailed to the wall. They turned left to collect their horses from the stables.

'We could leave them here,' Athelstan remarked, 'and take a boat downriver.'

'God forbid, Brother,' Cranston snapped. 'Have you no sense? The bloody ice is still moving, and I never fancy shooting under London Bridge even on the fairest day!'

They left the Tower and rode up Eastcheap, turning into Gracechurch, past the Cornmarket where St Peter on Cornhill stood, and into Cheapside. The roar from that great thoroughfare was deafening: traders, merchants and apprentices shouted themselves hoarse as they tried to make up for their previous loss of trade. The bailiffs and beadles were also busy: two drunkards, barrels placed over their heads, were being led through the marketplace, followed by a stream of dirty, ragged urchins who pelted the unfortunates with ice and snowballs. A beggar had died on the corner of Threadneedle Street. The corpse, now stiff, had turned blue with the cold. A small boy armed with a stick tried to beat off two hungry-looking dogs which sniffed suspiciously at the dead beggar's bloody feet. Cranston tossed him a penny and, standing on an overturned barrel, bellowed for half the market to hear how he was Coroner of the city, and would no one help the poor lad have the corpse removed?

'I don't care if you're the bloody mayor himself,' one of the traders shouted back. 'Piss off and leave us alone!'

Athelstan drew his cowl over his head and pulled his sleeves down. He knew what was coming next. Cranston, true to his nature, jumped down from the barrel and grasped the unfortunate trader by the throat.

'I arrest you, sir!' he roared. 'For treason! That is the crime you have committed. I am the King's Coroner. Mock me and you mock the crown!'

The man's face paled and his eyes bulged.

'Now, sir,' Cranston continued quietly as the other traders slunk back, 'I can ask the wardsman to convene a jury of your peers or we can settle on a fine?'

'A fine! A fine!' the man gasped, his face turning puce.

Sir John tightened his grip. 'Two shillings!' he announced, and shook the fellow so hard Athelstan became alarmed and took a step forward, but the coroner waved him back.

'Two shillings, payable now!' Cranston repeated.

The man dug into his purse and slapped the coins into the coroner's hand. Sir John released him and the fellow slumped down on all fours, retching and coughing.

'Was that necessary, Sir John?' Athelstan whispered.

'Yes, Brother, it was!' Cranston snapped. 'This city is ruled by fear. If a trader can mock me, in a week every bastard in London will follow suit.'

Cranston scowled as two beadles, summoned by the commotion, approached. The self-important looks on their smug faces faded as they recognised Sir John.

'My Lord Coroner!' one of them gasped. 'What is it you want?'

Cranston pointed to the beggar's corpse. 'Have that removed!' he bellowed. 'You know your job. God knows how long the poor bastard has been lying there. Now move it before I kick both your arses!'

The beadles backed off, bowing and scraping as if the coroner was the Regent himself. Cranston turned and flicked his fingers at the urchin. The boy, arms and legs as thin as sticks, his eyes dark and round in a long, white face, came over, his thumb stuck in his mouth.

'Here, lad!' Cranston pushed the two shillings into an emaciated hand. 'Now, go to Greyfriars. You know it?

Between Newgate and St Martin's Lane. Ask for Brother Ambrose. Tell him Sir John sent you.'

The boy, the money clenched tightly in his fist, stared back, spat neatly between Cranston's boots and scampered off.

The coroner watched him go. 'The preacher Ball is correct,' he murmured. 'Very soon this city will burn with the fires of revolt if the rich do not get off their fat arses and do more to help!' He turned, his face now grave and serious. 'Believe me, Brother, God's angel stands at the threshold, the flailing rod of divine retribution in his hand. When that day comes,' Cranston rasped, 'there will be more violent deaths than there are people in this marketplace!'

Athelstan nodded in agreement and stared around. Oh, the marketplace was full of wealthy traders, merchants draped in furs, the wealthy artisans in jackets of rabbit and moleskin. Most looked well fed, plump even, but in the alleyways off the markets, Athelstan saw the poor; not like those in his parish but the landless men driven from their farms, flocking into the city to look for work though none was to be had. The Guilds controlled everything and soon these vagrants would be turned out, forced across London Bridge to swell the slums and violent underworld of Southwark.

'Come on, Sir John,' he murmured.

They pushed on up the Mercery, standing aside as a group of debtors from the Marshalsea, linked by chains, moved through the crowd, begging for alms both for themselves and other inmates. They found the Three Cranes tavern at the corner of an alleyway just opposite St Mary Le Bow. Benedicta was waiting for them, seated before a roaring fire; beside her on the ground, crouched like a little dog, sat Orme, one of Watkin the dung-collector's sons. Athelstan slipped him a penny, patted him lightly on the head, and the boy scampered off.

'Well, Benedicta, you left my church in good order?'

The widow smiled and unloosed the clasp of her cloak. Athelstan suddenly wondered what she would look like in a bright dress of scarlet taffeta rather than the dark browns, greens and blues she always wore.

'All is well?' he repeated hastily.

Benedicta grinned. 'Cecily the courtesan and Watkin's wife were screaming abuse at each other, but apart from that, you will be sorry to hear, the church still stands. Sir John, you are well?' She twisted her head to catch the coroner's eye as he scowled across at the innkeeper who was busy gossiping to the other customers around the great wine barrels.

'My Lady,' Cranston retorted, 'I would feel better—' he raised his voice to a bellow '—I would feel better if I got some custom, and the attention due to a King's officer!'

The landlord kept chatting so Cranston strode across, roaring for a cup of sack and wine for his companions.

'What's wrong with Sir John?' Benedicta whispered.

'I don't know. I think the Lady Maude has upset him. She is being mysterious and secretive.'

'Strange,' Benedicta mused. 'I meant to tell you, Brother, Lady Maude was seen in Southwark over a week ago. She is so memorable, so petite and sweet-faced.' Benedicta screwed up her eyes. 'Yes, I am sure they told me she was coming out of Doctor Vincentius' house.'

'Is he a ladies' man?' Athelstan asked hastily, and wished he could have bitten his tongue out the moment he spoke. Benedicta stared coolly back.

'Brother Athelstan,' she replied, 'can you show me a man who isn't?'

Cranston's return saved Athelstan from further embarrassment. The coroner swept his beaver hat from his head, scratched his balding pate, winked lecherously at Benedicta and turned to watch a now frightened taverner bring across a deep pewter bowl of sack and cups of wine for his companions.

'You are not eating, Sir John?'

'No,' Cranston muttered. 'I don't feel hungry and I suspect the innkeeper, after my blunt speech with him, would poison the bloody dish!'

Benedicta laughed merrily. 'Sir John, you must calm yourself!'

'No,' Cranston replied, lifting the goblet. 'I'll find serenity at the bottom of this cup.'

Benedicta watched in disbelief as Cranston drained his drink in one large gulp and boomed for more, smacking his lips, gently burping and belching. Benedicta bit her lower lip to stifle her laughter.

'Well, Brother.' Cranston patted his broad girth. 'With apologies to the Lady Benedicta, what do you make of Mowbray's death?' Cranston licked his lips. 'Or Sir Ralph's?'

Athelstan leaned against the table and ran his finger round the rim of the wine goblet. 'First, we have found that Sir Ralph was probably murdered by someone who entered the Tower by crossing an ice-bound moat. Secondly, Mowbray was lured to his death by the tocsin sounding. Thirdly, both murders are certainly linked with Sir Ralph's dreadful betrayal of Bartholomew Burghgesh in Cyprus so many years ago.' Athelstan smiled at Benedicta's quizzical face. 'You are puzzled, My Lady. Well, so are we. First, how can someone enter the Tower, murder Sir Ralph, then leave the fortress without being noticed? Secondly, why did Sir Ralph just lie there and allow his throat to be cut so savagely that his head was almost hacked from his body? You saw the corpse, Sir John, and the chamber? There was no sign of any struggle nor did the guards hear anything. Thirdly, who rang the tocsin bell and, at the same time, so subtly arranged for Mowbray to fall from the parapet?'

The coroner's face grew longer at Athelstan's every word.

'And the list of suspects,' the friar continued remorselessly, 'still stands. We may have met the murderer, yet it may equally be someone in the Tower or the city about whom we know nothing.'

'I do not know the full story,' Benedicta interrupted, 'but there is rejoicing in Southwark at Sir Ralph's death.' She lowered her voice. 'Pike the ditcher says it is the work of the Great Community. The secret peasant leaders wish to weaken the city before they organise their great revolt.'

'Nonsense!' Cranston slurred, now on his third cup of sack. 'Pike the ditcher, with all due respect, My Lady Benedicta, should keep his mouth shut and his neck safe! Sir Ralph was not murdered by any peasant.'

Athelstan sipped from his wine cup and made a face at the sourness of the drink. 'One person we have not met, My Lord Coroner, is the merchant Adam Horne. Benedicta, before we go on to meet Simon in the Fleet prison, there are certain enquiries to make. You will accompany us?'

Benedicta agreed, so they rose and left, Cranston bawling abuse at the hapless taverner. Outside it was growing dark, and only a red glow showed where the sun had set.

Cranston steadied himself carefully on the icy cobbles and stared at the sky.

'Why is it always red at night?'

'Some say,' Athelstan replied, 'it's because the sun slips into hell, but I think that's an old wives' tale. Come on, Sir John.'

Athelstan slipped round the coroner, tactfully linked one arm through his and, with Benedicta on the other side, crossed the now deserted Cheapside. The stalls were being packed away, the last iron-rimmed carts crashed along to Newgate or east to Aldgate. Weary apprentices and traders locked their shutters and put out lantern horns. The bell of St Mary Le Bow began to toll the curfew, the sign that all trading should cease, as four urchins pulled a huge yule log up to the door of one of the great merchants' houses. Cranston stopped to enquire directions of one of the market stewards who sat in his little toll booth on the corner of Wood Street. The fellow pointed down to the corner of the Mercery and Lawrence Street.

'You will find the Horne house there,' he said. 'A fine place, with a huge, black-timbered door and a coat of arms above it.'

They turned, staying in the centre of Cheapside as the melting snow began to slide from the sloping tiled roofs. The Horne house stood deserted, no lantern above the door, only a tired-looking Christmas wreath. Cranston stepped back and looked up at the lead-paned windows.

'No candlelight,' he murmured.

Athelstan pulled Benedicta closer into the side of the house to protect her from any snow falling from the small canopied hood of the doorway. He lifted the great brass knocker, cast in the shape of a dragon's head and brought it crashing down. There was no answer, so he knocked

163

again. They heard the patter of footsteps and a whey-faced maid answered the door.

'Is Alderman Horne here?' Cranston slurred.

The young girl shook her head wordlessly.

'Who is it?' a voice asked from the darkness beyond.

'Lady Horne?' Cranston queried. 'I am Sir John Cranston, Coroner. You sent a message earlier today to the sheriffs at the Guildhall?'

The woman stepped out of the darkness, her drawn face bathed even whiter by the light of the candle she carried. Her cheeks were tear-stained, her eyes dark-shadowed and sad, whilst her steel-grey hair hung in untidy tresses beneath a white veil.

'Sir John.' She forced a smile. 'You had best come in. Girl, light the torches in the solar! Bring candles!'

Lady Horne led them up a stone-vaulted passageway into a comfortable but cold solar. A weak fire flickered in the hearth. Lady Horne told them to sit whilst behind them the girl lit candles. Athelstan gazed round. The room was positively luxurious with bright-hued tapestries on the walls, and exquisitely embroidered linen cloths placed on tables, chests and over the backs of chairs. Nevertheless, he could almost smell the stench of fear. The house was too quiet. He looked at Lady Horne who sat on the other side of the fireplace, an ivory and pearl rosary entwined around her fingers.

'You wish some refreshment?' she murmured.

Cranston was about to reply but Athelstan intervened.

'No, My Lady. This matter is urgent. Where is your husband?'

'I don't know,' she whispered. 'That terrible message arrived this morning and Sir Adam left immediately afterwards. He said he was going upriver to the warehouses.'

She clenched her hands tightly. 'I have sent messages there, but the boy returned and said my husband had already left. Sir John, what is the matter?' Her tired eyes pleaded with the coroner. 'What does this all mean?'

'I don't know,' he lied. 'But your husband, Lady Horne, is in terrible danger. Does anyone know where he has gone?'

The woman bowed her head, her shoulders shaking with sobs. Benedicta rose and crouched beside her, stroking her hands gently.

'Lady Horne, please,' Athelstan persisted. 'Do you know anything about the message or why your husband was so frightened?'

The woman shook her head. 'No, but Adam was never at peace.' She looked up. 'Oh, he was a man of great wealth but at night he would awake screaming about foul, bloody murder, his body coated in sweat. Sometimes he would tremble for at least an hour, but never once did he confide in me.'

Cranston stared across at Athelstan and made a face. The friar looked at the hour candle which stood on the table behind him.

'Sir John,' he whispered, getting up, 'it's almost seven o'clock. We must go!'

'Lady Horne.' The merchant's wife was about to rise but Cranston gently touched her on the shoulder. 'Stay and keep warm, the maid will see us out. If your husband returns, tell him to come to my house. It's not far. You promise?'

The woman nodded before looking away into the dying embers of the fire.

Outside Cranston stamped his feet, clapping his hands together. 'That woman,' he observed, 'is terrified. I suspect she knows the source of her husband's wealth, but what can we do? Horne could be anywhere in the city.'

Athelstan shrugged. 'Sir John, Benedicta and I must go to Fleet prison. We promised the parish we would visit Simon the carpenter.'

'Ah, yes,' Cranston replied tartly. 'The murderer.'

'You will go home?'

Sir John stared into the gathering darkness. He would have loved to but what was the use? All he'd do was sit and drink himself stupid.

'Sir John,' Athelstan repeated, 'the Lady Maude will be waiting for you.'

'No,' Cranston answered stubbornly. 'I'll go to the Fleet with you. Perhaps I can help.'

Athelstan glanced at Benedicta and raised his eyes heavenwards. The friar wanted Sir John to go; he was tired of the coroner's constant bad temper and sudden bouts of fury. He loved the fat knight, but on this occasion, dearly wished to see the back of him. Nevertheless, he agreed. They walked through the blood-stained slush of the Shambles, holding their noses against the sickening putrid smells from the slaughterhouses, and turned left into Old Deans Lane, a narrow alleyway ankle-deep in muck which ran between dark, overhanging houses. Somewhere in the distance a dog barked mournfully. At the corner of Bowyers Row, they stood aside as a huge, wooden wagon rolled by, pulled by four horses, their manes hogged, eyes blinkered and nostrils flaring at the corrupting smell of death. The horses' hooves and the wheels of the cart were muffled in straw so that it seemed to glide like a terrible phantasm. On one corner of the cart a torch flared, throwing the driver into ghastly relief as he sat cloaked and hooded, a grim death mask over his face.

'What is it?' Benedicta asked.

She brought up the hem of her cloak to cover her nose. Athelstan sketched a sign of the cross in the air and prayed the cart would continue, but it stopped alongside them. The driver tried to quieten the horses as two screeching cats, fighting over some vermin, scurried out of the shadows. Cranston knew what was in the cart. He had recognised the driver as the hangman from Tyburn.

'Don't look,' he whispered.

But Benedicta, her curiosity aroused, leaned on Athelstan's arm and, standing on tiptoe, peered over the rim of the cart. She stared in horror at the whitened, frozen cadavers which lay there under a tattered, canvas sheet. Their limbs hung all awry but round the neck of each was a thick, purple line, while the purple-red faces were contorted, swollen tongues held fast between ice-cold lips, eyes rolled back in the sockets.

'Oh, sweet Lord!' she breathed, and leaned against the wall as the driver cracked his whip and the cart rolled on.

'What was that?'

'The hanged from the Elms,' Cranston answered. 'At night the corpses are cut down and taken to the great lime pits near Charterhouse.' He glared at the widow. 'I told you not to look!'

Benedicta retched before, resting on Athelstan's arm, following Cranston through Ludgate and up towards the Fleet.

The prison did little to lighten their mood: grey frowning walls with a few sombre buildings peeping above them, and a black gateway with an arch which yawned as if it wished to devour any unfortunate who approached it. Cranston pulled at the bell and they were allowed through a wicket gate built into the ponderous door. A gaoler led them into the porter's lodge, the fellow bowing and scraping as he recognised Sir John. Athelstan was pleased then that the coroner had accompanied them. They went through a large hall where the debtors were jailed, furnished with side benches of oak and two long tables of the same wood, all covered in greasy filth. The people gathered around them were dirty and foul-smelling, men and women wearing threadbare jerkins and tattered cloaks. They pushed their way through the hall and up a stone-flagged passageway, past grated windows where poor debtors shook their begging bowls through the bars and whined for alms.

At last they went down slimy, cracked steps into the Hall of the Damned, the condemned hold, a massive, vaulted cellar with dungeons in the far wall.

'Who is it you wish to see?' the porter snapped.

'Simon the carpenter.'

The porter hurried across, chose a key and unlocked one of the doors.

'Come on, Simon!' he bawled. 'A rare treat! London's own coroner, a friar and a fair lady. Who could ask for more?'

Simon crept from the cell. Athelstan hardly recognised him: his face was a mass of sores, his hair long and matted with filth and vermin. The man's clothing had been reduced to rags and he was loaded with fetters. Simon shuffled awkwardly towards them, lifting his manacled hands to push his hair back. His lips were blue with the cold and his eyes, above sallow sunken cheeks, bright with fever.

'Father, you have brought a pardon?' he asked hopefully.

Athelstan shook his head. 'No, I am sorry. I just came to visit you, Simon. Is there anything I can do?'

The carpenter looked at him, then at Benedicta and, throwing back his head, laughed hysterically until the porter struck him across the face. The condemned man slumped to the floor, crouching like a beaten dog. Athelstan knelt beside him.

'Simon!' he murmured. 'Simon!'

The carpenter raised his head.

'Do you wish to be shriven? I will hear your confession.'

The man looked up despairingly.

'There's nothing left,' Athelstan whispered. 'This time tomorrow, Simon, you will be with God.'

The carpenter nodded and began to cry like a child. Athelstan turned. 'Sir John, Benedicta, please, give me a moment.'

They withdrew. The coroner bawled at the porter to follow them and, for the second time that day, Athelstan heard the confession of a man about to meet Death. At first, Simon spoke slowly and Athelstan had to fight hard to keep his composure as the chill of the dungeons seeped through his robe, turning his legs to blocks of ice, but then Simon allowed his emotions full rein. He talked of everything, a miserable litany of failure culminating in the rape of a child. Athelstan heard him out, pronounced absolution and rose, rubbing his stiff legs to make the warmth return. The porter came back.

'Tomorrow, Simon,' Athelstan whispered, 'I shall remember you. And, Simon?'

The condemned man looked up.

'You remember me before the throne of God.'

The carpenter nodded. 'I didn't mean to do it, Father. I was lonely, I'd drunk too much.'

'I know,' Athelstan murmured. 'God help you and her!' Athelstan turned to the porter and tossed him a silver coin. 'One good meal, sir.'

The porter caught the coin and nodded.

'One good meal,' Athelstan warned. 'I shall check on that.'

He was about to leave when Simon called out: 'Father!'

'Yes, Simon?'

'Ranulf the rat-catcher came to see me earlier today. He had been hired by a butcher in the Shambles. He said you were at the Tower because of Sir Ralph Whitton's death.' The carpenter grinned. 'Even though I have been shriven, it is good to know that bastard went before me. A strange place, the Tower, Father.'

Athelstan nodded. He felt Simon was only trying to prolong the visit. 'I worked there once,' the carpenter called out. 'A strange place, worse than this!'

'Why is that, Simon?'

'Well, at least here the cells have doors. In the Tower there are rooms, dungeons, where you go in, the doors are removed, and you remain until death behind a bricked wall.'

'Is that so?' Athelstan smiled. 'God be with you, Simon.'

Athelstan went back up the steps to rejoin Cranston and Benedicta. They never spoke until they were out of the prison, the wicket gate slamming shut behind them.

'The antechamber of Hell,' Athelstan murmured as they made their way down Bowyers Row under the dark mass of St Paul's. At Friday Street, Sir John made to leave.

Athelstan took him aside and stared into the bleary-eyed face.

'I thank you for coming, Sir John. Be at peace. Go home and talk to the Lady Maude. I am sure all will be well.'

Cranston scratched his head. 'God knows, Brother, but I feel the only good I did today was to listen to Fitzormonde and help that child. You know, the one who stood over the beggar man?'

'You came with us to the Fleet.'

'Aye,' Cranston muttered. 'I could not get a pardon for Simon, you know that, Brother, but I showed him one last mercy.'

'What's that, Sir John?'

'I left a coin for the executioner. Simon won't dance. He will be taken far up the ladder.' Cranston snapped his fingers. 'His neck will snap and it will all be over quickly.' The coroner stamped his feet and looked up at the star-filled sky. 'You had best hurry home, Brother. The stars await you.' He turned and tramped up the street. 'I only wish,' he called out 'we'd found Alderman Horne!'

Chapter 9

As Athelstan and Benedicta rode slowly back across the dark, choppy waters of the Thames, Adam Horne left the Crutched Friars monastery near Mark Lane just north of the Tower. He'd arrived just after Vespers to collect the message he had been told would be waiting for him. The grizzle-haired lay brother had smiled toothlessly and waved Horne into the door-keeper's lodge.

'It's been here all afternoon,' the lay brother murmured, handing him a thin roll of vellum. Horne anxiously un-folded the parchment and, begging the brother to bring a candle, hastily read the contents.

'Oh, my God!' he groaned as his hopes were dashed. Earlier in the morning he had received a piece of parch-ment with a sketch of a crudely drawn ship, and a flat sesame seed cake. He had tried to hide his fears from his poor wife and gone down to his warehouse, where another message had been awaiting him: he was not to return home, the short letter instructed, but to go to the House of the Crutched Friars where his anxieties would be resolved. He should fear nothing but put his hopes in the sender who wished him well. Now this short note cruelly dashed his hopes: the mysterious writer apologised for not meeting him but asked him to wait amongst the ancient ruins to the north-west of the Tower. Horne shredded the note, left the friary and made his way through the dark, ice-covered country lanes which cut round farms and smallholdings. He stared up at the starlit sky and shivered, not only from the biting cold but his own sombre fear of what might await him. Horne's common sense told him to run but he had waited too long. The threat had hung like a sword over his head for years and he wanted to confront it once and for all. A self-confident merchant, Horne also believed the meeting might end his fears for good. He could then go home, absolved from his part in that terrible crime committed so many years ago.

The line of trees ended and Horne stood on the edge of the common, in the far distance the lowering mass of the Tower. Perhaps he should go there? He sighed despairingly. Who could help him? Sir Ralph was dead and the surviving hospitaller would have no time for him. Horne gulped quickly at the realisation of his own guilt. Should he go on? He stared at the ice-covered ground and half listened to the cold wind moaning gently amongst the trees. Above him a raven cawed as it flew to hunt over the mudflats along the river. A fox barked. The sound was strident and made the hair curl on the back of his neck. Horne felt uneasy. He turned and stared back down the muddy track. Was someone there? Had he been followed?

Horne's face twisted into a snarl. He might be a fat, wealthy merchant now but fifteen years ago, he had fought as a knight, shoulder to shoulder with men who feared nothing on earth. Yes, he had been guilty. Even as much as Whitton, Fitzormonde and Mowbray had always been soft, they could whine and moan that they had not been to blame, but Horne had agreed to Whitton's plan and built a thriving business on the proceeds.

He fondled the long dagger he'd pushed through his wallet, drawing comfort from its metal-coiled handle. If there was an assassin about, he reassured himself, best to confront him now rather than be taken in the dead of night. An owl hooted. Horne snarled. 'Let all the hell hounds come from Satan's dark abyss! I will match blow for blow!' His empty words comforted him as he walked across to the ruins, a collection of snow-covered boulders. The old ones said the great Caesar once had a palace there. Horne, deeply agitated by a mixture of fear, terror and forced bravado, went and sat in the middle. He felt safer; despite the darkness, the white, snow-covered common and brittle ice would give him warning of any assassin's approach.

The merchant stared round the ruined Roman villa. A few yards away was a half-raised wall. Horne glared at it contemptuously. If any murderer lurked there, they would have to cover the ground and he had brought something special. A small arbalest, or miniature crossbow, swung from his belt, a bolt already in place. The darkness grew deeper. Horne studied the lights of the city. The wine he had drunk earlier in the day, his exertions and fear, made him feel warm and sleepy. A short stab of icy wind made him huddle deeper into his cloak and he stirred to keep the hot blood flowing through his veins. The merchant stared around into the gathering darkness and his courage began to ebb as he wondered who his strange benefactor might be. Horne closed his eyes, half sleeping, dozing. That's what Bartholomew Burghgesh had always told him to do.

'Rest whenever you can, my dear Adam. A true soldier always eats, drinks, sleeps and takes a wench whenever the opportunity presents itself.'

Horne smiled to himself. Brave, redoubtable man! A veritable paladin! Horne had liked him, but Ralph

Whitton had always been jealous of Bartholomew for being a better soldier than he. But surely there had been more than that?

Something about Whitton's wife being rather sweet on the young Bartholomew when he had, for a time, served as a knight banneret in the Tower. Horne sniggered to himself. Strange coincidence, the same place where Whitton had met his death. Horne looked up. Was that a sound he had heard? He sat still, his ears straining, but only the cawing of the ravens and the distant bark of some farm dog broke the chilling silence. Horne moved his feet restlessly. He would wait a few more minutes and then he'd go. He stared at the ground. Who was the murderer? he wondered. Could it be the hospitaller, Fitzormonde? Or Fulke, Sir Ralph's brother? He'd known Burghgesh quite well. Or someone else who believed he was God's vicar on earth to dispense justice and retribution? Or had Burghgesh survived, been taken prisoner, and then years later slipped back into England to reap bloody havoc on his foes? Or perhaps his son and heir? Had he really died in France, or else learnt about his father's terrible fate and secretly returned to stalk his sire's killers?

Horne chewed on his lip. He had to face the fact that he was a killer. He had been party to Burghgesh's murder. Sometimes at night this thought would rouse him screaming from his sleep. And was that why God had given him no son or heir? Was his wife's barrenness due to divine justice? Horne heard a sound, jumped up in terror and stared at the apparition just next to the old wall.

A man clothed in knight's armour, on his breast the red cross of the crusaders, his face hidden by that helmet! The same steel, conical shell with eagle's wings on either side and blue tufted crest on top. A chilling terror gripped

Horne's heart. 'My God!' he whispered. 'It's Burghgesh!' Or was it an apparition from hell? The armoured, visored figure just stood there, feet slightly apart, mailed, gauntleted fists gripping the handle of the great, two-edged sword with the blade resting on one shoulder.

'You are Burghgesh?' Horne hissed.

The apparition moved closer. Only the crunch of mailed feet on the hard ice broke the silence.

'Adam! Adam!' The voice was Burghgesh's, though it sounded sombre and hollow. 'Adam!' the voice repeated. 'I have returned! I come for vengeance! You, my comrade in arms, my friend for whom I would have given my life.' One mailed hand shot out. 'You betrayed me! You, Whitton and the rest!'

Horne moved suddenly, his hand going to the small arbalest which swung from his belt.

'You're no phantasm,' the merchant snarled. 'And, if you are, go back to Hell where you belong!'

He brought up the arbalest but, even as he did, the great two-edged sword scythed the air, neatly slicing the merchant's head from his shoulders. The decapitated head spun like a ball in the air, lips still moving; his trunk stood for a few seconds in its own fountain of hot red gore before crashing on to the blood-stained ice. Horne's mailed executioner carefully cleaned the sword, drew his knife and knelt beside the blood-gushing torso of his victim.

Some hours later, Sir John Cranston, muttering and cursing to himself, made his way from Blind Basket Alley up Mincing Lane into Fenchurch Street. Dawn had just broken and Sir John, unable to sleep, had risen early to confer with Alderman Venables about the continued disappearance of Roger Droxford, still wanted for the murder of his master, whose decapitated corpse Cranston had found. Sir John had spent a restless night tossing from side to side in his great double bed. He had tried to remain calm but still seethed with fury at Maude's continued intransigence in the face of his pleadings and questions: her only answer would be to bite her lip, shake her head and turn away in floods of tears. At last Cranston had risen and gone to his personal chancery but, finding himself unable to concentrate, had finished dressing and gone to rouse Venables. Cranston grinned wickedly. He'd enjoyed that, letting the good alderman know what it was like to be awoken just before dawn. The sleepy-eyed alderman, however, could give him no further information on Droxford.

'He can't have fled far, Sir John,' Venables murmured sleepily. 'God knows, in this weather only a fool would try to flee the city limits, and both the description and the reward have been circulated.' Venables had grinned. 'After all, Sir John, he's a man you would remember.'

'What do you mean?'

'Well, he had two fingers missing from one hand and his face was covered in hairy warts.' The alderman pulled his fur-lined bed robe around him, moving restlessly on the stone-flagged corridor and making it obvious the coroner should leave. 'What's so special about Droxford, anyway, Sir John?'

'He's special, Master Venables, because he's a murderer, a felon who has stolen over two hundred pounds of his master's monies, and it looks as if he has got away scot-free!'

Venables took one look at Cranston's angry face and agreed. Sir John had then stamped off, muttering curses about public officials who didn't seem to care. Yet, in his heart, Cranston knew he was a hypocrite. The business at the Tower was still shrouded in mystery. The fugitive Droxford, not to mention the easy-going alderman, were the nearest butts for Sir John's foul temper.

He turned into the still-deserted Lombard Street and up to the great stocks just before the Poultry. A group of beadles were standing around a beggar who sat imprisoned there, feet and hands tightly clamped, face frozen, eyes open.

'What's the matter?' Cranston bellowed.

The beadles shuffled their feet.

'Someone forgot to release him last night,' one of them shouted. 'The poor bastard's frozen to death!'

'Then some bastard will pay!' Sir John bellowed back, and continued up the wide thoroughfare, past a group of nightbirds, whores and petty felons now manacled together and being led down to the great iron cage on top of the Conduit. A frightened-looking maid let him in. Sir John suddenly stopped, eyes narrowing. Hadn't he glimpsed a shadow in the alleyway beside the house? He went back. Nothing. Cranston shook his head and, vowing he would drink less sack, brushed past the anxious-looking maid, down the passageway and into the stone-flagged kitchen. He thanked God Maude wasn't there. He was tired of their encounters.

'Any messages?' he barked at a subdued-looking Leif, still sitting in his favourite place in the inglenook of the great fireplace. The one-legged beggar lifted his head from his bowl of vegetables and spiced meat and shook his head.

'No, Sir John,' he replied. 'But I have polished the pewter pots.'

'Good,' he growled. 'At least someone in this city is working.'

Cranston poured himself a generous goblet of wine and seized a small white loaf the cook had left to cool on the kitchen table. The coroner stood snatching mouthfuls of bread and gulping noisily from a goblet whilst he stared angrily at the fire. What should he do? he wondered.

Whitton's and Mowbray's deaths at the Tower were still as unfathomable as ever. He had also failed to find Horne. Sir John knew it would only be a matter of time before his masters at the Guildhall or, worse still, the Regent at the Savoy Palace, asked for an account of his stewardship. He heard a sharp knock at the door.

'Go on, Leif,' he growled. 'I'm too bloody cold to answer it.'

Leif looked self-pityingly at him.

'Go on, you idle bugger!' Cranston roared. 'There's more to this house than sitting on your arse and stuffing your mouth with every bit of food you can lay your sticky little fingers on!'

Leif sighed, put down the bowl and hobbled out of the kitchen. Cranston heard the front door open and the man limping slowly back.

'What is it?' Cranston asked, winking good-humouredly at the maid who had also hurried down to see who was at the door. The girl smiled anxiously back and Cranston quietly cursed himself. He was frightening everyone with his foul temper. He must take a grip on himself. Perhaps he should ask Athelstan to intervene? 'Well, man?' he repeated. 'Who was there?'

'No one, Sir John.'

'What do you mean?'

'Well, there was no one there.' Leif steadied himself against the lintel of the door. 'Only this.' He held up a battered, leather bag tied at the neck and stained with watery dark marks around the base. 'I answered the door,' Leif ponderously repeated, 'no one was there, only this bag.'

'Then open it, man!' Cranston said testily.

The coroner turned away to refill his wine cup. He whirled around at Leif s horrified cry and the bump as the maid fell in a dead faint to the floor. The beggar man just stood there, eyes wide in horror, mouth slack; in his upraised hand he held by the hair the decapitated head of Adam Horne, alderman and merchant.

Now Cranston had seen decapitated heads, be they of murdered taverner or some lord executed on Tower Hill, but this was truly gruesome; it was not so much the half-closed eyes and still blood-dripping neck but the mouth forced open and, thrust inside, the mangled remains of the dead merchant's genitals.

Cranston grabbed the head from the horror-struck beggar's hand, thrust it back into the bag, stepped over the still prostrate maid and, roaring for Maude, dashed down the passageway to the door. He flung it open, rushing like an angry bull down Cheapside, but the snow-covered thoroughfare was still deserted, with no trace or sign of their mysterious, grisly visitor. Cranston stopped and, half crouching, retched violently as the true horror of what he had seen seized his mind and wrung his stomach as if it was a wet rag.

'Oh, the bastard!' he whispered. 'Oh, Lord help us!'

He staggered back inside the house. Maude, white-faced, stood at the foot of the stairs.

'Sir John, what is it?'

'Go back to your room, woman!' Cranston roared. 'Stay there!'

He turned to the grooms and servants now huddled together near the kitchen door.

'You,' Cranston barked at one, 'go for a physician! You,' he pointed to the cook and her assistant, 'take the maid into the solar!'

The poor, half-unconscious girl was hustled to her feet. Cranston walked back into the kitchen. Leif sat on the stool like a man pole-axed. The bag and its gruesome contents still lay where Cranston had dropped it. The coroner busied himself around the house. He shaved, changed his doublet, put on his sword belt and took his heaviest cloak from its hook outside the buttery. He found a heavy flour sack in one of the outhouses and placed the battered leather bag carefully in it.

'Leif,' he ordered, 'tell Lady Maude I am going to the Guildhall, then on to Southwark.'

The beggar, usually so garrulous but still dumbstruck at what he had seen, just stared and nodded, open-mouthed. Cranston swung the sack over his shoulder.

'Oh, Leif.' Cranston turned and grinned evilly at the beggar. 'There's more of that rich stew if you want it.'

Leif turned away, retching, whilst Cranston stalked out of his house muttering vengeance against all and sundry.

–

In St Erconwald's church, Athelstan had just finished the Mass for the dead and was now blessing the corpse of Tosspot, an old drunkard who'd lived in the cellars of the Piebald Horse tavern. Tosspot had been found dead the previous afternoon. Pike the ditcher and Watkin the dung-collector had, in the absence of any relatives, sewn the body into a canvas sack, placed it on a wooden trellis and brought it to lie in front of the chancel screen. Athelstan had always given strict instructions on this: any poor man or woman found dead in his parish was to be given honourable burial, so this included Tosspot. Athelstan sketched the sign of the cross above the corpse and sprinkled it with the Asperges rod. Around him the usual Mass-goers, Benedicta included, watched fascinated as Athelstan urged the soul to go out to meet his Christ whilst he, Athelstan, priest of that church, summoned God's army to meet this unfortunate man's soul; they were to lead it into Paradise and ensure it did not fall into the hands of Satan. Athelstan paused. And what about the body? he thought. Would that be safe? He looked down at his fingers and noted the chalk dust on their tips. Where had that come from? he wondered. It had not been there during Mass.

'Father,' Crim the altar boy whispered.

Athelstan, startled, looked up.

'Father,' the boy repeated, his face creased in a mischievous grin, 'you've suddenly stopped praying!'

Athelstan shook himself free from his reverie.

'We beg thee, Michael the Archangel,' he intoned the final prayer, 'to take the soul of this our brother.' He paused. What could he call him? Tosspot? What would the angels think of such a name? 'Take the soul of this our brother Tosspot,' he continued defiantly, 'into the bosom of Abraham.'

The friar glared at the congregation, but they all knelt, heads wisely bowed to hide their grins. Athelstan, trying to conceal his embarrassment, signalled at Watkin and Pike to lift the bier and follow him and Crim, bearing a lighted taper, into the cemetery. Outside the cold wind snuffed the taper out. Crim slipped on the ice and fell on his backside, cursing so loudly Athelstan had to bite his lip to keep his face straight. They crossed the lonely, haunted cemetery to the shallow grave Pike had dug in the ground. Athelstan caught a glimpse of the two lepers, shrouded in their hoods near the charnel house. He suddenly remembered the twig he had used to push the Hosts through the leper's squint for these two unfortunates to swallow. Athelstan smiled to himself. That's where the chalk had come from. They reached the grave. Pike and Watkin unceremoniously rolled old Tosspot into the shallow hole and, whilst Athelstan muttered some prayers, hastily covered it with icy lumps of clay. Athelstan then blessed the grave and with Watkin darkly hoping the body would stay there, they all trooped back into the church. Athelstan chose to ignore the dung-collector's dire speculation. The grave robbers, whoever they were, seemed to have disappeared. Perhaps moved on to vex some other unfortunate priest. He swept up the nave under the chancel screen and into the small, icy sacristy. Athelstan jumped as a large figure loomed out of the shadows.

'Sir John!' he snapped. 'Must you lurk like some thief in the night?'

Cranston grinned slyly. 'I must have words with you, Brother, and not here.'

Athelstan looked at him carefully. 'You've been drinking, Sir John?'

Cranston smirked. 'Yes and no. Quick! I'll wait whilst you divest.'

Athelstan hid his irritation. He doffed his chasuble, stole and cope, hastily hung them in the cupboard, gave a wide-eyed Crim a penny for his help then bustled Sir John back into the church. He beckoned to Benedicta who was standing near the baptismal font.

'Lock the sacristy, please,' he whispered to her. 'And then clear the church.' Athelstan looked around. 'Watkin!' he shouted. The dung-collector ambled slowly over, one eye on Sir John. 'Watkin,' Athelstan confided, 'I will be gone for some time. You are to ensure the candles are doused and the church is kept safe and, if you are so concerned about the cemetery, keep a watch there yourself.'

The sexton looked hurt and Athelstan could have bitten out his tongue. He had not intended to be so sharp, but Cranston's secretive arrival had unnerved him. The friar led the coroner out of the church. Cranston saw Bonaventure fairly skipping along to greet him but he had no desire to have that bloody cat rubbing up against his leg, so hustled Athelstan out to collect their horses.

'Follow me, my Mephistopheles,' he murmured. 'To a place of warmth and security.'

They crossed the beaten track, dodging between the heavy-wheeled carts, and led their horses down to London Bridge and into the welcoming warmth of the Piebald Horse tavern. Cranston loved this place, a veritable den of iniquity but one which sold good ales, fine wine and delicious food. Of course, the coroner personally knew Joscelyn, the tapster.

'A real sinner,' he had once described him as, 'who will get into heaven because he has stolen the gates.'

Athelstan agreed; the landlord of the Piebald Horse was a one-armed, reformed sea pirate who had confidentially explained to the friar how he would love to go to church but the smell of incense always made him feel ill. Athelstan smiled to himself. He found it strange that he had just buried Tosspot who used to clean the platters and tankards in this very tavern. The friar gazed round. The place looked cleaner; fresh plaster on the wall, the beams newly painted, whilst the rushes underfoot were fresh and sweet-smelling. Joscelyn waddled towards them. The old rogue's vein-streaked face was wreathed in smiles, his good hand scratching his chin as he relished the prospect of a fine profit. Sir John was a prodigious drinker and was well loved by the city's taverners.

'My Lord Coroner,' Joscelyn gave a mock bow, 'you are most welcome to my humble abode.'

'By the sod, you old bastard!' Cranston roared. 'Have you gone back to your old, wicked ways? Where did you get the sustenance to clean this sewer of iniquity?'

Joscelyn shrugged and spread his one good hand, fingers splayed out. 'I have a new partner,' he announced proudly, 'who sold his own tavern near the Barbican and moved across the river to be free from the prying of certain coroners!'

Cranston roared with laughter and led Athelstan over to the far corner where a table and stools were set apart from the rest of the customers. Athelstan felt rather embarrassed. Near the wine tuns, he noticed Pike the ditcher, the clay of the cemetery still fresh on his hands, deep in hushed conversation with a group of strangers. The Great Community, Athelstan thought, peasants from the snow-covered fields outside the city, slipping in to talk sedition, plan treason and plot rebellion. Pike noticed him and, eyes guarded, raised his tankard. Athelstan smiled back but watched as, a few minutes later, Pike rose and led the rest of his companions out of the tavern.

Cranston squatted down with his back to the wall, smacked his lips and gazed hungrily up at the hams and other meats hanging from ropes on the rafters to be cured. He watched a pot boy broach a new cask and through an open door glimpsed the kitchen with its huge oven where Joscelyn baked his own bread. A dusty-faced boy was now raking the coal and wood from this into a tidy, white pile of ash. The bread would then be slipped in, the oven door sealed, and when the oven cooled, the bread would be baked. A curious place, Sir John reflected, at the heart of Southwark's squalor, yet the ales and wine were always fresh and the food delicious. He glimpsed a table at the far end of the tavern with a huge silver nef, or spice ship. Cranston scratched his head. So much new wealth. He idly wondered if Joscelyn had returned to his old ways and was engaged in some petty smuggling.

Athelstan studied Cranston out of the corner of his eye. Sir John's temper had improved but Athelstan dreaded spending a day watching him guzzle one goblet of wine after another. The landlord waddled over.

'My Lord Coroner, you are ready to order?'

Cranston gazed speculatively at the ceiling.

'No fish!' he barked. 'Some pheasant or quail, cooked to a golden brown and stuffed with spices. I want the sauce thick. And some fresh bread!'

'And the Reverend Father?' Joscelyn asked sardonically.

'The Reverend Father,' Athelstan replied smoothly, 'would like a bowl of thick leek soup, some bread, and a cup of wine with more water than claret.'

They waited until Joscelyn had walked away, roaring their order into the kitchen.

'Well, My Lord Coroner?' Athelstan asked. 'What has happened?'

Cranston outlined in sharp, succinct phrases the grisly events which had taken place earlier in the day. 'I have also been to the Guildhall,' he mournfully concluded. 'The mayor told me in no uncertain terms how displeased His Grace the Regent Duke of Lancaster is at our lack of progress. Adam Horne was apparently a member of his retinue.'

'And what was your reply?'

'I told him that I didn't give a rat's arse, and that I was doing the best I could.'

'I suppose,' the friar answered, 'the mayor accepted your eloquent reply?'

Cranston slouched back against the wall. 'Oh, we had a quarrel, but I have more sense than to seek a confrontation. I explained we had searched for Horne but could not find him.' He glanced across at Athelstan, his face full of self-pity. 'I must resolve the matter with the Lady Maude,' he whispered. 'It's clouding my mind.'

Athelstan waited until the slattern had served them with goblets of wine.

'Look, Sir John, let us take these events from the beginning.' Athelstan raised a hand. 'No, it is necessary. And, if you'll accept my apologies, we must for the time being put the matter of Lady Maude to one side.'

Cranston nodded glumly.

'Sir Ralph Whitton,' Athelstan began, 'received a warning that he was going to die because of a terrible act of betrayal committed in Outremer some years ago. I know,' Athelstan quietly continued, 'Sir Ralph was guilty of such an act. That's why in the back of his Book of Hours, he scribbled those prayers to Julian the Hospitaller.'

'Who was he?'

'A knight who committed terrible murders and spent his life in making reparation. Anyway,' Athelstan continued, 'Sir Ralph moves from his own chamber to the so-called security of the North Bastion tower. He is frightened and even refuses to take his Moorish servant, Rastani, with him. He drinks heavily the night before his death and retires to his bed chamber. What happened then?' Athelstan asked, trying to draw Cranston from his own dark thoughts.

The coroner slurped noisily from his cup. 'Well, my dear friar, according to all the evidence we have, Sir Ralph went to bed, and locked the door behind him, keeping the key with him. The door leading to the gallery on which his chamber stands was locked by the guards, whilst the other end of the passage is blocked by fallen masonry. The guards are on duty all night just inside the entrance to the North Bastion. They are both trusted men and the key to both the gallery door and another for Sir Ralph's chamber hang on a hook beside them. We have established, on good authority, that neither sentry left his post nor did they see or hear anything untoward.'

'And now the murder?' Athelstan prompted.

'Young Geoffrey,' Cranston continued, 'whom Sir Ralph apparently doted upon, comes across early the next morning. The guards search him for weapons and open the door to the gallery. The same door is then locked, apparently on Sir Ralph's orders, and Geoffrey goes to rouse him. The guards hear him knocking and shouting but then our young hero comes back. He announces his inability to arouse Sir Ralph, is about to return and unlock Whitton's chamber himself, then changes his mind and goes for Colebrooke the lieutenant. They both return to Sir Ralph's chamber and open it. The room is undisturbed, but Whitton is lying on his bed, his throat slashed, the corpse icy cold, and the shuttered windows wide open. That, my dear friar, is where our problem begins.'

'Not if we accept our conclusion,' Athelstan replied. 'That someone crossed the frozen moat and, using the steps in the wall, climbed up to Sir Ralph's chamber. The assassin prised open the lever on the shutters, entered and committed the crime. Nevertheless,' he persisted, 'our conclusion has its own problems. Why did Sir Ralph just lie there and allow his throat to be cut? He was a soldier, a warrior.' The friar shook his head. 'All we do know,' he concluded, 'is that the assassin must have been a member of the community at the Tower who knew Sir Ralph had changed his bed chamber, and he or she either committed the murder or hired a professional assassin to do it for them.' Athelstan stared across at a group of dicers who sat playing noisily on the other side of the tavern.

'And Sir Gerard Mowbray's murder,' Cranston observed, 'is no clearer. Who rang the bell? How did Mowbray fall? Of course Horne's murder,' he continued, 'was relatively easy. The assassin played upon his guilt and fear and probably lured the hapless man to his grisly death in that lonely place.'

'Where did he die?' Athelstan queried.

'In the old ruins to the north of the Tower. And, before you ask, his murderer left no trace.'

'And the suspects?' Athelstan asked wearily. He leaned across and tapped Sir John on the arm. 'Come on, My Lord Coroner, apply that sharp brain of yours!'

Cranston shrugged.

'Well, it could be Sir Fulke. His buckle was found on the ice and he stands to gain from his brother's death. Sir Ralph's servant Rastani was lithe and able enough to climb up that wall.' Cranston made a face at Athelstan. 'By the way, I checked on their story for the night Sir Ralph died; both Sir Fulke and Rastani were absent from the Tower and there are people who can guarantee their whereabouts.'

'Master Geoffrey could be the felon,' Athelstan remarked. 'But on the night Sir Ralph died he was in Philippa's bed, and on the night Sir Gerard died, in his lady's chamber. True, he went to rouse Sir Ralph, but he was searched for any weapons, he had no key, and even if he had entered the room, favoured son or not, Sir Ralph would scarcely have offered his throat to be cut.' Athelstan rubbed his face. 'The possibilities are endless,' he said. 'Hammond, the felonious chaplain. Colebrooke, the envious Lieutenant. The gracious Mistress Philippa. Not to mention our hospitaller who may have told us a pack of lies.' The friar narrowed his eyes. 'We must check on them all,' he murmured.

'Or Red Hand,' Cranston observed. 'The mad man who may not be as insane as he appears.'

Athelstan looked up and smiled. 'But we have made some progress, Sir John. If Fitzormonde is to be believed, we know the reason for the murders: Burghgesh's death on that unfortunate ship in the Middle Sea so many years ago. The picture on the parchment is to remind his murderers of their foul act and the sesame seed cake a warning of their impending doom.'

'And that—' Cranston almost shouted, glaring across at the landlord to bring his food, for his stomach was growling with hunger '—leads us to another mystery. Did Burghgesh really die? Or is he back, hiding in London, even the Tower? Or is there someone else? Perhaps his son or some other friend?'

Cranston leaned back as Joscelyn brought across the steaming platters of food. The landlord served Sir John himself, cutting thick slices of pheasant breast and laying them deftly with his one hand on the pewter platter whilst a maid scurried up with a jug of steaming gravy in which the bird had been cooked. Sir John grinned his thanks, took his own pewter spoon from his wallet, drew his dagger and set to as if he hadn't eaten for days. Athelstan watched in astonishment: Sir John's permanent hunger always fascinated him. A slattern brought his own meal, a thickly spiced bowl of soup. Athelstan asked to borrow a pewter spoon and ate slowly.

'They've forgotten the bread,' Sir John grumbled.

Athelstan called the girl back and small, fresh white loaves, wrapped in a linen cloth, were immediately served. Whilst he ate, Athelstan reflected on what they had discussed. He waited a while until Sir John had taken the edge off his appetite.

'There is one matter we have overlooked.'

'What's that?' Cranston mumbled, his mouth full of food.

'Horne's murderer means the assassin knows us or why should he send such a grisly trophy to your house?'

'Because the bastard's mad!'

'No, no, Sir John. It's meant as a warning. This murderer sees himself as doing God's work. He is sending a message: keep well away until my work is done. Don't interfere.' Athelstan lowered his spoon. 'Such a terrible thing,' he whispered. 'A man's genitals hacked off and stuffed into the mouth of his decapitated head. Of course,' he continued, 'Fitzormonde mentioned that.'

'What?'

'Well, how the Caliph of Egypt would punish in such a way anybody who transgressed his command. The head and genitals hacked off and both exposed above the city gates in Alexandria. It's obvious, Sir John,' he continued, 'our murderer must be someone who has lived in Outremer, someone who knows about the Hashishoni – the flat sesame seed cake, and that awful way of humiliating the corpse of an executed criminal.'

Cranston lowered his knife. 'But who is the murderer, Brother?'

'I don't know, Sir John, but I think we should re-visit the Tower and speak to our group of suspects.'

'And then?'

'We go to Woodforde.'

Cranston groaned.

'Sir John,' Athelstan persisted, 'it's not far – a few miles through Aldgate and down the Mile End Road. We must find out if Burghgesh ever returned and what happened to his son. Moreover,' he continued, 'perhaps it may give you some time to reflect on the Lady Maude.'

Cranston jabbed the point of his knife into a piece of soft meat, mumbled his assent and continued to eat as if his very life depended upon it.

Chapter 10

Athelstan and Cranston finished their meal and crossed London Bridge. Beneath them the water moved black and sluggish and they heard chunks of ice crashing against the starlings which protected the wooden arches from the fury of the Thames. They passed through Billingsgate. The air stank with the odour from the stalls, now freshly stocked with herring, cod, tench and even pike as the fishing fleets took advantage of a break in the weather.

The Tower was all abustle when they arrived. Like any good soldier, Colebrooke had the garrison working to break the tedium caused by the freezing weather, as well as to take his own mind off the recent murders. The lieutenant was standing on Tower Green, shouting orders at workmen who were refurbishing mangonels, scorpions and the great battering rams. A number of archers stood ankle-deep in the slush, practising at the butts, whilst others were being mercilessly drilled by the serjeants. Athelstan vaguely remembered rumours about how, in the spring, the French might attack the Channel ports and even force their way up the Thames to plunder and burn the city.

Colebrooke's displeasure at seeing Cranston and Athelstan was more than apparent.

'You have found the murderers?' he yelled.

'No, Master Lieutenant!' Cranston bellowed back. 'But we will. And, when we do, you can build the gallows.'

Cranston stepped aside as a butcher and two fletchers rolled barrels of salted pork down to the store house. The coroner wrinkled his nose. Despite the heavy spices and thick white salt, the pork smelt rancid and his gorge rose as he saw insects crawling out from under the rim of the barrel. He quietly vowed not to accept any food from the Tower buttery or kitchens. Colebrooke, seeing his visitors would not be deterred, turned away to issue further orders. Athelstan took advantage of the delay to walk over to where the bear, squatting in its own filth, was busy plundering a mound of refuse piled high before him. The madman, Red Hand, sat like an elf fascinated by the great beast.

'You are content, Red Hand?' Athelstan asked softly.

The man grimaced, waving his hands in the air as if mimicking the bear. Athelstan crouched down beside him.

'You like the bear, Red Hand?'

The fellow nodded, his eyes intent on the bear.

'So does the knight,' Red Hand slurred and Athelstan caught the stench of wine fumes on his breath.

'Which knight?'

'The one with the cross.'

'You mean Fitzormonde?'

'Yes, yes, Fitzormonde. He often comes to stare. Red Hand likes Fitzormonde. Red Hand likes the bear. Red Hand does not like Colebrooke. Colebrooke would kill Red Hand.'

'Did you like Burghgesh?' Athelstan asked quickly. He caught the gleam of recognition in the madman's eyes.

'You knew him,' Athelstan continued. 'As a young soldier, he once served here.'

Red Hand looked away.

'Surely you remember?' Athelstan persisted.

The madman shook his head and stared at the bear, but Athelstan saw him blink away the tears which pricked his madcap eyes. The friar sighed and rose, dusting the wet ice from his robe.

'Brother Athelstan!' Cranston barked. 'Master Colebrooke is a busy man. He says he cannot waste the day whilst you converse with a madman.'

'Master Colebrooke should realise,' Athelstan replied, 'that it is a matter of opinion, as well as the judgment of God, who is sane and who is mad.'

'Father, I mean no offence,' Colebrooke answered, taking off his conical helmet and cradling it in his arms. 'But I have a garrison to command. I will do what you want.'

Athelstan smiled. 'Good! Mowbray's body, where does it lie?'

Colebrooke pointed to the Chapel of St Peter ad Vincula. 'Before the chancel screen. Tomorrow it will be buried in the cemetery of All Hallows church.'

'Is it coffined?'

'No, no.'

'Good, I wish to see the corpse, and after that My Lord Coroner and I would like to speak with all those affected by Sir Ralph's death.'

Colebrooke groaned.

'We are here on the Regent's authority,' Athelstan interrupted. 'When these matters are finished, Master Lieutenant, we shall report on the support, or lack of it, we have had in our investigation. We will meet the group in St John's Chapel.'

Colebrooke forced a smile and hurried off, shouting at his soldiers to search out Sir Fulke and others. Cranston and Athelstan walked over to St Peter's. The church was a dour, sombre place, cold and dank. The nave was shaped like a box, with rounded pillars guarding darkened aisles.

At the top a small rose window afforded some light. The chancel screen was of polished oak and before it, surrounded by a ring of candles, lay the corpses of Sir Ralph Whitton and Sir Gerard Mowbray. The embalmers had done what they could but, even as they walked up the nave, both Cranston and Athelstan caught the whiff of putrefaction. The two bodies lay under canvas sheets on wickerwork mats supported by wooden trestles. Cranston stood away, waving Athelstan on.

'I've eaten too richly, Brother,' he murmured. 'Look for what you want and let's get out.'

Athelstan was only too happy to oblige. He ignored Sir Ralph's corpse but lifted back the insignia over the hospitaller's and the canvas sheet which lay underneath. He did not wish to look at Mowbray's face. Athelstan had seen enough of death. Instead he examined the white, scabrous legs of the hospitaller, picking up one of the candles to study the purple-yellow bruise just above the shin on the corpse's right leg. Satisfied, he pulled back the canvas sheet, replaced the tallow candle, genuflected towards the sanctuary and left the church, Cranston following as quickly as possible. They stood on the porch steps and eagerly drank in the invigorating cold air.

'Good Lord, Sir John,' Athelstan murmured, 'I always thought St Erconwald's was bad but, if ever I moan about it again, remind me of this church and I'll keep my mouth shut.'

Cranston grinned. 'It will be my pleasure, Brother. You found what you are looking for?'

'Yes, I did, Sir John. I believe Sir Gerard was not pushed from the parapet. Someone laid a spear or a piece of wood at the top of the steps whilst the hospitaller was at his usual place at the far end of the parapet walk, near Salt Tower.' Athelstan pursed his lips. 'Yes, it could be done under cover of darkness whilst Sir Gerard was lost in his own thoughts.' He narrowed his eyes and stared at the distant wall of the Tower. 'The tocsin sounded. Mowbray hurried along the parapet. In the dark he would not see the obstacle. His leg struck it, he slipped and fell to his death.'

'But we don't know who rang the bell or placed the pole on the parapet. Remember,' Cranston continued, 'apart from Fitzormonde and Colebrooke, everybody was in Mistress Philippa's chamber.'

'Colebrooke might have done it,' the friar replied. 'He might have seen the knight standing on the parapet, crept up, placed the pole there, and somehow or other arranged for the tocsin to be sounded.'

'But we have no proof?'

'No, Sir John, we do not. But we are collecting it. In bits and pieces.' He sighed. Only time will tell if we are successful.

They found Colebrooke and the rest of the group sitting on benches in the Chapel of St John. Their displeasure at being summoned was more than apparent. Hammond kept his back half-turned. Fulke slouched, staring up at the ceiling; Rastani seemed more confident and Athelstan caught the sardonic mocking look in his dark, brilliant eyes. Colebrooke marched up and down as if he was on parade whilst Mistress Philippa leaned against the wall, looking sorrowfully down at Tower Green.

'Where is Geoffrey?' Athelstan asked.

'Geoffrey Parchmeiner,' Fulke replied, 'being a rather frightened, silly young man, may have many vices.' The knight ignored his niece's furious look. 'But he works hard. He has better things to do than hang around the Tower answering idle questions whilst good men are killed and the murderer walks scot-free.'

'Thank you for that speech, Sir Fulke,' Cranston replied, beaming falsely around. 'We have only one question and I apologise to you, Sir Brian, but it's a name, that's all. Bartholomew Burghgesh – does it mean anything to any of you?'

Athelstan was amazed at the transformation caused by Cranston's words. The coroner's smile widened.

'Good,' he announced. 'Now we have your attention.' He glanced quickly at the hospitaller's angry face. 'Sir Brian, you must not answer, and if you are patient, you will see why we ask. Well,' the coroner clapped his hands, 'Bartholomew Burghgesh?'

'Hell's teeth!' Sir Fulke snarled and walked into the centre of the room. 'Don't play games, Sir John. Burghgesh was one name my brother, Sir Ralph, would never have mentioned in his presence.'

'Why?' Athelstan asked innocently.

'My brother could not stand the man.'

'But they were comrades-in-arms.'

'Were,' Fulke emphasised. 'They quarrelled in Outremer. Bartholomew was later killed on a ship taken in the Middle Sea by Moorish pirates.'

'Why?' Cranston barked.

'Why what?'

'Why did your brother dislike Burghgesh so much?'

Fulke stepped closer and lowered his eyes. 'It was a matter of honour,' he murmured. He licked his lips and glanced nervously towards Philippa. 'Sir Ralph once accused Bartholomew of paying too much attention to your mother, Sir Ralph's wife.'

'Were the allegations true?' Athelstan asked.

Fulke's face softened. 'No,' he stammered. 'I'll be honest – I liked Bartholomew. He was funny, always thought the best of people. He was both gentle and courteous.'

Athelstan suddenly glimpsed the steel in Sir Fulke's character.

'You really did like him, didn't you?'

'Yes, yes, I did. I was much distressed at the news of his death.' Fulke shuffled his feet and looked down at the floor. 'I'll be honest,' he continued. 'When I was younger, I used to wish Bartholomew was my brother because, God forgive me, I did not like Ralph.' He looked up, his eyes sad. 'Years ago, he and Bartholomew served as officers here in the Tower.' Fulke coughed and cleared his throat. 'My brother was treacherous. He was cruel. He ill-treated Red Hand. He even beat the priest here when he was only a young clerk.'

The chaplain blushed with embarrassment.

'Come on, tell the truth!' Fulke now glared round, snarling like a dog. 'Sir Ralph was hated!'

Mistress Philippa stepped forward, her face white with fury. 'My father is sheeted, waiting for burial, and you speak ill of him!'

'God forgive me, Philippa, I only tell the truth!' Fulke flung out his hand. 'Ask Rastani! When he was a boy, who plucked his tongue out?'

The Moor just stared back. His eyes never flickered.

'It's true!' Fitzormonde intervened. 'It was over the Moor that the bad blood first surfaced between Burghgesh and Whitton.'

Fulke slumped back on the bench. 'I've said enough,' he snarled. 'But I'm tired of these questions. Mistress Philippa, your father was a bastard and no one here will gainsay me.'

Cranston and Athelstan just stood amazed at this sudden outburst of hatred and animosity. Good Lord, Athelstan thought, anyone here could be Sir Ralph's murderer. Burghgesh had been well loved. Did someone in this room believe he was God's executioner to avenge a good man's death? Athelstan looked around.

'Master Parchmeiner will not be here today?' he asked, taking advantage of the sudden lull.

'No,' Sir Fulke replied wearily. 'For pity's sake, Father, who would want to stay here? So many memories, so much hatred.'

Mistress Philippa sat huddled on one of the benches, her face in her hands. Sir Fulke went over to her and patted her gently on the shoulder. Cranston caught a smirk on Rastani's face. Was he the murderer? the coroner wondered. He recalled Athelstan's words, how the slayer of Adam Horne used a method practised in Moorish countries to desecrate the body of a criminal and traitor.

'We have seen enough,' Athelstan whispered. 'We should go.'

'Just one more thing,' Cranston announced. 'You knew Adam Horne the merchant?'

'Another bastard!' Sir Fulke hissed. 'Yes, yes, Sir John. Horne was my brother's friend.'

'Well, he's dead.' Cranston proclaimed flatly. 'Found murdered last night in the ruins just north of here.'

Fitzormonde swore quietly. The others looked up in alarm.

'I wonder where you all were?' Cranston asked.

'Hell's teeth, Sir John!' Colebrooke snapped. 'Now the thaw's come, anyone could slip in and out of a postern gate.'

Cranston smiled wanly. The lieutenant was right: it would be nigh impossible to make everyone account for their movements. Horne could have been murdered any time between dusk and dawn.

'Come, Sir John,' Athelstan murmured.

They took their leave unceremoniously, Cranston waving Colebrooke aside. They hardly spoke a word until they had collected their horses and left the Tower, going up towards Eastcheap.

'Oh, Lord save us!' Cranston suddenly broke the silence. 'What hatred exists in the human heart, eh, Brother?'

'Aye,' Athelstan replied, gently guiding Philomel away from the snow-covered sewer which ran down the middle of the street. 'Perhaps we should all remember that, Sir John. Minor jealousies and misunderstandings can fan the petty flames of bickering into the roaring fires of hatred.'

Cranston glanced at Athelstan out of the corner of his eye and smiled at the barbed reminder of what was true of Fulke and others in the Tower was also true of his relationship with the Lady Maude.

'Where to now, Brother?' he asked.

'To Master Parchmeiner's shop opposite Chancellor's Inn near St Paul's.'

'Why?' Cranston asked.

'Because, my dear Cranston, he was not present with the rest in the Tower and we must interrogate everyone.'

They rode up Candlewick Street and into Trinity, a prosperous part of the city Athelstan rarely frequented. The houses were spacious and grand; their lower storeys were built of solid timber, the projecting gables above were a framework of black beams and white plaster. The roofs were tiled, unlike the houses of many of Athelstan's parishioners who had to be content with reeds and straw. Many of the windows had pure glass and were protected by wood and iron. Servants from these houses regularly flushed out the sewers with the water they used to wash clothes so the streets did not reek as they did in Southwark. Before several of the imposing entrances stood armed retainers wearing the gaudy escutcheons of their patrons: bears, swans, wyverns, dragons, lions, and even stranger beasts. Stocky, well-fed merchants walked arm-in-arm with their plump wives, clad in garments of silk and satin, decorated with miniature pearls of exquisite delicacy. Two canons swaggered by from the cathedral, clad in thick woollen robes lined with miniver. A group of lawyers in gowns of red, violet and scarlet, trimmed with lambswool, sauntered arrogantly by, their cloaks pulled back to display decorated, low-slung girdles.

Pigs wandered here with bells slung round their necks to show they were the property of the Hospital of St Anthony and couldn't be slaughtered. Beadles armed with steel-pointed staffs dispersed fowl or curbed the yapping of fierce yellow-haired dogs, whilst bailiffs tried to move on a strange creature dressed like a magpie in black and white rags. The fellow loudly claimed he had in his battered, leather coffer some of the most marvellous relics of Christendom: 'One of Charlemagne's teeth!' he yelled. 'Two legs of the donkey that carried Mary! The skull of

Herod's servant and some of the stones Christ turned into bread!'

Athelstan stopped and restrained the beadles who were harassing the poor fellow.

'You say you have one of the stones Christ turned into a loaf of bread?' the friar queried, trying hard to hide his laughter.

'Yes, Brother.' The relic-seller's eyes brightened at the prospect of profit.

'But Christ didn't change stones into bread. The devil asked him to, but Christ refused.'

Cranston, also grinning, drew close to watch the charlatan's reaction. The relic-seller licked dry lips.

'Of course he did, Brother,' he replied in a half-whisper. 'I have it on good authority that when Satan left, Christ did it but then changed them back to show he would not be tempted to eat. It will only cost you a penny.'

Athelstan dipped into his purse and drew out a coin.

'Here.' He pressed it into the fellow's grimy paw. 'This is not for your stone. Keep it. It's your ingenuity I am rewarding.'

The man gaped, open-mouthed, and Athelstan and Cranston walked on, quietly laughing at the relic-seller's quick response. They passed the Littlegate of St Paul's where a lay brother was feeding a group of lepers with mouldy bread and rancid pork slices, as laid down by the city fathers who judged such food actually helped them. Cranston glared across in disgust.

'Do you really think it does?' he asked Athelstan abruptly.

'What, Sir John?'

'Such food, does it really help lepers?'

Athelstan gazed at the grey cowled figures with their staffs and bowls for alms. 'I don't know,' he murmured. 'Perhaps.'

The lepers made him think about the two who lurked in the cemetery of St Erconwald. A memory stirred but he could not place it, so pushed the matter to one side. They turned into an alleyway off Friday Street and Cranston began to bellow at passersby for the whereabouts of Parchmeiner's shop. They found it on the corner of Bread Street, a narrow, two-storeyed tenement with a shop below and living quarters above. There was a stall in front, but because of the inclement weather, this was now bare so they opened the door and went inside. Athelstan immediately closed his eyes and sniffed the sweet odour of fresh scrubbed parchment and vellum. The smell reminded him vividly of the well-stocked library and quiet chancery of his novice days at Blackfriars. The shop itself was a small, white-washed room with shelves along the walls stacked with sheets of parchment, ink horns, pumice stones, quills, and everything else one would need in a library or chancery.

Geoffrey himself was sitting at a small desk. He smiled and rose to greet them.

'Sir John!' he cried. 'Brother Athelstan, you are most welcome!' He went into the darkness beyond to bring back two stools. 'Please sit. Do you want some wine?'

Surprisingly, Cranston shook his head.

'I only drink when Sir John does,' Athelstan mockingly replied.

The parchment-seller grinned and sat down behind his desk.

'Well, what can I do for you? I doubt you want to buy parchment or vellum – though, Brother, I have the best the city can offer. I am a Guild member and everything I sell carries their hallmark.' Geoffrey's good-natured face creased into a smile. He shook his head. 'But I don't think you come to buy.' His face became grave. 'It's the business at the Tower, isn't it?'

'Just one thing,' Cranston answered, moving uncomfortably on the small stool. 'Does the name Bartholomew Burghgesh mean anything to you?'

'Yes and no,' Geoffrey replied. 'I never met him, but I heard Sir Fulke talk of him, and once Philippa repeated the name in her father's presence. Sir Ralph became very angry and stormed out. Of course, I asked Philippa why. She just shook her head and said he was an old enemy of her father's, and refused to be drawn any further.'

Athelstan watched the young man intently. Could this languid, rather effete fop be the Red Slayer? The terrible murderer who stalked his victims in the Tower?

'Geoffrey?' he asked.

'Yes, Brother.'

'You have known Philippa how long?'

'About two years.'

'And Sir Ralph liked you?'

The parchment-seller grinned. 'Yes, though God knows why. I can hardly ride a horse and the call of arms does not appeal to me.'

'You were with him the night he died?'

'Yes, as I have said, I was with him in the great hall. Sir Ralph was morose and became maudlin in his cups.'

'He was drunk?'

'Very.'

'You helped him across to his chamber?'

'Well, again, yes and no. Master Colebrooke assisted me. I took Sir Ralph to the top of the stairs into the

North Bastion tower but the passageway was so narrow Colebrooke helped him the rest of the way.'

'And you stayed with Mistress Philippa that night?'

The young man looked embarrassed and his eyes dropped. 'Yes. If Sir Ralph had known, he would have been most angry.'

'But,' Athelstan intervened, 'he favoured your court-ship of his only daughter?'

'Yes, I think he did.'

'Why?' Cranston barked. 'I mean, as you have said, you're no soldier.'

'No, I am not. I am not a lord or a knight but a merchant, Sir John, and a very good one. I am one of those who lends money so the King can hire his knights.' The parchment-seller gestured round his well-stocked shop. 'It may not look much but my profits are high. I am a wealthy man, Sir John.'

'One other matter.' Athelstan smiled. 'We have touched upon it before. You went to rouse Sir Ralph. What happened?'

'The guards opened the passageway door and locked it behind me as Sir Ralph had ordered. I went down and tried to rouse the constable. There was no answer, so I went back. I told the guards and took the key to Whitton's chamber. I was going to open it myself but changed my mind and went for Colebrooke.'

'Why did you do that?'

Geoffrey pulled a face. 'I knew something was wrong by the silence, not to mention the cold draught under the door of Whitton's chamber.'

Athelstan remembered the gap under Sir Ralph's door and nodded. Someone standing outside the room would have felt the powerful draught and know something was wrong.

'Why didn't you open the door yourself?' Cranston asked.

The young man smiled weakly. 'Sir John, I was frightened. Sir Ralph was not a popular man. Looking back, I suppose I was worried someone might be in the chamber.'

'And the night Mowbray died?'

'I was with Mistress Philippa, drunk as a lord. Ask the others.'

'And you never left?'

Geoffrey grimaced. 'Like the rest, I went to use the privy along the corridor. When the tocsin sounded, I lurched out with the others to see what was wrong. I didn't do much. I was drunk and I hate those parapet steps. I wandered around, looking busy, and found Fitzormonde and Colebrooke standing over Mowbray's body.' The young man paused and looked sharply at Athelstan. 'I know why you are here. There's been another death in the Tower, hasn't there?'

'Yes, yes,' Athelstan murmured and gave Parchmeiner the details of Horne's death.

Geoffrey leaned back in his chair and whistled softly. 'I suppose,' he said wearily, 'you wish to question me about that?'

'It would,' Cranston observed, 'be helpful to know where you were last night.'

Parchmeiner shrugged. 'I worked in my shop, then I got drunk as a bishop in a nearby tavern, the Golden Griffin. You could ask there.'

Athelstan smiled. What would be the use? the friar thought. Horne could have been killed at any hour.

He studied Parchmeiner's girlish face. 'You are London-born?' he queried, trying to look at the parchment lying on Geoffrey's desk.

'No, Brother, I am not. My family are Welsh, hence my colouring. They moved to Bristol. My father traded in parchments and vellum in a shop just beneath the cathedral there. When he died I moved to London.' Geoffrey picked up the piece of parchment. 'My sister, now married, still lives there; she has just written inviting herself to town for the Yuletide season. She, her husband,' his face grew mock solemn, 'and their large brood of children will bring some life to the Tower.' He turned to Sir John. 'My Lord Coroner, you have more questions?'

Sir John shook his head. 'No, sir, we have not.'

They rose, made their farewells, and stepped out into the cold, icy street.

'What do you think, Brother?'

'A young man who will go far in his trade, Sir John. He has his roots.' The friar grinned. 'Yes, Sir John, like you I wondered if he could be Burghgesh's son. But I am sure he is not.' Athelstan stopped and stared hard at the coroner. 'We are looking for a killer without ties, Sir John. Someone who is pretending to be something he or she is not. Someone who knows about the great act of betrayal so many years ago. The question is, who?'

'Well!' Cranston clapped his hands together. 'We'll not find it here, Brother, but perhaps in Woodforde...' The coroner wiped his nose on the back of his hand and stared up at the sky. 'I don't want to stay in London,' he murmured. 'The Lady Maude needs a rest from me. And you, Brother?'

'My parish,' Athelstan drily replied, 'will, I think, survive the continued absence of their pastor a little longer.'

They separated at the corner of Friday and Fish Streets, agreeing to meet within two hours at a tavern outside Aldgate on the Mile End Road. Sir John stamped off, leading his horse, whilst Athelstan continued down Trinity into Walbrook, along Ropery to London Bridge. Thankfully, he found St Erconwald's fairly deserted except for Watkin, to whom he gave strict instructions about the custody of the church, and Ranulf the rat-catcher who had come to remind him of his promise that if a Guild of Rat-Catchers were founded, St Erconwald's could be their chantry church.

'I promise you, Ranulf, I will think on the matter,' Athelstan replied, trying to hide his amusement at the thought of St Erconwald's full of tarry-hooded rat-catchers, all looking like Ranulf. The fellow's yellow, wizened face broke into a sharp-toothed smile. He skipped down the steps as happily as any boy.

'Brother,' Watkin mournfully moaned.

'What is it?'

'Well—' The dung-collector turned on the top step of the church and pointed towards the frozen cemetery. 'We still haven't set a watch.'

'Why should we, Watkin? The grave robbers have moved on.'

The dung-collector shook his head. 'I don't think so, Brother, and I am afeared worse might happen.'

Athelstan forced a smile. 'Nonsense. Now look, Watkin, I will be back late tomorrow evening. Take a message to Father Luke at St Olave's. Ask him to be so kind as to come here and say Mass tomorrow morning. You will know where everything is? And tell the widow Benedicta to help you. You'll do that?'

Watkin nodded and stumped off, muttering under his breath about priests who didn't listen to tales of the dark shapes which did dreadful things in city churchyards. Athelstan watched him go and sighed. How could he deal with the cemetery when there was no evidence of any danger threatening? He checked the door of the church was locked and stood engrossed in his own thoughts about Cranston. The Lord Coroner was proving to be as difficult a problem as the dreadful deaths they were investigating. What was wrong with the Lady Maude? Athelstan wondered. Why didn't Cranston ask her outright?

Athelstan smiled as he went across to his own house. Strange, he concluded. Cranston, who was frightened of nothing on two legs, seemed terrified of his little lady wife. Athelstan checked that the windows and doors of the priest's house were locked, slung his saddle bags over a protesting Philomel, and both horse and rider wearily made their way along the icy track. He stopped at an ale-house to leave further messages with Tab the tinker for Benedicta and Watkin; they were to lock the church after morning Mass and, if the widow felt so inclined, she should take Bonaventura back to her own house. The friar then made his way back on to the main highway, past the Priory of St Mary Overy and across London Bridge. He stopped midway to say a prayer in the Chapel of St Thomas for the safety of their journey and then continued on his way.

Cranston was waiting for him at the small tavern just outside Aldgate in the Portsoken overlooking the stinking city ditch. The coroner seemed in good spirits. Athelstan concluded it was due to the large empty wine bowl in front of Sir John but Cranston, winking and burping, staunchly kept his hidden resolve not to vex Athelstan further with his own worries and anxieties. The friar joined Sir John in one last cup of mulled wine, heated with a red-hot poker and spiced with cinnamon, before they reclaimed their horses from the stable and made their way along the darkening highway towards Mile End. Cranston remained full of good cheer, aided and abetted by an apparently miraculous wineskin which never seemed to empty. Athelstan, tired and saddle sore, prayed and cursed whilst Cranston, farting and swaying in the saddle, chattered about this or that. Finally Athelstan reined in Philomel and grasped the coroner by the wrists.

'Sir John,' he asked wearily, 'this business at the Tower – we are making no headway. How long can we spend on the matter?'

'Until we finish.' Cranston's eyes gleamed back. 'By the sod, Brother! Orders are orders, and I don't give a rat's fart about mumbling monks, icy roads or cold journeys. Now, have I told you of the Lady Maude's preparations for Christmas?'

Athelstan groaned, shook his head and kicked Philomel forward as Cranston regaled him with Lady Maude's intended banquet of boar's head, cygnet, venison, quince tarts and junkets of apple-flavoured cream. The coroner chattered like a magpie as the weak daylight died and dusk fell like a grey powder, shrouding the wide waste stretches of snow. The distant forest became obscured by a misty darkness which closed in round them, broken by the odd pinprick of light as they passed some hamlet or village. No wind blew but it was deathly still and bitterly cold.

'I am sure,' Athelstan mumbled to himself, 'the very birds will freeze on the trees and even the hares on the hill will remain underground.'

Cranston, the wineskin now surprisingly empty, only replied with a short stream of belches. They passed a crossroads where a cadaver hung, black and frozen, its head twisted to one side, face unrecognisable after the crows had feasted there. Cranston stopped and pointed down a track to a light blinking in the distance.

'We'll stop there for the night, Brother. A good, snug tavern, The Gallow's Friend.' He leaned over and smiled at Athelstan. 'Despite its name, you'll like it.'

Athelstan did. It was a clean, well-swept establishment with secure stables, a fresh herb-smelling tap room, and a large roaring fire with the logs piled high – though he baulked at the huge four-poster bed he'd have to share with Sir John.

'No, no, My Lord Coroner,' Athelstan murmured. 'I insist you sleep alone.'

'Why, monk?'

'Because, coroner, if you rolled over in your sleep, you'd crush me to death!'

Laughing and joking, they left their bags there and made their way down to the tap room where the landlord's wife served them huge fish pies, the crust, golden and crisp, hiding a savoury sauce which dulled the flavour of the rancid fish. Athelstan tactfully asked the landlord for a pallet bed to be placed in their chamber and sat down to eat almost as heartily as Cranston. Of course, the coroner drank as if there was no tomorrow and when he had had his fill, leaned back against the pillar of the huge fireplace, belched, and pronounced himself satisfied. Athelstan stared into the flames, half listening to a wind which had suddenly sprung up, now whining and clattering against the tightly secured shutters.

'Brother?'

'Yes, Sir John?'

'This business at the Tower, could it be black magic?'

'What do you mean?'

'Well, the head that was sent to me.'

Athelstan stretched his hand out to the flames. 'No, no, Sir John. As I have said, we are not dealing with a demon but something worse, a soul steeped in mortal sin. But whose?' He looked up at Sir John, who had his fiery red nose deep in a wine cup again. 'What's puzzling,' Athelstan continued, 'is why now? Why has the murderer chosen this moment? And how can they know about the dreadful events surrounding Burghgesh's death?'

'What do you mean?' Cranston slurred.

'Well,' Athelstan replied, 'we should be looking for a man or woman with no background, someone who has suddenly appeared on the scene, but everyone we have talked to has their own little niche.'

Cranston burped. 'I don't know,' he slurred. 'It could still be black magic because I'm damned if I can find a way through the tangle. Now, as I have said to Lady Maude...' The coroner suddenly stopped and stared into his wine cup, and the good humour drained from his face.

'Come, Sir John,' Athelstan said quietly. 'It's time we slept.'

Surprisingly, Cranston agreed, drained the cup and slammed it down on the table. He stood up, swaying and smiled benevolently down at his companion.

'But do you believe, Brother?'

'What, Sir John?'

'In the black arts? I mean, the business in your cemetery?'

Athelstan grinned. 'To be perfectly honest, Sir John, I am more frightened of the human heart than any mischievous demon. Now, come. Let's rest.'

Athelstan was pleased he had judged the moment right because, by the time they reached the top of the rickety wooden staircase, Cranston was half-asleep and beginning to mumble piteously about how he missed Lady Maude. Athelstan led him down the cold, darkened passageway and into the small chamber. He gently lowered Cranston on to the bed, pulled off the coroner's boots and made his companion as comfortable as possible. The coroner turned, belched, and quietly began to snore. Athelstan grinned and covered the huge frame with a coverlet. Sleeping, Cranston reminded the friar more than ever of the huge bear in the bailey of the Tower. Athelstan went over and knelt beneath the small, horn-glazed window, crossed himself and gently mouthed the words of David's psalm.

'Out of the depths have I called to thee, O Lord. Lord, hear my voice.'

By the time he had reached the fourth verse, Athelstan was already distracted. Was Sir John right? he wondered. Did the great demon, the Red Slayer, haunt both his cemetery and the Tower of London? He closed his eyes, finished the psalm and made his way to the pallet bed. For a while Athelstan lay listening to Cranston's heavy snoring and fell asleep almost at the very instant when, back in the darkened cemetery outside St Erconwald's, shadows flitted across the graveyard to crouch over a freshly dug grave.

Chapter 11

In his dream, Athelstan stood on a darkened ship. The bowsprit, mast and sails were covered in black crepe. Above him on the poop, a skeleton, its face a white, leering mask, held the wheel and grinned wickedly down at him. The sea was smooth and clear as thick, dark glass. The sky overhead was empty of stars and hung like a purple-blue cloth around the ship as it drifted towards the horizon where a fiery red glow lit the gateway to Hell. On one end of the mast a figure jerked spasmodically. Athelstan glimpsed the blackened, twisted face of Pike the ditcher hanging by the neck. The friar turned as someone tapped him on the shoulder. His brother Francis stood there: his face was blueish-white under a shock of black hair. A thin red snake of blood trickled out of the corner of his mouth; his chest was an open, bubbling mass of blood where he had received his death wound.

'You ran away from your monastery, Brother?' His voice sounded hollow.

Athelstan stretched out his hand. 'I am sorry, Francis,' he murmured. Athelstan stared around. Was Cranston here? He was sure he could hear the coroner's voice.

Athelstan walked to the entrance of the hold and gazed down. A naked woman squatted there, her face hidden behind a black veil; from her mouth came a foul toad and round her neck curled an amber snake, its red-slit eyes flashing like diamonds. A fat-bellied rat crouched beside her. Athelstan walked down the steps. Behind the woman, kneeling stern and impassive, was a knight in full armour, gauntleted hands resting on the hilt of his great two-handled sword. The hold stank of death and Athelstan could feel someone pressing close behind him. He squirmed violently as a hand seized his shoulder.

'Athelstan! Athelstan! Brother, for God's sake!'

The friar opened his eyes. Cranston, his fat face wrinkled with concern, stared down at him.

'Brother, what is the matter?'

Athelstan stared back. 'Good Sir John, I was dreaming.' He raised a clammy hand and rubbed his face. 'I was dreaming,' he repeated.

'And not a pleasant one!'

'No, Sir John. Some succubus of the night with the power of a thousand scorpions seized my mind.'

Cranston gazed quizzically back and Athelstan grinned.

'I am only joking. I think my nightmare was due more to the table than the grave. We dined too well last night.'

'Yesterday is gone and today is today,' Cranston pompously replied. 'Come on, Brother, it's daybreak.'

Athelstan rose quickly, said a hasty prayer and washed himself in the freezing water from a cracked pewter jug. They gathered their possessions and moved down to the cold, deserted taproom. The fire was not lit and the room didn't seem as cheerful and welcoming as it had the night before; they broke their fast quickly on warm oat cakes and mulled wine, saddled their horses and rode back along the track to the highway.

The day looked as if it would be a fine one. A weak sun was about to rise, turning the darkness to a dusty grey:

their horses plodded along the frozen track, both riders taking special care against the potholes, some as deep as a man, which could bring down and even kill both the unwary rider and his horse. The countryside was empty and silent. Athelstan shivered as he remembered his nightmare and the eerie stillness of that terrible dream. The hedgerows on either side were still thickly covered with snow and, beyond them, the fields lay iron hard under sheets of ice. A circle of hungry crows soared noisily above a clump of oak trees, branches black against the lightening sky.

'I wish I was back in London,' Cranston moaned. 'I hate the bloody countryside. I hate the silence!'

Athelstan caught a blur of colour in a ditch on the side of the track and pulled his horse over to look closer. The corpse which lay there was frozen hard, that of an old man covered from head to knee in a loose, threadbare gown. Athelstan closed his eyes and breathed a prayer as he glimpsed the blue-black holes where the hungry ravens had pecked at the scrawny, whitening flesh.

'God rest him!' Cranston murmured. 'Brother, there is nothing we can do.'

They moved on through a silent, sleeping village, only a few plumes of black smoke giving any sign of life. After an hour's ride they approached the village of Leighton. At the crossroads they glimpsed a group of villagers huddled round the blackened scaffold. Thankfully, the iron gibbet which swung from its hook was empty. The villagers were gathered round a corpse whilst beside it two burly labourers hacked the iron ground at the foot of the scaffold. Then hoes and mattocks cleared a shallow hole while their breath hung heavy in the frost air. Athelstan looked at Cranston. The coroner shrugged though his hand went beneath his cloak to ensure his dagger was loose in its sheath. The villagers turned at the riders' approach. An old woman, her face yellow and lined with age, scrawny body covered in the battered hide of a cow, shuffled towards them.

'Morrow! Morrow!' she cried. 'Travellers on a road like this?' Her milky eyes grinned slyly up at Athelstan. 'Good morning, Father. 'Tis rare to see a priest up so early.'

'Mother!' Cranston bellowed back, loosening the muffler round his mouth. 'It's good to see anyone in such Godforsaken weather. What are you doing?'

'Burying Eadwig.'

'Here?' Athelstan asked. 'You have no church, no cemetery?'

The old hag lifted her skinny hand. 'Come and see! Come and see!'

Reluctantly they pushed their horses nearer. Cranston's mount became skittish and even Philomel showed a lively interest in the group round the scaffold. The villagers parted as the coroner and his companion approached. Athelstan glimpsed red, dirty faces, greasy, matted hair, and the occasional glare of hatred at their well-fed horses and warm, woollen cloaks. Cranston took one look at Eadwig's body, closed his eyes and drew away. The peasant had been hanged. His face was black, tongue half-bitten off but still clenched tightly between yellow teeth, whilst one eye had popped from its socket and lay grotesquely against the bruised cheek.

'Good God!' Athelstan breathed. 'What happened?'

'He killed himself,' the old hag cackled. 'And you know the law, Father?'

'Oh, yes, Mother, I know the law.' He looked at the small, wooden stake leaning against the scaffold. 'Sir John, I suggest we ride on.'

The coroner needed no second bidding. They turned their horses, ignoring the soft cackles of laughter behind them. Athelstan closed his eyes, praying from whatever psalm he could remember to fend off the awful terrors which clung to the world of men. Behind him he heard the faint sounds of a wooden mallet driving the stake through the suicide's heart.

'Good God!' Cranston murmured. 'You priests, Athelstan, should change all that. Only the Good Lord knows why the poor bastard killed himself, but must a suicide be buried near a gibbet at the crossroads with a stake driven through his heart?'

'The bishops have tried to stop it,' Athelstan replied. 'But Christ's teaching, Sir John, in certain parts and over certain hearts, lies as thin and as loose as a spider's web.'

They rode through Leighton, following the track which skirted the dark mass of Epping Forest and into Woodforde just as the church bell tolled for Nones. The village was an unprepossessing one: a few villagers, hooded and cloaked against the cold, scurried about shooing scrawny chickens away from the horses. Some boys were bringing battered wooden buckets up from the well and the occasional housewife emptied the slops from the night jars out into the middle of the street. Even the alehouse was still shuttered and locked.

'Like a village of the dead,' Athelstan murmured.

'Aye, it might as well be, Brother,' Cranston replied through his muffler. 'The cold will stop all work in the fields.'

A young urchin, his face pinched white by the cold, suddenly appeared and walked solemnly alongside them, a dirty canvas bag clutched in one bony hand. Athelstan reined in Philomel.

'What's the matter, boy?'

The urchin just stared, round-eyed, at Philomel's tail.

'Come on, lad, what do you want?'

'Mother told me to follow. Told me to wait for the horse to lift its tail.'

Cranston chuckled. 'He is waiting for our horses to shit!' he exclaimed. 'It's good manure and, if dried, burns well and cheerily.'

Athelstan grinned, pulled back his hood, dug into his purse and threw the boy a penny. 'You can have everything our horses will drop, boy,' he announced solemnly. 'And there's a penny for your trouble. You know the Burghgesh family? They have a manor house here.'

'Oh, all gone,' the lad replied, his eyes still fixed on Philomel's tail. 'The house lies beyond the village near Buxfield but it is deserted and closed up. Father Peter will tell you that.' He pointed to where the tiled-roofed church with its grey, ragstone tower peeped above the treetops.

'Then,' Athelstan said, kicking Philomel into a trot, 'that's where we'll stop!'

They rode through the wicket gate of the church, following the pathway which snaked between the trees and overgrown graves to the Norman church which stood on the brow of a small hillock. Beside it was a modest, two-storeyed house, its roof made of yellowing thatch, the windows nothing more than wooden shutters. Athelstan looked back. The young boy still stood behind him, one hand gripping the bag, the other balled into a tight fist, guarding Athelstan's penny as if it was the key to heaven itself.

'Father Peter's in?'

'He will be there,' the boy replied. 'And, for another penny, I'll look after your horses.'

Athelstan nodded and another coin was tossed in the air.

'That young man will advance far,' Cranston murmured as they dismounted and knocked on the door. They heard bolts being pulled back, the door swung open and a clean-shaven, cheery-faced Father Peter peered out.

'Travellers in this weather?' His voice was burred by a thick country accent but, despite the snow-white hair and slight stoop of the shoulders, Father Peter was an active, cheerful man. He hardly waited for their introductions but ushered them into the warm, sweet-smelling room, chattering and asking questions like a magpie. He took their cloaks and told them to sit on a bench which he pushed towards the heat of the fire.

'A coroner and a Dominican come to visit me,' he announced in mock wonderment, and squatted down beside them on a stool. Father Peter took three earthenware bowls from a small cupboard near the inglenook and served them generous portions of soup from a black bowl which hung perilously from an iron hook above the flames. 'Bits of fish, some herbs, what's left of my vegetables.' The priest screwed up his eyes. 'Ah, yes, and some onions.'

Both Athelstan and Cranston gripped the warm bowls and sipped at the rich stew which scalded their mouths and lips but put some warmth into their frozen bellies. Father Peter watched, even as he sipped from his own bowl. Athelstan smiled back and put his bowl down.

'At the moment it's too hot to eat, Father,' he murmured apologetically. 'Even to hold.'

Cranston, however, had no such difficulty. He slurped as noisily as a ravenous dog, mopping up what was left with hard crusts of bread which Father Peter shoved before him on a wooden platter. At last Cranston burped, smacked his lips and handed the bowl back.

'The best meal in many a day, Father. We thank you for your hospitality.' The coroner stretched his great hands out towards the flames. 'We will not keep you long. You know the Burghgesh family?'

Father Peter's eyes narrowed. 'Aye,' he replied. 'I know of them.'

Athelstan began to sip carefully at his now cooling bowl of soup.

'Will you tell us, Father?'

The priest shrugged. 'What is there to say? Bartholomew Burghgesh and his wife lived in a manor house near Buxfield. Bartholomew was always a restless man, born to the sword and the horse rather than the plough and the bailiff's accounts. He went to London and served in the retinues of the great ones. In the old King's time, he was in the garrison of the Tower, then he went abroad with others to fight in Outremer.'

'And his wife?'

Father Peter made a moue. 'She was a quiet, sickly woman. They had one boy... what was his name? Ah, yes, Mark.' Father Peter sighed. 'Oh, they were well looked after. A steward administered the manor, and Bartholomew always sent gold. Then about – oh, some fourteen or fifteen years ago – news came of Bartholomew's death. He had been killed on board a ship taken by the Moors in the Middle Seas. By that time Mark was a young man. He took his father's death with little show of regret, but the mother became ill and died within a year of her husband.'

'And Mark Burghgesh?'

'He was like his father, his head full of stories about Roland and Oliver and performing marvellous feats of arms. For a while he was Lord of the Manor. After the old King's victories in France, he raised money from the bankers, bought a destrier, and armour, and formed a small retinue of archers of like-minded men from the village.' The priest paused and stared into the flames. 'I remember the morning they left,' he continued dreamily. 'A beautiful summer's day. Sir Mark on his black warhorse, his dark red hair oiled and combed; before him went his squire carrying a banner with the Burghgesh arms, and marching behind were six archers with steel caps, quilted jerkins, long bows and quivers full of goose-quilled arrows. A brave sight.' The priest rocked himself gently. 'None of them came back,' he murmured. 'They all died in the blood and muck.'

Athelstan caught his breath. So like his own story. He and Francis had joined such a retinue. Athelstan had returned but his brother's body still lay mouldering in some forgotten field in France.

'None of them came back?' Cranston repeated, fighting hard to control the excitement in his voice. 'So Mark Burghgesh could still be alive?'

The priest stared at him and shook his head. 'Oh, no, Sir John. I spoke wrongly. No one came back alive. Come, I'll show you where Mark is.'

They rose. Father Peter handed them their cloaks, taking his own from a wooden peg, and they followed him out into the cold. The young boy still stood like a soldier, holding the reins of the horses, his eyes looking eagerly at the piles of steaming dung obligingly dropped by both Philomel and Cranston's mount. Father Peter stopped.

'Boy, take the horses round to the stable. You'll find some oats there. Then go in and take some soup. Don't worry, the horses won't wander off.'

The urchin stared at Athelstan.

'Go on, lad,' the friar ordered. 'You'll freeze to death standing there. And, I promise, the horse dung's yours.'

They reached the church door. Father Peter unlocked it and they entered the darkened nave. It was cold, the air icy. Athelstan gazed at the square, squat pillars decorated with greenery like his own in Southwark, though not as beautiful. He hasn't got a painter, Athelstan thought. Father Peter caught his eye and Athelstan felt guilty at his petty pride.

'A fine church, Father,' he murmured.

Father Peter grinned. 'We try, Brother. But I would give a king's ransom for a good painter and craftsman.'

They went beneath the simple chancel screen, across the sanctuary into a small lady chapel which lay in the far corner of the church. A large wooden statue of the Virgin and Child stood on a stone plinth whilst around the walls were raised tombs, simple and square, lacking any effigy or ornamentation. Father Peter went across and gently tapped one.

'Sir Mark Burghgesh lies here,' he announced quietly. 'His body was sent back for burial.'

Cranston stared in disappointment at the grey ragstone tomb. 'Are you sure, Father Peter?'

'Yes,' the priest said. 'The embalmers did their best to dress the corpse: before the coffin was lowered, I looked once more at the face. Sir Mark had received a terrible death wound on the side of his head, caused by a battle axe or mace, but I am certain it was he.'

Athelstan hid his disappointment and gazed despondently at Cranston. Their cold journey through the bitter Essex landscape had been fruitless.

'Why do you want to know all this?' Father Peter asked as he led them out of the church.

'There's been a murder, Father, in London,' Cranston answered, chewing his lip. 'We hoped our journey here would yield fresh evidence. Have you noticed anything untoward in the village?'

'Such as?'

'Anything,' Athelstan pleaded. 'Any news or gossip about the Burghgesh family?'

The priest shook his head. Athelstan and Cranston looked at each other despondently as they left the church and re-entered the priest's house where the boy was lapping a second bowl of soup as hungrily as a starving dog. At their approach he scurried into a corner. Father Peter waved them back to their seats and went across and poured them generous stoups of ale from the jar just outside the small buttery door.

'No,' he repeated, sitting down on the stool and cradling the blackjack of ale in his hands, 'Woodforde is a quiet place. Even quieter now the Burghgeshes have left.'

'What happened to their manor house?'

'The King's Commissioners sealed it off. No one has been there since.' The priest coughed. 'I should know. The Sheriff of Essex pays me a small stipend to ensure the seals on the doors and windows are not broken.' He looked at Cranston. 'And they are still sealed. After all, there's nothing there. All the moveables have been removed, the roof has fallen in, the surrounding meadows and ploughlands been sold off.'

'There was no other heir?'

'None that I know of.' Father Peter suddenly took the tankard away from his lips. 'In heaven's name!' he exclaimed. 'There was something. Yes,' he murmured excitedly, 'about three or four years ago, something very strange. It was like a dream. Now, when was it? Yes, it was at the beginning of Advent. I forget the actual year. I had said morning Mass, gone across to the house to break my fast then went back to clear the altar.' Father Peter stared into the flames. 'I went up the nave and was surprised to see a man, cowled and hooded, kneeling at the entrance to the Lady Chapel.'

'Where Mark Burghgesh is buried?'

'Yes, yes. Now I trod softly, and at first the man didn't hear me. But when he did, he rose very quickly, pulled his cowl close about his head, and brushing by me, left the church, ignoring my salutation. All I glimpsed were a few strands of grey hair and a white, neatly barbered beard.' Father Peter picked up his tankard and sipped from it. 'Now, it had been years since I had seen Bartholomew Burghgesh and I considered him long dead, yet I am sure that man I glimpsed that cold December morning was Sir Bartholomew himself. He had his walk, the gait and stance of a professional soldier.'

Athelstan leaned forward excitedly. Was Sir Bartholomew alive? he wondered. Was he the bloody-handed slayer stalking his victims? 'Continue, Father,' he whispered.

'Well, I didn't mention it to anyone. The villagers would think I had been drinking or wandering in my wits.'

He grinned at Athelstan. 'You can appreciate, Brother, how the sheep like to gossip about their shepherd.'

Athelstan smiled back and stole a sideways glance at Cranston who was sitting, open-mouthed, at Father Peter's revelation.

'A year later,' the priest continued, 'on the Feast of All Hallows, I was in the village ale-house. Autumn was here, the countryside was fading under the colder, harsher weather. We were talking about death and exchanging gruesome ghost stories. The landlord, God rest him – the fellow has since died – suddenly spoke up, declaring that he had seen the ghost of Sir Bartholomew Burghgesh. Of course, the others laughed at him but he insisted and said that at about the same time I thought I'd seen Sir Bartholomew, a stranger had arrived in the village late at night and stopped at the ale-house for food and drink. The man had been cloaked and hooded and hardly ever spoke except to buy his meal.' Father Peter closed his eyes. 'The landlord said the fellow made it obvious he wanted to be left to himself. After all, Woodforde's on the highway into the city. We have many people who like to keep their business to themselves. Anyway, the stranger was about to leave when a slattern dropped a tankard. The man whirled round and for a few seconds the landlord saw his face. He swore it was Bartholomew Burghgesh.'

Father Peter sighed. 'Of course, I kept quiet about what I had seen, but I was intrigued. I journeyed out to the old manor house near Buxfield. If it was Burghgesh, I thought, surely he would have returned to his former home? Yet I discovered that nothing had been disturbed.' He shrugged and spread his hands. 'That's all I can tell you. Only God knows if the man I and the landlord glimpsed was Sir Bartholomew. I heard no other rumours about his sudden return, either from abroad or beyond the grave, so I let the matter rest.'

'Father,' Athelstan persisted, 'please, when was this? Three or four years ago?'

The priest stared into the fire.

'Yes, three years ago,' he replied. 'But,' he smiled, 'I can tell you no more.'

Cranston leaned forward and clasped Father Peter by the wrist.

'Father, your hospitality is only matched by the value of what you have told us.' The coroner glanced at Athelstan and smiled. 'Come, Brother, it's not yet noon. If we travel hard and fast, we can be back in the city before nightfall.' He looked across at Father Peter. 'I thank you for your hospitality, Father.' He turned and tossed a penny at the lad still squatting in the corner. 'You, boy, will either make a good squire or a merchant.'

They rose, gathered their cloaks, and within the hour were clear of Woodforde. They journeyed through Leighton, past the grisly scaffold with the freshly dug makeshift grave still visible at its foot, and back on to the Mile End Road. Cranston, who had stopped at a local tavern to refill his miraculous wineskin, was full of chatter and speculation.

'It's possible, Brother,' he boomed for the umpteenth time, his bewhiskered lips red from the juice of the grape, 'quite possible that Sir Bartholomew is still alive and hiding in or near the Tower to carry out his silent war of revenge.'

'Sir John,' Athelstan replied, 'I would agree, but where would Burghgesh hide? Is he a member of the garrison? A kitchen scullion? Some tradesman who has the right of access?'

Cranston made a rude noise with his lips.

'Or,' Athelstan continued, 'does Sir Bartholomew squat like some dark spider in the city whilst others carry out his dreadful commands?'

Cranston reined in his horse.

'Strange, mind you,' he murmured.

'What?'

'Well, three years ago Whitton was disturbed, agitated, as if he had seen a ghost. At the same time, Brother, a cowled and hooded figure was seen in the tavern near the Tower, and the same person, probably Burghgesh, also seen in Woodforde.'

'You're saying Whitton's agitation was caused by Burghgesh's reappearance?'

'Of course.'

'But, if that is so, what has happened to Burghgesh since?'

He and Cranston were still arguing rival theories when they reached Aldgate long after dark and made their way through a small postern door in the city gate. Cranston, full of wine and his own theories, was now certain they had grasped the truth. Athelstan did not demur. At least, he concluded, their journey to Woodforde had diverted the coroner's mind from his constant agonising over the Lady Maude's mysterious conduct.

–

As Athelstan and Cranston made their way back into the city, the hospitaller, Fitzormonde, was standing in the bailey of the Tower, staring at the huge bear now stuffing its cruel mouth with scraps from the Tower kitchen. Like Athelstan, Fitzormonde was fascinated by the beast and secretly admired the madcap Red Hand who was the only man who dared approach the animal. Fitzormonde, despite his travels, had never seen such a huge beast. Most bears were small and black, sometimes no higher than a man, but this great, shaggy-furred animal reminded him of stories he had heard from knights who had served with the Teutonic Orders in the wild black forests of the north. How they had seen deer twice the size of anything in England and bears such as this one, which would crush a horse in its huge, muscular arms.

The bear suddenly stopped eating and glared at the knight, its small, piggy eyes red with hatred. It opened its mouth, growling deep in its throat in a display of wickedly sharp teeth. The huge beast strained at the great iron chain clasped to the collar round its neck. Fitzormonde stepped away and the bear went back to its meal, shuffling its food into a dirty untidy pile as if it suspected Fitzormonde would like to take it away. The knight stamped his feet to keep warm. Tomorrow, he thought, he would leave the Tower. He had already said as much to Mistress Philippa when he had met her and her rather effeminate betrothed.

Fitzormonde gazed up at the cruel gargoyle faces on the Chapel of St Peter ad Vincula. Yes, he thought, tomorrow, he would pay the chaplain to sing one last Mass for his fallen comrades then go back into the city and request from his superiors some mission or task well away from this benighted fortress.

He started as he heard a whirring noise in the air. He looked up. A raven? No, what was it? The hospitaller suddenly stepped back in panic as the bear sprang into life, towering above him, its great paws clawing the air. The bear roared at him with fury, its black muzzle and huge jaws covered in a thick white froth. Fitzormonde's hand went to his dagger as the bear danced like a demon, pulling at the great chain clasped in the wall. What was wrong with the animal? What had happened?

Fitzormonde made to run but, even as he turned, heard the great iron chain spring loose and saw the bear rush towards him. He tugged at his knife but had it only half-drawn when the huge taloned paw of the bear smashed his head as if it was a rotten apple. Roaring with fury, the bear dug his claws into the dying knight's unprotected back and dragged him across the cobbles, bellows of rage proclaiming its triumph.

Chapter 12

Athelstan was furious. He felt the anger burn his innards until his heart pounded and the blood throbbed in his head. For a moment, the friar didn't give a damn about anything – the teaching of his Order to be gentle or the precepts of the gospels about kindness. All that mattered was the anger raging within him as he stood in the cemetery outside St Erconwald's church. The snow had now turned into an icy, grey slush which dripped off graves, trees, bushes and the low cemetery wall as the thaw continued under clear skies and a weak wintry sun. Athelstan cursed, using every filthy oath he had learnt from Cranston. He beat the staff he held against the loose brick, furious enough to grind the rock into sand.

Oh, he had found everything in order on his return: Bonaventura, asleep and well, curled up in the church like some fat bishop as Cecily cleaned and swept the nave. Benedicta and Watkin had set up the crib in one of the aisles, using figures carved by Huddle. The painter had also finished a vivid picture of Christ in the manger, just above the baptismal font inside the church door. Even Ursula's pig had resisted its usual forays into his garden, and Pike the ditcher had cleared the gravel-strewn path in front of the church.

Athelstan had pronounced himself satisfied and chattered about parochial matters as he stabled, watered and fed Philomel. But even then, he had sensed the anxiety in the faces of those who had come to welcome him: Benedicta, Pike, Watkin, Cecily, and Tab the tinker. They had followed him around the church, answering his questions whilst exchanging secretive, anxious glances.

At first Athelstan dismissed their concern as some petty matter. Had Cecily been flirting again, or one of Pike the ditcher's sons peed in the church? Perhaps Ranulf borrowed Bonaventure or Watkin's children had been drinking from the holy water stoup? The members of his parish council had fussed round him like noisy chickens. At last, just before he locked the church, Athelstan tired of their secrecy.

'Come on!' he demanded, confronting them. 'What has happened?'

They shuffled their feet and looked away. Benedicta suddenly became concerned about an apparent spot on her gown.

'It's the cemetery, Father!' Watkin blurted out. 'Tosspot's grave has been disturbed.'

'When?'

'The night you left.'

Athelstan had been so angry he'd used language which made even Pike the ditcher's face blanch.

'Perhaps Sir John will do something now,' Benedicta tactfully intervened. 'Or maybe if we make an appeal to the Alderman of the Ward?'

'Aye!' Athelstan rasped. 'And perhaps pigs will fly and we'll find pork in the trees tomorrow morning. The people who do this terrible thing are bastards! They are wicked and fear neither God nor man. Even the pagans honour the corpse of a dead man. Not even a dog would do this!'

His parishioners had withdrawn, more frightened of their gentle parish priest's terrible rage than the dreadful news they had brought. Athelstan had stormed off to his house and drunk a cup of wine with a speed Cranston would have admired. He slept fitfully that night, not even thinking of climbing the tower steps to study the stars. He'd tossed and turned on his pallet bed, fuming with rage at the sinful desecration of his cemetery. The next morning he rose early, opened the church, perfunctorily fed Bonaventura, skipped through the morning office and tried hard to concentrate whilst he celebrated Mass. Bonaventura, like the cunning cat he was, seemed to sense his patron's change of mood and quietly stole away. At the end of the Mass, before he gave the final benediction, Athelstan spoke in sharp, terse tones.

'Our cemetery has been violated once again,' he declared. 'I, Athelstan, priest of this parish, say this, as God is my witness — no further burials will take place until the ground has been re-consecrated and this problem resolved!' He glared round at his small congregation. 'I will go to the highest in the land, be it the young King himself or the Archbishop of Canterbury. Guards will be set and, God forgive me, I shall see these villains hang!'

His parishioners had quietly left and Athelstan, now calming, felt a twinge of guilt as he glared down at Tosspot's ravaged grave.

'Your fiery temper, priest,' he muttered to himself, 'is no more curbed than it was twenty years ago. And your tongue is as sharp as ever.'

He breathed deeply. Yes, he had been too hard, he reflected, far too brusque with Benedicta and the others, but especially with the widow. She had stayed for a few seconds after Mass, not to gossip but simply to say that the chief bailiff of the ward, Master Bladdersniff, had accosted her on her way to church. He wished to see Athelstan on an urgent matter.

'Oh, yes,' Athelstan muttered. 'Master Bladdersniff, as usual, closing the stable door after the horse has bolted!' Athelstan felt a fresh surge of rage. If St Erconwald's had been one of the wealthy city churches, guards would have been set immediately and this would never have happened. Even Cranston, that fat-arsed coroner, hadn't helped, wrapped up like some mewling maid in his own concerns. Athelstan stared once more round the cemetery, it was so cold, so bleak. He remembered Father Peter and envied the Woodforde priest's quiet domest-icity. 'Bloody Cranston!' Athelstan muttered. 'Bloody murder! Bloody Tower! The bloody hearts of men and their evil doings!' He kicked the icy mud. 'I am a priest,' he hissed to himself. 'Not some sheriff's man.'

'Father? Father Athelstan?'

The friar turned and glared at the young pursuivant who stood, cloaked and hooded, behind him. 'Yes, man, what is it?'

'I have been sent from the Tower by Sir John Cranston. He wants to see you in the Holy Lamb tavern off Cheapside.'

'Tell My Lord Coroner,' Athelstan retorted, 'that I'll be there when I'm there, and he'd better be sober!'

The young man looked surprised and hurt. Athelstan grimaced and spread his hands.

'Lord, man, I'm sorry. Look, tell Sir John I'll be there when I can.'

He took a step closer and saw the fellow's white, pinched face and dripping nose. 'You are freezing,' the friar muttered. 'Go across to my house, there's a jug of wine on the table. Fill a goblet. You'll find one on a shelf above the fire hearth. Drink some mulled wine, and get some warmth in your belly before you return.'

The pursuivant turned and scurried off like a whippet.

'Oh, by the way,' Athelstan yelled after him, 'I did mean what I said. Sir John is not to drink too much!'

Athelstan walked slowly back to his church, up the steps and into the porch.

'Father?'

Athelstan jumped as Master Luke Bladdersniff, chief bailiff of the ward, stepped out of the darkness, his lean sallow face and wispy blond hair almost hidden under a tattered beaver hat.

'Good morrow, Master Bailiff.'

Athelstan studied the ward man: his close-set eyes were dark-rimmed and looked even more like the piss-holes in the snow, as Cranston so aptly described them. Athelstan had always been fascinated by the man's nose. Broken and slightly twisted, it gave Bladdersniff a rather comical look which sat awkwardly with the fellow's usual air of bombastic self-importance. Athelstan wearily waved him into the church.

'Master Bladdersniff, I suppose you have come to dis-cuss why my cemetery is violated and its graves robbed whilst you and the ward council do nothing about it?'

Bladdersniff shook his head, while peering over his shoulder, back into the darkness of the church porch.

'What is it, man? What's over there?'

The bailiff's mouth opened and shut like a landed carp. Athelstan stared more closely. The fellow looked as if he was going to vomit. His white face had a greenish tinge and the dark eyes were watery, as if Bladdersniff had been violently retching.

'For God's sake, man, what is it?'

Again the bailiff looked back into the darkness. 'It's Tosspot!' he mumbled.

'What?'

'Tosspot! Or, at least, part of him,' Bladdersniff replied, beckoning the priest to follow him.

Athelstan took a taper and went to where the bailiff stood over a dirty piece of canvas in a dark corner of the church porch. Bladdersniff pulled this open and Athelstan turned away in disgust. A man's leg lay there, or at least part of it, cut above the knee as neatly and as sharply as a piece of cloth by an expert tailor. Athelstan stared at the bloody stump and mottle-hued skin.

'Good God!' he breathed, and caught the stench of corruption from the slightly puffed flesh. 'Cover it up, man! Cover it up!'

Athelstan doused the taper, walked out of the church and stood on the top step, drawing in deep breaths of fresh morning air. He heard Bladdersniff come up behind him.

'What makes you think it was Tosspot?'

'Oh, you remember, Father. Tosspot was always regaling his customers at the tavern with tales of his old war wound, an arrow in the leg. He was continually showing his scar as if it was some sacred relic.'

Athelstan nodded.

'Aye,' he replied. 'Old Tosspot would do that whenever he became drunk.' The friar looked at the bailiff. 'And that leg bears the same scar?'

'Yes, Father, just above the shin.'

'Where was it found?'

'Do you want to see?'

'Yes, I do.'

Bladdersniff led him down Bridge Street, across Jerwald and into Longfish Alley, which led down to Broken Wharf on the riverside. As he walked, Athelstan never spoke a word and the people who knew him stepped aside at the fierce, determined expression on the usually gentle priest's face.

Athelstan noticed little except the dirty, filthy slush of the streets they crossed. He ignored greetings and seemed totally unaware of the traders and hucksters behind their battered stalls and booths shouting for custom. Even the felons fastened tightly in the stocks failed to provoke his usual compassion, whilst he treated Bladdersniff as if the bailiff hardly existed. Athelstan felt sick at heart. Who would do that to poor Tosspot's corpse? he wondered. How would it profit them? They reached Broken Wharf above the riverside. Bladdersniff took the friar by the arm and pointed down to the dirty mudflats where gulls and crows fought over the rubbish left on the riverside. Athelstan looked out across the Thames. The water looked as dirty and dark as his own mood. He noticed the great chunks of ice still floating, crashing together as they swirled down to thunder against the arches of London Bridge.

'Where did you find it?'

'Down there, Father,' Bladdersniff brusquely replied. 'On the mud, wrapped in that piece of canvas. An urchin looking for sea coal found it and brought it to one of the traders who recognised old Tosspot's wound.' The bailiff coughed nervously. 'I have heard about the raids on your cemetery.'

'Oh, you have? That's good.' Athelstan smiled falsely at him. 'You think the limb was washed in by the river?'

'Yes, I do. Now, at any other time, Father, the river would have swept it away, but the heavy ice has interfered with the current and the canvas bag was pushed back to the bank.'

'So you are saying it must have been thrown in here?'

'Yes, Father, either here or some place very close.'

Athelstan looked to his left, along the mud flats and walls which stretched down to London Bridge. Too open, he reflected. No felon would dream of committing such a terrible act in a place where he could be seen. He looked to his right and the long row of great houses whose gardens stretched down to the riverside. A recent memory stirred. 'I wonder,' he murmured to himself. 'I really do wonder...'

'What, Father?'

'Nothing, Master Bladdersniff. Go back to my church. Collect what is left of poor Tosspot and bury it as you think fit.'

'Father, it's not my...'

'Do it!' Athelstan snarled. 'Do it now or answer to the City Coroner, Sir John Cranston!'

'He has no jurisdiction here.'

'Yes, but he can get it!' Athelstan retorted. 'Oh, for God's sake, man, do it for me. Do it for poor Tosspot, please?'

Bladdersniff stared, nodded, and strode away.

Athelstan walked back to St Erconwald's. He had recognised one of the houses down near the riverside and remembered how cleanly and sharply the limb had been cut. This stirred memories of his own military experience in the makeshift hospitals of the old King's armies in France. Athelstan thought of the cemetery. Where were the lepers? Why hadn't they noticed anything? Athelstan remembered the lepers he had seen near St Paul's the day he and Cranston had visited Geoffrey Parchmeiner. Their begging dishes!

Athelstan stopped in the middle of Lad Alley. 'Oh, my God!' he whispered. 'Oh, sweet pity's sake!' The white chalk he had found on his fingers after Mass when he and young Crim had pushed the sacred host through the leper's squint... The friar suddenly felt weak and leaned against the urine-stained wall. Other memories flooded back. 'Of course!' he whispered to himself. 'That's why the cemetery wasn't disturbed for a while. The thaw! But when the river was frozen, they couldn't get rid of what they'd stolen.' Athelstan's face contorted into a sudden snarl. 'The bastards!' he hissed. 'The evil bastards!'

He strode back down Lad Alley into one of the busy thoroughfares which ran parallel to the riverbank. A young urchin, running after a ball, bumped into him, slipping and sliding on the icy slush. Athelstan seized him tightly by the shoulder until the boy winced.

'Father, Father, I didn't mean to! Honest, I didn't!'

Athelstan looked at the urchin's pallid face.

'I am sorry,' he replied gently. 'No hurt was intended. But here, lad. For a penny, take me to Doctor Vincentius' house. You know the physician?'

The boy didn't know Vincentius and shook his head, but ran to a local stall-holder who provided clear instructions. The urchin then led Athelstan through an alleyway and into a quiet street of houses, grand, half-timbered affairs, though their paint was now peeling and their un-washed façades gave sad, mute witness to grander, more prosperous days. The boy pointed to the third one down with its windows shuttered, though the huge front door was freshly painted and reinforced with shining bands of steel. Athelstan handed the penny over, went across and pounded on the door until he heard the patter of quick footsteps and the bolts drawn back. A lank-haired young man opened the door, dressed in a blue cotehardie fringed with squirrel fur. His eyes widened in alarm when he saw the friar.

'Brother Athelstan!'

'How do you know my name, you bastard?' the friar shouted, and pushed him back against the wall. 'Where is Doctor Vincentius?'

'He's in his chamber.'

Athelstan didn't wait for the fellow to usher him in but strode along the lime-washed stone corridor and threw open the door at the far end. Vincentius was sitting behind a great oaken desk in his warm, dark, panelled chamber. Athelstan was aware of shelves stuffed full of parchments, a zodiac chart on the wall, the smell of herbs and spices, and a small log fire crackling merrily in the hearth. The doctor rose, his dark eyes guarded, tawny face creased into a smile.

'Brother Athelstan! What is the matter? What can I do...?'

'This for a start!' Athelstan punched the doctor as hard as he could, sending Vincentius sprawling against the wall, knocking over a small table and sending a yellowing skull crashing on to the map-strewn floor. The doctor got up and dabbed at the cut at the corner of his mouth with the back of his hand. His dark eyes now mocked the priest.

'You seem in a temper, Father?'

Athelstan heard the young man come up behind him. 'It's all right, Gidaut,' Vincentius murmured. 'But perhaps we'd better start to pack once again.'

244

Athelstan glared at the doctor as the door closed softly behind him.

'You are a bastard, Doctor! A heretic! A despoiler of graves! I have just seen what's left of poor Tosspot's corpse. If the wardsman had any sense, he would be here with the city guard. Only a skilled physician could cut a leg so cleanly.' He walked closer to the desk. 'And don't lie! You and your creature out there—' Athelstan indicated the door with a toss of his head. 'A clever pair. Dressed like lepers, your faces masked by skins covered with white chalk, you lived in my cemetery by day, or at least part of it, finding out what happened. And who would dream of approaching a leper? And, even if they did, you were well prepared. Your face was covered in a cloth mask, the skin of your hands discoloured. Then of course, you would come back at night and take whatever you wanted!' Athelstan breathed heavily. 'God forgive me,' he muttered. 'I'm no better than other men. Do you know, when a man is declared a leper, he attends his own requiem? We think of him as already dead, and so did I. The lepers in my cemetery were just shadows to me, walking bundles of rags. Only one thing was missing: I never saw them with begging dishes, and didn't realise that till this morning.' He glared at the physician. 'You really should have been more careful, Vincentius. You took those corpses and, when you were finished, ditched what was left into the Thames. But the river was sluggish. This morning the grisly remains of your macabre activities floated back to the riverbank.'

The doctor still kept his back to the wall and watched the priest guardedly. 'You are most observant, friar. Benedicta told me that.'

Athelstan flinched at the look in the doctor's eyes. 'Aye,' the friar replied, slumping down on a stool. 'But I should have been *more* observant. I found chalk on my fingers after I had passed the Host through the leper's squint.' He glared at the doctor. 'That's sacrilege, you know? To take the Eucharist as a cover for your blasphemous doings.' Athelstan glared around him. 'Yes,' he rasped, 'I should have been more observant. I never saw you with a begging bowl, nor could I remember you in the streets around the church.' He rose. 'You broke God's law as well as the King's. I am leaving now but I will be back with the city guard. Tonight you will be in Newgate getting ready to stand trial before King's Bench at Westminster!'

'Benedicta also said you were a tolerant priest. Aren't you going to ask me why, Father?' Vincentius replied softly.

The physician suddenly had a wary, frightened look in his eyes. 'I did wrong,' he muttered, slumping into his chair. 'But what real harm did I do? No, no!' He waved his hand at Athelstan. 'Listen to me! I have studied medicine in Bologna, with the Arabs in Spain and North Africa, and at the great school of physic in Salerno. But we doctors know nothing, Father, except how to apply leeches and bleed a man dry.' Vincentius laced his fingers together and rested his elbows on the desk. 'The only way we can learn about the human body is to open it up. Dissect each part; study the position of the heart, or the coursing of the blood, or the composition of the stomach. But the church forbids that.' He held up a beringed hand. 'I swear I meant no disrespect, but my hunger for medical knowledge, Father, is as great as yours for saving souls. And where could I go? To the execution yards or battlefields where the corpses are so mauled they are beyond recognition? So

I came to Southwark, outside the jurisdiction of the city. Yes, yes.' He saw the look of annoyance in Athelstan's eyes. 'To a poor parish where no one cared, just as they don't for the famished children who roam the streets near your church.' Vincentius played with a small knife. 'I took to imitating a leper to spy on the graveyard, taking only those corpses over whom no one had a claim.'

'I claimed them!' Athelstan yelled. 'God claimed them! The church claimed them!'

'Yes, I took the corpses,' Vincentius continued, 'and dissected them. Gidaut and I buried them at night in the river, but then we stopped because of the great frost.' He shook his head. 'I did wrong, but are you going to hound me for that? I did good work here, priest. Go out into the streets of Southwark, talk to the mother with the lanced cyst in her groin. To the urchin whose eyes are clean. To the labourer whose leg I set properly. And if I hang, what then, Brother? Who will give a damn? The poor will still die, and the physicians in Cheapside who milk their patients of both money and health will clap their hands to see me dance at the end of a rope.'

Athelstan sat down wearily on the stool. 'I don't want your death,' he replied. 'I want the dead in my cemetery to lie as God expects them to. I want you to go, doctor.' Athelstan rose and dusted down his robe. 'I am sorry I struck you.' He stared at Vincentius. 'But you must be gone from here. I don't know where to, and don't really care, but in a week, I want you out of the city!' Athelstan suddenly felt tired and weak, and realised he hadn't eaten for some time. 'I am sorry I struck you,' he repeated, 'but I was angry.' He suddenly remembered Cranston was waiting for him and looked back at the doctor. 'Oh,' he said, 'you owe me one favour.'

Vincentius sat back in his chair. 'What is that, Father?'

'Well, two to be exact. First, you had a visitor here – Lady Maude Cranston. Why did she come?'

Vincentius grinned. 'The Lady Maude, despite being in her thirtieth year, is now *enceinte.*'

Athelstan stared back in disbelief. 'She's with child!'

'Yes, priest. About two months gone. Both she and the child are healthy, but she is frightened of Sir John not believing her. She doesn't want to disappoint him. I believe they lost a child some years ago?'

Athelstan nodded and the doctor enjoyed the look of stupefaction on the priest's face.

'She told me about Sir John. I advised her most carefully against the pleasures of the flesh. I believe her husband is a mountain of a man?'

'Aye,' Athelstan answered, still dumbstruck at what he had discovered. 'Sir John is certainly that.'

'And the second favour, Father?'

'You served in Outremer?'

'Yes, I did. For a time I practised in hospitals in both Tyre and Sidon.'

'If you met someone there, how would you greet them?'

Now the physician looked surprised.

'*Shalom,*' he answered. 'The usual Semitic phrase for "peace be with you".'

Athelstan lifted his hand. 'Doctor Vincentius, I bid you farewell. I do not expect we will meet again.'

'Priest?'

'Yes, physician?'

'Are you pleased that I am going because of what I have done, or pleased that I am leaving and will not see the widow Benedicta again? You love her, don't you, priest? You, with your sharp accusations against others!'

'No, I don't love her!' Athelstan snapped. But even as he closed the door behind him, he knew that, like St Peter, he was denying the truth.

–

Sir John Cranston, Coroner of the City, squatted bleary-eyed in a corner of the Holy Lamb tavern and stared self-pityingly across Cheapside. He had drunk a good quart of ale. Athelstan had not arrived, so he'd decided to return home. He would deal with his wife like a man should, with abrupt accusations and sharp questions, but he wished the friar had come. He would have liked his advice on so many things.

Cranston leaned back against the wall and squinted across the tavern. The latest business at the Tower was dreadful. He had gone to see Fitzormonde's badly mauled corpse: half the face had been torn away and the man's body savaged almost beyond recognition. Cranston rubbed the side of his own face with his hand. At first Colebrooke had believed the death was an accident.

'It was just after dusk,' the lieutenant had informed him. 'Fitzormonde, as was customary with him, had gone to watch the bear. One second everything was peaceful, the next Satan himself seemed to sweep out of hell. The bear broke loose and mauled the hapless hospitaller. I ordered archers down and the bear was killed.' Colebrooke shrugged. 'Sir John, we had no choice.'

'Was it an accident?' Cranston asked. 'The bear breaking loose?'

'At first we thought so, but when we examined the beast, we found this in one of his hindquarters.' The lieutenant handed Cranston a small bolt from the type of crossbow a lady would use for hunting.

'Who was in the Tower at the time?'

'Everyone,' Colebrooke replied. 'Myself, Mistress Philippa, Rastani, Sir Fulke, Hammond the chaplain – everyone except Master Geoffrey who had returned to his shop in the city.'

Cranston had thanked the lieutenant and gone over to the shabby, dank death house near St Peter ad Vincula where Fitzormonde's mangled remains lay, waiting to be sewn into their canvas shroud. The corpse was hideous, nothing more than a scarred, bloody pile of flesh. Cranston had left as quickly as he could, questioned those he found, and concluded that the crossbow bolt had been loosed by some secret archer: this had goaded the bear to fury and, snapping its chain, it had attacked Fitzormonde.

Cranston gazed one more time round the tavern, sighed and closed his eyes. Was there no way of resolving this problem? he thought. And where the bloody hell was Athelstan?

'My Lord Coroner?'

Cranston opened his eyes. 'Where have you been, monk? And why are you grinning?'

Athelstan smiled and called over to the taverner. 'Two cups of your best Bordeaux. And I mean your finest.' He sat down, still beaming at Sir John. 'My Lord Coroner, I have some news for you.'

Chapter 13

Sir John Cranston sat in the high-backed chair in his spacious, stone-flagged kitchen and stared lovingly at Lady Maude, who was standing at the table filling jars with comfits. He couldn't believe Athelstan's news, not at first. The truth had only sunk in after three further goblets of Bordeaux and Athelstan's repetition of what he had learnt from Doctor Vincentius. At last, Cranston thought, it all makes sense…

He stole a glance at his wife's waist and realised Lady Maude's voluminous skirts would conceal any thickening of the waist; even her nightgowns were quilted, and of course the thought of another child had never occurred to him. After Matthew's death from plague so many years ago at the age of three, Cranston had given up all hope of an heir. He drummed his fingers on the arm of the chair. Lady Maude caught his glance and sniffed into a jar to hide her surprise at Sir John's sudden change of mood. Should she tell him now? she wondered. Or wait, as she had planned, till Christmas Day?

Lady Maude had been stunned by the realisation her monthly courses had ceased and a friend had recommended Doctor Vincentius. The physician had confirmed her hopes and given her sound advice on what to eat and drink and to be gentle with herself. She had to refuse Sir John's amorous embraces but could not tell him the reason. She had to be certain. Lady Maude bit her lip. There was another reason: once Sir John learnt the truth, she would know no peace. He would hang round her like a great shaggy guard dog, watch her every move and give her endless lectures about 'being safe and keeping well'. Lady Maude lowered her face. The child, she silently prayed, must be healthy. She would never forget Sir John when Matthew died. He, who had the courage of a lion, just sat like a little boy, with not a sound, not a moan, nothing save those streams of silent tears.

Sir John's thoughts followed a similar pattern; he had solemnly promised Athelstan not to broach the matter with his wife but wait for her to do so. He had also promised to allow Vincentius to leave London unscathed. However, Cranston narrowed his eyes, he would have to think again about that. Perhaps in the new year letters should be sent to every sheriff in England about Doctor Vincentius and his iniquitous activities in other people's graveyards? The coroner stirred and looked across at Athelstan, who was chatting merrily with Leif the beggar.

'Brother, you will stay for some dinner?'

'No, Sir John, I must go. Perhaps later?'

'And the business at the Tower?'

Athelstan rose from his chair. 'I don't know, Sir John. Perhaps it is best if you eat and reflect on what we have already learnt. We'll discuss it tomorrow, eh?' He looked admiringly at the jars Lady Maude was filling. 'You expect guests at Yuletide?'

'I thought so, Father,' she replied. 'My relatives from Tiverton in Devon.' Lady Maude threw a mock angry glance at Sir John's snort of displeasure. 'They were supposed to come but the roads are impassable, not even messengers can get through. I was talking to one of the aldermen's wives. She said her husband's trade had been badly hurt. All of his journeymen travelling to the south-west have had to turn back.'

Athelstan smiled and Lady Maude went back to her comfits. She strove to hide her agitation as Brother Athelstan informed Sir John that one of his parishioners, a Doctor Vincentius, was leaving Southwark and would not be returning. Lady Maude hid her face. She was sorry the doctor was going. He had been a most skilful man. She sighed and stared at the table. Now she would have to look around for a good physician, someone better than the usual leeches who lived round Cheapside.

Athelstan winked secretively at Cranston, made his farewells, and walked out into the darkening street. He collected Philomel from the stables of the Holy Lamb and rode back through the darkness, chuckling to himself at Sir John's reaction to his news. He hoped Lady Maude had heard his announcement about Vincentius' departure. Perhaps, the friar concluded, it was all for the best.

Philomel suddenly slipped on a strip of ice. Athelstan groaned in despair, dismounted and, gathering the reins in his hands, gently guided the old horse along the darkened pathway. Above him the houses rose sheer and sombre. Outside each of the great Cheapside mansions an oil lamp burned, but as Athelstan turned the corner at St Peter Cornhill and went down Gracechurch into Bridge Street, the tracks became darker. He had to pick his way carefully round the mounds of refuse, night soil and scraps of food where rats gnawed and scampered. Behind him a door slammed and a night bird nesting in the eaves of a house flew out in a burst of black feathers, making Athelstan jump. Beggars whined for alms. A whore stood on the corner, the orange wig straggling across her raddled face made all the more ghastly in the light of the candle she cradled in her hand.

She cackled at Athelstan and made a rude gesture. He sketched the sign of the cross in her direction. A city bully-boy leaning against the door of an ale-house saw the lonely figure and felt his wooden knife hilt. But when he glimpsed Athelstan's tonsure and the crucifix round his neck, he thought better of it.

Athelstan moved on, relieved to see the soldiers in the torchlight guarding London Bridge. Its gates were closed but the city archers recognised 'the coroner's chaplain', as they called Athelstan, and let him through.

The friar crossed the bridge, the sound of Philomel's hoof beats hollow on the wooden planks. It was an eerie experience. Usually the bridge was busy but now it was silent and shrouded in a thick river mist. Athelstan had the ghostly impression of walking across some chasm between heaven and hell. The gulls nesting in the wooden arches below flew out, shrieking in protest at this unexpected disturbance. Athelstan remembered the ravens in the Tower. Another death there, he thought, two if he included the bear. Athelstan felt sorry for the beast.

'Perhaps it was for the best,' he murmured to himself. 'Never have I seen so unhappy an animal.' He recalled the teaching of some of his Franciscan brethren who, following the preaching of their founder, maintained all animals were God's creation and should never be ill-treated or kept in captivity.

Athelstan passed the silent darkened Chapel of St Thomas of Canterbury in the centre of the bridge. The wardsmen on the Southwark bank shouted at him; some of them even wondered if he was a ghost. Athelstan sang out his name and they let him through, teasing him gently about his unexpected appearance.

The friar led Philomel through the dark alleyways of Southwark. He felt safer here. He was known and no one would dare accost him. He passed a tavern where a boy, to earn a few crusts, stood just within the doorway, sweetly singing a carol. Athelstan stopped and listened to words promising warmth and cheer. He patted Philomel on the neck. 'Where will we spend Christmas, eh, old friend?' he asked and walked on. 'Perhaps Lady Cranston might invite me, now her relatives are not coming from the West Country.'

He stopped abruptly. 'Lady Maude's relatives!' he murmured to the dark, quietened street, and felt a shiver go up his spine. 'Strange,' he murmured. 'Something so small, a mere froth on the day's happenings.' He rubbed the side of his face. Lady Maude's words stirred memories of something else he had heard.

He almost dragged Philomel back to St Erconwald's, so eagerly the destrier snickered angrily at him. Athelstan stabled the old war horse, ensured all was well in the church, and guiltily remembered his anger earlier in the day. Bonaventura was apparently out courting so Athelstan went across to the house, built up the fire and hastily ate a piece of bread. After a few bites he tossed it into the fire as the bread was stale, and poured himself a goblet of watered wine. He cleared the rough tabletop and began to list all he knew about the murders in or near the Tower.

The thought which had sparked his memory in the street outside might, he speculated, be the key to resolving the entire problem. He smiled as he remembered old Father Anselm's oft-repeated axiom in his lectures on logic. 'If a problem exists, a solution must exist. It's only a question of finding the path in. Sometimes it can be by the smallest chink of light.' Anselm would then cast a beady eye on Athelstan. 'Always remember that, young Athelstan. It applies as much in the realm of metaphysics as it does to a day's ordinary events.'

Athelstan closed his eyes. 'I still remember that, Father,' he murmured. 'God rest you.' He arranged his writing tray, marshalled his thoughts and dipped the grey goose quill into the ink, cursing when he found it was cold. He held the pot over the candle to warm it and hastily re-read the memoranda he had written when he was in the Tower. Once the ink was heated, he carefully listed his conclusions.

Primo – despite being well protected, Sir Ralph Whitton had been slain in the North Bastion tower. Sir Ralph had slept behind a locked door to which he held the key, as did the guards outside. The door to the passageway in which the chamber stood was also locked; again the keys were shared with his trusted bodyguard. Yet all these precautions had been brought to nothing. His assassin had apparently entered the chamber by crossing the frozen moat and, using footholds in the Tower wall, had climbed up, unlatched the window, entered and slain Sir Ralph.

Secundo – the assassin must have known the Tower well to use these footholds, yet why didn't the clamour of the shutters being opened, not to mention the assassin's entry into the chamber, arouse Sir Ralph? The buckle from Sir Fulke's boot had been found on the ice. Was this a clue to the possible murderer?

Tertio – the young man, Parchmeiner, had been the first person to try and rouse Sir Ralph but the chamber had only been opened by Master Colebrooke the lieutenant.

Did Sir Ralph's second-in-command have a role in this murder?

Athelstan gazed at what he had written, shook his head and smiled. 'No, no!' he whispered. 'All that must wait.'

Quarto – Mowbray had been killed by a fall from the parapet, but how had he slipped? Who had rung the tocsin bell? Who had been absent from Mistress Philippa's chamber? Only two: Fitzormonde and Colebrooke.

Again, Athelstan shook his head.

Quinto – Alderman Horne's death. Athelstan made a face. No clues there whatsoever.

Sexto – Fitzormonde's death? He and Cranston had seen that the bear's chain could have been clasped more securely, and Fitzormonde was in the habit of staring at the bear. But who had been the assassin who fired the bolt and roused the beast to such a murderous rage?

Septimo – Sir Ralph and others had died because of their terrible treachery towards Sir Bartholomew Burghgesh. Had Burghgesh died on that ship so many years ago or had he returned to England? The vicar of Woodforde claimed to have seen him, as had the landlord of the ale-house there. Was this the same mysterious person the landlord at the Golden Mitre tavern had also glimpsed? If so, Burghgesh had been seen by at least three people around Advent three years ago, the same time Sir Ralph Whitton had been in such a state of deep distress. But if Burghgesh had survived and returned to England, how and where was he hiding now? One further problem: Sir Ralph's distress had apparently diminished. Surely this would not have happened if Burghgesh had survived? Sir Ralph would only have taken comfort had he appeared three years ago and died.

Octavo – whoever had sent the sinister notes to Whitton and the others must have access to the Tower. Did Burghgesh or his son, hidden in the city, send their messages and accomplices into the Tower?

Nono – who stood to profit from the murders? Colebrooke? He wanted promotion and knew the Tower well. He had been present in the Tower when all three had died. Sir Fulke? He, too, benefited from his brother's death; his buckle had been found on the ice outside the North Bastion tower. He also knew the Tower well and had been there when the two hospitallers perished. Rastani? A stealthy, subtle man who might have taken his own vow of vengeance against Sir Ralph and his companions. He knew the fortress well and had been present when the hospitallers died.

Athelstan shook his head. The same applied to Hammond, that rather sinister chaplain. Or was it Mistress Philippa in collusion with her lover? And what about Red Hand, the mad man who perhaps was more sane than he appeared?

Athelstan looked up and gasped. Red Hand! The hunchbacked albino had mentioned secret dungeons being bricked up, and Simon the carpenter had mumbled something similar.

Athelstan sat for a while, head in his hands. He picked up his pen, stared round the darkening kitchen and glimpsed a bunch of holly in the far corner. Christmas in a few days, he thought. He got up, warmed his fingers over the brazier and wished Benedicta was with him to share a cup of mulled wine. He recalled Doctor Vincentius' words about his affection for the widow, and stared into the fire. Was it so obvious? he wondered. Did the other parishioners recognise his feelings as well? He shook his head to clear his mind. No, he must concentrate on the problem in hand. A shutter clattered and Athelstan jumped as a dark shadow pounced on to the rush-strewn floor.

'Bonaventura!' he muttered. The cat padded over and brushed majestically against the friar's leg. 'Well, Master Cat, you have come for something to eat?'

The cat stretched, arching his back. Athelstan went into the buttery, filled a cracked, pewter bowl full of milk and watched the cat lap it up before going to stretch out in front of the fire. Athelstan went across and fastened the shutters: windows, doors and passageways, he thought, recalling once again Red Hand's mutterings and Simon the carpenter's dark warnings. Athelstan looked enviously at the cat. 'It's all right for some,' he grumbled and sat down before his parchments to continue his study. He took each name, building up a line of argument as if he was preparing some theological disputation.

The hours passed. Athelstan rubbed his eyes wearily. Only one path remained open: the one shown by Lady Maude's innocent remarks which had so abruptly startled him on his journey back to Southwark. Athelstan drew a rough plan of the Tower and continued to pursue the conclusions he had reached. Just before dawn he pronounced himself satisfied. He had found the assassin, though very little else. For that he would need Cranston.

–

The next morning Sir John rode like a young knight down Cheapside to the Golden Mitre tavern near the Tower. The coroner felt as if he was riding on air. Even the cold morning breeze felt as warm and soft as the caress of a young woman.

Cranston had embraced the Lady Maude most passionately before getting out of bed that morning. She had clung tearfully to his chest and muttered about speaking to him soon. He had murmured sweet nothings, patted her on the head, rose, dressed and, going downstairs, bellowed for a cup of sack whilst a groom saddled his horse. Sir John felt as proud as a peacock to know he would be a father again. He rewarded himself with a swig from his 'miraculous wineskin', as Athelstan called it, sucking the robust red juice into his mouth. He beamed around expansively. Oh, it was a fine day to be alive!

Sir John scattered pennies before a group of beggars shivering on the corner of the Mercery. He shouted cheerful abuse at the poulterers who were cleaning and gutting chickens and other fowl in their huge iron vats for the Christmas season. A whore was being led bare-shouldered through the streets, her head shaved close under a conical white cap. A bagpiper went before her whilst a scrawled notice, pinned to her dirty bodice, proclaimed her a public slut. Cranston stopped the procession and had her freed.

'Why, Sir John?' the rat-mouthed bailiff asked.

'Because it's Christmas!' he roared back. 'And Christ the beautiful boy of Bethlehem will be with us once again!'

The bailiff was going to object but Cranston's hand fell to his dagger, so the fellow cut the woman's bonds. She stuck out her tongue at the bailiff, made an obscene gesture at Cranston and scampered off up an alleyway. Sir John rode on into Petty Wales. He arrived at the tavern and, tossing the reins of his horse to a groom, swaggered into the sweet-smelling tap room.

'Monk, where the hell are you?' he bellowed, giving the other customers the fright of their lives and bringing a wide-eyed taverner scurrying to attend to him.

'Sir John, you are happy?'

'As a fly on a horse's arse in summer!' Sir John bawled back. He threw the miraculous wineskin at the taverner. 'Fill that! The friar told me to meet him here,' he muttered. He gazed through the smoke and gloom and glimpsed Athelstan, nodding half-asleep over a table.

'Bring a cup of sack for me,' Cranston ordered the landlord. 'Fresh oatcakes, and a strip of dry gammon!' He smacked his lips. 'Some eel stew for the Brother and, even though it's Advent, he'll take a jug of watered ale!'

The coroner swaggered across and tapped the half-sleeping friar on the shoulder. 'Arouse yourself, Brother!' he bawled. 'For, by the sod, the devil walks, roaring like a lion seeking whom he may devour!'

'I hope he's not as heavy-handed as you, Cranston,' Athelstan grumbled, opening his eyes and gazing wearily up.

Cranston crouched down beside him. 'Good morrow, monk.'

'I am a friar.'

'Good morrow, friar. And why are you not so full of the joys of Yuletide?'

'Because, Sir John, I am cold, tired and totally dispirited.' Athelstan was about to continue the litany of his woes when he caught the mischief dancing like devils in Cranston's eyes. 'It's good to see you happy, Sir John. I suppose you have ordered food?'

Cranston nodded, swept his great beaver hat off his head and slumped down on the bench opposite.

They had eaten their fill and Cranston downed two cups of claret before Athelstan had finished his story. The coroner shook his head, asked a few questions and whistled softly under his breath.

'By the sod, are you sure, Brother? So much from an innocent little remark by the Lady Maude?'

Athelstan shrugged. 'Lady Maude's little comments have caused a great deal of consternation in the last few days, Sir John.'

Cranston belched, rose, and bellowed for his wineskin, tossing coins at the taverner. 'You have carried out my instructions, Sir John?' Athelstan asked.

'Yes, friar, I have.' Sir John stretched and yawned. 'All our suspects are waiting in the Tower, though Parchmeiner will arrive late. You want to see Colebrooke first?'

'And Red Hand?'

'Ah, yes, Red Hand.'

'You have the warrant, Sir John?'

'I don't need any bloody warrants, monk! I am Cranston, the King's Coroner in the City, and they will either answer the question or face the consequences.'

They made their way out of the tavern where they left their horses, down some alleyways and through the great yawning entrance to the Tower. Colebrooke was waiting for them at the gatehouse. Athelstan noticed he was wearing hauberk, mailed shirt and leggings.

'You are expecting trouble, Master Lieutenant?'

'Sir John's instructions seem most stringent,' Colebrooke replied.

'Where's Red Hand?'

'What do you want that mad bugger for?'

'Because I ordered it,' Cranston replied.

They crossed the green, the sparse grass now visible beneath the wide swathes of grey slush. Two soldiers trailed behind. Colebrooke sent one across to the small door in the base of the White Tower. Athelstan stared sadly across at the far corner where the great bear had sat, now empty and forlorn, but the ground still showed the marks of its occupation and a few pathetic scraps of food still littered the icy cobblestones.

'God rest the bear's soul!' Athelstan murmured.

Cranston turned. 'Do bears have souls, friar? Do they go to heaven?'

Athelstan grinned. 'If your heaven needs bears, Sir John, then there will be bears! But, in your case, I suppose heaven will be miles and miles of taverns and spacious alehouses!'

Cranston slapped his thigh with his gauntlet. 'Oh, I like you, Brother.' And he beamed at a surprised Colebrooke.

Suddenly the door of the White Tower was thrown open and the soldier re-emerged, dragging Red Hand by the scruff of the neck.

'Let him go!' Athelstan shouted. He went across, crouched and clasped the hunchback's hand in his. He stared into the madcap's milky eyes and saw the tear stains on his raddled cheeks. 'You mourn the bear, Red Hand?'

'Yes. Red Hand's friend has gone.'

Athelstan looked at the soldier and indicated he should move away. 'I know, Red Hand,' Athelstan whispered. 'The bear was a magnificent beast, but he will be happy now. His spirit's free.'

Red Hand's watery eyes caught Athelstan's. The madman smiled. 'You're Red Hand's friend?'

Athelstan studied the hunchback's face, his scrawny, white hair and grotesque mottled rags. He recalled Father

Anselm's other words of wisdom: 'Always remember, Athelstan, every man is in God's image. A flame burns as fiercely in a broken jar as it does in the most elaborately carved lamp.'

'I am your friend,' Athelstan replied. 'But I need your help.'

Red Hand's eyes became wary.

'I want you to show me your secrets.'

'What secrets, Master?'

'What the bloody hell are you doing, Brother?'

Athelstan threw a warning glance at the coroner.

'Look, Red Hand,' Athelstan whispered. 'You talked to me of chambers, dungeons, which were bricked up.'

Red Hand tried to prise his fingers free of Athelstan's, but the friar held firm.

'Please,' he murmured. 'Did Sir Ralph have such secret cells? If you tell me, Red Hand, I can trap the man responsible for the bear's death.'

The madman needed no further encouragement. He turned. 'Wait! Wait there!' he pleaded, and ran back through the small door of the White Tower. He re-emerged a few seconds later with a little bell which he tinkled. 'Follow Red Hand!' he shouted. 'Follow Red Hand!'

Cranston looked in disbelief at Athelstan. Colebrooke seemed angry.

'What's the little sod up to?' Cranston murmured as the scampering madcap led them across Tower Green to a door which had rusted firmly shut at the foot of Wakefield Tower. Red Hand stopped at the door, bowed three times and tinkled his bell.

'What's in there?'

Colebrooke shrugged. 'Some dungeons dug deep into the earth.'

'Open it!'

'I haven't got any keys.'

'Don't be obstructive,' Cranston barked. 'Open the bloody thing!'

Colebrooke turned, hands on hips, and yelled orders. Soldiers ran over. Under Colebrooke's instruction, they wheeled across a huge battering ram, swinging its iron head against the door until it buckled and swung off its hinges.

'Torches!' Cranston ordered.

Cressets were brought and hastily lit. Red Hand scampered down the slime-covered stairs, which fell away into icy cold darkness. At the bottom of the steps ran a small corridor, narrow, dank and evil-smelling. On the right nothing but mildewed walls; on the left two cell doors, their locks rusted shut. Athelstan stiffened as he heard squeaks and rustles and, spinning round, glimpsed a brown, greasy body slinking away into the darkness.

'Break the doors down!' Cranston bellowed.

The soldiers attacked the heavy but rotting wood, smashing open a huge hole. Athelstan took a torch and went in. There was nothing there except rats, squeaking and scampering on a rotting pile of straw in the far corner.

'Hell's teeth!' Cranston hissed. 'Nothing!'

They clambered out through the open door. Cranston held the torch up and examined the wall between the doors.

'Look, Athelstan!' he exclaimed.

The friar studied the wall carefully.

'There's another door,' Cranston continued. 'But it's been bricked up. Look, it bulges out and the plaster is fresher than the rest of the wall.'

'You found it! You found it! You found it!' Red Hand clapped his hands and jumped up and down like a child playing a game. 'They have found the secret door!' he sang out. 'They've won the game!' The madcap stopped shouting. 'I did that,' he announced proudly. 'Sir Ralph Whitton told me to do it. The door was locked and I bricked up the entrance.'

'When?' Athelstan asked.

'Oh, years ago. Years ago!'

Cranston snapped his fingers. 'Smash that wall down!'

The soldiers set to with iron-headed mallets and hammers. Soon the corridor was thick with a foul white dust.

'There's a door!' one of them exclaimed.

'And that too!' Cranston ordered.

In a few minutes the rotting wood behind the destroyed wall buckled and snapped, the soldiers creating a large enough hole for Cranston and Athelstan to crawl through. Torches were ordered and Cranston held one up.

'Oh, Good Lord!' Cranston whispered, staring at the decaying skeleton slumped on a bed of rotted muck. 'Who is that? And what terrible son of Satan ordered such a hideous death?'

'To answer your questions, Sir John, I suspect these are the mortal remains of Sir Bartholomew Burghgesh. And Whitton, a man steeped in murder, ordered it.'

'Look!' Sir John hissed, snatching the torch and holding it up against the wall just where the white skeletal arm rested. Athelstan peered at the crude drawing of the three-masted ship carved into the stone, the same as had been found on the letters sent to Sir Ralph and others. Cranston's eyes rounded in surprise.

'Brother, you are right.'

'Yes, Sir John. Now, let's see if the rest of my theory has substance.'

They told Colebrooke to leave guards near the cell and eagerly returned to the cold brisk air of Tower Green.

'What did you find?' the lieutenant asked anxiously, coming up behind them.

'Be patient, Master Lieutenant. But come, I have further favours to ask of you.'

Athelstan guided him by the elbow away from the rest. Cranston watched the friar and soldier talk quietly together.

'Is Red Hand needed?' The hunchback suddenly appeared, jumping up and down.

Cranston smiled, dug into his purse and pushed two silver pieces into the man's hand, patting him gently on the cheek.

'Not for the moment, Red Hand. But you have my thanks and that of the Regent, the Mayor, and the city of London.'

The hunchback's eyes danced with delight. He ran off, leaping with glee, cavorting and laughing at the dark ravens which cawed noisily above him.

'Red Hand's a champion! Red Hand's a champion!' he yelled.

Athelstan rejoined Sir John. 'The lieutenant has his orders,' he murmured. 'Come, My Lord Coroner, the drama is about to begin.'

The rest of the Tower household were waiting in Philippa's chamber. Sir Fulke was dressed most elegantly in a dark gown of gold-fringed murrey. Philippa, now wearing full mourning weeds and a black veil, sat in the window seat, head bowed over a piece of embroidery. Rastani crouched by the fireplace, the chaplain sat on a stool opposite. All except Philippa looked up and glowered as Athelstan and Cranston entered.

'We have been waiting for an hour,' Sir Fulke bellowed.

'Good!' Sir John replied. 'And, by the sod, you will wait another bloody hour if I want it! We are here on the King's business. Four men lie dead, one of them Sir Ralph Whitton, a high-ranking official, albeit a perfect bastard!'

Mistress Philippa looked up, her face a white mask of fury. Athelstan closed his eyes, even as Sir John gave the girl his most profuse apologies.

'So, shall we begin?' Sir Fulke shouted.

'In a while, in a while,' Athelstan murmured. 'We wait for Master Colebrooke and young Geoffrey, I believe.'

Cranston slumped on to a window seat next to Philippa but she turned her back. Athelstan brought a stool across and set out his writing tray, ink stand and pen on the table before him. Colebrooke, breathing heavily, pushed open the door.

'All is ready, Sir John.' The lieutenant went over to Athelstan. 'Here, Brother!'

Athelstan clasped his hand and hid up his voluminous sleeve what the lieutenant had given him. The friar stared round the silent chamber. It is here, he thought, we shall trap the murderer.

Chapter 14

Cranston twiddled his thumbs and beamed around. Athelstan noticed with quiet amusement that beneath his cloak Sir John was wearing doublet and hose of a deep bottle-green, with silver fringes and buttons to match. One of the coroner's best set of robes, a sure sign Cranston was in good fettle. The rest of the group, however, remained subdued: Hammond staring at the floor, Rastani gazing into the fire. Sir Fulke bit his lip and tapped his foot impatiently. Colebrooke fidgeted whilst Philippa stabbed furiously at a piece of embroidery. Footsteps sounded outside, the door swung open and Parchmeiner entered. Athelstan glimpsed the guards outside and was glad Colebrooke had the sense to have armed soldiers nearby. The young man was red-cheeked and breathless. He smiled at Philippa, crossed the room and kissed her gently on the lips before gazing round expectantly.

'Sir John! Brother Athelstan! Why the sudden affray?'

The friar rose. 'Shalom, Geoffrey!'

'Peace to you, Brother.' The young man's face was suddenly tinged a deep red.

Athelstan smiled. 'How do you know the Arabic word for peace?'

The young man shrugged. 'I buy and sell. I know more than one language.'

'Pull back your cuffs, Master Parchmeiner!'

269

The young man looked flustered. 'Why?'

'Pull them back!'

'I can't see...'

'Pull them back!' Cranston ordered. 'Now!'

Parchmeiner undid the embroidered cuffs and Athelstan gazed down at the white rings which broke the dark flesh of the man's wrists.

'How did you come by the marks of slave manacles?' Athelstan asked. 'Trading?' He moved quickly and suddenly pulled the man's knife from his belt and tossed it across to Cranston. 'And how are your relatives in Bristol? Have you heard from them?'

The young man's eyes narrowed and Athelstan noticed his determined mouth and chin. The veil was slipping. In future, Athelstan promised himself quietly, he would study faces more closely.

'Don't lie, Geoffrey. You have no relatives in Bristol. You sent no letters. The West Country has been cut off by snow. How could you be in communication with people in Bristol when the western roads have been impassable?' Athelstan smiled bleakly at Cranston. 'Isn't it strange how such an innocent remark brought all these matters to a head?' Athelstan stepped closer, aware of the sudden change of atmosphere in the room. Philippa now stood, her fist pressed to her mouth. The others were tense, immobile as statues.

'But your name's not Parchmeiner, is it?' Cranston barked.

Athelstan took a step nearer. 'Who are you?' he said quietly. 'Mark Burghgesh?'

A smile flickered across Parchmeiner's face as he tried to assert himself. 'What nonsense is this?' he snapped. 'Philippa, I have known you two years. I come from

Bristol. My sister lives there. She will be here in a few days.'

Athelstan shook his head. 'No, she won't, young man. That road is blocked, both literally and metaphorically. Moreover,' he continued, 'you still haven't told us about the rings round your wrists.'

The young man looked away. 'I used to wear bracelets,' he lied glibly.

'This is nonsense,' Philippa intervened. 'Are you going to accuse Geoffrey of my father's murder?'

'Yes, I am!' Athelstan announced.

'But someone climbed the North Bastion!'

'No, they didn't!' Athelstan looked at Colebrooke. 'Master Lieutenant, you have everything ready?'

Colebrooke blinked nervously and nodded.

'Then let us begin,' Cranston barked. 'Master Lieutenant, you have armed guards and archers, both in the corridor and downstairs?'

'Yes, Sir John.'

'Good. They will guard everyone here. If anyone attempts to escape, shoot them!'

With Cranston leading, they walked out of the chamber, down the stairs and out across Tower Green beyond the first curtain wall to where the lonely, bleak North Bastion stood. They entered the doorway and stood in the porch where the two soldiers stood expectantly on guard. On the far wall there was a wooden rack with metal hooks from which keys hung.

'Now,' Athelstan said to the guards, 'on the morning Sir Ralph was found dead... tell me again what happened.'

One of the soldiers grimaced. 'I takes young Parchmeiner upstairs,' he said. 'No, I take the key from the rack.

I takes him upstairs. I unlocks the door to the passageway, let him through, lock it and come down.'

'Then what?'

'Well,' the second soldier interrupted, 'we hear Master Geoffrey calling Sir Ralph.'

'What happened then?' Athelstan asked.

'He comes back and knocks on the door.' The fellow pointed to the top of the stairs. 'We unlock it, he comes down and sends for the lieutenant.'

'No,' Athelstan interrupted. 'Something else happened, or so you told us.'

One of the guards scratched his unshaven chin.

'Ah,' his companion spoke up. 'I knows what. Young Geoffrey said he would rouse Sir Ralph himself and we gives him the key. He then goes up the stairs, changes his mind, comes back, returns the key and goes for Master Colebrooke.'

'Good,' Athelstan smiled. 'Now, Sir John, I will retrace Parchmeiner's steps.' He glanced quickly at the young man, whose face was pale, eyes narrowed and watchful. Philippa was staring at him like a child who cannot explain the sudden, unexpected mood of a parent. Sir Fulke and the chaplain stood bemused but Athelstan noticed the mute Rastani had edged closer to Parchmeiner, his hand not far from the knife hilt stuck in his scabbard.

'My Lord Coroner,' Athelstan exclaimed, 'before we go any further, everyone should give up their arms except Lieutenant Colebrooke.'

There were mild protests, but Cranston repeated Athelstan's order and knives and swords clattered to the ground in an untidy heap.

'Now we shall begin,' Athelstan said. 'Sir John, you will start counting?'

The friar nodded to one of the guards. 'Unlock the door at the top!'

Cranston bellowed out the numbers as Athelstan went upstairs. The door swung open and was locked behind him. Cranston stopped for a few seconds at number twenty as he heard Athelstan call out Sir Ralph's name before continuing. He had just passed the number fifty when he heard Athelstan pounding on the door at the top of the steps. One of the guards ran up and opened the door. Athelstan emerged. He tripped down the steps behind the soldier.

'Now,' the friar exclaimed, 'I want the key to Sir Ralph's chamber!'

Athelstan took one of the keys from its hook and went halfway back up the stairs, shook his head and came down.

'On second thought,' he said, 'let us send for Master Colebrooke.' He handed the key back to the soldier. 'Tell me,' the friar asked, 'did I take any longer than young Geoffrey?'

'No, about the same. He was a little longer in the passageway, but not much.'

Sir Fulke pushed his way forward. 'What does this all mean?' he demanded.

Athelstan smiled. 'Now I will show you. Master lieutenant, re-open the door at the top of the stairs and let us all go up.'

The lieutenant ran to re-open the door and they all followed him down the cold, vaulted passageway. Colebrooke unlocked Whitton's chamber and they followed him in. Sir Fulke promptly cursed. Philippa gave a short scream. The chamber was icy cold, the shutters wide open, and the bolster on the dirty, grey mattress of the four-poster bed had been savagely slashed, the goose feathers trickling out in grisly reminder of Sir Ralph's murder.

'Who did this? What evil nonsense is this?' Hammond the chaplain spoke up.

Athelstan ignored him and confronted Parchmeiner.

'You know what I have done,' he said quietly. 'Exactly what you did on the morning you murdered Sir Ralph, and I'll tell you how. First, when Sir Ralph moved to the North Bastion, you acted the role of the obsequious future son-in-law. You helped him move a few possessions across. You see, the chamber was guarded when Sir Ralph moved in but not before, so you carefully oiled the hinges and the lock of the door, which explains the oil stains in the corridor outside. Secondly, the floor above is sealed off, and at the far end of the corridor outside is a pile of fallen masonry. You hid a dagger there amongst the rubble, as I asked Colebrooke to conceal Sir John's. After I slashed the bolster, I hid the dagger there again. On the night before Sir Ralph died, you sat with him at table. You helped him to drink deeply, aided probably by a fairly strong sleeping potion, enough to make him drowsy. Thirdly, you helped Sir Ralph to the foot of the steps, the guards took him up to his chamber, and it is probably then that you exchanged the keys. You took the one Sir Ralph left there for the use of the guards and slipped another on to the hook. I asked Colebrooke to do the same. He handed the real key to me when we were in Mistress Philippa's chamber.' Athelstan paused. 'The next morning you come across, the guards search you, but you have nothing except your own harmless possessions, which,' Athelstan touched the young man's side carefully, 'like any merchant, include a ring of keys. You climb the steps, the guards let you through, and you proceed to Sir Ralph's chamber. As you knock and shout, you open the door silently because the lock hinges are so well oiled. The rest was easy.'

'But—' Colebrooke intervened.

'Not yet,' Athelstan snapped back. He studied Parchmeiner's eyes carefully. 'Once inside, you move very quickly. The shutters are unlatched, the cold air streams in. You cross to Whitton's bed and yank his head back. Sir Ralph, still in a heavy stupor, may have opened his eyes for a brief few seconds as you slashed his throat. You wipe the knife on the bedclothes, lock the door, slip the knife back into its hiding place and stand knocking on the door at the far end of the corridor.'

Athelstan saw the faint look of amusement in Parchmeiner's eyes, though the young man's face remained cold and impassive.

'It was then,' Athelstan continued, 'that you slipped the key to Sir Ralph's chamber off your ring. You go downstairs, ask for the false key, go back up the steps and make the sudden change whilst your back is turned. You return the correct key to the guards. I have just proved two keys can look alike. You then go looking for Colebrooke.'

'Oh, no!' Philippa, her face now white and drawn, as she slumped against Sir Fulke, her eyes fixed on Geoffrey. 'Oh, please God, no!' she repeated.

'It happened that way,' Cranston airily declared. 'My clerk has proved it. The guards simply saw and heard what they were supposed to.'

'Brother Athelstan!'

'Yes, Sir Fulke?'

'My brother's body was cold when the lieutenant came up.'

'Of course it was,' Cranston snapped. 'The brazier and the fire had died, which makes me think Whitton was drugged. The murderer threw the shutters open and the icy air rushed in. Remember, it was a freezing cold morning, and of course Master Parchmeiner's delay in sending for Colebrooke would have helped matters.'

Athelstan suddenly caught a glimpse of colour from the corner of his eyes. 'Sir John! Rastani!'

The coroner, in spite of his bulk, moved quickly. He caught the mute even as the fellow sprang at his master's assassin. Cranston hoisted the struggling man by the front of his jerkin as easily as a baby.

'You, sir,' the coroner said quietly, 'will keep your place till these matters are finished!' He shook Rastani as if he was a rag doll. 'You understand?'

The mute threw one vicious glance at Parchmeiner.

'Do you understand?' Cranston's grip tightened.

The mute's mouth opened and shut, then he nodded slowly. Cranston gently lowered him and two of Colebrooke's guards now took up position on either side of the Moor.

'You will watch him!' Cranston ordered curtly. 'Well, come on, pull your swords!'

During this spectacle, Parchmeiner never turned a hair but looked coolly at the friar, who knew he was in the presence of a natural killer, someone who had seized his opportunity to wreak the most terrible vengeance.

'Master Colebrooke!' Athelstan called, not taking his eyes off the murderer. 'I want Master Parchmeiner's hands bound and a rope tied round his waist.'

Colebrooke rapped out commands and one of the guards forced Parchmeiner's arms behind his back, tying both wrists and thumbs together. Another soldier unloosed his belt and pushed one end through Parchmeiner's, wrapping the other end tightly round his own wrist guard. Athelstan relaxed. He gazed round the freezing death chamber.

'We need not stay here,' he declared. 'We may return to Mistress Philippa's chamber.'

The young girl hardly said a word but moaned softly as her uncle enfolded her in his arms. The group left the North Bastion. As they crossed Tower Green, Colebrooke, now aware of the danger, ordered a serjeant-at-arms to beat the tambour, calling the garrison to arms. Orders rang out, gates were closed, and as they went up the steps to Philippa's chamber, Athelstan heard men-at-arms and archers taking up positions below. He turned and smiled at Cranston.

'I must apologise. Your dagger is still in the pile of masonry in the North Bastion tower.'

'Don't worry,' he muttered. 'What I have seen is worth more than a thousand daggers.'

In the chamber, Parchmeiner stood between the two guards. Athelstan looked at him curiously for the young man was now smiling as if savouring some secret joke. The rest were a quiet, captive audience. Rastani, sullen and withdrawn, slumped on a stool between two burly serjeants-at-arms. Philippa moaned softly, lost in her own grief, flanked on either side by her uncle and the chaplain. Cranston filled himself a goblet of wine. Athelstan went and crouched near the fire, warming his hands over the flames.

'The other deaths were easy,' he continued evenly. 'The night Mowbray died, he went up on the parapet near the Salt Tower whilst the rest of you gathered here in Philippa's chamber for supper. I suspect Master Parchmeiner arrived last. You see Mowbray, like any soldier,' he turned and grinned at Colebrooke, 'was a creature of habit. Let us dismiss Master Parchmeiner's fear of heights as a lie. He knew Mowbray was on the far side of the parapet, standing in his usual spot, so he crept up and placed the butt of a spear or an axe pole at the top of the steps, wedging it neatly between the crenellations of the wall. He then comes to Mistress Philippa's chamber and the meal begins.'

'But he never left,' Sir Fulke interrupted. 'He never left to ring the tocsin bell!'

'Of course he didn't!' Cranston answered. 'Master Colebrooke, everything is ready? The garrison has been warned? Well,' Cranston slammed his wine goblet down on the table, 'I need to relieve myself. I understand there's a garderobe down the passage?'

Sir Fulke, a perplexed look on his face, nodded. Cranston went out of the side door. The rest of the group remained impassive like figures in a fresco. Suddenly everyone jumped as the great tocsin bell began to sound, followed by shouted orders, men's feet running, and then the bell stopped tolling. Cranston, grinning from ear to ear, sauntered back into the room.

'Who rang the bell?' the chaplain squeaked.

'I did,' Sir John replied.

'How?'

'What Sir John did,' Athelstan replied quietly, turning his back to the fire, 'was to go along to the garderobe. An archer, carrying a small arbalest, went with him. I noticed that the window above the privy overlooked Tower Green. The archer, standing behind the curtain which hides the privy, shot a bolt and hit the bell.' Athelstan shrugged. 'You know the mechanism. Once it is tilted slightly the bell begins to toll.'

'But it was dark,' Sir Fulke spoke up.

'No, Sir Fulke. As you may remember, at night there are torches around the bell.'

'But the bolt was never found!'

'Of course not. The snow around the tocsin was thick and undisturbed. The bolt would hit the bell and fall into the snow. When the soldiers from the garrison checked why the bell had been rung, they would be looking for footprints, not a crossbow bolt, no bigger than your hand, embedded deep in the snow and ice.'

'And the crossbow?' Parchmeiner spoke for the first time, his voice harsh and staccato.

Athelstan shook his head. 'Like the dagger, you could have left it in the corridor and, when finished, replaced it or dropped it down the privy hole. And who would notice? As you hastily left the garderobe and ran back to the chamber, everything was in uproar as the tocsin sounded. No one would see any connection between your leaving and the bell sounding. You had gone to the privy, not downstairs, and the guards had seen no one approach the bell. The rest was easy,' Athelstan murmured. 'In night-shrouded confusion, you ran up to the parapet and tossed the weapon over the wall into the ditch. If anyone saw you on the steps, you could always pass as a hero looking for the cause of poor Mowbray's death.' Athelstan looked at Cranston. 'When Sir John told me about the crossbow bolt found embedded in the bear, I suddenly realised how the tocsin bell could have been so mysteriously sounded.' Athelstan felt suddenly tired and rubbed his face with his hands.

'God knows,' the coroner boomed, going to stand legs apart in front of the prisoner, 'how you lured poor Horne to his death, though the man was so full of fears it would be easy enough to play on them.' Cranston clutched

Parchmeiner's face in his hand and squeezed it tightly. 'I saw the grisly remains of your work.'

Parchmeiner brought his head back, smiled, and spat full into Cranston's face. The coroner wiped the spittle from his cheek with the hem of his robe then, bringing his hand back, slapped Parchmeiner across the face. He turned and looked at Athelstan as the young man struggled between his guards.

'Don't worry,' Cranston said. 'I won't strike him again, but he deserved that for bringing his evil deeds into my house and under my roof.'

He went and refilled his wine goblet. He took it over and offered it to Philippa where she sat with her uncle, but she wouldn't even raise her head. Sir Fulke looked away so Cranston walked into the middle of the room, sipping from the cup. 'Finally, Fitzormonde's death.' He made a face. 'That was easy.' He gestured at Parchmeiner. 'Our young killer here pretends to leave the Tower, and with people milling about during the great thaw, no one would really notice him slipping back in again, perhaps wearing a different cloak or hood. There are enough shadowy corners in this fortress to hide an army. Every evening Fitzormonde always went to see the bear and Parchmeiner seized this opportunity. Once again armed with an arbalest, he fires. The beast, enraged, launches itself at Fitzormonde. The badly secured chain snaps and the hospitaller dies. Whilst Geoffrey exploits the chaos to slip through the main gate or one of the postern doors and be safe beyond reproach.'

'You have no proof!' Parchmeiner rasped. 'No proof at all!'

'No, but we can get it!' Athelstan answered. 'First, I can prove that a man may climb the North Bastion in the middle of the night and at the dead of winter. But could he climb down again? I can examine the rubble outside Sir Ralph's chamber for stains of blood from the dagger you hid there but undoubtedly collected later. Master Colebrooke can also make enquiries about who oiled the locks and doors of Sir Ralph's chambers. The tocsin can be examined for the mark of a crossbow bolt and the ground carefully searched, for it undoubtedly still lies hidden in the ice and snow. We could start making enquiries about who was where on the night Adam Horne died.' Athelstan walked up to the white-faced man. 'We can also hold you in a dungeon here until the snow melts, and make careful investigations after these friends and relatives of yours in Bristol.'

'But why? Why?' Philippa's gaunt face was anguished, dark shadows appearing under her reddened eyes. 'Why?' she screamed.

'Fifteen years ago,' Cranston replied, too full of pity to look at her, 'your father and the others whom Parchmeiner murdered served as knights in Outremer under the leadership of Sir Bartholomew Burghgesh. You have heard the name mentioned? Your father,' Cranston continued, not waiting for a reply, 'and the others cruelly betrayed Sir Bartholomew in order to seize certain treasure he had taken from the Caliph of Egypt. Now Sir Bartholomew left Cyprus for Genoa but the others, led by Sir Ralph, secretly informed the Caliph and the ship Sir Bartholomew was travelling on was attacked.' Cranston scratched his head. 'The accepted story is that Bartholomew died on that ship but, as we now know, three years ago, just before Christmas, Burghgesh came to see your father at the Tower. Sir Ralph, either by trickery or force, took Sir Bartholomew captive and imprisoned him in a dungeon beneath this very tower. He used the madcap Red Hand to block up the cell. After all, who would listen to the rantings of an idiot?' Cranston whirled round as the young man struggled between his guards.

'He is here?' Geoffrey shouted. 'Bartholomew's body is here?' Parchmeiner suddenly went limp. 'Oh, God!' he whispered. 'If only I had known!'

Athelstan crossed to his side. All the hatred and arrogance in the assassin's face had now fled and the friar felt a twinge of compassion at the tears brimming in the young man's eyes.

'Who are you?' Athelstan whispered. 'Tell me! You have my promise, you will see Bartholomew's last resting place.'

Parchmeiner looked down at the floor. 'Burghgesh was not my father,' he replied in a faraway voice. 'But I wish to God he had been. I was on the same ship as him when it was taken. I was only an orphan, so I clung to Sir Bartholomew.' Geoffrey smiled faintly. 'He protected me,' he whispered. 'He put me behind him and fought like a paladin until the Moors promised both of us our lives if he surrendered.' The young man looked up and blinked. 'They kept their word, but Bartholomew was beaten with the bastinado until the soles of his feet turned to raw flesh. Then we were sold as slaves to a merchant in Alexandria. Sir Bartholomew tended the garden and I was put to work in the scriptorium, curing and storing parchment. The years passed. Sir Bartholomew never gave up hope. He looked after me, treated me as a son, protected me against those who would have preferred to treat me like a woman. One night, Bartholomew cut our master's throat and rifled his treasure room. We fled across the desert to Damietta, bribed a merchant and took ship to Cyprus, thence to Genoa and across Europe to Southampton.'

'How long ago was this?'

'Three years ago. Sir Bartholomew had told me about Whitton and the treasure but,' the young man's voice almost broke, 'my master was good and true. He still couldn't accept that his comrades—' the words were spat out '—his *comrades* had betrayed him!' The young man shook his head, mouthing oaths quietly to himself. 'We travelled to London. Sir Bartholomew still had the treasure he had stolen from the merchant in Alexandria, gold and silver coins, so we lived like lords in a tavern near Barbican Street.' Geoffrey now stared at Athelstan. 'Can you believe that, Brother? He wouldn't accept he had been betrayed. He left me in the tavern and went to Woodforde, but returned disconsolate. His wife and son were both dead and the manor house in disrepair. We stayed for a while until Sir Bartholomew said his comrades would meet as planned near the Tower every Advent before Christmas.' The young man licked his lips. 'Sir Bartholomew made enquiries as to what had happened to each of his comrades. Two were hospitallers, one a merchant.' Geoffrey laughed. 'Sir Bartholomew, God bless him, was even pleased to hear that Whitton was now Constable of the Tower and told me all about this fortress, every nook and cranny.'

The murderer stirred restlessly between his captors, now lost in his own memories. 'Bartholomew went to meet Whitton. He said he would find out the truth, whatever it cost.' The young man made a grimace. 'But he didn't return and my own suspicions were proved correct. Whitton, who had betrayed him fifteen years ago, had now used his position to have Bartholomew killed.' He glared at Athelstan. 'I am glad I killed them! I gave them fair warning. I used the same sign Bartholomew always shared with me in our captivity – the three-masted ship which brought us together.'

'And me?' Philippa cried. 'What about me?'

'What about you?'

'Didn't you love me?'

The young man laughed. 'You need a heart to love, Philippa. I have no heart, no soul. Bartholomew was my life.' He dismissed the girl with a contemptuous glance. 'I used you,' he continued, ignoring her loud sobbing. 'I took Bartholomew's gold to plot Whitton's downfall. I knew about manuscripts and vellum, so I became Geoffrey Parchmeiner. Oh, by the way, Geoffrey is my Christian name. Geoffrey Burghgesh, you can call me. I sold the best parchment for a pittance to the Tower. I became friendly with the constable's daughter and wheedled my way into her affections.' The murderer smiled to himself.

'You studied the constable? His movements? His moods?'

'Oh, yes, Brother. I knew that each Advent he and the other murderers met to feast and glory in their sin. I became what he wanted me to be – a rich young merchant besotted with his rather plain daughter. You see, Brother, if you spend your youth as a prisoner of the Moors, you learn how to act. You have to in order to survive.'

'Why now?' Cranston barked. 'Why not a year ago?'

The young man shook his head. 'Sir John, I had to plan. I had to study my quarry, and when the Thames froze over, I struck. Oh, I enjoyed it. I would have been successful if it hadn't been for you, Brother. I sent Horne's head to Sir John to show justice had been done.'

The young man grinned at Cranston as if relating a good story, and Athelstan realised for the first time that Geoffrey's mind was disturbed.

'Of course,' he continued, 'my scheme might have gone awry, but if so, I would have plotted something else. After all, there's more than one road to Hell. And I waited because revenge, as you can all appreciate, is a dish best served cold.'

'You bastard!' Sir Fulke shouted.

'A limb of Satan!' Hammond cried.

'Perhaps,' Parchmeiner retorted. 'But they all deserved to die.'

'No, they didn't,' Athelstan said quietly. 'They did wrong but at least two of them were genuinely sorry. You could have brought an appeal against them at King's Bench. The very accusation would have destroyed Sir Ralph.'

'I am God's judgment!' Parchmeiner yelled, glaring round the room. 'I am their doom! Horne knew that when he saw me dressed in armour similar to that Sir Bartholomew had worn.' He turned and spat in Sir Fulke's direction. 'God damn you and all your family. I even took the buckle from your shoe and left it on the ice. It would have been a nice twist, eh? To be hanged for the murder of your own brother?'

Sir Fulke turned his back.

'The rest was so easy,' Geoffrey continued. 'The letters were sent. Sir Ralph moved to the North Bastion. I oiled both the hinges and lock of the chamber door, and hid a dagger in the rubble in the passageway. I changed the keys when I helped the drunken bastard to his last resting place.'

'And the rest?' Athelstan asked.

'Oh, Mowbray was easy, sulking in the darkness. I'd been up to the parapet before and he'd never noticed. I did place an arbalest in the corridor and hit the tocsin bell then threw it down the sewer hole.' Geoffrey giggled. 'Horne was a victim of his own fears, a veritable fool, and I did warn Fitzormonde about that bear.' The assassin bit his lip. 'I could have killed them by other means but, once Whitton accepted me, the game had to be played.'

Cranston walked up to face him. 'Geoffrey Parchmeiner,' he intoned, 'also known as Burghgesh, I arrest you for murder. You will be taken to Newgate prison and, at a fixed time, answer for your terrible crimes in the court of King's Bench.' He looked round and nodded at Colebrooke. 'Take him away.'

'I want to see Bartholomew's last resting place!'

'Yes, you may,' Athelstan replied. 'Master Lieutenant, let him look at what we discovered this morning, but bind him well!'

The murderer threw one ferocious look at Fulke before Colebrooke and his soldiers hustled him out of the door. Athelstan sighed and looked round.

'Sir Fulke, Mistress Philippa, I am sorry.'

Philippa buried her face in her uncle's shoulder and silently wept. Sir Fulke just looked away.

'Sir John,' Athelstan said, 'we are finished here.' He put his writing implements back into the canvas bag, bowed to Sir Fulke and followed Sir John down the now darkening steps.

Outside Cranston took a deep breath. 'Thank God that's over. Brother!'

They walked under the forbidding mass of Wakefield Tower where they waited whilst a servant scurried back to the North Bastion tower to collect Cranston's dagger.

'A true murderer,' Sir John said quietly.

'Aye!' Athelstan replied. 'Insane or possessed, driven by hatred and revenge.' He looked up at the ravens cawing noisily above them. 'I'll be glad to be free of here, Sir John. This place has the stink of death about it.'

'It is called The House of the Red Slayer.'

'It's well named,' Athelstan replied.

They stood aside as Colebrooke marched by, Parchmeiner now tightly bound, almost hidden in the middle of his guards. The servant came back with Cranston's dagger and they left for the nearest tavern.

Sir John, of course, demanded refreshment after what he called his 'arduous labours'. Athelstan matched him cup for cup until they separated. Sir John went back to continue his rejoicing whilst Athelstan led a protesting Philomel up Billingsgate and across London Bridge to the dark loneliness of St Erconwald's.

—

A few days later, on Christmas Eve, Athelstan sat at his bench just inside the chancel screen, cradling a purring, contented Bonaventura on his lap. The friar looked around the sanctuary. All was ready for Christmas. The altar had a fresh cloth trimmed in gold, the sanctuary had been swept, the altar decorated with holly and ivy, the greenery and blood-red berries shimmering in the candlelight. The children had rehearsed their mummers' play. Athelstan laughed softly remembering how Crim, who had played the role of Joseph, had disrupted the proceedings by a short fist fight with one of the angels. Cecily had swept the nave and dusted the ledgers, and tomorrow he would celebrate three Masses: one at dawn, one mid-morning and the other at noon. Athelstan closed his eyes. He would remember his dead, his parents and his brother Francis, the men killed so violently in the Tower, as well as young Parchmeiner, who would surely hang.

The bishop had given him permission to re-consecrate the cemetery and Pike the ditcher had announced that Doctor Vincentius had left. Benedicta had been upset and Athelstan still felt wracked by feelings of guilt. He absent-mindedly kissed Bonaventura between the ears. He had apologised to all concerned for his ill temper on the morning he had heard about Tosspot's grave being desecrated. Athelstan sighed. All seemed to be in order, but was it? Christmas would pass, the Feast of the Epiphany would come, and with it fresh problems. Perhaps he would arrange a feast, a banquet for the parish council, to thank them for their kindness? Watkin had given him a new spoon made of horn; Ursula the pig woman a flitch of bacon; Pike the ditcher a new hoe for the garden; Ranulf the rat-catcher a pair of moleskin gloves and Benedicta, God bless her, a thick woollen cloak against the rigours of winter. Yet tomorrow, after Mass, he would be alone. Athelstan stared at the candle flames. Did God hide behind the fire? he wondered. He closed his eyes.

'Oh, Lord of the hidden flame,' he prayed, 'why is it so terrible to be alone?' He jumped, then grinned as the church door was flung open. 'Good Lord,' Athelstan beamed. 'I have heard of the power of prayer, but this is truly miraculous!'

'Monk!' Cranston bellowed, standing like a Colossus swathed in robes at the back of the church. 'I know you are here, Athelstan. Where are you bloody well hiding? By the sod, it's too early for your damned stars!'

Athelstan rose and walked under the chancel screen. 'Sir John, you are most welcome.' He looked carefully at the coroner. 'Surely not another murder?'

'I bloody well hope not!' Cranston roared, walking up the church, beating his hands together. 'I need some refreshment, Brother. You will join me?'

'Of course, Sir John, but this time I pay.'

'A priest who pays for what he drinks,' Cranston mocked. 'Yes, it must be Christmas.'

Athelstan collected his cloak from where he had flung it over the baptismal font and they walked out into the cold afternoon air.

'Let us go to the Piebald Horse!' Cranston suggested. 'A good cup of claret and some hot stew will do us both body and soul the world of good!'

They walked down the alley and into the welcoming warmth of the tavern. The one-handed landlord bustled across to meet them.

'Sir John,' he greeted. 'Brother Athelstan.'

He ushered them to a table near the fire as Cranston bellowed out his order. Sir John slouched on the bench and beamed round the tavern.

'You are busy, Sir John?'

'I am still looking for Roger Droxford, who murdered his master in Cheapside. I have had news of him hiding in a tavern near La Reole so perhaps I may call there on my journey home. But, Brother, let us forget murder. The Lady Maude has invited you to dinner tomorrow at three o'clock in the afternoon. You and the Lady Benedicta.'

Athelstan blushed as Cranston grinned devilishly.

'Don't worry, she'll come. I have been to her house, had a cup of claret, and given her a kiss on your behalf.'

'Sir John, you mock me.'

'"Sir John, you mock me," Cranston mimicked. 'Come, Brother, there's no sin in liking one of God's creation. You'll come?' He added, 'I have a present for you.'

Athelstan nodded whilst Cranston wondered if the astrolabe he had bought would really delight this strange star-searching friar. The landlord brought their goblets and two dishes of hot spiced mutton.

'So, Sir John, everything is tidied away. Sir Ralph's murderer has been caught; Doctor Vincentius has left; my cemetery is safe; tomorrow is Christmas, and all is well.'

Cranston slurped from his cup and smacked his lips.

'Aye, Brother, but spring will bring its own basket of troubles. The Red Slayer will strike again. Man will always kill his brother.' He sighed. 'And Lady Maude must be looked after, she and the child must be kept safe.' Sir John lowered his head and glared at Athelstan. 'The child will be a boy,' he announced flatly. 'And I shall call him Francis, the name of your dead brother.'

Athelstan caught his breath and put down the wine goblet.

'Sir John, that is most thoughtful. It's very kind.'

'He will become a knight,' Cranston continued expansively. 'A Justice of the Peace, a man of law.' He paused. 'Do you think he will look like me, Brother?'

Athelstan grinned. 'For the first few months he will, Sir John.'

Cranston caught the humour in Athelstan's voice. 'What do you mean, monk?' he asked dangerously.

'Well, Sir John, of course he will look like you. He'll be bald, red-faced, drink a lot, burp and fart, bellow and be full of hot air!'

The rest of the people in the tavern stopped what they were doing and gazed in astonishment as Sir John Cranston, the King's Coroner in the City, leaned back against the wall and roared with laughter till the tears streamed down his face.

Athelstan grinned till he thought of dealing with two Cranstons. Then the friar closed his eyes. 'Oh, Lord,' he whispered, 'what happens if it's twins?'